Adams, Alice, 1926–
Superior women

36,953

DATE DUE			
DEC. 14 1984	SEP 2 0 1985	
DEC 1 9 198	JUN 4 1986	
JAN 3 1985	SEP 8 1986	
JAN 17 1985		
JAN 3 0 1985	NOV 1 1 1987	
FEB 1 2 1985	APR 1 1	
FEB 2 8 1985	SEP 1 6 1992	
	JAN 8 1994	
MAR 2 8 1985		
APR 1 5 1985		
JUN 3 1985		
JUN 1 2 1985		

MYNDERSE PUBLIC
LIBRARY

Seneca Falls, N.Y.

NOV 1 6 1984

ALSO BY ALICE ADAMS

Careless Love

Families and Survivors

Listening to Billie

Beautiful Girl (stories)

Rich Rewards

To See You Again (stories)

Superior Women

SUPERIOR WOMEN

Alice Adams

Alfred A. Knopf   New York   1984

36,953

THIS IS A BORZOI BOOK
PUBLISHED BY ALFRED A. KNOPF, INC.

Copyright © 1984 by Alice Adams

All rights reserved under
International and Pan-American Copyright
Conventions. Published in the United States
by Alfred A. Knopf, Inc., New York, and simultaneously
in Canada by Random House of Canada Limited, Toronto.
Distributed by Random House, Inc.,
New York.

Library of Congress Cataloging in Publication Data
Adams, Alice, [date]
Superior women.
I. Title.
PS3551.D324S9   1984   813'.54   84-47507
ISBN 0-394-53632-0

Manufactured in the United States of America
Published September 21, 1984
Second Printing, October 1984

Fic.

MYNDERSE LIBRARY
31 Fall Street
Seneca Falls, New York 13148

To Robert McNie, with love

Superior Women

1

All, or almost all, of the events of Megan Greene's life, its violent dislocations, geographic and otherwise, are set in motion in the instant in which she first sees a young man named George Wharton, an unremarkable person, and later not a crucial figure in her life, but at that moment, to Megan, he is compellingly exotic. This takes place in the Stanford Bookstore, where Megan has a summer job; she lives in Palo Alto. George is tall and lean, with brown hair, sand-pale skin, a bony face, strong prominent jaw. He looks like what he is, a post–prep school boy from New England, but Megan has never seen one before. And his clean white khakis, old blue Oxford-cloth shirt, cord coat, and once-white sneakers, while fairly standard garb for Harvard Square and environs, in California look almost foreign.

Entranced, and aware among other more subtle reactions of a seering lust, Megan believes that she has "fallen in love." Since this is 1942 and she is sixteen, a not unreasonable interpretation.

Megan understands that he is "Eastern," this tall young man who has just come in and is standing there in the sunlight, tall and helpless, but she adds, as she is prone to, certain romantic corollaries of her own; she believes that he is rich (he is, very rich, but being a New Englander he would die before admitting to more than the most modest wealth). She furthermore assumes that he is "brilliant," possibly with literary inclinations, as hers are (she is wrong on both counts there; George is premed, of average intelligence). She imagines him to be endlessly sophisticated, having been everywhere—an older man, at least five years older than she, of wide experience. All sorts of experience, but especially sexual (wrong again).

Megan herself is medium-tall and plump, heavy-breasted, with shapely legs. Brown hair and dark blue eyes, a pretty, smooth-skinned face, very serious. Her mouth is sweet and eager, her whole expression is eager, needful.

Aside from the obvious hungers that are the lot of every poor but very bright young woman, Megan is also avid for a quality that she has not seen much of and could not name; what she considers Eastern comes close. She covets style, the sophistication which she has instantly imputed to George Wharton, before hearing his voice or knowing his name—the very qualities which she deplores the lack of in her own surroundings, of course: her parents run a store on University Avenue, out near the Bayshore Highway, whose humiliating slogan is WE BUY JUNQUE, WE SELL ANTIQUES. And they do not do well at it, Florence and Harry, Mom and Pop. (George Wharton will never see them, Megan vows, almost in the first instant of her seeing him.)

He has noticed her too, Megan observes; what she does not know is that his awareness of her (yes, her breasts and legs) increases the strength of his so–New England vowels, the Yankee flatness of his speech, as he comes around the table where she is standing to ask, "Uh, I don't suppose you have many books on sailing?"

Wordlessly, at first, but smiling, Megan, who knows the stock, is able to point in the right direction before she just gets out, "Over there."

"Oh, really? Uh, great! Thanks!"

He smiles, and strides over to the shelves she indicated; he turns back to Megan to smile again, holding up a book to indicate that he has found just what he wanted, a book on sailing. Thanks to *her*.

With what Megan appreciates as true delicacy, he takes his book to another clerk for the actual purchase, but then, book in hand, he comes back to Megan, and stands looking down at her. He is five or six years older than she is.

"At least I can read about it," he says, with a twisting, large-toothed grin; he must mean sailing?

"There's supposed to be good sailing up in the San Francisco Bay," Megan offers.

They are standing there in the dust-moted bookstore, a table of remaindered books between them, as though for safety. Megan, in her flowered cotton dress that is too tight and cut too low (her mother mentioned both at breakfast, mean skinny blond Florence). And George, in his strict blue-and-white cord coat.

He tells her, "This summer I really don't have any time. I'm cramming chemistry, for med school, and staying with some ancient cousins. In Atherton."

Aware of surges of heat throughout her body, Megan nevertheless achieves a pretty smile. She says, "Well—"

Very indifferently he asks her, "You live around here? You're in school?"

Of course by school he means Stanford, and so, vaguely, not quite lying, Megan says yes. And in that instant she has decided to apply to at least three Eastern schools, for the fall after next, when she will have finished high school. She will begin with Radcliffe—so lives are patterned.

The next day is exceptionally hot. In the tawny hills that surround the Stanford campus the dark green heavy live oaks barely move; along Palm Drive the asphalt is melting. High up in those palm trees the green-gray fronds are hard, dusty, and dry, they rattle in the slightest breeze, like snakes.

Stacking books, in the not–air-conditioned store, Megan dreams of sailing, breeze-driven across a blue Atlantic afternoon—dreams of sailing to an island off the east coast, to a white, white beach; they would leave the boat and lie there, alone on the sand, lie kissing, kissing until moonlight. She with him.

It is quite possible, though, that he will never come into the bookstore again, that she will never even find out his name. However, that afternoon, as she looks up from those dreams Megan sees him enter the store, a little stoop-shouldered, since he is so tall, too tall for that room. Her heart lurches as he smiles and comes up to her, saying, "Well, no one told me it got this hot in California. This feels like Boston."

"Usually it doesn't, this is unusual—" It is hard for her to talk.

Not quite looking at her he says, "What I really need is a beer. But I guess I'll have to wait. Worse luck. I've got a lab, right this minute."

Megan smiles, barely breathing. She understands that he wants to ask her out for a beer, but she does not know why it is so hard for him to ask. He is not quite used to girls? Maybe he did not go to a public high school, where everyone did that every day. She asks him, "Have you been out to Rossi's? That's a beer place around here."

He takes this up eagerly, words hurrying out. "No, actually I've hardly been anywhere, between chem labs and my. relatives in Atherton. The summer plan is that I have to have dinner with them every night. They're quite venerable, and I'm afraid my family has 'expectations.'" His mouth twists sideways. "But maybe after dinner, could you get out? I could pick you up at your dorm? I do have a car, in fact I drove out here in it." He grins, more breathless even than she is.

"Well, why don't we just meet here?" Megan suggests, on an instant's inspiration; the women's dorms are not far away, and if he thinks she lives in one, well, why not? She can take the same bus that she always takes to work, and when he takes her home— another plausible story comes to her instant rescue: she will say that she is spending the night with a girl friend who lives (un-accountable! so odd!) out near the Bayshore.

Thus from its earliest beginnings there is an illicit element in their relationship, to which Megan is instantly acquiescent, in which she, like so many women, functions with instinctive, adaptive skill.

He tells her his name, George Wharton, and she says hers, and then he says, in that voice, "Well, great, then. I'll see you out front here about nine, okay?"

"Oh, sure. *Great.*"

. . .

A Model A is not what Megan would have expected, not yet knowing anything about reverse snobbery, or prideful New England thrift, but that is what George leads Megan to, his car, which is parked in an alley near the bookstore. Not touching her, he opens the door for her, and Megan climbs awkwardly up into the seat.

They start off, and George begins to talk about his car. "It's a great old machine," he says. "Really the greatest. Made it over the Rockies without a complaint. I hope I'll be in as good shape, at that age."

He laughs, as Megan does too. She has no idea, really, what he has been talking about, but she has begun to realize that he is not used to being with girls, not at all.

It is understood that they are heading for Rossi's, and at the edge of the campus he asks Megan where to go. She tells him: right, then left, then straight along a narrow white dirt road, between sweeping shadowed hills, dim black shapes of trees, under a huge black diamond-starred sky.

Discouragingly, the parking lot at Rossi's is very crowded, the Packards and Buicks and Ford convertibles of Stanford fraternity boys; some of them even belong to high school kids, but are borrowed from parents—the Buicks, probably. Megan is thinking that she would just as soon not see anyone she knows, especially not some friend from high school, who might speak to her, say something to do with school, which is Palo Alto High.

George too looks a little daunted by that crowd; Megan sees that he would much rather not spend any time there. She tells him, "They have beer to take out, if you want. It does look crowded."

"Oh great, terrific. I'll just go in and get it." He has opened the door on his side. Stepping down, and out, he then turns back to her. "You won't mind waiting?"

"Oh no, that'd be swell."

Hearing her own voice, which has hitherto sounded neutral to her ears, possibly slightly Midwestern, since both Florence and Harry come from Iowa, Megan now keenly feels the difference between her voice and his, hers and George's; it is almost as though she were hearing another language.

In five minutes, which have seemed very long to Megan, George is back with two large foaming paper cups. "We can always come back for more," he tells her. His narrow mouth smiles—not his eyes, which are regarding her curiously, intensely. He asks, "Do we drink them here?"

"We could, if you want to. Or we could drive somewhere." Megan has said this as softly as she can, as though to conceal both her accent, so suddenly disliked, and her certain knowledge of their true direction. They will go, she knows, to a certain cleared space, high up and very private, in those surrounding hills. And she knows what they will be doing, in ten or so minutes from now. Their not touching, so far, has acquired a sort of violence; they are like dogs on leashes, she suddenly, crazily thinks, and she smiles to herself, in the dark.

She directs him up Page Mill Road, jolting over gravel. He is driving very fast, so that they both spill a little beer, as they sip, or try to.

At last Megan says *Here*, and George stops the car. Clutch, brakes—very noisy.

They are in a fragrant, rustling eucalyptus grove, near a heavy thick clump of pines. Far below them, through the trees, a vast valley of lights is just visible. Above them an airplane lumbers through the hot dark sky, flashing landing lights—they are near the airport.

Megan has put her cup down on the floorboards.

George asks, "All through?" His voice catches.

Mid-seat they collide, then, their mouths, arms, breasts, and hands and legs all wildly seeking each other out. (The genital sources of all this passion are oddly ignored, not touched, only mashed together violently, through clothes.) "Kissing" is what both Megan and George Wharton think of themselves as doing, or "necking," that being the totally unspecific term then in use. They are kissing, their mouths devouringly open to each other, his tongue in her mouth, probing and tasting as she tastes his, his sexual tastes of cigarettes and beer, hers of summer fruits and toothpaste and beer.

Although they reach many climaxes, both of them, in the course of those hours of kissing and straining together, that first night—and God knows how many climaxes in the course of the weeks that they spend in that way, every night—those spasms are in a curious way passed over, made nothing of. George is ashamed: surely he is not supposed to be doing this with a girl, it is probably worse than doing it with your hand, in the shower. And Megan is similarly ignorant; the orgasm is the one part of the sexual act that no one has told her about, in terms of women; she has been vaguely told that "receiving seeds" is pleasurable, but in some unspecified way. Men "ejaculate," women "receive." Thus she is allowed to believe that she and George are kissing, are necking—neither of which is necessarily related to "sexual intercourse."

It is only a six-week chemistry course that George is taking, and then he is going back to Boston; he will spend the rest of the summer with his parents and brothers at their place on Cape Cod, "the Cape." Sailing, swimming, "clamming." Resting up for med school. To Megan it all sounds remote and glamorous, a movie about people in white flannel suits and yachting hats. Mostly it sounds most painfully distant from her, from California. She is sure that George will not write to her; in a way she does not even expect him to. But the pit of her stomach twists at the thought, the imminence of his departure.

It does not occur to her, as it might to some other girl (surely it would occur to Lavinia, later one of Megan's most important friends), that he could invite her to visit, to meet his family. Learn to sail. To "clam."

"I'm not much on writing letters," George quite unnecessarily says, on their last night together. Again, they are parked up on Page Mill Road.

Megan has determined not to cry, a resolve of steel, and she is not going to say anything silly, any high school stuff about love.

And she manages; she even jokes, "Maybe postcards?"

George laughs, very pleased with her: had he been afraid that she would cry, or make some dumb demand? He says, "Terrific, I'll send you a postcard." And then, out of many impulses, innate good manners among them probably, he says, "Megan, you don't know what a difference knowing you has made, this summer. You are absolutely the greatest girl—" He breaks off, having gone as far as he can, and maybe farther.

They fall to kissing again. His large hands, now experienced, reach up under her bra, touch her breasts, hard nipples. He does not touch her under her pants.

Clutching each other, they writhe and twist and strain together, thighs and legs entwined, sweat and sexual secretions wetting them everywhere.

They are kissing, they are necking in a car. They are not "going all the way."

You are absolutely the greatest girl. Those words, in George's often-hoarse, flat-voweled, and still (to Megan) exotic voice, form her winter treasure, a record that she plays and replays. It is an accompaniment to her memories of "kissing."

But, greatest in what way, did he mean? Sexiest, she is fairly sure that he must have meant that; she thinks he has not kissed many other girls. But is that good, is it good to be sexy? Or is there something seriously wrong with her, called nymphomania?

Or, did he possibly also mean nice, or smart, or even pretty? There was, certainly, a note of regret in his words, but regret for what? For the end of their summer time together, or for not being able to say more?

Did he love her?

Rounding any corner in Palo Alto, Megan imagines seeing George, with his narrow sea-blue eyes, his tall strong body, just slightly stooped. His shy New England grin. There he would be, and he would say something really silly, like *Surprise*. And then he would say, even sillier, "I had to see you, I couldn't stand another day or night without you. I love you."

No postcards, nothing at all until December, and then there is one, mailed in care of the Stanford Bookstore, that is signed, "Your old friend, George Wharton." No salutation, just beginning: "Remember me? Med school is really keeping my nose in the books. I hope you are well. I wish you a Merry Christmas and a Happy New Year. Your old friend, George Wharton."

The picture on the other side is of a dormitory, where he must live. Longwood Avenue, in Boston.

Not much to go on. Still, there is the fact of his having sent a card at all. Not having forgotten who she is.

Megan thinks about George all the time: while studying and getting straight A's, while walking and swimming a lot and trying not to eat; while parked and necking up in their place on Page Mill Road with some boy from her high school (in that slightly odd way, she is being true to George).

"Rad-cliffe?" says Florence Greene, mother of Megan; giving the two syllables equal stress, she has made the word bizarre. Thin, bleached-blond Florence does not look old enough to be Megan's mother.

Megan moves restlessly through the dingy, antimacassared living room of the small house that George Wharton never entered—but where, in the early morning hours, he often let her off: her girl friend was recovering from "an operation," Megan was staying on with her, "helping out."

"You noticed that new drive-in, a couple of blocks from here, out on the Bayshore?" now asks Florence.

"Uh, sort of." She and George once had hamburgers there; Megan recalls how they gobbled, so famished, after so much kissing.

"They're hiring," says Florence. "I'm really thinking I could get me a job there. They've got these real cute uniforms." Megan believes that her mother talks this way on purpose to irritate and embarrass her; after all, back in Iowa Florence taught school, before the Depression took her job and she and Harry came to California and started in with Junque. When Megan was younger, for a long time she refused to believe that Florence was her mother.

"Oh *Mother*," Megan now says—a frequent response to Florence. She has instantly imagined her mother coming up to their car, as a carhop. Coming up to George's Model A and—oh Jesus, what could she say? "Jesus, Mother."

At which Florence flares up. "Don't swear at me! You know you're just like your father, when it comes to me. Why shouldn't I get a job like that? You're both big snobs, that's what you are. Look, you want to go to Rad-cliffe, you go there, if you can get yourself a scholarship, to add to that money your granddaddy left for your college. And I want to be a carhop. I'm tired of that dirty store. Tired of being broke all the time. I want to *work*. And I want to wear something *cute*."

One of the things that Megan spends the second half of the winter doing is trying to answer George's postcard. Not that it needed an answer, she knew that, but she wanted to remind him of herself, and she wanted to sound light and lovable, not a fat girl who is seriously in love. She scribbles message after message on various scratch pads, and then on a variety of unsent Christmas cards. It always comes out wrong, whatever she says.

At last she writes what is a probably unconscious imitation of the very card that she got from him. Including no salutation. "Guess what: Radcliffe has decided to accept me and I start in June. Will live in Bertram Hall. Hope to see you sometime. Your friend, Megan Greene."

On the reverse side there is a picture of the Stanford Bookstore.

2

June 1943. Freshman Orientation Week is dizzying for Megan, in that heady bright New England air. Very much alone, and feeling herself to be a foreigner, a Californian, a hick, she looks and watches and absorbs. She smells new grass and hears old church bells, she observes strange buildings. And everywhere she sees new, alluring faces. Interesting clothes. And she thinks obsessively of George, now only a few miles away..

This is the week when Megan first sees what she takes to be a trio of old, close friends: Lavinia, Cathy, and Peg, in the smoking room on the third floor of Cabot Hall. They all look so Eastern, those three; Megan is powerfully drawn to them. Megan, in her denim skirt and shirt, California clothes, has been talking to a small, dark, rather nearsighted but pretty girl named Janet Cohen; they have exchanged names along with certain other information about each other. Janet is "practically engaged" to a boy who is in the army, somewhere in the South Pacific. His name is Adam Marr; he is a writer, a genius, probably, but Janet's parents can't stand him. Her mother cries when Janet goes out with Adam. Janet sighs, as Megan thinks how pretty she is, how enviably small—and how even more enviable is the declared fiancé. Janet seems very smart; Megan likes her already, she thinks.

And then, as they are talking, the tall Eastern trio comes in: Lavinia, in a white quilted satin robe, the lace just slightly bedraggled (a somehow endearing touch, that lace). She is laughing softly, with Peg and Cathy. Big Peg in blue chenille, Cathy in a tailored dark red flannel robe, white lotion dabbed on her face, her brown-black hair in pin curls.

Glancing over at Megan and Janet, Lavinia gives the tiniest, slightest frown, one of her most characteristic gestures. At the time, Megan is not entirely sure who has earned that negative response, she or Janet, and why? Was it simply the fact of their presence?

. . .

Later she will ask her close friend Lavinia, "But why don't you like Janet?"

The famous frown. "Oh, I don't know. She's just so—so Jewish."

"I don't know what you mean." Megan's voice is tight.

Lavinia laughs. "Megan, Megan, you're such a California innocent. If you'd ever lived in a big city where there're lots of them, you'd *know*."

Megan experiences the total frustration that comes of knowing you are right, but being for whatever reasons unable to argue. Lavinia's flawless sophistication, which is incredibly impressive in a girl of seventeen, makes Megan feel simple and silly. Lavinia is from Washington, D.C. She knows everything.

In the smoking room at Cabot, that first night, on the other side of the room Lavinia (no longer frowning; they come and go quickly, those little frowns) and Peg and Cathy go on with whatever they were talking and laughing about.

As Megan says to Janet, "There was this boy, I knew him last summer. He was taking a chem lab course at Stanford. He's at Harvard Med. I really like him, I guess, and I sent him a postcard, but I said I'd be in Bertram. I didn't know about Cabot, for this week. And it's four more days. I just don't know—"

"Well, if I loved him I'd certainly call him," says valiant Janet, who loves Adam Marr.

"Really, do you think so?" Megan is breathless at the very idea of calling George.

"Well, sure. But maybe wait until you move to Bertram. That way if you have to leave a message it won't sound confused."

Wonderful, practical Janet. Very smart indeed. Who goes on to say, "I know it's hard to wait, sometimes."

The sound of laughter from across the room has reached a higher pitch, and Megan imagines that they are talking about sex, sharing confidences, maybe. Gradually it dies down, those mingled laughs, and from the diminishing sounds one voice emerges, such a light and pretty voice that it must belong to the blond one, Lavinia, who says, "Well, the truth is I'm just terribly frustrated."

"*George!*" At the sound of his voice, having left her message and then waited four days for his call, all Megan's plans for cool control collapse; her *George* could be heard all over Bertram Hall.

At his end, presumably the med school dormitory, George chuckles. "God, you sound terrific," he says to Megan. "Are you liking it here? You like Cambridge?"

"Oh, it's fantastic. I'm absolutely crazy about it, it's wonderful—"

Another chuckle. "Well, I'm glad. It's a town I've always liked, especially there around the Square. But say, do they let you out at night? Could you come out for a beer?"

"Oh sure, I'd *love* to." So much for being coolly casual. Blasé. Sophisticated.

George, in army khakis, is something of a surprise. Unused to each other, in new surroundings, he and Megan sit facing each other in a booth in the Oxford Grill; two beers sit on the table between them, and a large wine bottle covered with candle drippings, years of multicolored wax, just now topped with a large red candle. Megan has not seen this done before, and she imagines it to have been accidental.

George still likes her. Megan can tell by his eyes and his smile, as he looks across at her; when he says, "Gosh, you really look great!" she can almost feel that love has been declared.

He tells her how busy he is in med school, how really hard they have to work just to keep up, not to mention his wanting to do really well. Last summer he had told her that his father and grandfather and his great-grandfather all were doctors, and now the weight of this reaches her, the pressure he must feel as fourth in line, generations of distinguished Boston doctors. No wonder he is paler and thinner now, the bony line of his jaw yet more pronounced.

Because of gas rationing George has taken the subway over from

Boston; leaving the O.G. (as Megan is quick to learn to call it) they walk very slowly, in the gentle June dark. Earlier he asked what time she had to be in, and Megan airily told him, "Oh, any time before midnight."

"Well, I call that really liberal," was George's comment.

Megan did not tell him that she had to ask for a special permission, with a lie about a friend's brother on his way overseas.

They are not heading toward the Radcliffe dorms, she notices, but are going in an opposite direction. They reach a boulevard which she knows to be Memorial Drive, beside the river, the Charles. They cross the street. Traffic is light, no one speeding. On the river bank George begins to talk in a nervous way about rowing, "crew," one of his favorite undergraduate pastimes, he tells her. Megan is reminded of their first drive together, from the Stanford bookstore out to Rossi's, George going on and on about his car.

They stop at a bridge, and George says, "I'm always curious about what's underneath a bridge, aren't you?"

Underneath that particular bridge is very hard, sharply sloping ground, onto which they nevertheless fall, and kiss, and kiss.

A few days later, walking along Brattle Street, Megan experiences an extraordinary recognition: she suddenly, blindingly sees that at that moment, in the brilliant June New England air—she understands that she is perfectly happy (in a way that most people, sadly, recognize only in retrospect: Ah, *then* I was happy). Everything that Megan could possibly want is either present or is imminently possible for her, just then. The new air is distinctly not Western, it could not exist in California; the air is as novel to her as the architecture is: she deeply responds to the bright strict lines of wooden houses, so much wood and paint and sometimes silvered shingles, or softly aged, rose-colored brick, and the violet-tinted, diamond-shaped glass, in rare ancient windowpanes.

Nowhere adobe or tiles, no California stucco, painted pastel. No Bayshore Highway. No Junque!

The air and Brattle Street form her most beautiful immediate present. And Megan's racing warm blood even suggests that George

Wharton could come to love her, and say so. And that those three
girls whom she first saw in Cabot, those so-Eastern girls, whom
she watches having coffee and muffins together in Hood's might
someday be her friends. (She understands that they all live in
Barnard Hall, just across the way from Bertram.) At this very
moment she is hurrying along Brattle Street, toward Hood's, where
they all might be.

However, on this particular day, the only one of the three who is
sitting in Hood's is Lavinia, the thinnest and blondest, the most
Eastern, richest-looking—the most lovely and delicate. The kind of
girl, Megan has decided, who does not even let boys kiss her, much
less all the writhing and touching that she and George do, every
time they see each other, ever more feverishly.

Very carefully not looking at Lavinia, Megan, who is still
perfectly happy, goes over to get her coffee; she takes out a book
and begins to look at French verbs—she has French next. She is
thinking that George could call her tonight; at that moment even
that seems possible. She smiles to herself.

Absorbed in that thought of George, Megan forgets the time;
looking at her watch, she sees that she is almost late. She picks up
her books and is about to hurry out when from behind her she
hears herself addressed, a light voice saying, "Well, good morning,
Bertram Hall."

She turns to find Lavinia, teasingly smiling, saying, "Oh! you're
always in just the biggest hurry!" Her accent is faintly Southern—
sometimes.

Megan grins, feeling heat in her face. "I guess so," she says.

Lavinia asks, "What do you have next?"

"French."

"Oh. I have Gov."

And so, within minutes Lavinia and Megan are walking up
toward Harvard Square, they are circling Brattle Street, passing the
Coop, and crossing through traffic, over and into the Yard. Anyone
seeing them would take them for good friends, the two of them,
chattering as they walk.

"You look to me as though you came from some place really far away," Lavinia observes, at some point along their walk. She has narrowed her eyes, as though her observation had been profound.

Megan says, "California. Palo Alto, actually. It's fairly near San Francisco."

"Ah, you see? I could tell—I know all about you, Bertram." Lavinia laughs provocatively.

"Oh, you do?" Eager, ungraceful Megan.

But Lavinia is leaving her, Lavinia is going into Harvard Hall, for Gov. She smiles delicately as she says, "Well, see you later, Bertram."

"Oh, yes. See you." Megan is left dizzy in the sun, and just slightly less happy than before.

3

Why is it, almost from that day of meeting at Hood's, that Lavinia quite aggressively invites the friendship of Megan—why does Lavinia so clearly seek her out? On the surface, as friends they seem a very unlikely combination: tall thin blond, impeccably expensively dressed Lavinia—and plump dark Megan, in her slightly wrong California clothes. And, as the two girls do indeed become friends, it often occurs to Megan that other girls must find their friendship strange, especially those who themselves would like to be friends of Lavinia's.

Lavinia, if asked, could easily explain; she would simply and quite emphatically say that Megan is one of the most brilliant people she has ever met. Megan has read everything; her term papers come back with invariable A's and flattering professorial comments. (Actually, perhaps surprisingly, Lavinia herself has a remarkably high IQ; in those numerical terms the two girls are identical.) Before Radcliffe, Lavinia went to a Southern boarding school (it is not true, as Megan at first imagined, that Lavinia and Peg and Cathy were all at school together); at that school, as well as being the prettiest girl, Lavinia was also by far the brightest, as well as the most formidably sophisticated. She enjoyed her position, all that devout praise from wondering teachers, themselves generally "unattractive" (a frequent word of Lavinia's, of course; one of the many that she generally sets off in quotes, for a special, private emphasis)—"unattractive" and nowhere near as bright as Lavinia. But Lavinia was often bored silly, at that school. She welcomes the intelligence and the wit of Megan, and of Peg and Cathy too, who are both, in their separate ways, also very smart.

A deeper reason for Lavinia's seeking her out, which Megan only comes to understand much later, is that Lavinia has two and only two patterns of serious friendship with women. Her first and most usual kind of friend is a not-very-attractive (as opposed to "unattractive"), somewhat maternal sort of girl, Peg being the perfect example, although of course there were others, quite as perfect in their ways as Peg. The other kind of friend is pretty, *attractive*, also bright, but sexy, *wild*. Lavinia's wild friend at boarding school, Kitty, was finally thrown out, having been discovered in a "compromising position" (how Lavinia relished that phrase!) with a boy from St. Christopher's ("We both had our pants down, it was really terrific," Kitty reported to Lavinia) in the chapel of the school, an episode much enjoyed by Lavinia, all around. Actually, although less apparently, Lavinia's own sexual impulses are also wild, strong and imperative, but her deepest nature is intensely conservative; appearances are almost everything for beautiful Lavinia.

Many years after college, still puzzling over it all, Megan wonders if maybe, at first, Lavinia could have chosen her, Megan, as another in her line of exploited maternal friends, perhaps equating fat with motherliness, as people frequently, so mistakenly will. It would have been only later, as they began to talk, that Lavinia recognized Megan as the wild and sexual sort of friend, the kind whose sexuality would get her into various forms of trouble— whereas sexy Lavinia just liked to hear about others' escapades.

.   .   .

Peg's function in Lavinia's life was absolutely clear, even in those earliest days. Peg mothers Lavinia, in a jolly, masochistic way. And sometimes she scolds, as mothers will: "Lavinia, you've gone and lost four boxes of my bobbypins already this month." (Bobbypins: in those war years a valuable commodity.) And so Peg jokes, the tiredest, heaviest joke of all by now: "Don't you know there's a war on?" (Actually it could of course be said that none of them do.)

The connection between Cathy and Lavinia is less clear to Megan, beyond the fact that Cathy has simply fallen prey to Lavinia's powerful charm, as everyone does.

One afternoon, in August of that first Cambridge summer, Megan walks that short distance from Bertram Hall to Barnard; that morning in Hood's, Lavinia, there alone, has said, "You never come to see me! You just stay stuck over there in Bertram all the time. But I'll bet you have some terrific night life going on, now don't you, little Megan?"

Megan blushes. Could Lavinia know about George, or has she just made a wild and accurate guess? But the fact is that Lavinia would find it very unlikely that Megan would "have someone." Megan instantly grasps this, and uncomfortably she realizes that she is being teased, and not kindly.

Barnard Hall, where she has not been before, feeling not invited, is considerably bigger than Bertram, and probably newer. The girl at the switchboard (this duty is passed about; it is called being on bells), says to Megan, "Oh, they're all up on the fourth floor."

And so Megan begins to climb up the wide, dead-white brown-banistered stairs.

And the first person she sees, at the top of the stairs, is small Janet Cohen, sitting out there alone, smoking, a heavy book across her blue-jeaned knees.

In the split second before they greet each other, Megan sees that for an instant Janet has believed herself to be the object of the visit. Just as quickly, and as visibly, Janet sees that she is not. I might have known you wouldn't come over here just to see me, is what Janet's second expression says.

But, "Well, how've you been?" they both say, warmly, and at precisely the same instant. And, as a muttered afterthought, Megan adds, "I told Lavinia I might come by."

"*Oh.*" That is all that Janet says, but her sharp upward look continues a sentence: Oh, you're friends with *them*?

"I don't really know them very well," Megan has felt it necessary to explain. And then, "What're you reading?"

Janet shows her. Dos Passos, *U.S.A.*

"Adam gives me these reading lists," Janet proudly explains, and complains, "Honestly, it's all I can do—"

"I'd love to read it, when you're through," says Megan. "Maybe I could borrow—"

"Oh sure, I'll be through in a week or so. I read a lot every night, since of course I don't go out."

"Oh—" Megan has suddenly remembered that she has Janet to thank for having urged her to call George. "Oh, I did what you said, I called that guy I know at Harvard Med. Remember I told you, and I didn't want to call?"

"You did? That's wonderful! You see him a lot?" Janet is beaming, and her instantaneous vicarious pleasure is so warm and true that Megan is tempted to lie and to say, Yes, we see each other all the time, and it's wonderful, we're really in love. But some quality in Janet precludes such lies, and so in a wry way Megan (honestly) says, "Well, sometimes it's wonderful, sort of."

Janet laughs, perhaps because she recognizes just that wry sadness as a frequent mood of her own; and the two young women part on that note, having exchanged a warm smile of mutual recognition.

"Well, see you later," they both say, as Janet lights another cigarette and Megan pushes through the wide swinging doors that lead to the open hall, the top floor of Barnard.

Lavinia's room is at the farthest end, Megan has been told, and she walks that echoing distance with something akin to stage fright: of course this is just a casual visit, but will she behave quite casually enough? For instance, what will she do if Lavinia isn't there? Suppose there is only Cathy, or Peg; how could she explain having come over at all?

But Lavinia is there, with Cathy. The door is open, and Megan sees them sitting close together on what must be Lavinia's bed. And they are both in the robes in which Megan originally saw them, in the smoking room at Cabot, Lavinia's bedraggled white satin and lace, Cathy's red wool.

Seeing Megan, Lavinia jumps up and comes to the door; she greets Megan as though she, Lavinia, were wearing something very elegant, or at least a clean, untattered robe. "Well, here's our little Megan! You came to see us! We'll have to make tea. Wicked Cathy, you go on down to Peglet's room and borrow some tea bags."

Cathy, not glad to see Megan, mutters that she thinks Peg is out doing archery.

"Just take them, then, and some of those really good cookies her mother sent. The chocolate chip. Megan will love them, I can tell." Megan is given a complicitous smile as Cathy leaves; and Lavinia confides, with a small laugh, "Cathy was *very* naughty last night. On her very first date, with a brand-new boy, in the ROTC. The good Lord is punishing her with a terrible hangover." She laughs again, very gently, as though to prove a lack of real malice.

Some of Lavinia's hair is up in pin curls, and there are traces of cold cream around her eyes, but still, despite all that, despite the untidy robe, her presence is impressive. Also, scrupulously analyzed, Lavinia's features are not actually beautiful; she simply gives a strong impression of beauty. Her hair is not blond but an ashy color, an ashen light brown; her large gray eyes are too close together, and her nose a shade too large. Her upper lip is short, and her chin rather long, almost a Habsburg chin. Her skin is fine but uniformly white, too pale. She is very thin, with small breasts and long narrow feet.

Lavinia knows what she looks like. "Actually I'm not at all prettier than you are," she is to say, to Megan. "We just have opposite defects. I'm too thin, and you're a little plump. I'm flat-chested, and you're—you're 'overendowed.' My skin is dry, yours isn't. And my feet are too big, and too narrow for most shoes."

However, although it has a sound of reason, even of fairness, this diagnosis fails to cheer or even to convince Megan. Only years later is she able to diagnose its basic fallacy, which is that the defects Lavinia mentions as her own are quite acceptable—are classy, "aristocratic," even. Of course it is preferable to be too thin, and to have dry skin rather than a face that perpetually shines and is often red, not to mention a tendency to bumps. And small breasts surely suggest greater refinement than large ones do. And what could be more regal than a long, narrow, high-arched foot?

Lavinia has a carefully, delicately nurtured air about her; her look is ethereal, and certainly nonsexual. Whereas Megan looks strong, and clearly sexual. She sees herself as a peasant, in contrast to Lavinia.

Cathy comes back into the room, and Megan thinks how *punished* she looks; wicked or not, Cathy looks miserable. Her pale skin is mottled, as though on the verge of breaking out, and her eyes are clouded. Megan feels a surge of sympathy for Cathy which is almost as strong as her curiosity as to what really happened. How awful Cathy must feel, and obviously does feel—but what exactly did she do, with the boy from the ROTC, besides just drinking too much?

With what is either an intuitive flash, a look into Megan's mind, or is more probably the continuation of an earlier conversation with Cathy, Lavinia now tells Megan, "She won't say exactly what went on, so we can all think the worst." She shoots a look at Cathy.

Sounding more guilty than defensive, Cathy gets out, "I keep telling you, we just drank a lot of stingers at the Pudding, and then on the way home I guess we necked a lot."

"Well, I only hope his hangover is worse than yours is," severe Lavinia pronounces, piously adding, "And I hope he calls you very soon."

At that last Cathy looks so stricken that Megan grasps that Lavinia has probed to Cathy's darkest fear: Cathy is afraid, she *knows*, that the ROTC boy will never call her again; he is the kind of boy who would not approve of a girl who would neck on a first date, the kind of boy that in fact George Wharton could have turned out to be, and maybe really, basically, he is.

None of which Lavinia could know about—or could she? Just

how good-natured is her teasing? For the moment Megan cannot decide, or rather, she decides to avoid such conclusions.

Lavinia makes their tea on a hot plate, and distributes it very grandly, in the thick white dormitory mugs, along with Peg's mother's chocolate-chip cookies, from a cracked blue plate.

"Tea is the best possible thing for a hangover," Lavinia instructs. "The morning after my cousin's coming-out party, oh, I wanted to die! A friend of mine, Kitty—Kitty and I were so thirsty we drank a gallon of water, and that just made us drunk all over again! You must never drink water the morning after champagne. Anyway finally somebody, the maid, I guess, fed us both some tea, and by the time of the lunch party we felt almost human again. Kitty, now there's a wild girl—" And Lavinia laughs, in a nostalgic, reminiscent way, as vividly glamorous images flow into Megan's receptive imagination, a compound of literature and Hollywood: she sees a debut, a Scott Fitzgerald party. Bare powdered shoulders, corsages of orchids, gardenias. Floating chiffon, and men in tuxedoes, or gold-braided uniforms these days. And Lavinia (Carole Lombard! Daisy Buchanan!) lightly dancing, sipping champagne.

Lavinia does have beautiful hands, Megan notices, as Lavinia pours out more tea. The white nails are perfect ovals, fingers long and narrow; even the tight white skin on her hands looks polished. Megan resolves to do her own nails more often; maybe you have to do them every day, to have them look like that?

Now in her most serious voice Lavinia is asking Megan, "But do you really like it, living over there in Bertram?" Concern fills those wide gray eyes.

Actually, Megan is so delighted, still, to be at college, at Radcliffe, at all, that she has not conceived of possible improvements in her state; she has not thought about liking Bertram or not. And so she says, "Well, I guess so. It's really all right. Actually I haven't got to know anyone there too well. They're mostly juniors or seniors, and they already know each other."

With one of her most intense, entirely concentrated looks, Lavinia remarks, "You don't have to stay there, you know. You could tell them you want to move between terms, in September. You could come over here."

Surprisingly, Cathy adds, "You could have the room across the hall, actually. She's moving into Cabot, she thinks it's a little more 'grand,' over there."

(They all, the three and then four friends, acquire from Lavinia this verbal trick of emphasis, of just slightly setting off words; perhaps Cathy does it first. Later, reading Proust, they see it as Lavinia's Duchess de Guermantes device, to which Lavinia readily agrees. "Of course, Proust has always been my absolutely favorite writer. I feel so at home in Proust.")

Loud clumping noises just then sound from down the hall, increasingly noisy, until there in the doorway is Peg, big Peg, looking bigger yet in her white gym uniform. She makes enthusiastic welcoming sounds at the sight of Megan—"Well, little Megan, our visitor for tea! Well! Welcome to Barnard!"—in her deep jolly voice.

Responding politely, if not precisely in kind, Megan is darkly aware of some negative reaction to big Peg. I don't like you, she is thinking, as she smiles up at Peg; but this is inadmissible, she will not allow herself not to like Peg. Lavinia and Cathy like her, so why should Megan not—what's wrong with her?

Peg says, "Well, I'm glad you girls appreciate my mother's cooking," and she laughs, very loud.

"We're just trying to see that you don't eat too much, and put on weight," Lavinia chides.

"I'm starting my diet tomorrow." An old joke, at which Peg laughs again. "Actually this dormitory food makes things a little difficult. It's all so fattening. Have you noticed that too, little Megan?"

I am nowhere near as fat as you are, Megan wants to say; we do not look in the least alike. But Peg's tone has been one of polite inquiry, even concern, and so she only says, "I haven't thought about it much. It is pretty fattening, I guess. So much starch."

It is Lavinia who says, "Peglet, Megan is nowhere near as big as you are. Now, really." She has spoken very lightly, but definitively, with her tiny frown.

Poor Peg flounders. "Oh, I didn't mean—" She now sounds so distressed that Megan is touched, and likes Peg better. She herself sometimes says things that she has not quite meant to; feeling awkward herself, too often, she is moved by awkwardness in another person. But she is even more touched by Lavinia's defense.

"As a matter of fact Megan's moving over here in the fall, and you both can go on diets," Lavinia at that moment announces.

Peg's enthusiasm is noisy: Terrific, wonderful, *neat*—she says, while Megan smiles, feeling fairly foolish.

Matter-of-factly, a welcome contrast to Peg, Cathy states, "It will be better, there being four of us." But what did she mean?

"I just love Barnard Hall," Lavinia declares, at her most Southern. "And this top floor, our end of the hall. It's our own private quarters." She laughs, admitting that what she has been saying sounded a little silly, but then she says, "In fact I like it so much that I don't think I'll even bother going home between terms. I'll just stay here and read up for next fall and take walks. And go to museums in Boston."

"Oh, Lavinia, you'll be so lonely, you won't like that at all," Peg clucks worriedly. "If you don't want to go all the way home you could come down to Plainfield with me. My mother would love—"

"You're so sweet, but not going home isn't the point. I want to be here, by myself. And I won't be lonely at all, I like being alone."

Megan has been listening rather breathlessly to this exchange. She too is going to stay at college between terms; her parents have said that coming back to California for such a short vacation is out of the question (although Florence has written enthusiastically about her new job, the great tips; mother the carhop, Megan can hardly bear to think of her). Megan's imagination races ahead: she sees herself and Lavinia taking long walks, all over Cambridge, and going into Boston on the subway, going to museums. But then she wonders: will Lavinia want to do something expensive, like a matinee, or even dinner out? That thought scares her deeply for a moment, but her excitement is even stronger; she and Lavinia will talk, talk for hours. Tell each other things. Become real friends.

Some instinct for caution, however, prevents her from mentioning this coincidence of plans to Lavinia. Not now. She does not say, Oh great, I'll be here too.

. . .

But that is how she feels; she leaves Barnard Hall in a state of elation that afternoon, going back to Bertram. She will move to Barnard in the fall, she thinks, as she sits at her desk in her single corner room, trying to read a few pages of Chaucer before the dinner bell. She and Lavinia will have ten days, or a couple of weeks, of walking, conversation.

Outside her windows, the golden Cambridge air is soft and gentle. Yellow leaves fall slowly, singly, to the drying grass; the sound of evening bells is distant, indistinct. Pale stars have just appeared in a paler sky; it is the faded-out end of a lively brilliant day. Barely thinking at all, Megan lets herself be filled with that view, with the evening air. It is another moment of great happiness for her; she is again aware of wonderful possibilities, golden chances.

Just then the hall buzzer shrills out, a phone call for someone. In a minute a voice can be heard answering, "Third floor," and then, more loudly, "Greene! Call on Line One!"

It could only be George, Megan thinks, as she rushes toward the phone booth, takes up the receiver, and pushes down the button. And it is, George saying, "Well, I've really been hitting the books, but how about tonight? Could you possibly? Are you free?"

Five minutes later, as she pins up her hair in bobbypins, hurrying—it is almost dinnertime—it strikes Megan that her visit to Barnard Hall has functioned as a good omen in her life: from now on she and Lavinia will be true friends, and her life will take on Lavinia-like qualities—she will lose weight, be thin, wear better clothes, and George will fall seriously in love with her.

At the sound of the dinner bell she wraps her hair in a scarf, which is acceptable practice at meals; also, everyone knows that a person thus gotten up has an important date that night.

Which leads to another small piece of luck for Megan, that day, enough to make her think that her fate has indeed taken a new direction: a girl from Chicago, a senior, known to be as rich as she is lazy, indolent, who has never bothered speaking to Megan before, addresses her from across the table: "Greene—" in her arrogant, idle nasal voice, "Greene, since you're going out tonight, how would you like to be the proud recipient of a new white sweater that an aunt of mine just sent me? She means well but she's a little dim about my size." Betty, from Chicago, is tall, exceptionally thin, scrawny, actually. "Perfect for you, though, I think," drawls Betty.

Megan flounders, "Oh well, I'd really like to see it, but how—I mean, could I—" She is unable to say, Couldn't I pay you for it.

Betty's laugh is harsh. "You could write to the aunt for me," she suggests.

"Oh, I'd be glad to."

"I'm kidding. Come by and try it on after coffee."

"You look, uh, terrific," George says to Megan that night, in the Oxford Grill. He almost never remarks on how she looks, and the compliment has been an effort, he almost stutters over it.

"I do? Well, thanks." Megan feels a blush on her neck.

"Something, uh, new? Your hair is longer?"

"I don't know. Maybe." Megan does not say, as she might have, that in the time since they have seen each other her hair could indeed have grown.

"Well, how about another beer?"

At a certain point George always asks that, and always Megan demurs. "Oh no, not for me, no thanks. But if you want another one—"

Tonight, however, as he says those ritual words, what she thinks is, I'd really like another beer. And she further thinks, I wish we spent more time talking. And so, rather airily (in a Lavinia voice?), she says, "Actually I'd love another beer."

"You would? Well, in that case I'll have one too."

No waitress is immediately present, and as they wait there Megan realizes that she is expected to withdraw; now she should say, Well, I really don't need another beer. (George is very, uh, thrifty, Megan suddenly and meanly thinks.) But she does not withdraw; in fact she has another new thought that shocks her a little: Why don't we ever go out to dinner? is what she thinks. Other people seem to. He must sometimes eat out?

"I guess I'd better hustle up a waitress," George says resignedly, getting up. And, watching his thin, lanky, khaki-clad body as he crosses the room, Megan retracts; she forgives the lack of dinner, food. He is so beautiful, so perfect, as a man.

Setting down the new beers George says, "Well, I suppose you're looking forward to getting back to California, after the summer term."

"Actually I think I'll stick around here," Megan tells him cautiously. "I've got a lot of reading to do, and I'd like to take some walks around Cambridge. Go into Boston and see a couple of museums."

"Oh, you'll be around here, will you?" George seems to digest this slowly. "Well, we'll have to get you down to the Cape sometime. Do you think you'd like sailing?"

"Oh sure, I think I'd love it."

"Well, we'll definitely have to think about that. Some Saturday. Usually the folks are around on weekends, and my brothers, but they're a pretty good gang. Maybe you could stay over. Spend the weekend."

"I'd love that." Out of breath with sheer pleasure, Megan looks up at him. It is the moment of her life in which she is prettiest, so far; she is almost beautiful, in her shining happiness. Which unfortunately she does not know, and George is not able to tell her.

The only problem, as Megan thinks of it, will be Lavinia: Will going to the Cape with George come at a time when Lavinia was counting on going in to Boston, or just somewhere to talk? For an instant this is very worrying, but then Megan decides that she will simply have to tell Lavinia, in a straightforward way: Look, there's this boy, and he wants me to come up and meet his family.

Isn't that what Lavinia herself would do? Megan is almost certain that she would.

That night, furiously necking on the hard ground under their bridge, beside the Charles, George does what he has not quite done before: he reaches down inside her panty girdle, forcing back the tight elastic, reaching and reaching, and touching, touching her where she is so hot and wet, very wet. Dimly Megan wonders how he can want to do this, all that slime. (The function of sexual secretions in women is something else, along with orgasms, that she has not been told about. She does not know that other women function in this same way; vaguely she imagines that she is supposed to be cool and dry, in there—Lavinia would be, probably.) But George seems to notice nothing wrong. He is if anything more excited, more violent in his thrusting against her, his heavy breath.

At last, almost limping with exhaustion, they are walking back across Cambridge, to the Radcliffe dorms. They can hardly speak. Megan thinks of nothing to say, nor does George. The night air is cooler than it has been on most of the nights of that summer, and Megan wonders, what about winter, rain and snow? Where will they go, then, for love, or whatever it is that they are doing?

But in the meantime she more brightly thinks there is going to the Cape, and sailing. Meeting his family. "Clamming."

And Lavinia, her new friend.

4

"Guess what? I'm not frustrated anymore!" This is the first thing that Lavinia says, with a small happy laugh, on the first day of the between-terms vacation. September 1943. She and Megan are sitting on the broad back steps of Bertram Hall, facing the deserted quad where now, in this warm slow start of fall, the grass is gradually drying out, slowly yellowing.

. . .

That September is also the scene of bloody battles: the invasion of Italy and Italy's surrender; ferocious fights in Pacific jungles, Asian seas. But although these events are viewed almost daily in newsreels at the University Theater, on Harvard Square, the war is still essentially unreal. Even the fact of uniforms everywhere is suggestive less of blood and death than simply of high drama. The war is like background music in a movie; it serves to heighten and intensify private experience—especially for girls like Lavinia and Megan, or Cathy and Peg, whose only concentration is on their own personal lives.

"I went out with this ROTC," Lavinia continues. "Gordon Shaughnessey, isn't that the most divine name? and is he handsome! We went dancing at the Fox and Hounds, with a whole bunch of people, and then some drinks at the Napoleon Club—when I think of what that evening must have cost! Aren't you glad you're not a boy? I am! And Gordon's not rich, I can tell. Anyway, after that we all ended up in separate cars, Gordon and I in this funny Caddy, he said it was his roommate's, 'Potter' something, now there's a name, *Potter.* Anyway, we ended up parked by the Charles, somewhere, and he must have been as hard up as I was, we were really all over each other, and is he fun to kiss! I think I'm in love!" Lavinia laughs again, in her light cool way; she can take or leave being in love.

Megan has reacted to this recital with an uncomfortable mixture of excitement and envy. Her imagination takes in and vividly dramatizes all the scenes that Lavinia has named: the group all dancing in an expensive nightclub—all beautiful girls like Lavinia (and Katharine Hepburn, Ingrid Bergman, maybe), ROTC boys in their dark officers' uniforms. Dim lights, small tables, a band. And then drinks at the Napoleon Club, probably smaller and darker. More "intimate."

Parked by the Charles, "all over each other." Well, Megan can easily imagine herself in that scene, in "Potter's" old Caddy. Herself all over someone who is fun to kiss. (Is George fun to kiss? She had not thought of it in just that way.) And Lavinia did all that on a first date? And—what about Gordon Shaughnessey? Was he shocked, will he ever call her again? And is Lavinia worried that he won't, as Cathy was, last summer, when she went out and necked with her ROTC boy, who never did call back?

Megan is certain, somehow, that Lavinia is not worried. Either way will be all right with her, whether she sees this boy again or not. And Megan is also certain that Gordon Shaughnessey will call.

Megan herself is both worried and unhappy when she thinks of George, which is almost all the time. Although he knows that she is there, between terms, and although he talked in such a definite way about sailing, the Cape, his parents—he has been absolutely silent, unheard-from, absent from her life. And as always, during such lapses of time, Megan imagines that she will never see him again, never, gone, no more of George. And this time her fears seem very solidly, fatally grounded, else why, having talked about such clear plans, would he then not call? Unless he really meant not to see her again.

This is only the first day of vacation, of course, but if he meant for her to come to the Cape for a weekend, surely he would already have called her. George is not casual; he is in his way rather formal. And surely his parents would be the sort who plan ahead, inviting guests, discussing train schedules.

But "Oh God!" Lavinia suddenly cries out, interrupting Megan's unhappy train of thought. "Oh God," cries Lavinia again, "he's coming over in half an hour, and I've got to change. Why don't you come up and talk to me while I get dressed?"

Although that sentence was phrased as an invitation, it was actually an imperative; Lavinia has risen without looking around for an answer. Of course Megan would follow her over to Barnard, and Megan did.

Lavinia's room is in the sort of total mess and confusion that Megan has begun to see as characteristic: clothes everywhere, cashmere sweaters carelessly wadded up or strewn about, silk slips, tiny white lace bras, and the sheerest, palest (that year, infinitely valuable) nylon stockings, scattered about, hung over chairs.

"Well, obviously I don't have time for a bath," says Lavinia, with her tiny concentrated frown. "I'll just go and wash the essentials." And she gives Megan her knowing, complicitous laugh.

Not at all sure what is meant, Megan ponders: essentials? Her face and neck and under her arms, of course, but does she also mean *there*?

While Lavinia is in the bathroom, which is some ways down the hall, Megan looks around (of course she does, given her fascinated curiosity about Lavinia), although (of course) she feels guilty, furtive. But the room does not yield up much beyond expensiveness and confusion. A pair of earrings that, if real, are diamonds and rubies, lie across an open book, and the book turns out to be Hobbes, instead of some romantic poetry, as it should be, for those earrings.

But, having got up to inspect the earrings and to identify the book, Megan next sees a drift of envelopes scattered across the desk, where the book was lying. Several are addressed in the same hand, a strong, passionate forward slant, very masculine but curiously ornate, and the envelopes themselves are most ornate, a heavy vellum. Others with airmail stamps are from some naval officer, overseas. Several typed envelopes have the return address of a law firm in Washington; her father? Megan looks more closely at the first and largest, most interesting group: that violent hand. She sees that the man's last name is Rodman, clearly, and the first is—Harry? Harvey?

At just that moment, perhaps fortunately, there is a loud distracting noise from the quad below; the WAVES who live in Briggs Hall are marching, singing something Jolly Sixpence, as usual. Thus Megan is at the window, looking down, when Lavinia comes back, hurrying, into the room. Megan is not poking around Lavinia's desk, reading names from envelopes.

"Well," laughs Lavinia, smelling of flowers, "if I can just come up with some decent underwear I'll be okay. He'll fall more and more in love with me—"

Decent underwear? More in love? Breathlessly, Megan considers implications.

In any case, what Lavinia seems to have meant by decent turns out to be a tiny white lace bra, a white satin garter belt and some white silk panties, the kind that button at the side, like shorts. Not at all like the panty girdles or plain white briefs, so protectively tight at the legs, that Megan and most girls wear.

"Do you think he'll hate me because my panties haven't been ironed?" asks Lavinia, with her laugh.

Megan tries to answer with her own laugh, or with any sound at all, but fails. She is thunderstruck: does Lavinia mean that she has let him touch—that she will again—?

"Oh, I'm afraid I've shocked you, Megan baby. I forget how pure you are."

Megan rather unsuccessfully gets out, "Oh, I'm not all that pure," and again, she tries to laugh.

"Oh, really, that's good. We must talk about it sometime." They exchange a long look, and then Lavinia, seeming to pull herself together, says that she thinks she had better go on down-stairs. "I don't think there's anyone on bells."

By now Lavinia is fully dressed, gray flannel skirt, pale pink sweater, cashmere. (Megan for some time has puzzled over the fact that Lavinia's sweaters and skirts look much better on her than anyone else's do, and now she arrives at a simple explanation, which is that they all fit her, perfectly. Whereas, that year, almost everyone else has carefully cultivated the sloppy look of oversized clothes. Including overweight, bosomy, overshy Megan.)

Lavinia picks up her dark red coat from its heap at the foot of her bed, together the two girls leave the room; they start down the hall, toward the stairs. Just at the top landing Lavinia pauses though. She touches Megan's arm for an instant, holding her back, and with one of her most intent looks, Lavinia says, "Oh, I forgot, there's something I really need you to do for me. A favor." She looks down the stairs, and then turns back to Megan as she says, mysteriously, "I need you to come to the Ritz for lunch with me next Thursday. There'll be someone else along. A person I know. I can't explain right now, but you will? Okay?"

Before Megan can say anything at all they start down the stairs, but even if Megan had meant to refuse, what could she have said? Although she is already thinking, God, the Ritz, whatever can I wear? And if the other person is a girl we'll split the check three ways, probably, and it could cost—anything!

From the foot of the stairs, from the front desk Megan and Lavinia can see into the small, rather shabby visitors' room; they can both see a tall, dark, thin young man, in a neat ROTC uniform. He is sitting there alone, staring at his hands.

Megan has begun to say to Lavinia, "Well, so long, I'll see you," when Lavinia takes her arm and pulls her into that tiny room. The boy stands up politely, but his face has fallen, as he visibly (to Megan) thinks, Oh God, she's bringing a friend along. A fat friend.

Lavinia is saying, "This is Megan. Megan, I want you to meet Gordon Shaughnessey."

"Nice to meet," Megan and Gordon Shaughnessey mutter simultaneously, and then, more coherently, Megan says, "Well bye. See you later."

Lavinia looks at Megan with an expression which would seem to say, Help me, I'm scared. Or, on anyone else that is what that quick look would mean. But Lavinia is never frightened, is she?

Of course not. In a firm way, with her knowing smile, Lavinia says, "Goodbye, little Megan. See you later." She then turns on Gordon her look of absolute, concentrated attention; it is also a very sexy look, Megan observes. And to Gordon, Lavinia says, very softly, "Hello."

Megan leaves. Going down the front steps of Barnard she feels as though she is stumbling, falling—but she is not, not really.

If she hangs around the dorm all day and night, waiting for George to call, two things will surely result, Megan knows: one, George will not, will most certainly not call; and, two, she will go out of her mind, go nuts.

Therefore, she forces herself out on long walks; she walks everywhere, all the environs of Harvard Square. She forces herself to think about houses, architecture. She regards the hard spare elegance of the big houses out on Brattle Street, contrasting them to the softly styled Spanish stucco houses in Palo Alto, or on the Stanford campus. Even the Protestant churches back in California have a Spanish mission look, she remembers, her stoic gaze fixed on the severe white lines of Christ Church, near Harvard Square.

Certainly the New England air is different, too, especially now in mid-September, with the perceptible approach of fall. Even sorely troubled as she is (for surely George had promised, promised her sailing and the Cape, and meeting his parents), even so sad and distracted as she is, Megan catches the lively cool vibrations in that deep blue New England air, before the faintest yellowing of leaves, the autumnal desertions of birds.

Every day she walks for hours and hours, and back at home in the dorm she does reading for a course to be given that fall, called Criticism of Poetry. They will study Donne and Yeats, Dryden, Pope and Keats. She has read at least some of all those poets but Donne, of whom she has barely heard before.

When she is not walking, or seriously reading, she thinks painfully, and sometimes bitterly, of George.

Also, she worries about the lunch at the Ritz with Lavinia, which has been several times postponed. Selfishly, she wishes that Lavinia were not so totally occupied with her new love affair, with Gordon Shaughnessey. She and Lavinia have hardly had a conversation, much less "really talked."

She is much lonelier than she can afford to admit to herself.

"—and he's terribly old, he must be thirty-something," Lavinia is saying.

They are not at the Ritz at lunch, but at a delicatessen up on Mass. Avenue, at night. Gordon has guard duty, and thus for the first time since he and Lavinia met, Lavinia is free to spend some time with Megan.

Lavinia is in the midst of explaining what she has not had time to say before, that the Ritz lunch is not, after all, to take place: the man who was coming up from Washington, and from whom, it turns out, Lavinia wanted some sort of protection, will not, after all, arrive. Lavinia has brought along a two-page telegram from him. Megan has never seen such a telegram before, and when Lavinia remarked, "You see, he's really crazy," she had to agree, in a way. But of course she responds to extravagant gestures, having experienced rather few, only read of them. This is how love should be, Megan thinks.

And now, over roast beef sandwiches and coffee frappes, Lavinia is telling the story of that love affair, hers with Harvey, whom Megan has instantly identified as he of the thick vellum envelopes, the impassioned forward slant to his hand.

"I met him at some friends' house in Georgetown," Lavinia is saying, "and since he was so old I didn't pay much attention. Anyway, we were leaving for the country, Fredericksburg, the next day. This was last summer. But he must have got our address in Fredericksburg from someone because—well, you would not believe the flowers. Every day, at least fifteen dollars' worth of flowers. So when he called and asked me to meet him for dinner at the Shoreham, I sort of felt I ought to."

As always, when Lavinia tells a story, Megan is there: she is in the Shoreham's dining room, where she has never been. And she can see Lavinia, in some pale summer dress, see candles and roses and glasses of wine, on a white linen table. With an indistinct "older man," who is terrifically in love with her (Laurence Olivier?), who fell in love at first sight, who would be permanently in love.

"Well," Lavinia says, with the smallest frown, and the slightest blush, "well, I'd never had anyone in love with me like that. You know, before him I just knew *boys*. So I sort of fell in love with him too, although now I think I was mainly in love and excited by the way he felt. Anyway, it kept on like that all summer, this literal barrage of flowers, and these letters, and then I'd go into town, to meet him. It turned out that he had a suite at the Shoreham, he lived there. So, after dinner we'd go up to his room, and, uh, neck. Well, I must say, his technique was really smooth, his being older and all. Well, I'm just lucky I'm still a virgin. But we certainly did everything else."

Megan is barely aware of the food that she is eating—although the sandwiches are very good, and the frappe thick and sweet and cold—so enthralling does she find Lavinia's story, and so *right*: perfect that a rich older man should be insanely in love with Lavinia (Jane and Mr. Rochester!)—and all those flowers, those heavy letters. A suite at the Shoreham, where every night they would "do everything else," probably on a bed.

"But then when I went back to school last fall," Lavinia goes on, "I still thought I was in love but it got sort of embarrassing, all those letters. Sometimes two special deliveries a day. It was so *conspicuous.* And he wasn't someone I could tell anyone about, like the boys everyone else was writing to. He wasn't some freshman at Princeton (although he did go to Princeton, a long time ago). Or a senior at St. Paul's."

She looks at Megan: a question—how is Megan taking this? Seemingly satisfied, she continues. "I saw him when I went home for Christmas, and there certainly was all that old excitement, but then at some parties I heard a couple of things about him. People were getting a little suspicious about all that money. I mean, he didn't *inherit* it, not any of it. Even if he did go to Princeton.

"You know, basically Washington is a very small town, people know everything. And I began to think that if there was something even the tiniest bit wrong about his money, and if my father found out, well, actually if anyone found out—well, I began to think that I had to get out of it somehow. For one thing, I didn't want to come up here to college with something like that going on in my life. So, I began to hint that I thought I was too young to be so serious, corny stuff like that, and how I was going to need all my time at college for work. Well, that's a good laugh, isn't it, baby Megan?"

"Uh, I guess." But Megan cannot help feeling a little sad for poor Harvey.

"Well, I was saying stuff like that. And he would not listen to one word I said. And then instead of letters I began to get these crazy long telegrams. He must be spending a fortune."

Megan finds that she has finished her sandwich and her frappe, although she was not aware of eating. Lavinia has hardly touched her food, but then she has been doing all the talking. Now, as Megan watches, Lavinia takes a reluctant bite from her sandwich, a small sip of her frappe. "I guess I don't really feel like eating," she complains. "But I really should. Gordon says my bones stick into him," and she laughs.

Initially relieved about not having to go to the Ritz (money, and the problem of what to wear), Megan is now experiencing considerable regret about not meeting Harvey; for one thing, obviously he would have paid for the lunch. And in this cooling weather she could have worn her one good suit (a birthday present from Florence, from Joseph Magnin, the best store in Palo Alto; blue, really nice); everything would have been okay. Mostly though she is aware of the most intense curiosity about Harvey: the knight (ah! Mr. Knightly!), the perfect figure of romance. And a millionaire, or almost, probably.

"What does he look like?" Megan asks.

"Gordon? But you met him, silly Megan. Honestly, you do live in a dream world. How could you forget the handsomest man at Harvard? Honestly—"

"No. Not Gordon, Harvey."

"Well." Surprisingly, Lavinia looks both uncomfortable and displeased; she might almost be on the verge of saying that Harvey's looks are none of Megan's business, except that Lavinia is never so overtly rude. But she seems then to come to some sort of decision; the frown disappears, and in a confiding way she leans toward Megan. "Well, he's blond, and rather handsome, if you see him sitting in a restaurant, just his head and shoulders. But I guess he had polio or something, we never talked about it and I couldn't ask, but he's really crippled. Even on crutches he can hardly walk. And that's something that really scared me off. I mean, of course I never saw his legs, we never went that far, I told you, but the very idea— Really, I wasn't sure that I actually could—"

Lavinia's tone has been deeply, genuinely troubled, and sad. But then she shrugs, and the tone shifts. "Oh!" she cries out, "if he'd only leave me alone! Why won't he catch *on!*"

Megan is wholly concentrated on absorbing the fact of crippledness, Harvey's legs. And her mind has made a connection, which she would like to reject, between crippledness and romantic extremity; she thinks, and she wishes that she did not think, that of course (and maybe only) a crippled man would fall in love like that, and especially with Lavinia, so tall and blond, so *perfect*.

And she further makes another, highly unwelcome connection, this time between crippled and fat. She thinks of herself, fat Megan, and "madly in love" with George Wharton, who in his way is also perfect. She thinks of her own obstinate refusal to "catch on" to the fact that George Wharton does not love her.

Escaping back to Harvey, she sees too that he would have to be rich; otherwise, a cripple, he would not have dared, would not even have aspired to Lavinia. (Would George love her if she were rich?)

And: of course Lavinia would have to break it off, eventually. Even being seen with a crippled man must have been acutely painful to her, actually more painful than rumors of financial insecurity, irregularity. Megan starts to say, You know, really you're still a virgin because of Harvey's crippled legs. But of course she does not say that.

"Oh, *shit*," then says lovely Lavinia. "I've forgotten my billfold. Darling little Megan, would you pay? I'll get it next time, okay?"

"Of course."

5

"I just don't know," Lavinia's mother, who was once a fabled golden Southern beauty, is saying, vaguely, fuzzily, to her daughter. "I just don't know," Mrs. Harcourt repeats; she smells of lavender, and of sherry. "If this boy is coming all the way down here, I just don't see—" As so often happens, she then forgets what she is talking about, beyond a distant sense that she was about to say something important.

Lavinia's stomach knots in a familiar way, and she thinks as she has a thousand times before, Thank God, I don't even look like her.

She tries then to remind her mother of their earlier conversation, to bring her back. "But we always used to have Christmas at Fredericksburg," Lavinia states, "and I thought it would be so nice. It has nothing to do with Gordon."

That last was a total lie. The fact is that Lavinia is anxious, desperately anxious, that Gordon not visit them in Georgetown, in the huge house in which she and her mother now sit, in what is called the breakfast room, although no one has ever eaten a breakfast there. The Fredericksburg house is big too, but it is simpler; it can be passed off as a farm, and so it is called, by the Harcourts. But this Georgetown house, set back from P Street, with its weight of marble, and family portraits and delicate French antiques and ponderous draperies—this house could intimidate anyone, and especially Gordon, with his strong feelings about being Boston Irish, his father a policeman, living in Dorchester. In a house that Lavinia has never been allowed to see.

The irony of this fear, this anxiety about the impressiveness of her family house, is not lost on intelligent Lavinia; it is very ironic that she who has always loved her house so much should now be worried about its effect. She has even thought of it as her perfect setting (Harvey used to say, "It's the perfect house for the childhood of a princess. Now I'll have to get you an even bigger house, and don't think I won't." Well, probably he would have). And prior to the advent of Gordon in her life, Lavinia also saw her house as her perfect refuge; it kept people away, it put off those whom she chose to be put off. And now, for her to worry that Gordon, whom she absolutely loves, in this setting will love her less—well, it's very funny, very funny indeed—but whom could she tell?

"Well," says Mrs. Harcourt, blinking pale blue eyes in the general direction of some feeble Washington winter sunshine, just visible through one narrow leaded window, "well, I suppose you'd better talk to your father." And then, with one of her odd lurches into clarity, sobriety: "And in that case I'll start my packing."

The prospect of introducing Gordon to her mother is of course a further source of anxiety to Lavinia, but if her plan of Christmas in Fredericksburg, at "the farm," succeeds, that too will be resolved: Mrs. Harcourt so dislikes the country, and particularly that house, its wrap of river mists, its drafty rooms, that she generally takes to her bed and stays there, during long family stays in Fredericksburg. With luck, her mother will not even appear for meals, Lavinia calculates; Mrs. Harcourt subsists at such times on bouillon and soft-boiled eggs, which the maid takes up on trays, at intervals. She can easily be described to Gordon as "not very well," which is, God knows, the truth.

Another virtue of Fredericksburg is just that, the maid situation: at Fredericksburg there is only one, the inconspicuous brown Bessie. Whereas in town, along with Bessie, there is Clarissa and her husband, Oscar, who is not actually a butler, but he looks and acts like one, in his formal black suits, serving dinner. (Well, at least all of them are Negroes, none of them Irish, Lavinia suddenly thinks, wanting both to laugh and to cry at the very thought of Gordon confronted with Irish help. Jesus, with her luck they would turn out to be his distant relatives. At which Lavinia does laugh a little, to herself. She wishes Kitty were around.)

Six months of exposure to Boston have instructed Lavinia in certain social truths: while "Gordon Shaughnessey" sounded, at first, so romantic and glamorous to her, and sounds so still—so redolent of kings and castles, Irish poetry—in Boston it is not a "good name."

But she does not care anymore about those distinctions, those family-money-position badges that used to mean so much to her, about which she has always been so finely acute. None of that is important, of course it is not; she is so much in love with Gordon, and only love is really important. Only love.

Besides, Gordon is a National Scholar, and he belongs to the Fly Club, despite his name, and the Fly is really tops.

Lavinia looks like her father, the same gray eyes, same delicate, fine nose, and longish chin. And perhaps this striking resemblance is one of the things that makes her father adore her; more and more he adores his mirror, this increasingly beautiful young woman, his only child. Middle-aged, almost fifty at her birth (her mother, the beauty, was twenty-five years his junior), Mr. Harcourt's self-image has been kept young by his daughter, almost atoning for such disappointment with his wife. He is not old and gray and paunchy; he is young!

But he does not always yield to the whims of his beautiful daughter; of course not, he won't spoil her.

And so he now says, "But you know your mother, she isn't happy at Fredericksburg, Lavinia."

He looks at her sternly, and Lavinia returns the look. She does not say, however: Mother isn't happy anywhere. Neither of them says this, but the sentence lies there between them; it is the truth.

Mr. Harcourt sighs. "Well, we'll have to see," he says.

Knowing that she has won, they will spend Christmas at Fredericksburg, Lavinia retains a sad smile: it would not do to show triumph over an issue that will surely make her mother unhappier yet.

But.

"My mom's that upset," says Gordon over the phone, that night. "She'd planned on me being here all the time. And when I said Washington—"

"Oh, *darling*," Lavinia cries out, at this announcement of Gordon's that he is not, after all, coming down to Washington. It seems the worst thing that has ever happened to her: things gone all wrong, for almost the very first time. "I've missed you so much!" she cries out, uncontrollably.

"I've missed you, kid."

But something is wrong, Lavinia can hear it in his voice. Is he embarrassed to be giving in to his mother, a man of nineteen? Or could there be something else? Gordon has sometimes mentioned an old girl friend, Marge, whom Lavinia has understood to be his parents' choice for him. Is Marge around, is she, too, home for the holidays? Is Gordon more interested in her than he has admitted? This possibility causes Lavinia genuine pain, along with quick murderous impulses; however, at the same time she knows that it is extremely important, always, to pretend to believe whatever a man is saying. She figured that out a long time ago, on her own: never accuse them of lying. And so now she says, "Well, darling, maybe I could get my parents to let me come back a day or so early. We could have fun in Boston. Just see each other. You could meet me at South Station."

"Oh, great. Say, that would be terrific."

Something *is* wrong; his voice is wrong. However, she will not let herself think about it; that would be fatal. She will go back early to Boston, and when he sees her again everything will be all right, Lavinia is sure of that—sure of her power, in that way. Her beauty.

"I'll let you know when I'm coming," she says to Gordon. "Darling, I can't wait to see you." She will get all new clothes, everything new and beautiful, herself all beautiful and new. New lovely underclothes.

"Kid, me too," says Gordon.

It is quite true that she can't wait to see him again. To kiss him, to be kissed.

There is no point, then, absolutely no point in going to Fredericksburg for Christmas—and no point either in Lavinia's not taking moral credit for this shift in plans.

"I've been thinking," Lavinia says to her father, in the dark red leather library, full of books that no one reads. "You're really right, Mother does hate it at the farm. It doesn't seem fair to wish that on her, at Christmas."

"Ah, that's my considerate girl." Mr. Harcourt suppresses a sigh of relief.

Her gray eyes meet his, so similar, in a level, serious look. They appear, father and daughter, to be two people speaking the truth; they both appear to be kind and concerned.

Mr. Harcourt then asks, "How about your young man, though? It won't be too hard to entertain him here?"

"Oh no, there's always something to do. All the parties. You know." Not quite looking at her father, speaking vaguely, Lavinia adds, "Besides, he might not even be able to come. Those ROTC guys are always getting restricted."

"Oh." If Mr. Harcourt senses duplicity in all of this he gives no sign; perhaps he is relieved not to have to meet the boy? He next asks, "Well, have you given any thought to your Christmas present?" and he smiles.

Lavinia looks down modestly before she answers, "I really need some clothes. Maybe a coat?"

In a pleased, surprised way her father's smile deepens. "You've read my mind!" he tells her. "I've been giving some thought to coats for young ladies, in all that famous Boston cold. I thought—well, what would you say to a really good fur coat? A good dark mink? It would be a sort of investment."

He is always generous with Lavinia; still, this offer comes as a surprise. A couple of years ago, when she was at boarding school, Lavinia wanted a nice fur coat, just a simple sheared beaver, and her father really hit the ceiling: remarks about new-rich Jewish girls ("Jewesses"), vulgar little fifteen-year-olds in fur. So that now, when he offers mink, Lavinia is sorely tempted; she can so easily see herself in mink, she knows that she is perfect for some dark, glossy fur, her hair the perfect contrast, her height perfect to carry it off. Harvey was dying to give her a mink coat. *But*: she cannot appear in mink, meeting Gordon, mink would be something that neither he nor anyone in his family could afford. She will have to settle for a really good black wool coat; no one not knowing a great deal about clothes, and Gordon knows nothing at all, would guess how expensive it will be.

Demure, Lavinia says to her father, "Oh honestly, Daddy, I just don't know. Don't you think that maybe, with the war on and all, I should just get a plain black wool coat?"

"Well, of course. Whatever you say, my darling. But come to think of it I'm sure you're right. And I'm proud that you had the thought."

Gazing at each other in mutual satisfaction, Lavinia and her father lift similar long chins, in similar gestures of pride and self-deception.

"Look, I can't even listen to your excuses for not doing my coat on time. I am leaving for Boston on Friday morning. I am coming in here on Thursday afternoon to pick up my coat. At that time you will have it ready. Is that clear?"

Gray eyes flashing, chin raised, Lavinia delivers this not-pretty speech to the large pale-brown woman who is sitting on the floor, her face on a level with the hem of Lavinia's new coat, her mouth full of pins, her right hand clutching a stubby piece of chalk. Lavinia does not look beautiful, at that moment, but her pale face has terrific power, nobility, almost. At boarding school, in the senior play she was Joan of Arc, and she could be playing Joan right now, so convincing, so driven by a sense of mission is she.

The pins prevent the Negro woman on the floor from saying anything at all, but her eyes express acquiescence. Resignation (she hardly has much choice).

Lavinia smiles. "You do the most wonderful work," she says, and now she is very pretty. "And it's not quite right around the waist. I want it to fit perfectly. Like all my clothes."

Getting off the train, on a Friday night that is also New Year's Eve, Lavinia is very beautiful. With the perfectly fitted, perfectly simple black coat (that cost more than the month's salary of the Negro fitting woman), she wears perfect black suede shoes, with high thin heels, and a filmy pale pink scarf at her throat. As she steps down carefully from the high train, off and into Gordon's arms, she sees her own beauty reflected in Gordon's eyes. In his kiss.

Whatever has been wrong will now be all right. He loves her entirely, as she loves him. They are perfect for each other, perfect together.

They break apart to look at each other, and kiss again.

Gordon says, "Well, we'd better start. I've got the car, old Potter's off skiing in New Hampshire, the bum."

"Oh, Gordon, that's perfect."

He picks up her bag. "Say, what've you got in this thing, your rock collection?"

She laughs, although she has heard the joke before; it is what Gordon says whenever he carries anything of hers, even the green book bag that he bought for her at the Coop. His first present. Thinking of this, of presents, it comes to Lavinia that later that night, at midnight, maybe, Gordon will give her the tiny gold fly, the emblem of his club. You are not supposed to give them away, and if he did it would mean—not exactly an engagement, but something important. A symbol. A little frightened (suppose he does not give it to her, ever?), Lavinia realizes just how much she wants that tiny fly.

"Well, how about it?" asks Gordon. "Dinner at the Pudding, okay?"

Well, it is not okay; they go to the Pudding all the time, and now, in wartime, the Pudding is not an exclusive place; it has been turned into an officers' club, officers from everywhere, all over the place. All kinds of men, who would not under normal circumstances belong to a club at Harvard, or even be at Harvard. Lavinia is more than a little tired of dinner at the Pudding, although tonight, for New Year's Eve, there will be a band, and dancing. But she had been hoping, well, hoping for dinner in Boston, maybe dancing there: the Ritz, or at least the Fox and Hounds. However, however, she firmly tells herself, nothing like that is important, really. What matters is how handsome Gordon is, with his thick almost blue-black hair, his lovely fine mouth and clear pale skin. His blue eyes. What matters is love. "Oh, wonderful," says Lavinia, convincingly, smiling up at Gordon, clutching his arm delicately against her breast.

At the Pudding Lavinia and Gordon know a lot of people, but tonight fewer than usual of their friends are there for dinner. They are all having dinner in Boston, Lavinia imagines. However, she is pleased to see that Gordon leads them to a small table, where they will be alone. They can talk.

They have had a couple of old-fashioneds in the bar downstairs;

they are seated and talking about their dinner—maybe some wine?—when suddenly there is a loud clumping noise in the dining room, above all the din of silver and glassware and conversation. Everyone looks up, Lavinia and Gordon too, and there is Potter, who is supposed to be skiing in North Conway. Here he is, though, with a huge cast on his leg. Potter Cobb.

Laughing, his face flushed and his pale blond hair less sleek than usual, he is moving toward their table, hobbling along. As he approaches they can see that both his progress and his balance are impeded by two heavy bottles, one carried in each hand. French champagne—Lavinia knows that label.

Potter is in love with Lavinia, he has been since they first met, last fall, at an after-game party. But he loves her in a pleasant, silent, untroubling way. Lavinia is used to inspiring such feelings, and she really likes Potter, he reminds her of some of her very nicest cousins. But tonight her heart sinks a little at the sight of him.

Potter is sensitive, generally, and his manners, of course, are impeccable. And, tonight, he seems to sense that he should not be there with them, with Gordon and Lavinia, despite his gifts of champagne. "Well, talk about barging in with four left feet," he says, somewhat breathlessly. "But I couldn't resist showing you this terrific piece of contemporary sculpture that seems to have landed on my left foot. And just as I was going out of the house the old man pressed these cold bottles into my moist hot hands. As a matter of fact I wasn't at all sure you'd be here tonight."

"Well, where else?" To Lavinia, Gordon's voice has an uncharacteristically hearty sound; it seems to boom. "And pull up a chair if you can make it," Gordon says. "Of course you'll have dinner with us. And you can tell us all about your bloody skiing accident."

Lavinia smiles in an automatically flirtatious way at Potter, who responds, "Our Southern beauty is yet more beautiful, wouldn't you agree, Gordon, old man?"

"Definitely, definitively. Come on and sit down, you old fool."

Potter really didn't have to sit down and have dinner with them, Lavinia is thinking. He could have one glass of wine, and tell them about his stupid ankle, all in about ten or fifteen minutes. Not stay all through dinner, ordering even more wine, and until dessert and coffee. *Brandy.*

But that is exactly what Potter does; he stays and stays and talks and talks and talks, and orders drinks that he insists are to go on his tab, like some garrulous rich old uncle. "In all my skiing years I never saw ice like that," he seems to have said several times.

"What you mean is that you *didn't* see the ice," chimes in Gordon. To Lavinia, it is not an especially funny remark, but the two men really break up over it. In fact Gordon seems to be having a wonderful time, and worse, he does everything to encourage Potter to stay with them.

At some point in all the ski talk, Lavinia catches a familiar name: George Wharton. A demon on skis, according to Potter. George Wharton, the beloved of foolish Megan, although Megan doesn't seem to see him very often.

And so Lavinia asks, "George Wharton, really? Was he by himself up there?"

"Oh, you know George? Well, he was with Connie, of course. Connie Winsor. They're practically engaged. But you must know Connie too, if you know old George."

"Well, not exactly. He's just sort of the friend of a friend."

By that time they are drinking brandy, and the dining room is almost empty; everyone else is downstairs, dancing, celebrating New Year's Eve.

Potter says, "Well now, I insist that you two kids go on down and rush into the fray on the dance floor. I absolutely insist."

Well really—at last. But when Lavinia looks over at Gordon she sees that his pale face is paler yet, is dead white, and breaking out in sweat across his forehead and on his upper lip. Gordon is drunk; he is going to be sick.

Probably just in time, he gets up and lurches across the room, to the men's room. Lavinia does not watch him go, nor does she look up when Potter says, "Well, the poor old guy. All my fault, really. Ordering all that stuff," and he looks regretfully in the direction of his departed friend.

Gordon does not come back. More time passes; a weak conversation limps along between Potter and Lavinia, and still no Gordon.

At last Potter says, "Well, I'd really better check." He gets up and clumps across the floor.

In his absence Lavinia peers at her own face, in her small gold compact; she is okay, she sees, nothing smeared or shining, or out of place.

Looking embarrassed, Potter comes back alone. "I think I'd better take you home," he says. "He'll be okay, but it may take some time. I'll come back later and pick him up."

Lavinia smiles, radiantly. "I'd love for you to take me home," she says.

Potter drives slowly, in the big car that, although actually his, Lavinia thinks of as Gordon's; they have spent so much time necking in it. In the streets of Cambridge people are blowing horns, making noise, all over Harvard Square. There is a near traffic jam; it takes almost twenty minutes to get from the Pudding over to the Radcliffe dorms—twenty minutes during which Potter and Lavinia do not speak. It is easy not to, with all that noise outside.

Somewhat surprisingly, Potter parks the car at the far end of the quad, near the tennis courts, where Lavinia and Gordon often have parked; it is darkest there. Potter's intentions seem innocent, however; he only asks, "Want a cigarette before you go in? Actually it's quite early, for New Year's Eve."

Not answering him, on a quick impulse which she neither understands nor examines, Lavinia moves toward Potter; her hands reach and clasp the back of his neck, her mouth presses his.

For an instant Potter simply allows himself to be kissed, like a man savoring some new sensation, passively. But then, very gently, smoothly, knowingly, his hands reach into her coat; he pulls her to him, and he is kissing her deeply, as Lavinia thinks, How odd this is, we might be anyone at all, any couple on New Year's Eve. How impersonal sex is, really, after all. She thinks all that even as she responds, returning his kiss and the pressure of his body.

At last they separate. For a moment Lavinia is afraid that Potter will say something wrong, will say that he loves her, or something, ruining it all. Instead he reaches into a pocket, probably for a handkerchief. She is also afraid that he has come to some false conclusion, that his silence is ominous.

Having found the handkerchief, Potter offers it. "You need this?"

"Thanks, I have one." Lavinia applies her own small handkerchief to her mouth, and then, expertly, fresh lipstick, as though she could see in the dark.

Potter says, "You're very beautiful, you know, Lavinia."

She smiles, as she thinks that that was the perfect thing for him to say. Exactly right, not spoiling or defining anything. She smiles upon him, in the dark, as she says, "I'd better go in now."

He clumps along beside her to the steps of Barnard Hall, where, of course, they do not kiss again. Lavinia touches his arm. "Thank you, Potter. Really, thanks very much."

"My pleasure." He makes a gesture as though touching his hat to her (so like Potter, that) and then he is gone.

Lavinia does not hear from Gordon all the next day, New Year's Day. Rather expecting that he will just come over, in Potter's car, probably, and take her somewhere (she plans to be very kind and understanding; anyone can drink too much) she spends the day alone, reading, but she is all dressed, all day, in one of her best white sweaters, and she stays carefully within range of the floor phone; she has let the girl on bells know where she is. Thank God the dorm is almost deserted, and especially that none of her friends are around: no Peg with her booming questions, "Well, where's Mr. Shaughnessey keeping himself today?" Or Megan, with her too-intelligent, hypersensitive eyes; Megan would not ask but she would visibly wonder. Cathy at least would be incurious; in fact heaven knows what Cathy is thinking, most of the time. Very possibly she disapproves of a nice Catholic boy like Gordon taking up with a wicked Episcopalian. (Gordon has told Lavinia that his religion is not very important to him, but sometimes she wonders: does he only say that for her benefit, in the same way that he says that he never really cared for his old girl friend, Marge?)

· · ·

No word from Gordon, not that day or the next, and then vacation is over, and everyone is back. Lavinia tells all her friends that Gordon has been restricted, such a bore.

She admits to herself that she is suffering, and admits it to no one else, of course not. She is in actual pain, and it takes all her tricks of makeup, eye cream, and varieties of powder, not to let it show. When Megan was suffering most over George Wharton, she used to slop around in her Levi's and a torn old sweater, no makeup, her broken heart all over her silly fat face. (But Lavinia really likes Megan, the little fool. She will never tell Megan about Connie Winsor; Megan will find out for herself, and Lavinia will be as comforting as she can. She has even thought of introducing Megan to one of Gordon's friends, maybe Potter?—but then Megan is so— so fat, and her clothes are never right.)

And how ridiculous all this *love* is, Lavinia concludes. She is deeply contemptuous of her own pain, as she was of Megan's; she is aware of being extremely foolish, she knows. "Love," finally, turns out to have no meaning at all. Harvey was madly in love with her, and she was (she *is*) madly in love with Gordon, who (quite possibly) still loves Marge. And Megan is in love with George, who is practically engaged to Connie Winsor.

Nevertheless, she will not allow Gordon to drift off from her like that, or whatever it is that he imagines himself to be doing.

She sends him a telegram, at Eliot House. "Please meet me at St. Clair's for tea at four on Thursday."

Lavinia, in her softest sweater, looks fragile, delicately bruised, rather than accusatory. And she speaks very softly. "I just wanted to see you again," she says. "I missed you, and I wondered."

"Ah, Lavinia, you're too good and beautiful for me, I always knew it. And there's things, things with my family, friends of my family. Things you'd never understand."

Smiling sadly, "understandingly," Lavinia is at the same time thinking how *Irish* he sounds; God, almost a brogue. She says, "You mean your family won't approve of me? Of us?"

"Well, that's a hard way to put it, but you could say that, you could indeed. But Lavinia, when I see you I only know that I love you. Ah, beautiful Lavinia—"

Dear God, is he going to cry? The cheap lower-class mick. "I love you too," she says.

Gordon leans toward her, and there are indeed tears in his eyes. "Besides," he says, "no one's supposed to know this, but we're shipping out next week."

"Shipping out?" For a moment sheer panic makes it hard for Lavinia to breathe. A second later, though, she is able to wonder just what it is that she fears: his being away? being killed?

"Yes, just for a practice cruise. On the *Enterprise*." He looks at his watch. "Look, I have to get back now. I'm on duty. But I'll call you tomorrow. We'll see each other for sure. I have to see you."

Gordon does not call, not that day or the next. Lavinia continues to keep herself looking beautiful, and to say that Gordon is restricted, on duty—as she feels her thin blood blacken with rage and pain.

Only to Peg does she confide that Gordon is shipping out, and only that; she does not mention not hearing from him. "Oh Peg, I'm so frightened! I don't know what to do."

"Poor little Lavinia—oh, poor thing! But you mustn't worry, Gordon will come back safe and sound to you. No one gets hurt on a practice cruise. And in the meantime, would you like a nice back rub?"

"Oh Peg, you're so nice. Whatever would I do without you?"

Big kind Peg, whom Lavinia secretly suspects of being a lesbian.

At last, beneath Peg's big strong clumsy well-meaning hands, Lavinia allows herself to cry.

.   .   .

A week later, on board the *Enterprise,* on the trial cruise, Gordon Shaughnessey dies of a burst appendix. Only the circumstance of its happening on an aircraft carrier makes it seem a military death.

6

By early spring of that year, 1944, the four friends have divided themselves into twos; it is now Lavinia and Peg who are always together, and Megan and Cathy. By everyone else the four are still perceived as a group (to which Megan was once so eager, so desperate to belong), and they are still friends; there has been no falling out. But Megan, for example, has spent no time alone with Lavinia, has had no private conversations with her since Christmas vacation; nor have Cathy and Lavinia spent any time together. Cathy and Peg were never more than friends of friends, and so it is less remarkable that they have hardly talked; they never really did. All in all there has been a distinct change, though, in the four-way relationship.

Undoubtedly the death of Gordon Shaughnessey had something to do with this new patterning. Since that happened Lavinia has spent even more time with Peg; they go to movies in Boston, even out to dinner together. It is as though Lavinia were newly widowed, and being cared for by her friend.

Megan and Cathy find it interesting to talk about.

"It's very strange," Megan says, one morning in Hood's, between bites of bran muffin, sips of coffee. "It's as though in some way she's happier now; she'd almost rather be going to matinees with Peg than waiting around for Gordon, the way she did all last fall."

"I know what you mean." Generally Cathy simply listens and agrees, she is not inclined to put forward theories of her own. But sometimes there is a sharp thrust to her observations. "Lavinia does everything in such a beautiful, ladylike way," she now says. "And 'war widow' is an especially good thing for her to do."

They laugh, and Megan agrees, "Oh *yes.*" She enjoys Cathy so much, she finds Cathy so very bright, and funny. She adds, "Lavinia is a terrific widow, one of the prettiest and youngest around the Square."

They laugh again, until at the same moment the possible unfunniness of being a war widow strikes them both, in a sobering way. But they do not express this perception to each other; they never talk about the war. It isn't funny.

"And Peg is the perfect comforting friend." Megan carries it on, in their usual tone. "Peg's not going to like it when Lavinia gets tired of being a widow and starts going out again." Some time ago Megan faced the fact that she just does not care much for Peg, jolly noisy old good-hearted Peg.

"Oh, you're so right," agrees Cathy. "This is the best time of all for Peg."

Megan is aware that envy, sheer unacceptable and generally inadmissible envy, is making her more malicious toward Lavinia than she should be. Whatever was going on between Lavinia and Gordon (and Megan sometimes caught a vague sense that Lavinia was not quite as "sure of him" as she sounded), it is probably easier to bear a lover's death than his living absence in your life, which is the case with Megan, who now hears from George Wharton perhaps once a month. One beer at the Oxford Grill and then some furious necking, somewhere, and then a miserable month or so of silence. Megan has wished that George were dead; if he were dead she would behave much better, she is sure. "I'm surprised Lavinia isn't wearing black," she now says, quite viciously, to Cathy.

Cathy looks at her and giggles, as in a somewhat academic way she says, "Actually in some cultures white is the mourning color. And she is wearing mostly white these days, if you'll notice."

"God, what she must spend on clothes." This remark does not make Megan feel guilty: it is okay to envy someone's large clothes allowance, whereas it is certainly not okay to envy the death of a friend's lover.

Cathy suddenly giggles again, clearly at some random thought, as she asks, "Did you ever read those really old books about girls' boarding schools? Grace Harlow or someone? There were a lot of them at a resort we used to go to. Anyway, there were always four girls. One beautiful and rich and wicked, and one big and fat and jolly. That's Lavinia and Peg, of course."

"I'm not the big jolly one?" Megan asks, somewhat anxiously.

"You're not so jolly. And Peg is much bigger than you are."

"Well, thanks."

Cathy goes on. "I'm not too clear about the other two. I think one was poor and virtuous and the other one was very smart, or some combination like that."

Megan laughs. "Well, I'm poor and you're virtuous, and God knows both of us are smart, so I guess it'll work out all right?"

"I guess. But is Lavinia wicked, really?"

In a speculative way they regard each other, and then, again, they both begin to laugh. Later Megan wonders: was Cathy thinking of the four girls in those books when she said that it would be better if there were four of them?

One of the things that Megan thinks about a lot, that spring, is her own virginity, her "virtue." Despite all that violent necking with George, she is still technically a virgin; hands don't count.

"Technical virgin" is a favorite phrase of Janet Cohen's, with whom Megan has continued to be friends. "All those technical virgins from Cabot Hall," Janet will say, indicating an especially good-looking, mostly blond, and handsomely dressed group of girls, who all live in Cabot Hall.

Uncertain as to her exact meaning, Megan cannot quite ask; she is forced to conclude, on her own, that the phrase could apply to herself; she herself is someone who has gone "almost all the way." But does that mean that Janet and Adam Marr really do it, go all the way? She supposes that it must; they would surely feel that real sex is more honest.

Megan wonders: should she and George have done it? Would he then have loved her, and taken her to the Cape, sailing, meeting his parents? Would he have said that he loved her? Megan believes that Janet is right; actually doing it would have been more honest, and somehow cleaner.

That winter, curiously, there was also a lot of talk about virginity in Megan's Criticism of Poetry class. It came up particularly in discussions of Donne, and the sexual symbolism in the religious poetry: "I never shall be chaste, unless you ravish me." And then, when they got to Auden, there was the difficult "distortions of ingrown virginity." *Well*.

The professor, a dark, very pale-skinned man, almost luminous with intensity, had an odd gesture: with both hands stiffly outstretched before him, in a sudden motion he would dip them down, like opposing wings; he did this often, as he spoke of Donne. He talked about "the breaking through of virginity into wholeness," a phrase that resounded in Megan's eagerly receptive mind. Breaking through, virginity into wholeness.

Walking back along Garden Street to the Radcliffe dorms, in the wild blue air of a New England spring, Megan decides that what she and George have been doing is really dirty: perverted, wrong. All that squirming around together, tugging inside constricting clothes, pretending just to kiss. She decides that the next time she sees George they will go all the way. They will "do it."

However, as she crosses Cambridge Common, past the benches of young wives, some with babies or little children, others pregnant, Megan then begins to think of practicalities: just how will she go about altering their usual procedures, especially if George really does not want to do it? As she thinks of it, he is the one who has remained untouched; she has never touched him there, touched his, uh, thing. He is always fully clothed, his khakis firmly zipped. Whereas lately, desperately, Megan has left off wearing a panty girdle; she bought herself some open-legged silk panties, to be worn with a garter belt, the sort that Lavinia wears, so that he can more easily touch her. There. How possibly could she be more available, should he want to enter her? Does she have to reach for him, unzip and grab? Can men be raped?

She smiles to herself, at that thought, and then she thinks, Well, maybe George just isn't the one. But I have to stop being a virgin. A technical virgin.

Arrived back at the Radcliffe quad, and approaching Barnard Hall, Megan sees a man in khakis, a soldier, sitting on the front steps, and for an instant her silly heart leaps up at the thought that it could be George.

It is not George, of course, but someone smaller and thinner and far messier than George could ever be. Light brown curly hair, a big nose, thin face, and large, intense blue eyes. A face, in fact, that Megan recognizes, having so often seen its picture, on Janet Cohen's bureau. Without thinking, Megan says, "Oh! You're Adam Marr!" A severe infection on his left foot has brought Adam home from the Pacific.

"You want my autograph?" This comes in an exaggerated Brooklyn accent, with an Irish grin.

"Oh. I'm, uh, a friend of Janet's. Megan Greene." Abashed, Megan has muttered her name.

But Adam caught it. "Well, Megan Greene." He looks her over, as Megan stares at his eyes. She is thinking that she has never before, on anyone, seen such a hot, hot blue; he has literally burning eyes.

Still not getting up, still looking at her, hard, Adam Marr then pronounces, "You know, Megan Greene—by the way, I like your name, are you going to be a writer?—if you'd take off a few pounds, you'd be one terrific tomato."

He has a fairly deep, very attractive voice; the voice and the grin combine to make what he has just said inoffensive, so that Megan is more pleased than not. She is flattered, actually, at the attention being paid her.

She says, "I guess. I mean, I know I should lose some weight."

"Yeah. Shed the baby fat along with the cherry." Adam has said this in, again, a burlesque Brooklynese, and then, somewhat jarringly, he continues in what Megan has learned to recognize as

"Harvard." "But actually," he says, "it's nice to see a few young virgins around these days." The grin appears and remains.

How can he tell, though; does it show, her "ingrown virginity"? Would he say such a thing to Lavinia? (Lavinia too is still a virgin, Megan is sure.) Wondering, and blushing, Megan is at the same time thinking that Adam Marr's eyes are very sexy; he is an exceptionally sexy-looking boy—young man. Of course he and Janet do it. They go all the way. Make love.

"Well, I guess Janet will be along soon," Megan manages to say. "I'd better go in and check my mail."

"Okay. See you later, Megan Greene."

"Well. Bye." He is somehow hard to leave, perhaps because he continues to look at her, in his particular way. Megan feels herself transfixed there, but at last she does walk past him, faintly smiling, and she pushes open the front door.

Thinking of Adam Marr, and wondering if she should have stayed on and talked to him, Megan goes over to the wall of pigeonholes, where the mail is distributed.

In her box are a letter from her mother (that too familiar hand, small and rounded, reaching forward) and a postcard, in a hand that she also recognizes instantly, although she has seen it only once before, on another card. It is George's writing, and with a swift closing of her heart, like a fist, Megan knows that what it says will cause her pain.

"Guess what?" the postcard begins; as on the postcard in which he wished her a Merry Christmas, there is no salutation. "It seems I'm going to be married, in June. Girl name of Connie. Then probably OCS. Hope you're well and happy. All best wishes. George Wharton."

"Men are very different from women, you have to remember that," says Lavinia to Megan, that afternoon. Megan has been crying, in a messy, uncontrolled way; she still is, off and on.

"Actually," Lavinia continues kindly, "I had heard something from Potter Cobb, about a girl named Connie, and George

Wharton. But you know how people talk, it could have meant absolutely nothing. She could have been just some skiing pal, or something. And I knew if I said anything you'd be upset. Honestly, Megan—"

"But Christ," Megan then gets out, between large gulped sobs, "what did he think we were doing? What was all that about?"

Cool Lavinia, in what has come to seem her habitual white, looks speculatively at Megan. "Now Megan, you're not going to tell me—"

It is quite clear what she has meant, and so Megan answers, "No, of course we didn't. But you know, almost. I just don't see how he could."

"Men are different," Lavinia repeats, with emphasis. Her gray eyes are serious, and genuinely pained. She still suffers, thinking of Gordon Shaughnessey, although she is less pained by his death than by his previous defection (it has even occurred to her that if he had not died he might have married *Marge*); but fortunately no one, not even Peg, or Potter, knows how things were between them, at the end.

"I guess," sniffs Megan.

"My old pal Kitty always says that the best cure for one man is to go out and neck with another," says Lavinia, smiling wanly.

"Oh, maybe. But I really don't feel like doing that. And I hardly know anyone else," Megan accurately says. "But do you think that's true? I mean, have you ever?"

"No, but I'm sure thinking about it." Lavinia's smile, which tearful Megan does not quite see, is both bitter and determined. It is high time that she gave up this pretense of mourning for Gordon's death, Lavinia thinks, and next she thinks, Well, how about Potter, who is really in love with her, and rich? Her father would like Potter, very much.

"Janet Cohen's going to fix me up with her brother, he's at MIT," says Megan, a little later, thoughtlessly having forgotten Lavinia's not liking Janet.

And so Lavinia frowns. "Now Megan, you know that Janet is all very well, I'm sure she's perfectly nice. But I've told you,

you must not start going out with Jews. What you don't know is, if you go out with one of them, all his friends will be after you."

"But what's wrong with that?" Megan has a sudden, vastly cheering image of herself, pursued by a host of Jewish men, all dark and brilliant and mysterious. And sexy, all of them: no problems there with zippers, no more ingrown virginity, her own virginity broken through into wholeness. And everyone knows that Jewish boys are smarter; they have to be if they get into Harvard, what with quotas. And often they like music, even poetry.

A quick side thought distracts her then: Megan wonders, Does Irish Adam Marr have this same view of Jewish girls? Is Janet sexy for Adam, in a way that an Irish girl could never be?

"You really don't understand about Jews," Lavinia is saying. "It may be different in California. But if you'd ever lived in a big Eastern city, you'd know what they're like."

Megan begins to cry again.

7

After a couple of weeks, although occasionally a poem or certain music (Janet Cohen playing Beethoven quartets, on her record player) can still move Megan to tears, and although she still ascribes that emotion, that sense of loss and yearning, to the loss of George Wharton, in another way Megan feels considerably better for having digested his cruel announcement. She is given, really, neither to excessive mourning nor to self-pity, and she grasps at her sense of relief, at no longer jumping at the sound of the phone, or staying in the dorm and hoping he will call (well, she never did too much of that). Now she is free to do anything that anyone suggests.

Unfortunately, though, for a while, no one makes an interesting or plausible suggestion. It somehow does not work out for her to meet Janet Cohen's brother, who is involved with a girl at Wellesley, or somewhere.

As she walks across the Yard, and in and out of classrooms, walks around the Square, Megan stares at the numerous handsome men and boys, and she thinks, Why is it that no one sees how available I am? Why isn't it clear that I don't *choose* to be an ingrown virgin?

She takes to wearing more makeup, pancake and mascara, and darker lipstick, even to classes, until Lavinia tells her to stop. "Megan, it isn't you, you look kind of scary like that, and a little cheap." Which was very likely true.

It is also possible, Megan later considers, that sheer need shows on her face, which could well be frightening, especially to boys as inexperienced as she herself is. She washes off her face, and she concentrates on a carefree look, a happy person who does not need anyone. She works on losing weight.

There is a man, though, who seems to be following her around. He is an instructor in her survey philosophy course, at Harvard what is called a section man. Mr. Jacoby, Simon Jacoby, who is at least ten years older than Megan. But everywhere she turns, there he is: in the poetry section of the book department at the Coop; in St. Clair's; back and forth across the Yard—there he is, slyly ducking his head, saying, "Oh, Miss Greene. Good morning."

Well, it can't be an accident, can it? this always being where she is? Megan decides that in some way she will confront him; well, what the hell, she thinks. And so, late one morning in the Coop, in front of the few shelves of new poetry, new thin volumes of Auden and Spender and Delmore Schwartz, she says, "Oh, good morning, Mr. Jacoby," with a very wide, blue-eyed California smile.

"Oh, Miss Greene, how are you? It's, uh, really spring now, isn't it?"

Megan agrees, having planned to agree to almost anything. She offers suggestively, "It's really hard to study in this weather, though."

He smiles and shrugs, his gesture saying, Yes, how true, how very right you are. "I live out near Concord," he tells her. "I keep all the windows open and the country smells are, uh, really terrific. But very distracting. I'm from New York City," he adds.

You are really terrific, and very distracting, is what Megan understands is really being said to her. And so she only smiles, in a pleased, receptive way. So that he has to continue.

"I don't suppose," he begins, "uh, would you ever be interested in a drive out there? Out to Concord?"

If you'll promise to take me to bed, take off all my clothes, and really make love to me. These words occur to Megan, who does not say them, of course, but they make her smile instead—perhaps seductively. "Oh, I'd love to," she says, quite possibly with more fervor than Simon Jacoby had expected.

"Well, um, are you busy this afternoon?"

She is not, and twenty minutes later—after a brief stop at Barnard Hall, ostensibly for Megan to pick up a sweater, but during which she actually changes from an ugly panty girdle to the silk pants originally bought for George's ineptly probing hands—twenty minutes later they are racing along, over the wide highways, the broad and gentle hills that lead out to Concord.

Simon's car is an impressively long, open, dark gray convertible, with red leather lining, smelling new. To Megan it is an exciting, almost an erotic smell, and it is reassuring to her that Simon Jacoby should turn out to be rich, as well as Jewish and interested in poetry, probably music. And maybe sex.

The true countryside, soon reached in that heavy, powerful car, is alive with spring: in steep meadows the long gray-brown grasses, beaten down all winter by the snow, now seem visibly to rise. White water leaps up from the swollen, rushing brooks, and on fruit trees the newest, palest boughs of blossoms sway very gently in the breeze.

Simon's house is an odd box of glass and steel, set up on what look like stilts, at the edge of some thick dark woods. "I know, it's terribly Bauhaus," he explains (to Megan, incomprehensibly) as they leave the car and approach this structure. "Some students of Breuer's did it for kicks, I guess. But the price is right—some friends of my parents own it. I like the privacy and the isolation. Sometimes."

"There's a Frank Lloyd Wright house on the Stanford campus," Megan offers. "It's really odd."

Going up the steps Simon takes her arm, and at that very slight touch Megan thinks, Ah, good.

There is not much furniture inside, just bookcases lining the one wall not made of glass, a big desk, a record-playing machine, and records. On the floor there is a wide, wide mattress, covered over with bright wool rugs. Nowhere to sit but on that mattress, and so Megan does sit there; she perches rather primly, and crosses her legs.

Simon hovers about her; this host-guest phase of their time together was not quite anticipated by either of them. Nervously, Simon says, "I didn't even ask, are you hungry? I always keep a lot of snacks around."

Megan has never been less hungry in her life, and so she can assure him, "Actually not." And, in a nice-guest way she remarks, "It's really pretty here. The woods."

"It was wonderful last winter," he tells her. "The snow. Little animals." And then, still an uneasy host and a not-quite-experienced seducer, "Well, maybe some wine? We can eat something later, if you want."

"Okay. Swell."

He goes into another room, as Megan thinks, This is extremely interesting—I am perfectly happy, I am having a good time, and it's less than a month since I got the postcard from George. Am I shallow? or what?

Simon comes back with a tall green bottle on a silver tray, two glasses, a small dish of peanuts. He opens the bottle and pours, and hands Megan a pale yellow glass. He says, Cheers.

Megan sips. It is cold and a little sour, but she smiles, and is about to say, What delicious wine, when Simon leans toward her. "You'll have to put down your glass," he tells her. "I can't wait another minute to kiss you."

At some moment, after they have made love for the third or perhaps the fourth time (their passages together tend to continue, or to merge), Simon begins to talk; he is naked, they both are, between fine sheets, beneath dark blankets. "I have to tell you, Megan," he says, raised up on an elbow, looking down at her, "you are the most terrifically amazing woman. You really are. I mean, you come the minute I do, or before. You're a living sexual fantasy, you know that? And you feel so smooth and slick, oh, beautiful! Do you have any idea how extraordinary you are? Most women—well, you're really exceptional."

In a dazed, pleased way Megan smiles up at him; evidently he could not tell that she was a virgin, which she is sure is just as well. He may even think she has spent a lot of afternoons like this, with men she picks up in bookstores (which is, come to think of it, exactly where she also met George Wharton, in the Stanford Bookstore). Curiously, it is perfectly all right with her if he does make these assumptions. If only there were something good to eat she would be perfectly happy, Megan thinks.

"I haven't even let you drink your wine," exclaims Simon, just then. And, telepathically—or perhaps he too is hungry?—"Couldn't you eat something now? Let me fix us a snack."

"Oh, sure," politely agrees Megan. "That would be great." She watches with interest as he emerges from under the bedclothes (on the way in, as it were, they were both too hurried to look at each other). Now she observes his thin dark muscular back, flat buttocks, black line between buttocks, black pubic hair. He has bent over to look for something on the floor, which he does not find. He mutters, Shit, and then, standing up, he turns to her. "I seem to have lost my shorts," he tells her.

It is pointing straight up, pointing toward her. Dark red, with an interesting tulip-shaped head. Simon looks down at himself, and he smiles as he says, "You see? You're a witch. A sex witch."

He gets back into bed with her, and they do it again.

A little later he says, "Oh, here're my shorts. No wonder."

Getting up, he puts them on, and this time he makes it into the next room, which must be the kitchen.

Lying there alone, still somewhat dazed, Megan considers what he has told her: Could it be true, that she is in some way amazing? some sexual way? Certainly, if all women experienced what she just has, they would do it all the time, every chance they got. Instead of so often pretending not to want to. In the phrase then current, playing hard to get. And so, she, Megan, must be different, in this way?

Simon comes back with some cold sliced meats and cheeses, butter and dark bread, on paper plates. Satisfied love has made him less formal, as well as more loquacious.

"But maybe in a way I always knew what you would be like," he now tells Megan. "I could never keep my eyes off you. I guess you noticed?"

"Sort of." Megan is concentrating on the food, which is mildly exotic to her. Delicious, she thinks, biting the dark sour bread, chewing, savoring.

That afternoon marks the beginning of a relationship that is, for Megan, somewhat exotic in itself; it falls into none of the categories that she has ever heard or read about. Certainly it cannot be described by any of the phrases current with college girls in those rigidly romantic times—even if Megan felt the need to describe it to anyone.

Surely one of the things that it is not is a great love affair: Simon continuously praises her in bed, he says that her body is beautiful, that he loves to look at her, as well as to touch, but he has never said that he loves her, nor ever asked her how she feels about him. He likes her, Megan is certain of that. He always behaves affectionately toward her, he even seems interested in her literary opinions. He is pleased by her enthusiasm for her poetry course, for Donne and Auden.

But: he makes no claims on her, and he does not take her out on weekends; he generally goes down to New York on Saturdays, he says. They see each other once or twice a week, on Tuesdays or Wednesdays, usually. Nor does he ask her about what she herself does, or has done, on weekends. If she goes out with anyone else, for instance: quite possibly he imagines that she does? And nothing about love, not ever.

Megan is less bothered than she is puzzled by this somewhat

curious behavior; it would be interesting to discuss with someone, she thinks. However, she knows no one who would not be shocked, in some way. As a Catholic, Cathy would disapprove, probably, of sex not only with no thought of marriage, but not even with love. Lavinia would be even worse: not only sex without love, but sex with a Jew. Peg—well, she never talks about anything with Peg. Maybe Janet Cohen, but then Janet is so manifestly in love with Adam, she would probably not understand just making love, for fun.

But Adam Marr would understand, Megan suddenly thinks. Adam would understand, and his opinions on the subject would be very interesting. Probably he could explain to her just exactly what is going on, between her and Simon. But you can't have that sort of conversation with men, Megan thinks. Or can you?

She is aware that the popular view would hold that Simon is "just out for what he can get," the ugly phrase most applicable to their situation. But Megan knows too that those words are quite wrong, for them: inaccurate, incomplete, as well as ugly, in their implication.

In the meantime, another boy asks her out, for a Saturday night. Stanley Green. Because of their names, Greene and Green, they are seated next to each other in the 19th Century Novel course. Stanley is a small, handsome blond boy, from Atlanta. He takes her to the Buena Vista for dinner; there, imperiously, he orders frozen daiquiris and lobster salad. And then they go over to the Hasty Pudding, to dance. Stanley seems happy and proud about his membership in the Pudding; he just got in, he tells Megan.

The floor is crowded, people dancing up on the stage, couples moving in and out of the bar, still pressed together, still in motion. Once, at a distance, Megan thinks that she sees Lavinia, that disdainful blond face pressed against someone's gold-buttoned blue blazer. Megan wonders who Lavinia is with, and if she is going to try the recommended cure for getting over Gordon (neck your head off with someone else), and if it will work. She thinks of Simon then, and she smiles; certainly Simon has been a marvelous cure for George.

Stanley Green is a good dancer, light and graceful, holding her close and sexily when the music slows. He talks quite a lot, in an easy Southern way; hardly saying anything at all, just a pleasant drawling comment on the other couples, compliments on her dancing, a few remarks about his postwar plans: he wants to go back to Georgia, to go to law school there, and maybe, eventually, go into politics.

Later, as Megan has known they would, they drive down to the river, where they park, near the Browne and Nichols boathouse, and they neck, steamily, passionately.

And that becomes Megan's program for Saturday nights, that spring: she goes out for dinner and dancing, and necking, with Stanley Green.

She believes that everyone she knows would disapprove, on several grounds: you are not supposed to "kiss" more than one boy at a time, as it were; certainly you are not supposed to spend Thursday afternoons in bed with one boy, and Saturday nights necking with another. And, two, if you do any of those things, with anyone, you are supposed to be madly in love. While Megan feels a certain affection for both Simon and for Stanley, she is nowhere near in love with either. (She cares more for Simon, actually; he is more fun to talk to, he is smarter, and God knows love in bed is more fun than necking in cars.)

Megan is forced to conclude that in a sexual way she is indeed different, not quite like other girls. Simon often tells her so, by way of high praise, and he must be right—experienced, Jewish-intellectual Simon. However, Megan knows that in her life she has never felt so well, nor has she ever looked better. She is clear-skinned, bright-eyed, is even a little thinner.

It is very hard to summon up the guilt that, in a way, she believes her sexual activities call for. After all, as she sometimes reasons, she is not hurting anyone, no, not at all.

Also, the excitement and the eventual anguish that she experienced over George Wharton have both begun to seem unreal to her. She can look back to all that as to a distant episode, and she can think: Well, if that's being in love, I won't do that again. I'll settle for sex.

8

Nineteen forty-four, the springtime of romance:

"Because I'm a Jew, of course!" Janet Cohen cries out, through furious tears. "She would rather see her son dead than married to a 'Jewess'—that's the word she actually uses. Can you imagine, she'd rather see him dead? And probably she would, the stupid old Irish sow."

Listening to this outburst, Megan is violently shaken. It has sometimes, recently, seemed to her that most of the people she likes best are Jews: Simon, Stanley Green, and Janet. And she has been deeply struck by the way in which Janet has said, Because I'm a Jew, her pride and despair and rage. The rage of course is directed at horrible Mrs. Marr, mother of Adam, who has announced that if they marry she will die.

Attempting lightness, Megan asks, "Do you think she possibly could? Die?"

Janet takes this question more seriously than Megan had expected. "Well, she's a powerful woman. She just could, you know. Bring on a stroke, or something. Sheer willpower, just to show him. Actually I had an aunt who died, she actually died, because her daughter married a Catholic. Pretty funny, huh? Needless to say, it did a lot for my cousin's marriage: they were divorced in three years, and all the relatives could say, 'So, you see?' "

"I can't believe it," states Megan, and this is true; she can't, none of this unfamiliar drama. How can they? she thinks, considering what is going on in the world. Hitler, concentration camps.

Janet gives her a look. "But what about your parents? Wouldn't they act up if you married a Jew?"

"No, actually I don't think so. So many of the people they know are Jewish, in the antique business. My father says Jews are the best at business, and my mother says they make the best husbands. And in San Francisco it does sometimes look like all the best people are Jewish, the ones who support the symphony and everything."

Janet makes a sound of disbelief. "Well, California," she says.

Megan laughs at her. "Maybe you and Adam should move out there. Why not?"

California is clearly too peculiar and too remote for Janet even to contemplate. "We want to go to Paris," she says. "Adam has a fixation on Paris, the theaters there. God, can you think of anything more wonderful? Once this fucking war is over." Her eyes fill with tears, at this splendid but distant prospect, before she sighs, "If only that old bitch doesn't manage to stop us. If only Adam could stop listening to her."

"What does he say?"

"Well, he's very upset." For a moment Janet is quiet, just sitting there. As often, they are out on the stairwell, on the top stair, where it is permissible to smoke. Janet now lights a new cigarette, fumbling with matches, and then she bursts out, "But sometimes he's so fucking unfair, it's like he's mad at both of us, me and his mother. At women. Shit. Can I help it if I'm Jewish and his mother's nuts?"

Megan has been somewhat taken aback by Janet's repeated use of "fucking," and then "shit." But she works it out: this is how Adam talks, of course. He has a strong, a political, belief in such words; Janet has said so. And Janet will do anything for Adam, Megan understands, and she understands too that Janet's power will win out, finally. Her sheer will to hold and keep Adam Marr.

One of the bits of popular wisdom at that time is that any girl can "get" any boy she wants, if she really wants him enough. And while to Megan this has often seemed untrue (could Peg, for example, get anyone at all?) now she seriously wonders: if she had been dedicated to George Wharton, in the sense that Janet is to Adam, could she have got him?

The thought is strangely appealing, and for a wild moment she considers a letter to George; after all, she never answered the wedding announcement card. You're making a big mistake, she could write to him. Before you do anything final, let's go down for a weekend in New York together. A weekend in bed, in some hotel. You don't even know how terrific that would be, George Wharton.

Instructed by Simon, so to speak, Megan herself does know; she can imagine it all quite vividly. And she thinks, Oh George, how could you have let me go? The intensity of that inner cry is odd; these days George is rarely in her consciousness at all.

Janet is still talking about Mrs. Marr. "With Adam's politics, I don't see how he can even listen to his mother," she now says. "Jesus, she sounds like a fucking Nazi."

Megan agrees, "She sure does." She has just imagined Mrs. Marr as a female Dr. Göring: shouting, bursting out of her ugly Nazi uniform.

"Shit," says Janet. "I've got a chem lab in half an hour. Of course the old bitch is also dead against Adam marrying a doctor. Garbage about competition. How I'd hurt his career."

"A lot of mothers would think it was terrific, your being a doctor."

"Yeah, Jewish mothers, probably. But I don't like Jewish boys. I never have."

"Janet."

"Well, it's the truth. You know that line from your favorite Mr. Auden, 'You are not free whom you may choose to love'? Well, it's true, we're not."

"I guess."

Peg has a date.

This at first unannounced fact has emerged in the course of the day, a Saturday. Momentous news: the date is for that night, dinner and dancing.

The first clue is that Peg shows up for lunch, in the dorm, with her hair in pin curls. It is all neatly tied in a scarf; still, this is unlike her. And so Lavinia demands, "Peglet, what is that—self-improvement day?"

"I just washed it." But Peg blushes, earning a long, speculative look from Lavinia.

The food that day is especially bad, heavy and soggy. Fastidious Lavinia barely touches hers, and about halfway through lunch she lights a cigarette and announces, "Well, I can see that I'll need more sustenance to get me through this day. Anyone for tea at the Window Shop? About three, if I can hold out that long."

Megan says, "I'd better not," at the same time that Cathy has said, "I don't think so."

"Well, okay for you two girls," Lavinia scolds. "Big Peg and I will have to eat your share. How about it, Pegeen?"

Another blush. "Well, I really don't think so."

And so Lavinia attacks. "Peg, what on earth are you up to? You're hiding something from me, I can tell."

"Well, actually I have this date, I was going to do my nails."

"Oh, a date? Well, that's terrific! My, how cozy you are, not a word. But Peg, who is he? Now you have to tell."

Megan and Cathy stare uncomfortably, as Lavinia is speaking.

And, in an embarrassed, hesitant way, Peg gets it out: the date is with someone named Cameron Sinclair. She has known him a long time. Well, not actually seen him for quite a while. He goes to Yale. And then, after a lot of steady, not wholly unkind probing from Lavinia, the true facts emerge: Cameron Sinclair is the son of old friends of Peg's parents; they met a couple of times as little children, at Rehoboth Beach. They have not seen each other since. He wrote (very likely his mother's idea, Peg supposes) and said that he was coming up to Cambridge this weekend; he wanted to look over the law school, and maybe Peg would like to have dinner? He is picking her up at seven.

Having triumphed, found out everything she wanted to know, and that Peg was reluctant to tell, Lavinia then can afford to be kind. "Oh, what're you going to wear, Pegeen? We'll have to work out something really good. And I'll do the manicure, great manicures are one of my true specialties."

Thus it works out that getting Peg ready for her date is a group project. With a variety of emotions that includes both genuine kindness and an incredulous condescension (*Peg,* on a date? what will he think when he sees her, no matter what she has on?), the three friends, her "best friends," gather in her room; they watch and they make suggestions, helpful and otherwise. They make silly jokes. Megan and Cathy and Lavinia, all concentrated on poor Peg.

And not one of them has the slightest idea of what is going on in Peg's mind. In close physical proximity to her, looking at her and talking, not one of them recognizes what is actually a serious anxiety attack; they do not feel Peg's genuine panic.

What Peg is mostly thinking is: *Suppose he is shorter than I am?*

She has been scouring her memories of Rehoboth Beach, desperately, searching for a little boy, with whom she supposedly played. She thinks he was blond. But what size little boy? And at the same time she realizes that even if she could remember his size, back then, it would not signify: a remembered tall little boy could, at eighteen, be a rather small almost-man, in fact he could be several inches shorter than she is—oh, dear Lord, please not. Just as blond hair could darken. She herself, big dark Peg, was once a blond little girl, described as cute.

And even aside from height, that problem, what does Cameron Sinclair imagine that she, Peg, now looks like? Suppose—oh, Lord!— suppose he is expecting a girl who looks like Lavinia?

At that moment Peg is struck by the fact that, really, she does not have to go out on this date; precisely because he has not seen her, grown up, and does not know what she looks like, she could get out of it. "Lavy," she says, and she tries to laugh, as though she were about to say something funny. "Lavy, I've got this great idea: why don't you go out with him tonight? Wouldn't that be funny? Just pretend you're me, I can fill you in on a few things. He'd never know. I just don't really feel—"

Lavinia frowns, in her most serious, scolding way. "Now Peglet, none of that. You are going out on this date and you are going to have a *very good time*. And as a matter of fact I'm seeing Potter tonight."

. . .

By 7:09, when the buzzer on the top floor of Barnard Hall announces that there is a caller for Peg, she is in a state of extreme exhaustion; exhaustion has almost replaced anxiety. Like an automaton, a zombie, she makes her way down the four flights of stairs. Only when she is a couple of steps from the bottom does she think that she could so easily have fallen, broken her neck, or at least an arm, or a leg. She could have avoided this whole impossible situation.

But there he is, standing at the bell desk. It must be he, Cameron Sinclair. Extremely tall, maybe six five or six, with a large red raw-looking face, red hair, so that what Peg actually thinks is, Good, we sort of look alike.

She immediately perceives that he is much more nervous about this occasion than she is even. Which helps to soothe her. A natural comforter, Peg is given something to do by his discomfort; she will concentrate on putting him at ease (this is always a recommended course for girls, and one that Peg takes to instinctively). Never mind how she herself feels, about anything.

Outside the door, Cameron tells her that Cambridge is "absolutely unfamiliar territory" to him, and he feels pretty much at a loss without his car.

For such a large man his voice is rather high, but this could be sheer nerves, Peg instructs herself.

Just how do they go about getting in to Boston? he asks her. And maybe they could stop off somewhere for a quick drink first?

Helpful Peg tells him that the subway at Harvard Square is an easy walk, and then just ten minutes in to Boston. And if he would really like a drink on the way, well, there's a very nice bar in the basement of the Continental Hotel, which is right on the way to the Square.

In the pleasant, dark leathery bar, Cameron seems visibly to relax. "I suppose they know how to make a really dry martini?" he asks, in a deeper voice than he has used before. "It's an okay place, I like it."

Pleased by his approval of her choice, Peg says that they make quite good martinis, she believes (she and Lavinia used to come here, in the early days of mourning Gordon Shaughnessey).

They have two double martinis each, which is more than Peg wants or is used to, but it is her vague feeling that a girl should go along with a man's drinking habits when out on a date.

They discuss his courses at Yale, his summer plans, and his chances of going to Harvard Law. A few perfunctory remarks about their families are thrown in for good measure.

"Well, how about getting in to Boston, getting some chow?" asks Cameron, during a pause. "I could use some grub about now."

Peg sees that this is indeed quite true. He should eat something very soon, or else he'll be drunk; Peg's father "drinks," she knows a thing or two about that problem. "Actually we don't have to go all the way into Boston," she says. "There's a very nice place near here, good steaks. Italian things. The Buena Vista. We could walk there in five or ten minutes." And get some fresh air on the way, she is thinking.

"Well, if you don't mind taking a rain check on Boston, that sounds like a splendid idea," says Cameron. "Lead on."

He *is* drunk, Peg realizes, as they lurch toward the Square, heading for the B.V. He is drunk and I will be too, if I don't eat something very soon.

Saturday night: the restaurant is crowded, and so they have another martini, waiting at the bar. Peg gulps down some peanuts, along with the gin.

Over dinner—the huge, probably black market steaks that finally arrive—Cameron confides his political ambitions to Peg. As he sees it, after the war there will be a reaction to all this pals-with-Russia business, as he puts it; people will stop worshiping Roosevelt and all the "sob-sister semipinks in Washington, not to mention all the New Deal Jews."

Peg, who is considerably more intelligent than any of her friends then realize (except possibly Lavinia, with her accurate personal assessments), is certainly far brighter than Cameron Sinclair in his ego-driven drunkenness has grasped. She is seriously offended by this nonsense; she has deep, personal feelings about Mr. Roosevelt (never mind what Lavinia would think; they do not discuss politics) and she is impressed by what she knows of the New Deal (also,

Cameron's views are painfully close to those of her father). But she does not say any of this. "That's really interesting," is what she says.

Which leads Cameron to think that she might at least be intelligent, after all.

Dinner somehow serves to sober Cameron and to make Peg more drunk. She is not quite sure what is wrong, she feels dizzy and vaguely sick; how she wishes that she were safely back in the dorm. And, even drunk, all her instincts urge her away from this Cameron Sinclair, but she is incapable of saying the simple words needed to get her home: if she says, I don't feel well, he will think she's having her period, and men always hate to hear about that, don't they?

And so, when Cameron hails a cab, just outside the restaurant, and grandly announces that they are going in to Boston, after all, she even smiles up at him, and she says, Oh, terrific.

Bitter bile is jolted up into her mouth, as they tear across some bridge or other, crossing the Charles.

Later, in the pink-frilled Ladies' of a nightclub, where (God help her, and her feet) they have danced and danced, she does throw up. Lacking a mouthwash, she fastidiously washes her mouth out with soapy water.

During another cab ride, the final one, a couple of nightclubs later, Cameron begins to kiss her—but "kiss" does not quite describe that sudden plunge in her direction, that thrusting of a thick, bad-tasting tongue into her mouth, while his hands, strong and enormous, tear at her blouse. Peg is caught somewhere in that limbo between fighting him off and responding, both of which she knows that she is supposed to do simultaneously; she is supposed both to make him want to see her again and to convince him that she is not "fast," or, worse, "easy to get." However she does manage an amazing feat of strength: she manages to remove his hand from its approach to the top of one of her stockings, but this is less from virtuous impulses than from fear that he will also feel the heavy stays in her girdle. But the effort is almost too much for her; she is nearly sick again, and she cannot be, not with his tongue in her mouth. She manages to swallow more bile, and to remove another strong hand from her breast.

And then, mercifully, they have reached Barnard Hall.

Peg realizes that it is extremely late, and she thinks, Good, no one will be around to see me. At that moment being unseen is more important to her than any possible punishment for lateness. With a quicker kiss than she had feared, at the door (possibly he did not want to keep the cab waiting?) Cameron is gone. Sure that she will never see him again, and relieved (although she has not admitted to herself her true view of Cameron Sinclair), Peg lets herself into the dorm, and she puts her key on its hook. If the night watchman has checked, she is in trouble, but she then thinks, So what? Why should she mind being campused (which is the almost automatic punishment for lateness), since no one will ever ask her for a date again?

She goes up the stairs and has almost reached the top floor when she realizes that someone is sitting out there, smoking. Someone in a pale blue quilted robe. Lavinia.

Who looks at her and cries out, "Peg! My God, are you all right? God! Look, no one must see you like this. I'll go ahead into the bathroom and check. You stay here." She leaves, with a quick backward look of sheer dismay, and of true sympathy.

Alone, waiting for Lavinia to come back—chilled and still somewhat drunk—Peg's eyes fill with tears of gratitude: Lavinia is taking care of her, Lavinia cares.

"Oh now, don't cry, old Peg. It can't be all that bad. Come on, quick, there's no one in the bathroom. You can get all cleaned up in a minute." Lavinia bustles her along the hall, and into the large bright empty bathroom. "Now, take off that blouse. God, what a mess you are! And wash your face. Peggy, for God's sake, stop crying. He didn't rape you, did he?"

"No—"

"Well, next time don't drink so much. It's *very* bad for your skin."

Lavinia does not let Potter Cobb touch her in any of the ways that Gordon Shaughnessey did, although they go out a lot that spring, and they neck, after dancing at the Fox and Hounds, cocktail parties at Adams House. Lavinia manages, always, to stay his hands;

she believes, and is probably correct in her idea, that this prim behavior will both indicate to Potter that she and Gordon did not do much either, in a sexual way, and also that it will make him love her even more than he already does.

In a way she too loves Potter, though, she really does. She loves his clothes and the way he combs his hair, his accent and his car, and actually his *ideas*. He is a conservative, and does not mind saying so. He quotes from Edmund Burke and Hamilton. "I distrust the mob," he says, "besides which I really don't like many of its representatives. Those should rule who have been educated to do so." He would like to go into the State Department; he has been in Washington a lot; he likes it there. He thinks he remembers Lavinia's house. He does not really remind Lavinia of her father, nothing Freudian like that, as awful Janet Cohen might put it; her father is a more forceful (she has to face it), a stronger person—but they sound alike, at times. If she had any sense at all, Lavinia thinks, she would marry Potter, and have with him the sort of life that she is supposed to have. Who needs another Gordon Shaughnessey, she thinks, or that sort of "love."

During that same spring an odd thing happens to Cathy Barnes, which is that a very rich, not bad-looking (if he is a little short) boy from Cleveland, Shaker Heights, falls wildly in love with her. He drives a red convertible and he wears Sulka ties, does not shop at Brooks or J. Press, and is thus called Flash by the New England clubbies, by those who speak to him at all; most do not. His name is Phil.

Flash Flannigan and Cathy, an unlikely couple from any outside point of view, first meet because in a careless way they both show up for an economics class, in Sever, that has in fact been canceled— Cathy, on that cool spring day, in a just-cleaned white cashmere sweater, and Flash-Phil in camel's hair (he is 4-F because of a dubious knee, and a little political pull on his father's part having to do with defense contracts). Phil looks at Cathy, and maybe he does fall in love right there and then, as he is later to claim. What he says is, "Well, a free hour. How about some coffee at St. Clair's?"

At St. Clair's, Cathy sees Lavinia across the room, having coffee with Potter; the two girls exchange small waves, each indicating to the other that it is okay not to come over and say hello.

Almost right away, as they talk, Phil and Cathy establish what strikes them both as a remarkable list of things in common: both are majoring in economics; both are Catholic; both plan to make a lot of money after the war. They do not plan to go to graduate school; they are not sure how they feel about Harvard and Cambridge; they would like to know where there's a really good steak dinner in Boston. They like the big bands, like Miller or Dorsey, Charlie Barnett.

Cathy to Megan, hesitantly: "I met this really strange guy."

"What's so strange about him?"

"Well, he wants me to go out with him tomorrow night. Dinner and dancing. I guess in Boston."

"Well, that sure does sound strange. He must be some kind of a freak."

They laugh.

Then Cathy adds, "He drives this big red convertible. I just don't quite see myself in that."

"Why not? Just don't wear bright pink, you'd look silly. But go along with it. Have fun. Honestly, Cathy—"

"Well, okay. But he's so—so Midwestern."

"Oh, come on. You sound like Lavinia. Or Potter."

Cathy giggles, blushing a little. "He's not very tall. I'll have to wear my flats."

They begin to go out all the time, hitherto quiet Cathy racing around in that long red car with Phil-Flash, as she has begun to call him. They go everywhere for really good steaks: is Locke-Ober's really better than Durgin-Park? They go dancing, at the Palace and the Statler, the Fox and Hounds, and out to the Totem Pole. They neck a lot.

· · ·

"I feel as though I'm drunk all the time," says Cathy to Megan.

"Well, maybe you are."

"Do you think I'm in love?"

"I guess. Do you think you are?"

"I'm not sure. I'll have to ask my priest."

They laugh.

"Honestly, she's beginning to sound Midwestern herself," says Lavinia to Peg. "Have you listened to those vowels?"

"Well, I hadn't exactly thought about it. She sure looks happy. But, uh, Lavy, this funny thing happened. I got a letter from Cameron Sinclair."

"From who?"

"Cameron Sinclair. The boy I went out with that time."

"Oh."

"He wants to come up and see me. Again."

"Well, honestly, Peg, what's so funny about that?"

"Nothing, but I just thought—I don't know."

"He must have liked you. But you just remember what I told you, and don't drink so much this time."

"Oh, I won't!" cries out Peg, who in fact drinks considerably more the next time she goes out with Cameron, and she passes out in a borrowed room, in the law school dorm—unfortunately not before Cameron has succeeded in ending both his own and Peg's virginity.

Although she could joke about asking her priest whether or not she was truly in love, still, Cathy is deeply concerned with possible sin; she knows perfectly well that she is committing sins of the flesh, and doing it often, almost every night. She is also going to Confession and not truly confessing. She wonders what Phil-Flash is saying to his priest, and decides that probably he is not fully confessing either. And what does this say about his true character—or for that matter about hers? What does it say about their relationship?

And Cathy inwardly notes that she has not in any way mentioned Phil to her mother, not even very casually. "I've been going out a lot," she might have written to her mother, whose affectionate interest is often thwarted by Cathy, Cathy knows. Her mother would have liked to hear such an intimate fact, and surely if Cathy means for them to meet, eventually, she could have made this small preparation?

Already Phil is pushing for an early marriage, but Cathy just isn't sure, for many reasons.

In some dim corner of her mind, and perhaps her heart, she does not believe that this is true love. She does not believe that she and Phil will marry.

9

Simon is stroking Megan's back, his hand firm on her shoulder blades, pressing in at her waist, back and forth, caressing her buttocks. It is late on a Thursday afternoon. In an idle way he then says, "Ah Megan, the loveliest skin in town. Why can't I take you down to New York with me?"

And Megan, who tends to take people more or less at their word, answers him, "Well, why not? Sometime."

Simon removes his hand too quickly. Then, as though to make up for the abruptness of the gesture, he pulls up the sheet, covering naked Megan. He tucks it in around her neck, and he announces, "In some ways I really feel like a shit."

Something cold within her suddenly and inexplicably makes Megan think of George Wharton, all that old pain. In a forced, light way she asks Simon, "Why? What do you mean?" She has turned and propped herself up, the sheet still shielding her breasts; she and Simon face each other.

He says, "Well, I guess I should have said this before, but it never seemed important. But in New York, you see, there's this woman that I'm engaged to. Uh, she goes to Barnard. Her name is Phyllis. I see her on weekends."

"You do?"

"I know, I should have mentioned it, but it really didn't seem to have anything to do with us," Simon repeats.

Megan instantly sees the logic of his not mentioning his fiancée, in a way; she can even agree that his New York life has nothing to do with them. Phyllis. She supposes that if she were smarter about such things she would have worked it out for herself already; certainly Lavinia would have known that a young man who spent every weekend in New York surely "had someone" there; he would not just be going down to see his parents, not a sexy, handsome young man like Simon, at his age. Well, how dumb of her.

"You look upset," Simon is saying. "I don't blame you. I've been a shit." (Is he taking some pride in this, this shittiness?) "But being with you, making love to you is the greatest thing, you are the greatest woman—"

"You and Phyllis don't make love?" Megan has a quick, intuitive flash that this would be the case; perhaps at last she is catching on to how things are?

"Oh no."

"You just neck?"

"Well, yes. You could put it like that." Poor guilty Simon blushes, and now he seems to feel an obligation to tell her everything. "I've always known Phyllis," he explains. "Our families moved from Brooklyn to West End Avenue at about the same time, and my parents, God, they'd die if I didn't marry a nice Jewish girl. From their point of view Phyllis is ideal. And she really is okay, in a way. She's bright."

"It's so funny," Megan muses. "I know someone, a girl, who's Jewish, and she wants to marry this boy, who's Irish, and his mother hates her." She is not sure why she thought the story of Janet and Adam would be helpful; in truth, she does not really want to talk to Simon anymore, that day. In fact she has a deep conviction of total wrongness, somewhere; the equations of sex and love and marriage are coming out all wrong, at least as far as she is concerned. Which is not at all to say that she would like to marry Simon, she would not; and probably in the long run she would not want to marry George Wharton either. *Still.*

"Megan, I can't tell you how awful I feel," Simon is saying. "I could kill myself."

It is not necessary that he tell her how awful he feels; Megan can see him, a dark young man, overwhelmed with guilt and confusion. In a comforting way she says, "Really, it's okay. You're right, it doesn't have anything to do with us, really. I guess I'm just, uh, surprised. Although probably I shouldn't be."

"God, I can certainly see how you'd be surprised. Oh, Megan, I do feel terrible. You probably won't even want to see me, after this."

"Oh, Simon. I didn't say that. But I would like to go back to the dorm now. Okay?"

"Oh, *sure.*"

They both rush through what has sometimes been a languorous ritual of getting dressed, often interrupted by passages of love—but not today. Dressed, they hurry out to Simon's car, and he drives her back over the hills of Cambridge, to her dorm, driving much faster than usual. As though to excuse their haste, at some point Megan remarks, "I've got this hour exam tomorrow. I almost forgot."

At the door Simon asks her, "You will see me again?" (He has made a clear effort not to plead.)

"Oh, Simon, don't be silly. Of course I will. Sometime."

Megan gives this episode considerably less thought and less emotion than she might have been expected to—than, in fact, she might have expected of herself. Perhaps, she thinks (she hopes) that she was inoculated against certain emotions by the experience of George Wharton.

And then she stops thinking of such things altogether, for the moment, and she decides that she wants to go out for honors;

maybe she could make Junior Phi Bete? As long as she's here she might as well learn all that she possibly can, mightn't she?

None of Megan's friends, at that moment, that May of 1944, share in her (at least temporarily) high-minded preoccupation with work. Cathy is always out somewhere with Phil-Flash; when she comes in late at night she is often a little drunk, her makeup all smeared; she is vague and exhausted and exhilarated and, for Megan, in a conversational way quite out of reach. Although, over late night cigarettes, they sometimes try to talk.

Lavinia is usually out with Potter, and Janet Cohen is either writing to Adam or talking about him—or off to some chem lab. Even Peg seems mysteriously preoccupied; she is known to have had several more dates with Cameron Sinclair, but she does not look happy.

Preoccupation with these various men thus isolates the four young women from each other—an accepted, even expected state of affairs at that time, but Megan feels it keenly. I sometimes have no one to talk to, is what she thinks.

If Megan has not been thinking of Simon, he seems to have thought of her a great deal, however; he telephones and asks her how she has been, and then, before she can get out more than a couple of words, he asks, "How about coming down to New York with me next weekend? I'm serious, I've got it all worked out. Where we'll stay, and everything. This great hotel, on Eighth Street. The Marlton."

It is odd, the way you get things you used to want, is what Megan is thinking. But she also thinks, New York, how terrific, if only I could. Lack of money has kept her in Cambridge and Boston, so far, and this week is no better than any others, financially.

"We'll take the train down," Simon says. "Go down Saturday night, if that's okay with you. Have dinner, maybe hit some spots on Fifty-second Street. Then Sunday we'll have all day, I'll just put in a quick appearance at my parents'."

And a quick spot of necking with Phyllis? Megan wonders; but that is unfair, she knows, unfair and ungrateful to kind, on-the-whole fastidious Simon.

She then wonders about train tickets: how much do they cost, and is she supposed to pay for hers? These worries make her tentative, as she says, "Well, that sounds really nice—"

"Megan, come on, it'll be terrific, and it's all arranged. I got our train tickets and I called the Marlton. You'll love it, and we have a suite."

"A suite?"

He laughs. "A couple of rooms, with a kitchen we won't use. And you'd laugh if you knew how much it costs. How little, I mean."

Megan does laugh, from sheer relief, and pleasure at the prospect of New York.

The train trip, the five hours from South Station, Boston, down to Grand Central, is all new to Megan, exhilarating: the lovely New England countryside, the fields and woods of Rhode Island, Connecticut, the vistas of sea and seashore, lined here and there with clusters of gray battleships. And the shirt-sleeve summer dusk of industrial cities, all revved up for war.

Megan is headily aware of possibilities, as on the verge of love. Cambridge recedes, now as invisible to her as California is, and she thinks, New York!

In the train's jolting club car they drink old-fashioneds, and then they have another in the dark bar of the Hotel Commodore, in the lower reaches of Grand Central—in the glamorous wartime atmosphere of reunions, dramatically heightened moments just prior to perhaps-final partings.

Megan watches everything, intensely feeling it all, drinking everything in with her strong sweet fruity cocktail.

From Grand Central they take a cab down Fifth Avenue to the Marlton, on Fifth and 8th Street. As the cab hurries downtown

Megan never turns from its window; she is dizzy with the excitement of those moments, breathing an air that is absolutely new to her: the thick hot New York June night air, an element entirely unlike that of San Francisco on summer nights, with its foggy gusts and salt hints of the sea. Unlike Palo Alto (very), unlike even Boston, or Cambridge. The white or colored neon lights are more brilliant here than anywhere else, more violent. The people on the sidewalks walk much faster.

Megan for the first time in her life is aware of being in a city.

The Marlton: big shabby rooms, a small kitchen which, as Simon predicted, they will never use. A high, wide, lumpy-looking bed.

They do not, however, linger in the room; Megan's impatience carries them both outside. "Can't we just walk on the street—I mean avenue, Fifth Avenue?"

"Sure, and I have a great idea. Where we'll have dinner. It's right *on* Fifth Avenue."

They go outside, and he leads her up a few blocks, and across the street to a terrace that is sheltered by an awning, and surrounded by low boxwoods. The Brevoort. That night, a Saturday, it is crowded with uniforms, ribbons and decorations, braid; and with women both beautiful and chic beyond the dreams of San Francisco, the capacities of Boston.

Dimly, fleetingly, Megan wishes that her white linen dress were black; she feels, though, that she is an invisible observer, and thus a participant in all those vivid lives around her.

The men on that terrace who are not in actual uniform wear a uniform of their own: dark blue blazers, white shirts, and dark striped ties, Simon like all the rest. Very much at home in that expensive atmosphere, he achieves a corner table with a view of both the terrace and the throbbing adjacent sidewalk, the traffic of the street. He asks Megan what she would like to eat, and at her look of utter confusion, smiling solicitous Simon competently orders vichysoisse and lobster salad.

If, at just that moment, he had told Megan that he could not, after all, possibly marry Phyllis, and if he had asked her, Megan, to marry him, then and there, that night (as in many ways he would strongly like to do), Megan would have said yes; she would like to marry New York—she would have said yes, at that moment, to anything at all.

After dinner, another taxi takes them up Fifth Avenue, through thicker, faster crowds, sounds of horns and music from car radios, blaring from the wide-open doors of bars, and clubs. Shouts, and the loud murmur of a thousand cars, all driving all over the city.

Fifty-second Street. They go down a few steps, into a narrow, black, and entirely packed room, what looks to be a hundred people, all crammed around tiny tables, in the din, the smoke, and the wild hot crazy sound of a trombone solo. The man out in front, playing in the spotlight, is so tall and lithe, swaying, dancing as he plays, thrusting out his long silver horn into the black smoky air—air smelling of gardenias and bad Scotch and mingled perfumes and sweat. The man thrusts and raises up his bright trombone, blasting out his passionate sounds.

Just as Megan and Simon are being seated, then, their two small chairs jammed together at a table already occupied by six other people, strangers, just then that man, the trombone player, puts down his horn, and he comes over to the mike to sing. He is still swaying, dancing; the movement is all over his body, even his hands move, dancingly. When he sings his voice is somewhat high, and husky—a seductive voice, its range insinuating. "I want you, baby, You the one for me, baby—"

Fully visible now, in the spotlight, he has brownish-yellow skin and wide-apart dark slightly drooping eyes, eyes that look directly at Megan, she feels—into and all over her. "I know you, baby, You are meant for me, baby—," he sings, directly to her. He stops and smiles—at Megan, a wide flashing grin that goes pointedly to her, eyes washing over her, saying more than any words she has ever heard. And then very slowly, gracefully, he moves offstage, to the sound of frantic applause; Megan is clapping until both her hands and her wrists are sore.

When it is possible to speak she asks Simon, "Who is that?"

"That's Jackson Clay. He's really good, isn't he. He used to play with Lunceford, and then Goodman for a while, I think."

Megan is transfixed, wholly concentrated on waiting for him to come back—Jackson Clay; she is almost holding her breath.

She would not, even then, have called that seizure falling in love; this is not like looking up to the sight of George Wharton, in the Stanford Bookstore, and realizing that George is going to speak to her. This is an excitement and a compulsion of quite a different order; if fewer imaginative emotions are involved, her eyes and ears, her breath and her breasts, her arms and her legs and her place all yearn toward his absence.

Suddenly, then, she sees him, sees Jackson Clay, not on the stage but just standing there in a doorway, lounging; is he staring in her direction, looking for her? The doorway in which he leans leads to a staircase, up which there is (there must be) the ladies' room. And so that is where Megan says she is going. "I'll be right back," she tells Simon.

She pushes through tables, past knees and elbows, past waiters and an ugly, pushy flower vendor, to where he is standing, as though in wait for her. "I think you're wonderful," Megan says, with what is almost her last breath, and she hears her own high strained voice.

"You do, now? That's real nice." Jackson Clay's dark look takes her all in, his white smile dazzles her, as he reaches for her arm. They start up the stairs together, he guiding, propelling her, until he turns her toward a door, which he opens. An empty room— lockers, chests, suitcases. He closes the door. Pulls her body to his, their entire lengths touching, merging, melting. His mouth and his tongue incredible—all *new*. Jackson Clay.

When at last they break apart he is out of breath too; he can barely say to her, "You are some beautiful girl, you know that? Say, when can I see you, you ever free?"

"Well—" Megan gets out. "Tomorrow—"

He grins; in that darkness she can see the white shine of his teeth, just tasted. "Well, tomorrow, that is the greatest. Tomorrow is my night off, Sunday night. How about you meet me here? Out front, say, nine o'clock?"

They kiss again. Prolonged.

At the head of the stairs at last they separate, touching hands. They both whisper, "I'll see you tomorrow." And Megan sees that there is indeed a ladies' room, where she goes to rearrange her disordered face. She is quite oblivious of anyone else who might be in the room.

Simon asks her, "Want to stay for another set?"

Sharply torn—she is dying to see and hear him again, hear him sing and play, to *her*—Megan at the same time feels that that would be dangerous, and so she asks, "Couldn't we walk home, down Fifth?"

And that is what they do; they walk all those brilliant hot early summer blocks, late Saturday night, down to 8th Street, to the Marlton.

The long walk, though, has done nothing to exhaust what Megan feels, to quiet her blood. In the high wide lumpy bed she and Simon fall upon each other, almost impersonal in their furious need. If Jackson Clay is present in Megan's wild state of arousal, it is also possible that Phyllis exists, at these moments, somewhere in Simon's consciousness.

"There's too much—I don't know what to show you," Simon tells Megan at breakfast the next day, Sunday, at Schraffts', on Fifth Avenue and 14th Street.

"But I want to see everything!"

He laughs at her; then suggests, "In that case the boat around the island?"

"Oh, wonderful!"

Jackson Clay of course has no intention of coming to meet her, Megan tells herself, on the deck of the excursion boat—at the railing, as fresh salt winds and spray lash her face and flatten down her hair, as she stares and *stares* at the kaleidoscope of skyline and wharves, traffic, trains, cars, boats. The brown river, and lost dipping sea gulls. She was just a dumb girl with big breasts, a hick from out of town, whom Jackson Clay kissed just because she was there.

"That's New Jersey," Simon tells her, pointing to rocky white cliffs. "The Palisades."

Megan has, however, invented a California friend who she will see, she says, after dinner tonight, when Simon has to go up to see his parents. She has even said that he might as well spend the night "at home." "I mean, won't they think it's sort of funny if you don't?" Aware of extreme disingenuousness, Megan widened her blue eyes very consciously, saying this.

"Well, actually they would. It's nice of you. We'll meet at Grand Central in the morning, then?"

But Jackson has no intention of meeting her at nine, on 52d Street, in front of the club.

They have dinner in a Village restaurant called the Jumble Shop, where everyone looks—to Megan—"literary," vaguely foreign, and all absorbed in conversations that she yearns to be a part of, or simply to overhear. "This is wonderful, I love it here," she whispers to Simon, her eyes pursuing a tall man in a black beret, with a woman in a violet feather boa, just leaving.

But Megan can barely eat.

"Shall we, uh, share a cab partway uptown?" Simon asks rather tentatively, after dinner. Megan's "California friends" are staying in a hotel near Times Square, the Woodstock—a name she picked from the phone book as she thought, What a waste, all this cleverness and ingenuity wasted on a man who won't even be there.

But: "Oh no," she says to Simon. "I think I'll walk for a while. There're lots of cabs," she adds vaguely.

"Okay, then. Grand Central tomorrow, at ten, at the Information Booth."

Both guilty, in separate ways, they kiss and separate.

Unsure how much a cab will cost—and then suppose she has to take another one, back to the Marlton, when he isn't there?—

Megan does walk about ten blocks uptown, up breathtaking, dusky Fifth Avenue, with her heart at the top of her throat.

At a quarter to nine, at the corner of Fifth and 21st Street, she does hail a cab, and she gives the address on 52d Street—where Jackson Clay, who by now has forgotten that he ever saw, much less kissed her—where Jackson Clay surely will not be.

But he is! He is there, he is early, it is only five of nine when Megan's cab arrives. Jackson, tall and wonderful in a long polo coat, standing there, looking around; he is waiting for *her*.

He gets into her cab as they pull up—and among other things Megan thinks, Oh good, I won't have to pay.

Jackson smiles. "You here! I was scared you'd forget, that you hadn't meant about coming to meet me."

He was scared. Megan smiles weakly, as he takes her hand and gives an address to the driver. And, as the cab rushes back up Fifth to the park, in the black night, winding, they begin to kiss. There has never been the slightest question of their intentions toward each other; this is not a date in the ordinary sense.

Jackson Clay lives in Spanish Harlem, 110th Street. The other side of the park.

His building has a small dim strange lobby, and the elevator is small and creaking. Jackson leads Megan down a hall, to a door. She is a little surprised, at first, by the nondescript dinginess of Jackson's apartment, until she thinks, He must spend hardly any time here, none at all, it's just a place to keep things.

He asks her, "You like a drink? You smoke?"

Okay, she would like a drink, Megan says.

As he leaves she sits down primly on a large, wide, fairly lumpy sofa; crossing her legs she senses heat there, and wet—oh, what will he think?

Coming back into the room, Jackson Clay puts their two drinks on the coffee table, he sits down and takes Megan wholly into his arms. She feels herself leaping against him, like a fish.

The most unusual feature of their actually making love, to Megan, is the way Jackson uses his tongue, his tongue all over her, beginning with her hands. He kisses the sensitive palms and in between her fingers.

At some point, when she has cried out over a "kiss," in a gentle way he says to her, "And I'd really like it if you'd kiss me too." But surely that is what she has been doing?

In a few intervals of exhausted cessation they drink their drinks, and they talk, a little. Jackson is from Oklahoma, he tells her; he is half Indian, Cherokee. He grew up on a reservation. (Megan can imagine none of this, Indians, a reservation, but she listens with awe and total interest.) He has been married four times. "The last one, she really embarrassed me, the way she talked," he says. "You talk so nice, like somebody English." (As Megan thinks, Well, I must have changed, I have picked up a Harvard-Cambridge accent, without even noticing.)

Out of the 52d Street club Jackson himself speaks differently; now he uses a normal, somewhat Southern speech, whereas in the club, in the clowning asides between songs, he was heavily "Negro."

They do not talk very much, but Megan receives a strong and certain sense of his niceness; Jackson is a genuinely kind, nice man, perhaps the nicest she has ever met. And she wonders: Maybe they should marry? (In 1944, there are not many alternatives available, to marriage, for nice young middle-class girls.)

Jackson has the same idea. As he takes her home, somewhere near dawn, Jackson says, "If you find out you pregnant, I'll marry you, quick as a flash. But you know, I was real careful." (She had not known that, actually; he did not use rubbers, as Simon carefully does.) Jackson says, "I'd like that, being married to you, I really would. But marriage with a musician is real tough on a woman. Always on tour. Out late. Women can get real restless." He laughs, but in a kindly, sympathetic way.

By then too tired for further speech, as they part Megan breathes out, "I love you, Jackson." "Me too, baby. I love you too, I surely do."

· · ·

Although she knows that she is not in love with Jackson Clay, back at college Megan gives a fair imitation of someone in love. She buys all his records, all the money from a birthday check from Florence (who seems to be getting rich!). She plays the records, she listens in a sort of swoon.

She writes him long letters; she plans and fantasizes about their next meeting; she sees herself walking into a club where he is playing, and his startled look of recognition.

But there is no urgency or anxiety in her obsession with Jackson Clay. It does not bother her that he does not answer her letters; she would not have expected him to. And it does not matter, to Megan, just when their dramatic reunion will take place; she sees it as simply (and wonderfully!) somewhere ahead.

10

Because of the war, at Radcliffe it is possible to stay in school all year round, several terms in a row, and thus graduate in a shorter time than the usual four years. This process is called Acceleration, and it is viewed with enthusiasm by most of the girls. The dean is against it; she has stated that four terms in a row is too much for anyone, and is quite possibly deleterious to young women's health.

Megan and Lavinia, Cathy and Peg are among those who think that Acceleration (any acceleration, probably) is a very good idea. Although none of them could have said just why, they think that getting out of college in three years instead of four is wonderful— despite the fact that all four of them are enjoying their Cambridge lives, in one way or another.

Megan has the most (perhaps the only) practical explanation for this haste, which is quite simply that less time in college for her will mean less expense for her parents. She is also drawn to acceleration because of the decreased time at home on vacations; these days she hates the very idea of California, most especially (if half-admittedly) she hates her mother's job, hates seeing Florence as a carhop, in her perky uniform, looking not many years older than Megan does, and *thin*, and *blond*. Talking that way.

In any case, all four of them elect to spend the summer term in Cambridge, in school. The summer of 1944.

On a hot morning in July, Megan and Peg find themselves alone in Hood's, having coffee. Theirs being the thinnest wire in that finely balanced four-way friendship, it is odd that this has came about; they are slightly awkward with each other. And it seems to Megan that Peg, who at best is not notably attractive, now looks quite terrible. Her skin, which is too pale but generally clear, is blotchy now, and her big blue eyes are dull. And instead of her usual hearty, blustering self, this morning Peg is very quiet, subdued, and somewhat unnecessarily polite, as though Megan were someone whose approval (or possibly advice?) she sought. Peg urges Megan to eat the bran muffins which she, Peg, has ordered and paid for, and she goes up to the counter to get more coffee for them both.

Megan's response to all this strangeness on Peg's part is a sort of sympathetic curiosity, and a revival of the guilt that she has always felt over her own negative reactions to Peg. Very possibly she has misjudged her all along? Peg, inwardly, could be as delicate, as vulnerable as anyone, or possibly more so?

Coming back with their coffee, setting it on the table and then lowering herself heavily into her chair, Peg looks even worse. She smiles faintly at Megan, to whom a wild thought has just come: Megan thinks, Peg is pregnant. And then she thinks, Oh no, that's impossible. How could she be? Peg wouldn't.

Just then in a violent way Peg belches, which seems to cause her real physical pain, so that Megan asks, "Peg, honestly, are you all right?"

Clearly not all right, Peg blinks back tears; in a strangled voice she says, "Well, not exactly. I seem to be—Megan, I think I'm pregnant."

They stare at each other, as large tears roll slowly down Peg's large face.

"Oh Peg. Jesus, do you really think so?"

"I'm next to sure," Peg miserably gets out. "And Megan, I wanted to ask you, if you possibly know anyone, uh, anywhere—?"

It is a minute before Megan understands what is being asked of her, and another minute before her mind forms the word "abortion." The next thing she thinks is, Why me? Why are you asking this of me? But in a heart-sinking way she knows; she knows just why Peg would choose her, why Peg has engineered this time together.

As though she had asked, Peg explains, "You're the only one I could—and I thought maybe you might know. You might have heard of some, uh, doctor." She reaches into her bag for Kleenex, and sniffles into it loudly. "Lavinia would never speak to me again, and Cathy, well, you know, a Catholic."

"I honestly don't know anyone," says Megan, honestly. "But maybe I could ask." Ask who? she wonders. Simon, whom she has been more or less refusing to see? Innocent Stanley Green, whom she is not seeing either? (It is hard for Megan to "see" anyone these days, Jackson Clay being so much on her mind.)

Anxiously Peg insists, "And you won't tell? I just couldn't stand—"

"No, of course. I won't tell anyone."

But why me? Alone, Megan in her mind renews this question; again she asks of Peg, But why me? Because you think, or assume, that I'm not a virgin either? That I've made love with two different people by now, and sometimes have worried that I was pregnant? And if you know all this about me, all of which is true, then *how* do you know it? And does everyone else know too?

Or is it just that I come from California, and you think all Californians have sexy lives, and lots of abortions?

Still, Megan feels herself burdened with Peg's problem, her unimaginable pregnancy.

And the father must be that guy from Yale, son of parents' friends.

. . .

"Why do you come to me with this?" asks Janet Cohen. "Because I'm a Jew?"

"Oh, Janet, of course not. I just thought—well, I don't honestly know why. Maybe because you're from New York."

"If you mean Brooklyn why don't you say so."

"I didn't especially mean Brooklyn."

Janet sniffs; she has said that Cambridge in the summer is bad for her allergies. She asks, "Are you trying to tell me that they don't have abortionists in Washington, D.C., or wherever your other friends come from?"

"Janet, please, forget it. Please. I'm really sorry I asked you."

They are sitting out on the stairwell, at the top of the long flight down. Smoking, late at night. As they begin fresh cigarettes Megan can see that Janet is somewhat pacified, although she says nothing to indicate a change of mood, nor does Janet smile.

A few minutes later, though, in a kindly way, Janet asks, "But Megan, honestly, why do you have to tell me this 'friend' story?"

In the harsh overhead light Megan feels herself blush; small-voiced, she says, "Janet, please, it's not me. I'm not pregnant. If I were I'd tell you, or I think I would." She considers this. "Yes, I would tell you. But this is someone else. And I can't tell you who."

For a moment they look at each other. Janet then says, "Well, I'm glad it isn't you."

Megan is thinking how pretty Janet is, with her fine dark coloring. And how nice she is, really. Janet simply has to be repeatedly reassured that everyone she meets is not a threat. Everyone is not Adam Marr's mother.

Loudly and surprisingly, Janet laughs. "Well, I know it can't be any of your closest buddies, here in Barnard. Can it? Lavinia the ice queen would never do it without a twenty-carat engagement ring, and Cathy would have to get a dispensation from the pope. And Peg, well, good luck finding anyone who'd do it to her."

Although Janet has never spoken quite so harshly of Megan's other friends, her "group," Megan is not surprised; the four of them as a group pay no attention at all to Janet, so small and shy that she is easy to overlook. Lavinia is the only one who mentions Janet at all, and she only says, "Little Megan seems to have this thing about Jews."

At this intimate moment with Janet, Megan would be inclined to go along with Janet's own views of the others, of her own group of friends. And what fun it would be if just now she could say to Janet, Well, actually it is one of those three, see if you can guess. And Megan imagines the joy of her final revelation: Well, you won't believe this, but it's Peg, she actually got herself knocked up.

Megan manages to resist this strong temptation, however.

And Janet says, "Well, I'll ask Adam. He's coming up on Saturday."

Adam Marr announces to Megan, "Well, actually I don't believe in abortions. Although not for any of those asshole Catholic reasons."

Sunday morning. Adam and Megan have been pointedly left alone by Janet, who is upstairs washing her hair. They are perched together on the brick railing of Barnard's wide terrace. Small groups of WAVES, in their trim dark uniforms and spanking white gloves and hats, pass by at intervals, returning to Briggs from church. Across the terrace from Megan and Adam is a cluster of dressed-up Barnard girls, who eye them (a couple?) from time to time. Megan is wishing that Adam would speak less loudly, especially since he uses those *words*, so often.

"A woman is there to receive a man's seed," he is now saying loudly. "That's what she's for. That's what fucking is for. Otherwise it's incomplete. Abortions are a form of castration, they kill the male seed. His life force." Adam seems to be enjoying this conversation tremendously. His voice rises in pleasure. "I start where the Church leaves off," he proclaims to Megan, and in effect to the terrace at large. "I left those jack-offs a long time ago."

It is his eyes that make Adam Marr seem attractive: intensely blue and hot (Megan has never seen such a heated, brilliant blue), his eyes dominate an otherwise undistinguished face: too curly brown hair, a medium-large nose, small mouth, flat chin. He is medium tall, medium thin—a perfectly okay build, Megan decides, but nothing special (Simon is much better built, and Jackson Clay a hundred times better). Only Adam's eyes are compelling, and the force of his voice.

"But it's your choice," he now says to Megan. "Maybe you're not ready for true, complete great sex."

Megan feels a blush as she whispers, "Adam, I keep telling you, it's not for me."

"Okay, okay. I'll have to talk to a buddy of mine. I'll call him and call you tomorrow."

You could just give Janet the message, Megan starts to say, but then she does not. She understands how fully Adam is enjoying this exchange, and she realizes that in a curious way she is too. She says, "Thanks, Adam. This is really good of you."

"Shit." He laughs. "My pleasure, as we say around the Yard."

Phil-Flash, who graduated in June, has gone back to Cleveland, but he flies in to Boston to see Cathy almost every weekend, or so it seems to Megan; undoubtedly Cathy believes that she sees him less than when he was in Cambridge. And between the weekends there are long phone calls, and boxes of flowers, sometimes a piece of jewelry. It is the most elaborate and expensive courtship that Megan has ever witnessed, by far. She is unable not to say to Cathy, "Why don't you just elope? Think of all the money you'd save."

"Well, I must admit, that's been considered as a possibility. Usually quite late at night, after quite a lot of brandy. Fortunately."

From this, imaginative Megan is able to conclude that Phil and Cathy do not go all the way, which of course she has wondered about. Late at night, fairly drunk and really wanting to do it, instead they consider an elopement. Cathy cannot have sex until she is married.

"What's worse, for Catholics?" Megan now asks. "Premarital sex, or abortions?"

Cathy laughs, presumably at Megan's extreme seriousness, and her laugh reinforces Megan's view as to her virtue. "Well," Cathy says, "we very much frown on both, as you know. They're both mortal sins. I would guess, maybe just for me, abortions are a bit worse. They're murder, after all. Killing a soul."

"Well, what would you do if you were pregnant and not married?" Megan persists.

"I would have the child and put it up for adoption. Or keep it. Those are the only possible Catholic solutions," says Cathy, in her wry, tight voice. But of course she is describing exactly what she herself would (or will) do, should the situation arise, later in her life.

"I just don't know," says Lavinia, with her small inward frown. When Lavinia frowns in that way Megan senses that she is re-establishing connection with her own inner self. Megan has learned too that such frowns are apt to precede some alarming and usually accurate statement, or judgment, as though Lavinia, in the course of her frown, has received a message, like a medium. She now continues, "I don't know, but I just don't trust Phil-Flash."

"You mean you don't like him," Megan argues, but she has felt a premonitory chill of sympathy for Cathy; so often Lavinia's harsh judgments are correct.

In a reasonable way, though, Lavinia agrees with Megan. "That's true, I don't like him. But no one likes him, Potter says. Everyone makes fun of the way he throws money around, and that *car*. But that isn't what I mean. There's something hysterical about the way he's gone after Cathy, who, let's face it, is not some exceptional beauty. I think it could all stop just as suddenly as it started."

As always, Lavinia's logic is impressive; Megan cannot help seeing exactly what she means. Lavinia seems somehow to be in touch with some of the inexorable laws of life that Megan has missed, and will no doubt continue to miss. Megan says, "I hope you're wrong," hearing her own small hopeless voice.

"But it might be the very best thing for Cathy, breaking up with him," ponders Lavinia. "He's so—so tacky." And then she laughs. "As long as she doesn't run off with some priest."

"Oh, Lavinia!"

One of Lavinia's special tricks is a look that combines high seriousness with great amusement—her expression now, as she says, "Well, don't be so sure. I knew this girl from Baltimore, a Catholic, of course, and she fell madly in love with a priest. She was very good-looking, and I guess he loved her too. Anyway, she ended up pregnant, and she had to go away to Arizona, or somewhere."

"Oh, Jesus." To Megan, all Lavinia's stories of wickedness, those about her friend Kitty or other wild folk, including, now, this poor girl from Baltimore—all such stories are particularly convincing. Megan can see the beautiful girl and the priest, he young and handsome, of course, and the girl weeping, despairing, pregnant, and off to Arizona, never to see her child or the priest again. She asks Lavinia, "If you were pregnant, is that what you would do, would you give up the baby?"

This time Lavinia's frown is one of simple displeasure. "No, of course not. In the first place I would never allow that to happen. *Never*. But if it should, I'd get married. Instantly."

"You're against abortions?"

Lavinia shudders. "I can't think of anything more sordid." She looks hard at Megan, then, and with a tiny smile she asks, "Little Megan, are you trying to tell me something?"

"Oh no, Lavinia, honestly. In fact I just got the curse. I have cramps."

"Please spare me the details. As long as you're okay. But Megan, you've got to be very careful. Those Jewish boys you go out with, they're all most terrifically oversexed."

On Monday afternoon, Megan is summoned to Peg's room. Armed with an address and a phone number, which Adam has supplied, she is startled to find Lavinia and Cathy already there. And there is Peg, in the process of passing around a giant box of chocolates. Peg is saying, "Well, girls, I want you three to be the first to hear my big news. You'll never guess. Cameron and I—" And then she bursts into tears, loud and choking, and heaving sobs.

It is Lavinia who goes over and puts her arms around Peg, and

MYNDERSE LIBRARY
31 Fall Street
Seneca Falls, New York 13148

strokes her hair. "Now little Peggy-poo, you mustn't cry. This is lovely, lovely news! I think it's wonderful, and oh! I'm so jealous!"

Lavinia and Peg often address each other in this sort of semi–baby talk, but today Megan finds it especially embarrassing. And what can Peg be thinking? Is she really going to marry Cameron Sinclair, whom Megan does not believe she likes? Just because she is pregnant? Or is she pregnant, after all?

Through tears, between sobs, Peg gets out, "It's really funny that I should be the first one, huh, girls? Who'd ever have guessed."

"Oh, I'm so jealous!" Lavinia cries out, again. "Well, you know what they say about still waters. But we'll all still be virgins while, while you're going to be 'experienced.' *Soon*. Now Peglet, you've got to promise to tell us all about married love."

Cathy, who is obviously meeting Phil-Flash later, has her hair up in pin curls, and some new white cream with which she seems to be experimenting spread over her face. She is smiling in Peg's direction, saying, Swell, how great. But her round brown eyes, meeting Megan's, are quite opaque, impossible to read. Is she thinking of herself and Flash, their possible wedding, and if so, thinking *what*?

Megan has observed that Peg is assiduously not looking at her, and she wonders if she should stick around after the others have gone and give Peg the information from Adam Marr, anyway. Should she say, Look here, you don't have to marry him?

Megan feels as though she is in fact at their wedding, Peg's to Cameron, and that the minister has come to the part about obstacles to the union, anyone knowing why it should not take place. And Megan, like that almost always silent presence, decides also to keep silent.

For all she knows Peg really wants to get married. To Cameron Sinclair.

11

Lavinia and Cathy and Megan all three decide to take the winter term off, winter of 1945. Peg was married quietly in Plainfield, in her parents' house, in September; she and Cameron then took off for Houston ("of all places!" as Lavinia puts it) in September. Cameron, who did not after all get into Harvard Law, is now interested in oil. Only Lavinia, of Peg's three friends, was in attendance at the wedding. ("Well, our little Peglet actually comes from a great deal more money than I had imagined," admits Lavinia, reporting back. "Lucky Cameron!" she adds.)

It is unlikely, though, that either the stern warnings of the dean or the absence of Peg played a part in anyone's winter plans. More probably they all simply needed a change; in any case that is how they put it to each other. And so they are scattered apart: Lavinia is in Washington, Cathy in Philadelphia, and Megan in calm and sunny Palo Alto (so boring! she often remarks, in her letters).

And all winter, as though they had nothing else to do, they all write long letters to each other. Especially Megan, who writes at length to both Lavinia and to Cathy; she and Peg do not communicate, and Megan has come to feel that in some way she behaved badly toward Peg, although she could not say just how: was finding an abortionist bad? In any case, Megan writes the most frequent and the longest letters, possibly because she now feels so isolated, out there in California—her own true center having shifted eastward, as it were. And she is lonely: her mother, Florence, works late at her carhop job, down the Bayshore, and then sleeps late; she and Megan find little to say to each other, in their infrequent encounters. Occasionally Megan helps out her father in his WE BUY JUNQUE store. She never mentions either parent in her letters.

Besides writing letters east, Megan's only real diversion is a course that she is auditing at Stanford, with an old high school friend. Without paying, of course.

. . .

Megan to Cathy:

You won't believe this, but this morning in my lit. class the professor, a "famous writer" (he writes very long novels about life among Mormons) actually said that "for his money" Jack London was a much better writer than Henry James. Truly, he said that. I almost choked. Oh Mathiessen, where are you? And there was an article in the local paper about the writers at Stanford, and one of the heads of the "creative writing department" said, he actually said, "Most of us are married. You don't see much Eastern effeminacy around these parts." Well, you don't see many brains or good writing either.

And the students. Boys in jeans and white T-shirts, girls in pastel cashmere and pearls, all of them, all the time. How I do miss the Yard and those nice coats and ties, and the girls not looking alike.

How are you? Does Phil come to Philadelphia? Do your parents like him? If you get married behind my back, so to speak, I will never speak to you again.

Lavinia to Megan:

Well, the most interesting news from our little Peglet: she's pregnant. I can just see her with a whole family of great big children, can't you? And she will get bigger and bigger. So much for all those silly people who used to say she was a dyke.

Last week I had to go up to New York to do some shopping and I called little Cathy. I thought she could just hop on a train and meet me for lunch. But she said she had a bad cold and she sounded terrible. In fact a little strange. Do you think everything is all right with her and Phil? I didn't want to ask. Between us, I think our Cath is a very strange and complicated girl.

Potter's letters are very satisfactory, both as to frequency and content. In fact he is a perfect darling, and I miss him very much.

Please be careful of all those California boys, dear little Megan. I hear they are really wild.

Cathy to Megan:

I don't know quite how to say this, but I guess Phil and I are divorced, without getting married, that is. He just suddenly stopped doing everything he had been doing, no more phoning or flowers or anything. He never said why, in fact he never said anything at all. My guess is a combination of pressure from his parents, since I am not just what they had in mind for their only son and heir, probably, and knowing him, some girl closer to hand, so to speak. I rounded up all his presents and sent them off to Cleveland, but he didn't even say if they had come. I guess he is not a very nice person, but I also guess that my judgment is not very good.

What have you been reading? I could use something good. I guess you are not recommending Jack London. I don't think I've ever read a book about life among Mormons. Probably they would be on the Index, whose proscriptions as you know I scrupulously follow.

Not being any longer a fiancée, or whatever I was, I am getting fat.

Janet Cohen to Megan:

Guess what? I am not going to med school after all because Adam and I are *getting married.* On New Year's Eve, because that is also his birthday. We are going to live in Brooklyn in the cheapest place we can find. I will get a job and he will work on his play and we will save all the money we can, and then the year after that we are going to Paris. I guess when all our twenty kids are grown up I will go back and finish college. Adam says I could even go to med school later on, but I am not so sure I will want to, by then.

After you graduate I really think you should come to see us in Paris. Adam likes you very much, and we could have fun.

Megan to Lavinia:

Actually I thought Cathy sounded okay, when she wrote, but of course even if she were dying of a broken heart she would not say so. You and Potter certainly were right about Phil-Flash. He is absolutely an SOB, I think. It is really lucky that Cathy didn't marry him. I hope she meets some nicer man this spring.

I am just back from four days in Los Angeles, which is the worst place in the world. You really would hate it. But actually I was there seeing a friend of mine from New York, who is a musician. A trombone, of all things. We went to a lot of jazz places and interesting restaurants. I never got any sleep but it was a nice change from Palo Alto.

But no, Lavinia, I am not "serious" about him. I am not getting married. Maybe not ever. I feel that marriage is probably overrated.

Occasionally, unavoidably alone with her mother, in the small ugly kitchen or the smaller "breakfast nook," having coffee, Megan experiences a jarring combination of strong emotions, almost unbearable, as Florence sighs and says—wistfully? accusingly?—"Seems like you just got here and now you're off, back to Boston."

"But, Mother, I've been here all winter."

"Well, probably it's gone faster for me than for you." Another sigh, but the remark at least sounded merely factual, descriptive.

"Well, you were working. I wasn't, really." Despite herself Megan is defensive.

Still another sigh as Florence, who may also have run out of things to say to her daughter, gets up and begins to rinse out the cups. "It's got to do with age," she throws back over her shoulder. "The older you are the faster time goes by."

"But, Mother, you don't look much older than I do." And you should look older, you're supposed to look like a mother, not a carhop, Megan does not add.

"Megan honey, what a sweet thing to say. I just never—"

As Florence turns away, too quickly, Megan is left with a sense of having somehow given the wrong present, and to the wrong person.

Although Florence is surely, surely her mother. Their bodies are so different in size and shape, and their hair is different, but their hands are almost identical, Megan has noticed, and her mother's still-eager mouth is very much like her own.

12

There is at Radcliffe, in these mid-forties war years, a small but highly visible group of girls who seem to do nothing but study. They are of a slightly older generation than Megan and her friends, and they chose the college for its academic excellence, or in some cases geographic necessity; many of them commute from Boston and environs. They did not arrive in Cambridge filled with fantasies concerning all the men around Harvard Square, as the Cabot Hall technical virgins did (probably), nor were they prompted by some flimsy summer love affair, as poor Megan was.

Megan knows a few of these heavy studiers in a more or less peripheral way, through an accidental walk with one of them between the dorms and Harvard Yard, an encounter in the smoking room. She likes them, on the whole, but she imagines (probably correctly) that in their eyes she is seen as entirely frivolous, fat but an intellectual light-weight (despite all her A's); they would know that she cares about boys and dates, sex, even clothes—whereas they would seem to care for such things not at all; they are seldom, if ever, seen wearing anything but jeans and baggy sweatshirts.

It is astonishing, then, to Megan, to realize that almost behind her back Cathy has become a part of that group. Cathy, who the previous summer was always pincurling her hair for her next date with Flash, now rarely even bothers to wash her hair, much less to curl it; she goes around in dirty Levi's and baggy gray sweatshirts. She spends almost all her time with a strange girl called Vince, who is also studying economics. Instead of Levi's, Vince wears gray slacks, as heavy and shapeless as Vince herself is large and un-indented, with dark gray-blond hair and skin of about the same color. Even Vince's eyes are gray and dull, behind heavy glasses.

Or, Megan wonders, is she seeing Vince in such a harsh light out of sheer jealousy, because she misses Cathy? And if that is so, just exactly what does it mean? She has to face the fact that the sight of Vince and Cathy, always together, makes her truly unhappy.

Megan knows, she knows perfectly well that this is not something that she should discuss with Lavinia—Lavinia the merciless, with her relentless intelligence, her overwhelming sophistication.

Nevertheless, there Lavinia is, often present and available for conversation, when she is not off somewhere with Potter. And finally the temptation is too much for Megan, who says (as casually as she can, which is not very casual), "It's funny, isn't it? Here we were hoping Cathy would meet some really nice guy this spring, and instead she's taken up with Vince." That was not exactly what she had meant to say; it came out wrong, but having spoken there was no way for Megan to amend her words, especially not under Lavinia's cold clear scrutinizing gaze.

And Lavinia has obviously given this odd new pairing considerable thought, herself, for she answers judiciously, "Well, I wouldn't worry about it if I were you. I mean, I'm quite sure it isn't what it may look like. Cathy isn't, uh, like that, we both know she isn't." (This with the sidelong, complicitous smile.) "And actually Vince isn't either. I can always tell. A couple of girls like that were thrown out of the school I went to, our senior year."

And Lavinia, in detail, tells a long story of lesbianism at boarding school: the discovery of love notes passed back and forth at chapel, the expulsion of both girls, and the reigning silence as to its cause.

"But of course we all knew," proclaims Lavinia, in her satisfied way.

But is that what she, Megan, really thought about Cathy and Vince? Megan uncomfortably wonders, and she is more uncomfortable yet after talking to Lavinia.

"The real point about our little Cathy," Lavinia explains, "is that she is basically a follower, like most Catholics. And don't ignore the fact that Vince is a Catholic too."

"Really? How do you know?"

"Her name, for heaven's sake. Clara Vincent. Anyone named that has got to be a Catholic. Besides, she's from Somerville, or one of those Irish places."

"Oh."

"Anyway, for a long time Cathy seemed to be following you around, she even began to sound like you. And then Flash, and now Vince. They always have to have a stronger personality."

Not feeling that she has an especially "strong personality" and unable to see herself as an object for imitation, Megan is less convinced than she generally is by Lavinia's arguments. Also, since the episode of Gordon Shaughnessey, Lavinia's anti-Catholicism has got out of hand, Megan thinks.

Lavinia and Potter plan to be married a year from the following June, in 1946, just after graduation. But their engagement will not be announced until Christmas. "There's no point in my being tied down for longer than that," Lavinia confides, with a sexy laugh. "And besides, Christmas seems a perfect time for engagement parties. Potter and I will go to all the regular parties, plus our own. It will be just right for him to meet everyone then."

As always, listening to Lavinia, Megan's imagination creates glamorous (if more than a little celluloid) scenes: crystal chandeliers glinting candlelight, above silver-laden tables. Marble mantels, blazing aromatic fires in huge fireplaces. And the rooms all filled with exceptionally beautiful people, in satin and velvet and furs, laughing and talking and drinking champagne and eating exotic, wonderful food. Christmas parties in Washington. Christmas engagement parties.

But in the meantime, Lavinia has a curious escapade with a young man named Russell Finnerty, which Megan finds out about only by accident.

Seated alone in the stairwell, on the top step where she used to sit and smoke with Janet Cohen or with Cathy, Megan first hears and then she sees Lavinia, who trips several times as she makes her way slowly up the stairs: Lavinia, with a white, clean-washed look on her face, her lipstick and powder clearly all kissed away, to reveal her own fine white dry skin—unlike other girls, who come in from sexy evenings with their lipstick smeared, their faces a mess. Lavinia also looks just slightly, delicately drunk. She and Potter must have been to another Porcellian party, Megan thinks, or something at the Pudding.

Lavinia sits down beside Megan and gets out a cigarette, as Megan, in a fairly perfunctory way, asks her how Potter is.

She is not at all prepared for Lavinia's snort and giggle. "Oh, little Megan, how sweet and naive you are, *au fond*. I was with the most divine *new* boy, named Russell Finnerty. I think I'm in love."

Very surprised, Megan asks what is to her the obvious question: "Oh, you and Potter broke up?"

Another giggle. "Of course not, silly. I'm going to *marry* Potter. We're *engaged*. Russell is just, just someone very cute. And the most terrific fun to kiss."

At what must have been a look of even greater surprise on Megan's face, Lavinia begins to scold. "Honestly, Megan, it's time you found out a few things. Marriage is one thing, and love and sex are two entirely others, and if you can have a little sex and love mixed up in your marriage, you're just damn lucky, but that's not what it's *for*. Potter and I were brought up in exactly the same way, we might as well be *related*. And I do love Potter, he's a dear sweet man, and I think the sex part will be okay. But I'm nowhere near *crazy* about Potter, not sick over him the way I was with

Gordon, and the way I could be with Russell Finnerty, if I didn't know any better. I know how to handle things now."

Vastly interested (of course she is), Megan admits, "Well, I had sort of worked out that love and sex are different. I mean, I was *in love* with George Wharton, and kissing him was terrific, and then he goes off and marries Connie Winsor."

"Exactly," Lavinia cries out. "Connie Winsor is one of the richest girls in Boston. George Wharton is no fool."

"Well, I guess not. But what I mean is, after George there was Simon, and I was not in love with him, but kissing him was even better than with George. He was more fun to kiss, I mean." (Saying this, Megan wonders: Does Lavinia also use the word "kiss" as a cover term for, uh, everything?)

Suddenly looking absolutely sober, Lavinia comes close to answering Megan's not-spoken question. "Megan, you'd better be very careful with those 'Simons' you insist on going out with. You just be careful that kissing is all you do, or nearly all." She giggles then, and in quite another tone she adds, "Honestly, Potter is really too funny, wanting to know just how far I went with Gordon. As far as he's concerned I'm as pure as Ivory Flakes, but he keeps asking these questions about Gordon, and of course I'm not about to tell him. He knows perfectly well that my precious virginity's intact, and that ought to be enough for him, I think."

Megan is still caught up in earlier parts of Lavinia's not-quite-coherent conversation, and she has been thinking of several things at once. One of them is how totally, unbelievably shocked Lavinia would be if she knew about Jackson Clay. Lavinia, who worries about Megan "kissing" Jews. If she knew what Megan was actually doing, with a *Negro*, a jazz musician, would she die of shock? Would she never speak to Megan again? Would she tell the dean, and get Megan expelled?

Of course there is a strong part of Megan that has always judged Lavinia very harshly, coldly, even; that part of Megan has (silently) called Lavinia a rich Republican bigot, an immoral person. And in that way Megan is strongly tempted, for a moment, to tell Lavinia everything, in full detail, about herself and Jackson

Clay, including how they met. How she "picked him up" and went to bed with him the very next night.

In that way she could clarify her connection with Lavinia, once and for all; they would have it out, as the girls sometimes did in the old boarding-school books that she and Cathy talked about, *those* four girls—and at that moment beautiful rich Lavinia would be exposed for the wicked person that she truly is.

However, Megan does not tell Lavinia anything about Jackson Clay; they do not have anything out, and the moment passes, or nearly, but not before clever (rich and beautiful, wicked) Lavinia has read a little of Megan's mind. "You're not telling me something, baby Megan," Lavinia croons. "Mustn't keep things back!"

"Really, there's nothing to tell. Honestly, I haven't done a thing but study lately. I'm turning into one of those grinds. Soon I'll look just like Vince."

As usual, in her way Lavinia has been right: even apart from (well, quite aside from) Jackson Clay, there is something else that Megan is not telling, which is her increasing obsession with the works of Henry James.

She began, as in academic circumstances so many do, with *The Portrait of a Lady,* which she liked very much, but no more, perhaps, than many favorite novels. Then, though, she read all the later novels, starting with *The Ambassadors,* and from then on everything by James that she could find, the stories, introductions, notebooks, travel notes—a considerable undertaking, even an impressive one.

And that obsession, that literary mania has for Megan the magnitude of an actual move to another culture; it has, in her life, an impact comparable to that of moving from California to New England. This is a move to the climate of Henry James. Her mind has become filled with vistas of perfectly smooth green lawns, large houses, long conversations at tea and over formal dinners, and everywhere manners so exquisite that the slightest deviation from that perfection has the force of an earthquake. Gilbert Osmund seated, as Mme. Merle is standing. And what is more exhilarating even, to Megan, than the perfection of lawns and the length and frequency of conversations, the perfection of manners—more thrilling still is the Jamesian exaltation of personality, the infinitude of human possibilities, the personal capacity for grandeur. Very heady stuff, to a girl from Palo Alto High.

But, to see the world in Jamesian terms, or rather, to imagine that one lives in such a world, can impose some fairly strange distortions on ordinary life—and so it is with Megan. Certain people, including Cathy and her grimy new friends, and certain circumstances, such as not having five dollars for a new sweater that one wants, must be simply and absolutely ignored.

Lavinia, however, in a Jamesian way becomes considerably more interesting. She is perfect for a certain sort of antiheroine: richly evil, infinitely manipulative. Megan now spends more time with Lavinia than formerly she did, thus (possibly spuriously) motivated. They have long conversations; Megan notes Lavinia's perfection of manner.

And Megan, as a friend for Lavinia, at this particular time in Lavinia's life, her "free" pre-engaged senior year, works out well too. Megan is interested, admiring, noncensorious (or so Lavinia believes), and undemanding. Almost anyone else would expect to be included in Lavinia's life, at various lunches or teas at the Ritz, for example; Megan seems to like to hear about such occasions, but she would never imagine or presume her own inclusion. Or so Lavinia imagines.

Thus, with their somewhat conflicting, erroneous but convenient ideas of each other, the two young women become even closer friends, that spring and summer of 1945, and from then on into another vibrantly beautiful New England fall, during which Lavinia continues her clandestine connection with Russell Finnerty, but manages to preserve both her virginity and her engagement to

Potter Cobb. And Megan discusses Henry James with her tutor, and the thesis that she intends to write, on the significance of private incomes in Henry James. Megan, the ardent disciple, fears that this is rather a vulgar choice of topic, but her tutor, a young Marxist, assures her that it is both original and of great potential interest.

Meanwhile, the war in Europe ends, the bomb is dropped on Hiroshima, then Nagasaki, and then that war is over too, and the end of the world has quite possibly begun.

Megan plans not to go home for Christmas, that winter of 1945. She will stay in Cambridge and work on her thesis for most of the time, and then of course she will be going down to Washington for at least a few days, for some of Lavinia's announcement Christmas parties.

She also spends Thanksgiving in the dorm, and very much alone, Lavinia having gone home to begin arrangements for the coming season, and even Cathy off to Somerville, with Vince. But Megan's thesis, just begun, is going well, excitingly, and the weather is golden and lovely. She is less lonely than she might have been, in fact hardly lonely at all. She looks forward to Christmas and then more distantly to June, the receiving of Honors.

Soon after Thanksgiving, though, when Lavinia is just back from D.C., Lavinia and Megan have what is to Megan a curious conversation. It has to do with Peg, big Peg, who of course is married now, and the mother of twin daughters. She is living in a place called Midland, Texas.

"Poor Peglet," Lavinia sighs. Once more, she has just come in from a late encounter with Russell Finnerty, and she is a little tipsy. Conveniently for her, Potter is spending a lot of time down in New York, being interviewed up and down Wall Street, as Lavinia in her amused, pleased way likes to put it. "Poor poor Peglet," Lavinia repeats. "She thinks she just may be preggers

again. Honestly, that Cameron must be some kind of a stallion."
Lavinia giggles sexily. "I've told her she absolutely can't be, though.
I can't have a pregnant matron at my wedding."

Peg, then, is to be matron of honor? Not knowing how to
respond to what seems startling news, Megan is silent.

Slightly tipsier than usual, Lavinia fails to notice this silence,
or to find it significant. She giggles again, and then she says, again,
"Honestly, that Cameron must be a real stallion. They must do
it all the time. But just wait until next summer, little Megan. I
can tell you all about married love, and I will, I promise."

It occurs to Megan to say what Lavinia must know, that you
don't have to "do it all the time" to get pregnant. She does not
say that, however. She has just been struck full force with the fact
that she herself has in no sense even been asked to be in Lavinia's
wedding. There has been no mention, actually, of her possible
attendance, even. Nor has Lavinia made any mention of Megan's
coming down to Washington at Christmas. Engagement parties.

So much for Henry James; I do not belong to his novels, Megan
concludes.

Later, lying in bed, in the chilly Cambridge dark, Megan tries to
fight off a deep, sharp pain that is somewhere in her chest. You are
being ridiculous, she tells herself. Why would you even want to
go to a bunch of parties with people you never saw before and very
likely would not like? Why would you spend all that money, which
you don't even have, for train tickets and new clothes? And
wherever, even, did you get this idea about going down to Washington? Lavinia never said any such thing—it was all in your head,
not in hers.

But she is hurt, and it takes her longer to recover from that
hurt than she believes it should.

"My mother told me a long time ago," says Cathy to Megan, "that
if you don't expect very much you'll never be disappointed."

This conversation occurs sometime in the middle of the following spring, the spring of 1946. Christmas has come and gone, Lavinia is back from Washington and is officially engaged. Somehow she and Megan have little time for each other, these days, at least in part because Lavinia, true to her own social rules, no longer goes out with Russell Finnerty; she no longer comes home tipsy, for a final cigarette with Megan on the stairs.

These days, again, Megan and Cathy have schedules that perfectly coincide; they both are writing theses, both studying for finals. Cathy and Vince are still friends too, but they seem to see each other less.

Megan has of course got over her hurt about not going down to Washington—*of course* Lavinia would never have asked her to. She has even been able to tell Cathy about that ludicrous fantasy, which has become another joke between them, and the occasion of Cathy's remark about her mother's theory of disappointment. To which Megan responds, "Of course your mother's absolutely right."

"Lavinia lives strictly by rules of her own," Cathy adds. "But of course I guess we all do?"

"I guess. It's just that hers are really far from mine," answers Megan, at the same time thinking that very likely Cathy's (Catholic) rules are also unlike hers, whatever "hers" are. But very likely Cathy and Phil-Flash never actually did it?

Telepathically, it seems to Megan, Cathy then asks, "Can you guess what I got in the mail from Phil-Flash?"

"No."

"An invitation to his wedding. Can you believe it?"

"No. Oh, *no.*"

This sets them both off laughing, possibly because there is no other available reaction; they literally shriek with laughter, they almost cry, until finally Megan gets out, "I think you should go! We both should go, I'll go with you. It's so wonderful, not being invited to Lavinia's wedding—I wasn't even invited to George Wharton's, come to think of it. And going instead to Phil-Flash's. Whatever shall we wear?"

"Oh, I think both of us in black crepe, don't you?"

They go on laughing.

. . .

In June, both Megan and Cathy graduate with Highest Honors, both Summas, whereas Lavinia is only Cum Laude. But the following week Lavinia, in Washington, is splendidly married to Potter Cobb, unattended by any of her college friends. Her old friend Kitty is her maid of honor, Kitty being only six weeks pregnant, which no one knows, or could possibly see.

13

Two letters, from the summer of 1946:

One, from Megan Greene, in Palo Alto, to Janet Cohen Marr, in Paris:

I could hardly believe it, three thousand dollars. My parents are not rich, my mother works at a really dumb job, and they have always been thrifty as hell, but my mother said they just inherited a farm in Iowa, which they sold, and this is my share. I was tearing through college partly to save them the dough, and now my mom is saying how they appreciated my efforts, how proud they are of my Summa, etcetera. And so, three grand. I am not sure what they expected me to do with it, probably some neat little savings account, so that in fifty years I would have ten thousand (is that right? I was never good at compounding).

I am pretending to be thinking it over, and also pretending to be thinking a lot about a Ph.D. at Stanford. I could live at home. Whereas, actually, truthfully, I am thinking all the time about Paris. Never mind Henry James in London, I just know that Paris is my place, especially with you and Adam there. Do not worry, I won't hang around.

So, please, could you and Adam sort of work it out, and tell me how little I could live on? Subtracting about six hundred right away, for the train to New York and then the boat, leaves twenty-four hundred. So, could I live there for two hundred a month? I will diet and give up cigarettes. I will do anything for a year in Paris.

I would really appreciate a really specific letter from you.

Adam Marr, in Paris, to Megan Greene, who is still in Palo Alto:

You delicate bourgeois bitches really kill me. Don't you know that two hundred dollars a month, which comes to about eight thousand francs on the black market, is about four times what the average worker makes, to support a whole family? Or do you plan to stay at the Ritz, like your old asshole buddy Henry James?

Christ, Megan, just get on the fucking boat and come on over. Take your chances with the rest of us. And remember, everywhere you look there are people poorer and hungrier than you, much poorer, whose parents do not give them handouts of money, no matter how swell they are.

P.S. If you can ever get your nose out of the aforementioned H. James (and I meant that just as it sounds) you just might try reading Marx. He just might improve your alleged mind.

P.P.S. Janet and I will be glad to see you.

Megan does just as Adam bids: she takes the day coach, exhaustingly but without adventure to New York, where she does not call anyone she knows: not Simon, who is now married to Phyllis; not Lavinia, who is married to Potter and living in the East Sixties (of course). She does not even call Jackson Clay, who is probably off somewhere on a tour.

From New York to Cherbourg she takes a converted troopship, which is filled with college kids like herself, all off for their first look at Europe, postwar. Megan has three foolish, fairly unpleasant roommates, Holyoke girls, and so she spends most of her nights up on deck, necking near the lifeboat station with a rather handsome (though chinless) blond boy whom she knew at Harvard, though not very well: Price Christopher, from Toledo, Ohio. Price is going to study at the Sorbonne, something quite grandly called *Cours de la civilisation française.* You just sign up for the course and that way you can collect the G.I. Bill, Price explains. (Which is what Adam Marr must be doing, Megan reckons.) Price has heard that you can get a room on the Left Bank for twenty or thirty dollars a month, and the student restaurants around there are very cheap.

Handsome Price, however, being of an exceptionally calculating nature, has another plan, which he confides to Megan; he has correctly gauged her relative lack of interest in himself, beyond a certain fleeting sexual attraction. He plans to cruise the expensive bars, he says, and he will take in most of the better concerts, check out bookstores, until he meets an attractive French girl, preferably a rich girl, of course; he will move in with her for the duration of his stay in Paris, thus both saving some money and at the same time improving his French. He is so convinced of the feasibility of this plan that Megan believes in it too; of course he will meet such a girl. Megan can almost see her.

The room that Megan herself finds, at last, is three stories up, in the Hotel Welcome, on the Rue de Seine. Its shape is peculiar, trapezoidal. It contains a very wide, low bed, two chairs, a desk, a sink, and a bidet: the French essentials. Its long shuttered windows look out and down on that narrow street, its fishmarkets, galleries, bookstores, and flower stalls, and over to the wider, grander Boulevard St. Germain.

The toilet is down the hall, but this is Megan's first room of her own; she finds it wonderful. Among other things, she wonders with whom she will first make love, in that bed—in Paris, France.

Somewhat surprisingly, Adam and Janet are not living in one of the cheap hotels, as everyone else is. They have a small, quite comfortably arranged apartment, on the Rue de Tournon, near the Luxembourg Gardens. "Okay, no cracks about our bourgeois mode of existence," is almost the first thing that Adam says to Megan, although she had not been about to make such a crack.

What has struck her most, and what she could never say, on first seeing Adam and Janet is the intensity of their affection for each other. What can be recognized only as love is present in the very air between them, surrounding them; it is visible on both their faces. Their affection is like a steady fire that warms a room, and for that reason, that year in Paris, that winter, people gather around Adam and Janet, everyone wants to be with them. (There is also Adam's wonderfully energetic intelligence, and Janet's slyer, wittier perceptions.)

Megan especially wants to be with them. She wants to see them almost every day. And Adam and Janet make it clear, in one way or another, that they want to see her too, every day. Closest friends.

A party at the Marrs'. "Come any time after dinner, and bring a bottle of something," is how Adam's invitations ran, which led to considerable divergence as to hours of arrival, and also among choices of drink. People began to arrive at Rue de Tournon about eight o'clock, and continued to do so until after midnight. And everything was being drunk, from the most sensible *vin ordinaire*, to Pernod, to the Scotch that some misguided person brought along.

Adam would seem to have walked through the central courtyard of the Sorbonne and to have invited everyone he saw. Surely, Megan thinks, he can't really know all these people, or not by name? She tries to work out a guiding principle.

To begin with, they all look fairly poor. The men are in old army clothes, in various stages of shabbiness, and the girls wear old sweaters and skirts, last year's college clothes. The exception is a dazzling young blonde, a Smith girl on her Junior Year Abroad, who looks uncomfortable in her smart blue velvet and pearls. She arrived, it turns out, with Price Christopher (who must not yet have found just the right French girl). Price introduces his blonde to Megan: Lucy Wharton. Even now, Megan jumps at the name— Lucy *Wharton?*

There are five, then six young Negro men there, Megan observes, which is all the American Negroes at the Sorbonne. Does Adam have some special feeling for Negroes?

And, that night, Megan notices an odd fact about Adam, which is that his accent changes, perhaps unconsciously, according to the person with whom he is speaking. Megan has usually seen him alone, with Janet, and at those times Adam, like Janet, and probably like Megan, speaks a somewhat Harvard-modified version of Brooklynese. With the Negro men, though, his voice becomes markedly Southern, or, actually, Negro. Later still Megan is amazed to hear his accent in French; someone has brought along a very pretty dark French girl.

"I used to know someone named George Wharton," Megan says to Lucy Wharton, when she can.

"Oh, you know George? My absolutely favorite cousin. And Connie, isn't she divine? Not exactly pretty, is she, but such a dear."

"Uh, actually I met him a long time ago. When he was out at Stanford, actually. One summer."

"Oh, George's California experience. I'd forgotten all about that. In fact he was very cozy about the whole thing, we heard practically nothing." Lucy looks over toward Price, who is headed for the pretty French girl. Not turning back to Megan, Lucy goes on talking nevertheless. "I asked Price if by any chance he knew George, but he didn't. They must have been in different houses, or clubs, or something."

Price would not have been in a club at all, Megan thinks, but does not say. She further thinks it is more likely that Price would have known Phil-Flash, also from the unclubbable Midwest. "Harvard's awfully big," she weakly lets drop.

Beautiful Lucy, whose eyes are a true dark azure, gives Megan a consummately scornful look. "Oh, I know. Actually everyone in my family's gone to Harvard for *generations*. Of course I thought of Radcliffe, but Mummy's an old Smith girl."

"You probably wouldn't have liked it there anyway," says Megan, intending unkindness.

But Lucy might not have heard her; she is still looking worriedly over at Price, who is being very gallant to Odile, the pretty French girl. He is bent over her in a classically romantic pose; even his French has improved for the occasion.

Megan thinks, but does not say to Lucy: You don't have to worry, really. She's not rich enough for Price. She's pretty, but her dress is much too shabby for Price's ambitions.

"I did meet one absolutely divine Cliffie," says Lucy, with a somewhat tactless emphasis on *one*. "Lavinia Harcourt. In fact she's married to someone I practically grew up with. They had the most divine wedding, down in Washington. But you probably wouldn't have known her."

"Actually I did. In fact we lived practically next door to each other."

A quick look from Lucy brings Megan to an odd realization, which is that she herself has been doing exactly what she observed in Adam: she has been aping Lucy's very Bostonian accent, so much so that even preoccupied Lucy notices. But in her own case the intent, although unconscious, was surely parodic, wasn't it? Whereas Adam would never parody Negro voices, would he?

Because of the variety of things to drink, the guests at that party all tend to get drunk at uneven rates, and in divergent, incompatible ways. Poor Lucy Wharton, predictably enough, being unused to such rough social scenes as well as to the *ordinaire* Price brought—poor Lucy gets sick; she is led off to the bathroom by kindly Janet, and soon taken home by another of the Smith girls, as the whole scene is almost ignored by unchivalrous Price, who is still occupied with gallantry to Odile.

Adam, drinking Pernod, is a wild manic drunk; his loud energy gives the nonparty whatever life it has. All night his voice can be heard over everyone else's, in those impossibly crowded, overfurnished, overheated, and now extremely smoky rooms. Adam is shouting Marxist theory or newly acquired French obscenities. He is in love with his new Marxist culture, and in love with words.

And he is deeply in love with Janet, Megan feels, observing the two of them at the door, near midnight, as finally people begin to leave. Adam's arm clutches Janet's much smaller shoulders, drawing her close, as he shouts good nights: *"Ecoute, mon vieux, soyez sage, eh? Et bien, bon soir, mon gars, ma fille—"*

At last only a few people are left, of that original throng: there are Adam and Janet and Megan, and a fragile-looking French boy, a painter named Danny, who has somehow attached himself to Megan. And Price Christopher. And the French girl, Odile. And somehow it is then decided (Adam decides) that they must all go on to a place called Bal Nègre, on the Rue Blomet.

They all troop through the blackened streets, in a direction which Adam, mysteriously, is sure is correct, and he turns out to be right. Adam has a photographic memory for maps; he has already memorized Paris.

They arrive at last at a door, which is easily opened—opened to an absolutely jammed, brightly lit, enormous room, incredibly noisy; from a block away they were able to hear the wild West Indian music, the shouts, the pounding, dancing feet. Just inside, as they enter, there is a long crowded bar, at which they all stop for drinks. Adam insists on Pernod all around, his new addiction, before they climb some rickety steps to a balcony that overlooks the dance floor.

And somehow Adam commands a table. And, almost immediately, before sitting down, he asks Odile to dance.

Megan involuntarily looks at Janet, whose face is a blank; then Adam looks at her too, and he kisses her neck, and he says, "You don't mind?"

She frowns, just a little. "No, of course not."

But she does mind; Megan has seen it on her face.

Price has not liked this either, his new French girl off with Adam, now down there dancing with Adam to this crazy, manic music. Very carefully he does not watch them, but instead turns his attention to Megan.

Danny, Megan has begun to realize, is fairly drunk, slouched silently in his chair.

Price makes a curious speech to Megan, its curiousness including the circumstance of time and place. "I've been thinking a lot about you, Megan Greene," says Price, above the noisy music and the shouts.

"Oh?"

He makes her wait, smiling down at her—superior, withholding. "In some ways you're much more like a man, despite that body," he at last tells Megan, with a further smile.

"Oh, really?" Price has spoken as though he were giving her a compliment, but Megan has failed to understand. *How,* like a man?

"About sex," he explains. "You aren't silly about it, the way most girls are. You don't take it too seriously."

Is he referring to the fact that she was able to neck with him on the boat, coming over to Cherbourg, without falling in love with him? Of course, he must mean just that; and he is praising her good judgment, isn't he? But Megan still feels somehow vaguely, quite subtly attacked. Why, she wonders, is it "like a man," necessarily, to exhibit simple good sense? Or, can he possibly believe that only a woman who was "like a man" would not fall in love with him?

Wanting to change the subject, then, and certainly to shift it from herself, from Price's idea of her, Megan remarks that it is too bad poor Lucy got sick. "She'll feel awful tomorrow," Megan says.

"Maybe just as well," Price oddly answers, and then he laughs. "If she'd stayed sober I might have taken her home for an old-fashioned rape scene. And I must not do that to a nice girl like Lucy. In fact I really should stay away from that girl altogether."

"Why on earth? She's so pretty, and probably rich."

"Exactly." Price beams at Megan (again approving of her "male" intelligence?). "She'd be the perfect girl for me to marry, and I don't need anything that serious. Not yet."

Price has said this so earnestly, so pompously, really, that Megan is tempted to tease him. "First you have to find that nice rich French girl to move in with?"

"Oh Megan, you really know how to hit a guy below the belt." But he laughs, appreciating her, or seeming to—for whatever reasons of his own.

Price has succeeded in making her uncomfortable, though,

Megan recognizes, despite the fact that on the face of it he has been talking to her as to a friend. As a male friend, in fact, which is perfectly all right with Megan; God knows she would not want to be courted, as a woman, by Price Christopher. But what is bothering her, she decides, is that she does not especially want to be his friend at all. On some important level she is deeply distrustful of Price.

Later Adam dances with Janet, and everything between them is immediately all right, Megan feels (or hopes). Price dances with Odile, and Megan with small, thin Danny, who is really too drunk to dance. "You aire so beautiful," he keeps crooning into Megan's ear, as they jump about, not at all in time to the music.

By the time they leave the Bal Nègre, the Métro has long since shut down, and so the six of them troupe home, through the shuttered, gray deserted streets; they say good night to Adam and Janet at the Luxembourg Gardens, to Price and to Odile a few blocks later on. Price lives on Rue Monsieur le Prince; it is not quite clear where Odile lives.

At the entrance to her hotel, the Welcome, seeing that Danny is in a state of near collapse, Megan simply propels him inside the door and then she half-pulls, half-pushes him up her stairs—a relatively easy task, since, even drunk, Danny is light, nimble-footed.

They fall into bed and both fall immediately asleep. They sleep until fairly late the following morning, when some harsh sunbeams bring them simultaneously awake. They regard each other, then, with a shared mixture of surprise and amusement. And then Danny begins to make love to her.

Although all his motions are practiced—he is highly educated in ways of pleasing—Megan feels—something is wrong. He does not really want to do this, she thinks, and, ludicrously, he is just being polite.

Which is not quite a sufficient reason for making love, or so she believes.

As she half-responds, politely, Megan longs for an instant im-
provement in her French. "This is not necessary" sounds crude in
any language, as does, "You don't have to make love to me." And,
under these circumstances, does one use the familiar form?

Sensitive Danny, though, has understood without any words.
From her breast he reaches to stroke her face, as, smiling, he asks
her, "Ah, you do not feel at this moment 'in the mood'?"

"Well, no."

Megan too is smiling, and next they both begin to laugh, having
perfectly understood each other, with remarkable clarity. Having
begun to be friends.

Danny seems to have no home. "I generally stay with some
friend," he says to Megan, early on. And, "I paint in the studio of
a friend." Also, he has no money. Or rather, he has just enough
money, always, for the two Métro tickets, which he invariably,
chivalrously pays for. He wears tattered pants that have the look
of some army or other, and clean white shirts, never ironed.
Blondish curly hair, light eyes, a delicately graceful body. A street
child. Megan likes Danny very much, from the start, and she
worries about him, although he does not seem to worry about himself, any more than a sparrow would.

That first day they go out to lunch, at Benoit, just down from
the Flore. "I have no money," he has already said to her. "You
don't mind to pay?"

"No, of course not. I have plenty."

"If I had—" He smiles at her, charmingly, and shrugs.

It is not important to Megan which one of them pays; since
she is the one who has money, it seems natural that she should pay.

They are friends. He is an amusing companion, a gentle friend.

In quite another way, Adam is also a good friend to Megan, that
year. The friendship between the two of them has grown, somehow,
whereas the connection binding Janet and Megan is just slightly
diminished. The two young women never spend time alone; they
do not go out for lunch, for example, and Megan finds it hard to
imagine what they would talk about if they did: how much Janet

loves Adam, how happy she is with him? Because it is true that Adam takes up the whole of Janet's life; he surrounds and encompasses her. While Adam and Megan are violently talking, arguing, or while Adam argues with some other friend (ferociously, often, with Price Christopher), Janet will simply watch and smile. In love and loved.

Megan and Adam have two major arguments, which they repeat, with minor variations, with varying degrees of heat, over that whole long winter. The first is political; it has to do with the strong possibility of war between the United States and Russia: should the war come, which side should win? Which victory would, finally, improve the world? Adam is far more certain than Megan is that such a war will in fact occur, and he is certain too that a Russian victory would be preferable. Preferable, not wonderful; he is not an absolutely committed Stalinist, being already prone to deviationist tendencies. But Russia's winning would be just a little better, Adam says.

Much less certain than Adam that such a war will occur at all, partly because it is too catastrophic for her to contemplate, Megan believes that if such a war does happen it will not matter much who wins. She also thinks, and she says, that very likely she does not know what she is talking about—a view with which Adam is only too ready to agree.

Their other argument has to do with chess, strangely enough. Adam considers chess an admirable intellectual exercise. Megan calls it a waste of time. "Honestly, Adam, it's just a *game.*"

"You don't approve of it because it's a discipline you probably could not master, even if you weren't too lazy even to try. Most women can't play chess."

"We have better sense than to waste our time like that."

"You do not. You have almost no sense at all, you dumb cunt."

"Stupid prick."

They go on like that, in a friendly rage, while Janet silently, smilingly sides with Adam.

Good friends, the three of them.

14

None of them goes to the popular Flore, or the Deux Magots, where everyone else goes, that year. Not Janet and Adam, nor Megan, with or without Danny. "Rich assholes, on the prowl for gen-u-ine existentialists," is how Adam characterizes the students who do go to those cafés, which from the look of things seems accurate enough. And the Montana Bar, around the corner from the Flore, is even worse: "Cunts from Bennington and Princeton pricks," says Adam Marr.

But one bright December morning, after weeks of dark and cold, Megan finds herself drawn to an empty table at one corner of the terrace of the Flore—the corner nearest that lovely small stone church, St. Germain-des-Prés. She sits down and orders coffee.

The Left Bank at that time has a leisurely, small-town quality. Faces once seen tend to reappear, to become familiar, even; there are a great many people whom one almost knows, or so Megan felt, after almost three months in Paris. Still, it is surprising, even startling, that morning, to see the very familiar face of Adam Marr, in his usual battered army fatigues, and more surprising still to see that with him is the less familiar, strikingly pretty dark face of Odile. Walking past the terrace, they are smiling and talking in an animated way, entirely engaged in their conversation. However, Adam's sharp glance is still able to take in Megan, there in the sunshine, waiting for her coffee. Adam salutes her with one raised hand, an eyebrow cocked in her direction—and very likely all this is accomplished without disturbing the rhythm of his sentence. And then they are gone, Adam and Odile, down the boulevard, in the direction of the Sorbonne. Probably.

Digesting that tiny encounter, along with her just-arrived hot coffee (like all the coffee in Paris, that year, it tastes very strongly of chicory), Megan tries to turn her attention toward the church across the street, its darkly shaded, dark green churchyard, the blackened stones, the high black iron spiked fence. And she thinks how very odd it is that in months of exploring the farthest corners of Paris (an expert guide, Danny has taken her everywhere) she has never once entered this church, the oldest in Paris—and so near at hand. She will have one more cup of coffee, she then decides, and go into the church. At last.

She is imagining the dark cool interior, sunlight filtered through ancient stained glass, when suddenly there is Adam, at her side, seemingly having appeared from nowhere. He is flushed and sweating a little, as though he had run back to her, from wherever he was. He is smiling, saying, "Did I make it in time for coffee? Never mind what you're doing in this jack-off place."

"I was just going to order some more," Megan tells him; she is aware of a nervous flutter in her throat, as she wonders why. Why should the prospect of coffee with Adam make her nervous? They have had dozens of coffees together, with or without Janet.

"This seems to be coincidence day," Adam remarks. "First I run into Odile, then you."

"She's awfully pretty," Megan offers, blandly.

"You think so? I guess. No tits though. That's a French girl for you." And Adam looks glum, as though Odile's small breasts and the breasts of all French women were a genuine deprivation to him.

"I think Price really has the hots for her." Megan hears this strange sentence from herself, and she thinks, But that isn't how I talk. Am I trying to imitate Adam, instead of talking to him?

"Actually," Adam says—and in those few syllables Megan notes that he has shifted from belligerent Brooklyn to purest Harvard Square, the Yard—"Actually," he says, "it's all like a rather bad play. Poor Lucy loves Price, and Price has the hots, as you put it, for pretty Odile."

Unthinkingly Megan carries his idea along; like a stooge she asks, "Does Odile love anyone, do you think?"

"She loves me, or she thinks she does." Adam looks fully at Megan, saying this, giving her the full, powerful effect of his eyes, so hotly blue, so intense in their regard. And, at this moment, they contain a certain despair ("an existential despair," Adam himself would probably call it; of course he is reading Sartre).

In a then more normal voice Adam begins to talk. He tells Megan considerably more than she would have chosen to hear, had she been given a choice. "I never meant to cheat on Janet," he starts right out by saying. "I knew I'd be tempted sometimes but I thought I could make it." He laughs, presumably at the presumption of his suppositions. And he goes on. "Maybe the worst of it is that sometimes I've used you for an excuse. It's funny, but that's what I really feel crummiest about. Telling Janet I was taking a book or something over to you, when I really was meeting Odile. She lives near you, that made it easy. Or saying I'd run into you somewhere, to Janet." He laughs again, without amusement. "And now I have—I really did run into you."

Megan sees that by now this confession has cheered him; he has managed to shift some of his guilt onto Megan, or rather, he believes that he has.

Something in her face, some judgment, then, must have prompted him to ask, "Is that all right? You understand, silly Megan? You don't really mind?"

She bursts out, "Of course I mind, and I don't know what you mean, 'understand.' Christ, Adam, why me? If you had to lie like that you could have used someone else. Price, even. Christ, I really hate it."

Adam leans back in his chair, regarding her from a greater distance thus, and with almost pure irritation. "Boy," he says, "you women sure stick together, don't you. Shit, Megan, you were just the most plausible person. Can't you see that?"

"Of course I see it, you stupid prick. It just shows how little imagination you really have."

Adam looks stung; he is ready with a cruel answer, Megan can see that—but then he seems to decide to shift his approach. His eyes go sad, and his voice deepens; his accent is very Cantabridgian. "You're right," he says. "I've been rotten. I've felt rotten about what I was doing. And really bad toward you, Megan. I respect your attitude in this."

It is the winter solstice; there in the cold Paris sunshine, Megan and Adam stare at each other. Both are silent, having said enough, and possibly too much. Until Adam, for whatever reason, is compelled to add, in his more ordinary voice, "And you know what? The fucking wasn't even all that great. We were like two well-trained athletes going through our paces. You know what was missing? *Love*. I love Janet. Maybe I had to find out the hard way." This has been said with great earnestness.

"Oh, *shit*, Adam. Today you're absolutely full of it."

Adam grins, quite suddenly all pleased with himself again (his mother's darling bad boy). "Aaaah—" He makes his most Brooklyn sound. "You dumb cunt. What do you think you know, about anything?"

He summons a waiter—"*Eh, garçon!*"—and insists on paying for their coffee. He and Megan get up, they say a few words in parting and go off in their separate directions, Adam toward Janet, Megan heading for the Hotel Welcome.

Alone and upset, for no reason walking very fast, Megan forgets that she had meant to go into the church.

During the next few weeks Megan is aware of serious distress, over Janet and Adam. Irrationally, perhaps, she feels that Adam's defection has somehow undermined their three-way friendship, so that for a while she barely sees either of them. And, as trouble will, that problem seems to bring along other worries in its wake: Megan begins to worry about everything in her life.

For instance, whatever will she do the following year? Once back from Paris, where will she go? Her parents expect her to be in California—in San Francisco, at least, if not with them in Palo Alto. Megan would like to live in New York, she thinks, but how?

And what will become of Danny? How will he feed himself, once she is gone? He has told her that the winter before he was sick, "from the *malnutrition*"; suppose he should be sick again? Another calmer part of her mind tells her that Danny will of course meet someone else, another American girl or boy, or man, or older woman: she understands that the nature, or gender, of his friends is not important to Danny any more than whether or not they make love is important. Danny is a true street child, a little cat, or a sparrow. Still, she does worry about him.

Also, and more pressingly, Megan wonders if she can make what money she has left last until June; she counts and calculates, and she comes up with a variety of answers, the variety having at least a little to do with the fluctuating franc, which no one can calculate.

That year all the young Americans in France exchange their dollars on the black market, except perhaps for the very rich, the totally innocent, or the incredibly high-minded. The legal rate is ridiculously low, it seems to them, these "poor" Americans; they cannot afford to use it. They have convinced themselves that trading on the black market is not immoral; it does not seem so, nor is it much discussed in moral terms. The fact that most of the money dealers are concentration camp survivors, with crude numbers tattooed on their wrists, makes the question of morality almost irrelevant. The logic being, if logic could be said to exist in this situation, that those men are now entitled to make their own laws. Having suffered such extremes of horror, whatever they want to do now has its own sanction.

And so, in certain parts of Paris, near the Opéra, especially, and American Express, on Rue Scribe, the Americans are continually accosted by shabby, thin dark men. In an intense undertone these accosters ask, "Got anything to sell? You got dollars? Good rate today."

(How can they always tell that you are an American, Megan has wondered. It cannot be a matter of clothes; hers are all old and shapeless, and the cheap walking shoes that she wears she has bought over here. There must be some total effect, some radar to which these men are particularly attuned.)

The American, if he or she is educated in this process, as most of them quite quickly are, will then stop, and in an indifferent, idle way will ask, How much?

"I give you three-fifty. You got dollars? Traveler checks?"

"Don't waste my time. I know where I can get three-eighty."

At this time the legal rate would be about two-fifty. (The black market rate is determined by the Swiss franc, which is published every morning in the Paris *Herald*, and duly noted by the Americans.)

Once the bargain is accomplished, the Americans follow their guide, at what is in theory a discreet distance, to some local café of the street banker's choice. Fairly often this turns out to be a tiny bar on a side street just off Rue Scribe, called the Café Légal— a heavy irony of which Adam is especially fond.

In fact the whole experience of going with Adam to change money, as Megan often does, is intensely dramatic.

In the café, after the not quite furtive exchange of dollars and francs, Adam likes to offer the man on the other side of the table a glass of wine. "*Et toi, tu prends un coup de blanc?*" Which is as often as not accepted, with a small smile that shows, usually, dark neglected teeth.

The ensuing conversation, if it can be called that, is difficult for Megan to follow, since by now Adam has taken on the other man's accent, be it Polish, Hungarian, Moroccan; Adam's French takes on those accents. Then, at a certain point Adam will point to the numbers tattooed on the dark, extended wrist, and he will ask, From where? *D'où ça?*

Buchenwald.

Auschwitz.

Dachau.

I was there for three years. Five years. Four months. My parents killed. I lost my wife. My child. My health is not good.

Megan is never able to look at the man who recites these horrors. These men always speak in a monotone; they are devoid of self-pity, of conviction, even. They are no longer sure that such things have happened to them.

Adam will respond to all that with a few spat-out expletives, violent and obscene—his version of sympathy. But it seems to work; the man will smile, in a friendly if hopeless way.

Then there is an ironic chuckle from Adam, which says, probably, Well, what can we do, we poor dumb humans?

Slowly, then, they all get up and leave the café, the money changer going off in his own direction, his eyes and posture no longer indicating that he is in any way connected with Adam and Megan, who follow at a distance, before making their own turn.

These encounters leave Megan weak, near tears, of which she is ashamed.

It is hard to tell what Adam feels. Certainly he too is genuinely moved; Megan has even seen tears brightening those brightest, bluest eyes.

But it is also true that he invites—he even creates these scenes.

When Danny and Megan go out to eat together, on his insistence they always head for the cheapest possible restaurants, of which he is a remarkable and wholly reliable connoisseur. One of their favorites is luckily a couple of blocks from Megan's hotel; it is a small steamy cave of a room, dominated by a pale, dark-haired giant of a woman who cooks, and serves, and shouts the menus to the patrons, along with strong advice about what is best, that day.

"You should have the kidneys, you, you always love my kidneys, and the fresh green beans," she proclaims, addressing herself to Danny, one Thursday afternoon. They are having a late lunch, one day in March.

Danny laughs at her; he shrugs delicately, implying with the gesture his total helplessness in the face of her superior strength, her power.

"It's like visiting your mother, coming here," Megan has observed, although she too very much likes this restaurant, and Danny's "mother."

"I have a lot of mothers, is the truth of it," Danny admits, with another small shrug. "But you of course are not among them, my most dear Megan. You are my true friend, for me the first sympathetic American."

Megan has heard this small speech before, with variants, but he says it so gracefully, with such an intelligent, amused quick look in his wide gray eyes that she is always pleased, and touched. And that is as far as they ever go, Megan and Danny, toward a discussion of their slightly odd connection. For the most part, Paris itself is their subject matter, Megan's endless, greedy curiosity about the city, and his special forms of knowledge.

That day, however, they are interrupted almost as soon as Danny has made his speech, and Megan has smiled, responding— interrupted by Price Christopher, with Lucy Wharton. Price, in a crisp seersucker suit for which the day is too cold, and Lucy in her Smith-girl skirt and sweater. They are quite obviously just out of bed together; they both have just-combed, slicked-down blond hair, and the pinkish look of recent sleep, and love, on their similar blond skins.

Although the room is almost empty, with plenty of tables, after greetings Price asks, "You mind if we join you?" But the question has come out hurriedly; he is already in the process of sitting down at Megan and Danny's table. With a shy look, lowered dark blue eyes, Lucy sits down beside him.

Price then asks, "You two just get up too?" This, delivered with a small grin, is even less of a question than his may-we-join-you was.

Megan is about to explain that actually they are having such a late lunch because they just got back from St. Denis, where the restaurant turned out to be closed (a special cheap find of Danny's: "one of the most cheap in Paris, and the best") and that they had not spent the night together. They never do. However Price, along with Adam and probably Janet and everyone else whom Megan knows that year in Paris, must assume that she and Danny are lovers —an appearance that somehow, she feels, protects her, and that she and Danny have allowed to persist without ever referring to it.

And none of that is remotely Price's business, she decides.

But Danny does answer, in French. "Actually, as you might say," he says, with one of his most charming, fleeting smiles, "we have been out to the Faubourg St. Denis, where we thought also to have lunch, but where, alas, our chosen restaurant was closed."

This has been said in a curiously challenging way, with a very direct look across the table at Price.

Because of the language difficulty, Danny and Megan have not been given to elaborate conversations about mutual (or rather, her) friends. And now Megan wonders just how Danny, the classically starving French painter, does feel about Price, that quintessentially American blond, well-fed, and expensively educated boy.

Startlingly, at that moment, in a mock-sexy hoarse falsetto, Price begins to sing. *"Je suis nais, dans le Faubourg St. Denis,"* he chants. *"Je suis Paris—"*

Embarrassed for him, and for poor Lucy, who has not spoken since they sat down, Megan half closes her eyes. When she opens them she finds Price and Danny smiling at each other like old pals, as Danny says, "But exactly. And may I compliment you on a charming voice."

"I accept your compliment, sir."

All that was in French, and Megan has to admit that Price's accent is admirable. Something in that small exchange has made her uncomfortable, though, and in an uncharacteristically aggressive way, she turns to Lucy and begins to tell her about a movie that she and Adam and Janet saw, *Quai des Orfèvres.* It was marvelous, Megan says.

Well-bred Lucy listens quietly, from time to time stealing an adoring glance at Price, who now is telling Danny about the Right Bank *boite* where he first heard that song, *"Le Boeuf sur le Toit."*

"I have been there myself," says Danny, with a quick, oblique, and pretty smile.

In April, which is the coldest, wettest April in anyone's memory, Adam Marr gets wonderful news: his agent has found a producer for his play; not only that, he has also found a backer, who is both enthusiastic and very rich. A famous director is very interested. Adam and Janet have to go back to New York as soon as they can pull themselves together for the trip. Before the first of May, they say.

And, more great news, to be shared immediately with Megan, their true best friend—Janet is pregnant! "Just look at those tits, and that belly!" Exuberant Adam, and happy blushing Janet.

"Should we give a party?"

This is discussed for a while between Janet and Adam, Megan being the most interested observer.

At first a party seems an obviously good idea. "With all our new dough we could even pay for all the booze ourselves," Adam calculates. "Even serve something fancy. Pernod, or champagne."

But then, as they get to the guest list, the plan begins to fall apart. For one reason or another, they do not seem to like anyone anymore—or rather, Adam doesn't.

Two of the Negro men who once were their friends are by now assumed to be a homosexual couple. Adam frowns. "I don't know," he says, "I'm sure it proves something terrible about me, about my own sexual drive, but I just plain don't like queers." (He is obviously sure that nothing terrible about his sexual drive could possibly be proven, ever, by anyone.) "They don't make me uncomfortable," he continues confidently, "I just don't like them. For one thing, they're all such lightweights, intellectually. Can you imagine a Marxist fairy? It's almost a contradiction in terms."

Megan starts, and then decides against telling him about her former tutor, a Marxist and a "fairy," in fact a member of a Marxist–homosexual–Anglo-Catholic group, at Harvard. But Adam undoubtedly disapproves of Anglo-Catholics too, she decides, and by this time she is tired of arguing with him; he tends to be a bully, "dialectically," as he himself might put it.

They run through various other friends, arriving at last at Price and Lucy. "I don't know," says Adam. "I don't think I really feel like inviting that Arrow Collar boy."

"He's very anti-Semitic," Janet puts in, surprisingly; Adam and Megan both look at her with interest.

"How do you mean?" Adam asks.

"I can just tell. The way he is with me."

"But how, how is he?" Adam persists.

Expressing herself verbally is hard for Janet; it is not her role. She has chosen to be a supportive listener—but now for Adam she makes an effort. "It's just that he's, uh, different with me than he would be if I were a gentile," she says. "He acts like I'm a little bit, uh, foreign. Maybe a little inferior. He's, uh, more familiar."

"I'll break his ass. Stupid cocksucker."

Megan at that moment feels an odd need to defend Price; she still believes that he is not quite as bad as they think, and that it's silly to call him anti-Semitic, really. But, as is becoming usual with her, she stifles her impulse to start an argument with Adam.

And Adam, aroused, rants on. "And as for that Miss Lucy Wharton, she's the kind that makes you want to stuff it in her mouth. All the way. The biggest hard-on in the world. And choke her on come."

To which Janet says, as she often does, "Oh, *Adam*," embarrassment and pride confused in her voice, and on her face.

It occurs to Megan then that Adam is so like a wonderful, wayward child himself, to Janet, and she wonders: how will Adam take to being a father, to giving up that much of Janet to another person? As quickly as the question arrived its answer follows: he won't like it much, not after the first flush of pride in what he will see as his own achievement. He will get back at Janet for having had a child with more and more serious affairs.

"What it comes down to, fat old Megan," Adam just then, most disarmingly, says, with great affection, "is that we don't really like anyone but you," and he gives her one of his warmest, bluest looks, as he turns to Janet. "Isn't that right, you beautiful knocked-up Jewish cunt?"

"It's true," agrees Janet, and she smiles toward Megan.

"We're ending up just the way we began," Megan comments, not quite knowing how else to respond, and feeling a little guilty about her newest perception of Adam.

"Your Danny, though. I really like him," Adam continues. "You know, if it weren't for the language thing, I could make a terrific actor out of that kid."

"But he's a painter," literal Megan objects, with a small frown.

"That's what he says. But have you ever seen a drawing, or anything he's done?"

"Well, no."

Triumphant Adam. "You see? The kid's an actor. He acts out

being a painter, because that is the Left Bank thing for a poor young man to do this year. The existential thing. But as a painter he is inauthentic. On the stage his true nature would emerge. Haven't you watched him walk? Christ, he could almost dance."

"Okay, so he's really an actor." Megan laughs, but at the same time she is inwardly admitting to revelation: what Adam says is absolutely true. The very emotional versatility, and the quick range of its expression, in Danny are indeed the qualities of an actor (and qualities that perhaps have kept her own emotions at a distance from him). And about his walk Adam is absolutely accurate: Danny's range of physical motions is amazing; just walking along he can, and does, express extremes of happiness, or fatigue, or humor, even lust. "I think you're at least almost right," she says, somewhat grudgingly to Adam.

"Almost! You retarded bitch, you don't know a fucking thing. But I tell you what, instead of a party, Jan, let's take these kids out for a farewell dinner. What's the most expensive restaurant in Paris? Maxim's or the Tour d'Argent?"

And that is how the four of them, Adam and Janet, Megan and Danny, come to be sitting near a window of the Tour d'Argent, with a view of the Seine and of Notre Dame, on one of the last nights of April 1947.

They look a little out of place, Megan observes, with a slight embarrassed twinge. Pregnant Janet's sweater is a little too tight, and Adam's coat and his tie have a prewar, maybe a Harvard freshman look, as does his too curly, unsuccessfully slicked-down hair. Megan herself, in her college good-black-dress, is pleasantly aware of having lost a lot of weight—a surprise, she thought she was eating a lot, but the dress does not fit anymore. It hangs off her, unevenly. It is too long but it is not a New Look dress, like the others in that richly populated room, the new ankle-grazing skirts, above high thin shoes.

Of them all, Danny looks most at ease, and most correct. His gestures and his whole posture serve to impart elegance to a suit that must in fact be old. He now looks as though he spent all his evenings in just such an environment—in the most expensive restaurants in Paris, instead of the very cheapest. Adam is right, Megan thinks; his "actor" perception of Danny is truly brilliant.

But despite Adam's brilliance, and his probable good intentions for the evening, it gets off to a bad start right away, with the arrival of their first waiter.

"We'll have some champagne, and caviar all around," Adam grandly commands.

Adam's tone and his by-now excellent French have almost no effect, however. The waiter frowns, and from a deep pocket he extracts a slip of paper. He scribbles, then shows the paper to Adam.

Adam scowls. "What's this?"

"It is the price of caviar, Monsieur."

"Well, what's the problem? Do I look like I can't afford it? What's the matter with you? I ordered caviar, and I know it's expensive. Believe it or not, we have it in America. Even in Brooklyn." By the end of this tirade he is shouting, and his proficient French has almost deserted him.

Placatingly, Janet murmurs, "He was just trying to warn you, honey."

The waiter, an old man in wire glasses, stiffly retreats.

"Stupid cocksucker, doesn't he know a world-famous playwright when he sees one?" Sipping champagne, which has fortunately arrived with amazing speed, Adam by now is laughing—one of his most appealing qualities at this time is his ability to see his own foolishness.

As might have been expected, though, none of them likes the caviar very much, when it finally arrives, and is served to them on thin cold toast. It is possible that the insistence on its cost has spoiled it for them all.

Nor is the famous pressed duck a great success, dutifully ordered by them, in turn. "Actually I can think of many better things to do with a good, tender duck," says Danny, thoughtfully, in the tone of a superior cook.

"Yeah, you could fuck one," says Adam, at which not even loyal Janet is able to laugh.

All in all, it is a farewell evening that has almost no connection with any of the days and months, all the evenings that went before it. It makes as little sense as most parting celebrations do.

15

Pink to silver pink to silver lavender: these are the colors of Lavinia's bedroom, on East 63d Street, in New York. A bedroom that she shares, sometimes, with her husband, Potter. His dark leather study-bedroom adjoins hers—like the toolshed at the bottom of a garden, Lavinia has unkindly, unfairly, and uncontrollably thought.

But her own room is beautiful and perfect, and French; all the fabrics, the silk-hung walls and even the pale pink bed linen, are imported from France. Heavy silver toilet things on her glass-lined dressing table, small crystal perfume bottles, and a three-way mirror, ornately framed, in silver.

Just now she is staring into that mirror, the contemplation of her own face being Lavinia's form of meditation. In that way she can concentrate, and sort things out.

One of Lavinia's minor problems at this moment, this sunny fall morning, early in October 1949, is where to meet Megan for lunch. Minor, and perhaps easily solved; still, any area has its implications. For example, Lavinia does not want an uptown restaurant, partly because she does not want to be in a position of having to say, after lunch, Well, since this is so near to where I live, how about coming back with me for coffee? (Well, of course that is unlikely; "uptown" is an enormous area and besides, Megan will have to get back to work, won't she?) The real reason for not wanting an uptown lunch, which Lavinia faces with a slightly embarrassed smile into her mirror, is simple, obvious, and inadmissible: she does not, *does not* want to run into anyone she knows. When she is with Megan. Having to introduce Megan, and later to explain to whoever, whomever, why it is that Megan does not lose weight. Why she wears those clothes. Even after that year in France, in Paris!—and her really good job.

However, since Megan is working somewhere almost in the Village, some publishing house near Union Square, Megan has said, she, Lavinia, will simply get into a cab and go down there. Let Megan choose a place she knows. Her own turf, as it were.

Lord knows what Lavinia should wear, though. Probably not too dressed, so far downtown. And it actually, almost, doesn't matter what she wears, or infinitely less so than usual. Maybe she should wear Levi's, for a joke, the way they all used to, all the time, back in Barnard Hall.

The truth, though, the frightful, ghastly truth that has been pushing toward the forefront of Lavinia's mind, is that it does not matter where she and Megan have lunch, or what she wears— *Lord*, not in the least, of course not. Because she has recently realized, or faced a fact that diminishes all other possible problems, which is that already, at twenty-three, she has made a fatal, absolute mistake: *she should not have married Potter Cobb.*

Lavinia's true, main, basic problem is that simple and that terrible, and it has taken her three years to bring herself to admit and even partially to face it, three years and all her strength (Lavinia, in her way, is an honest woman).

This gradually and painfully emerging view is not the same as a mere discontent with Potter would be; that could be taken care of, in one way or another. No, in his way Potter is perfectly nice, a perfectly okay husband, very presentable and rather quiet (and if in some ways he is a little less than nice, well, only a very naive person, like Megan, probably, would expect good sex in marriage). Lavinia can even appreciate the irony of its being she, wise Lavinia, who made this mistake, she who did not confuse sex and love with marriage, who *knew* what marriage meant.

It is simply that having seen as much as she now has of New York, Lavinia has also seen how much better she could have done. Dear Lord, how infinitely better, a young woman like herself, with *everything*. (A girl who has everything: that is a perfectly fair description of herself, Lavinia somewhat bitterly decides.) .

And part of the excruciating pain that she is experiencing (and it is excruciating: the face that she sees before her in the mirror is anguished, almost too anguished to be beautiful, she looks almost *old*)—much of that pain comes from her recognition of how *dumb* she was, how deeply stupid, to take Cambridge and Harvard standards for the world's. What looked superior, what looked to be the cream of the crop, as it were, at Harvard, is very small potatoes in New York. If she had come down to New York after graduation, a pretty, single girl, with a pretty, small apartment (something on Sutton Place? her father likes that neighborhood; he would have paid for it, probably), oh! then she could have met anyone at all. She could have not married until she was twenty-five or twenty-six, even. And then have really chosen well, instead of taking the first "suitable" person who came along.

For an instant, in a quick hot flash of rage, Lavinia blames Gordon Shaughnessey for this terrible, this fatal error. It is all his fault. If he had not ditched her, they could have gone along and had a nice college romance, until she was ready to ditch *him* (as she surely would have, eventually; never in the world would she have married a person with that name, in Boston). And she would surely *not* have married his roommate. A moment of colder reflection, however, forces her to abandon that view, and the comfort of that anger. Besides, it's difficult, with Gordon dead.

In any case, New York is full of really superior men; cruelly, almost all the men she meets are superior to Potter. Or does she simply think that, is—oh, God!—sexual frustration actually damaging her mind? Is that possible? A monstrous notion—she pushes it away. Even thinking of sex will only confuse what is already irreparably bad. Her marriage.

In any case, almost everywhere Lavinia goes she sees wonderful-looking men, sleek blond men, with great tans, wearing marvelous tweeds and rich silk ties, or dark interesting men in dark (bankers') gray flannel. Men who all stare at her, and who smile, acknowledging her beauty.

Most recently, there has been a man whom she seems to have seen everywhere, has met at a lot of parties. Henry Stuyvesant. Not handsome, he is almost funny-looking, really: too tall, six feet five or six, with big ears, a long nose, wearing glasses. Once he took off his glasses, though, and Lavinia saw the most remarkable eyes, so dark, so liquidly deep. There is something about Henry Stuyvesant that is very interesting. He is obviously intelligent—very. (At Harvard he was on the Advocate *and* in the Signet Society, she has found out that much.) He is usually with someone very beautiful, some deb, or young divorcée, but she has never seen him with the same woman more than twice. No one seems to be sure exactly what he does, and therefore, Lavinia believes, he must be very rich. Also, she has given his shoes a very careful look (a sure test, in her view): his are invariably dark English wingtips, still new-looking, very well polished. Maybe he is the richest man in town?

So far, they have had only a couple of silly party conversations. But Henry Stuyvesant likes her, Lavinia can tell. She will see Henry tonight, she then remembers, cheeringly; she and Potter and some friends, including Henry, are going out.

She will not have an affair with Henry Stuyvesant, though. But even this thought makes Lavinia smile, however, and she notes that the very idea is making her prettier. If we even go out to lunch together, ever, she thinks, it will have to be in a very public place. Maybe the Oak Room, where everyone will see us.

Lavinia next telephones Megan. "Megan baby, I know you're terrifically busy, with that job and everything, so I'll just jump in a cab and come down to you. We can go wherever you like, down there. Well, where do you usually go? There must be some place. Megan, why are you sounding so difficult? There's no point in your coming all the way uptown, and then having to go all the way back. Of course I know where Gramercy Park is, some cousins of Potter's live there. We had dinner down there last month, a beautiful old apartment. Well, of course I can find the hotel. Honestly, Megan, you're not in California. Cabdrivers know where they are. Okay, I'll see you at twelve thirty. In the lobby—okay, the dining room."

The Gramercy Park Hotel turns out to be perfectly okay, quite a pleasant dining room. Actually, had she known it was going to be so attractive, all the nice white linen and fresh flowers on the table, quiet waiters, Lavinia would have worn a newer suit, she now reflects. Not this leftover from college, her old Blackwatch plaid; too good to throw out, it seemed both appropriate and amusing, for a downtown lunch with Megan.

Sipping from her frozen daiquiri, Lavinia frowns as she realizes that Megan is now ten minutes late, and in an idle way she scans the room. Her wandering gaze is unfocused, until it is caught by a perfect gray flannel suit, long full skirt and short trim jacket, on a thin young woman who looks very much like—dear Lord, it is, it is Megan. Megan, who comes up to Lavinia, smiling and blushing. Very pretty, and *thin*—Lord, she must have lost thirty pounds. Even her breasts are much less visible.

Megan sits down, saying, "I'm really sorry I'm late. There's so much work, and more this afternoon." To the hovering waiter, who seems to know her, she says, "I don't think I'll have a drink, thanks, Bill. A glass of tomato juice?" Her smile at Lavinia indicates, somehow, that being late is not nearly as important as her work.

Lavinia gives her own smile. "I hardly know my baby Megan without her baby fat," she says.

Megan blushes again. "What's funny is that I actually don't think of myself as thin."

"Oh, I've heard about that. People who have plastic surgery and think they still have big noses. Or breasts."

"Well, yes." Megan's tomato juice arrives. She squeezes lemon into it, somehow managing to squirt juice into her left eye. "Oh, *shit*." She wipes at the eye with her napkin.

Lavinia giggles, briefly. "Well, I can certainly hear the effect of Adam Marr."

Megan seems not to understand, at first, but then she grins, and acknowledges, "Well, he certainly is, uh, influential. And I did see them quite a lot. In Paris."

"You don't see them now?"

"Not nearly as much. They're up in Connecticut, and Adam's so busy. And Janet and the baby." Megan looks slightly uncomfortable.

In her old way, Lavinia presses on. "From what *I* hear, Adam's giving her a really bad time."

Megan's eyes cloud, unhappily, as she says, "Well, you hear a lot of gossip, when someone gets really famous."

"Where there's smoke there's always fire, I always say," Lavinia remarks, and she wonders: Can one drink have made me drunk? How silly I sound. She feels herself not quite in control, a condition she despises. She sips at ice water, which does not alleviate the burning intensity of an emotion which she is forced to recognize as the purest rage: rage at Janet Cohen (Janet *Cohen*!) for being married to a famous man, even to a vulgar theatrical success like Adam Marr, a success that will never last. And Lord, for having a baby. A boy. (And horrible Adam is supposed to be very sexy; he probably does it to her all the time, when he's not doing it to someone else.) "I've heard a lot about Adam Marr and 'aspiring young actresses,'" Lavinia manages to say. (She is as angry now at Janet Cohen and at Adam as she was earlier this morning at Gordon Shaughnessey, and quite as fruitlessly; there is something wrong with her, clearly.)

Propitiously, at that moment the waiter arrives to take their order. They both want seafood salads, coffee later.

Pulling herself together, as best she can, Lavinia in her cool social voice asks, "Well, Megan baby, now tell me all about your life as a working girl."

Megan's face, divested now of what Lavinia has chosen to call her baby fat, reveals strong bones; even her small nose looks stronger. Irish peasant bones, Lavinia decides; she is barely listening, as Megan names books and writers dealt with by her publishing house. e e cummings, Robert Frost. Not exactly what you would call a best-seller list, but then Megan has never been practical.

"—of course if you don't care a lot about poetry it doesn't make a lot of sense, what I'm doing," says Megan. Does Lavinia hear a certain sharpness, a small rebuke in that last sentence? She is hypersensitive today, she reminds herself; she feels fragile. She is getting the curse, probably. Again.

"But tell me all about successful young married life," Megan is saying, with what looks like an innocent, inquiring smile.

At that, unaccountably, what Lavinia had not at all meant to say bursts out (or one of the things that she had not meant to say). "I want to have a baby, and I never do. Every month, it turns out that I'm not pregnant, again. And everyone is having them but me. Peg, twins, and now that boy, Rex, and now she thinks she's pregnant again. And Janet Cohen, I mean Marr, and her boy. And I've taken tests, and there's nothing— Oh, I don't know why I'm saying all this!"

"Oh, Lavinia, that's really too bad. But you haven't been married very long, really. Doesn't it take some people years?"

The intensity of Megan's concern further mortifies Lavinia; Lord, what's wrong with her? She does not "confide" in people, and now, seemingly, she is unable to stop. "I just have this feeling," she says. "This sense that it won't work out with Potter. Pregnancy, I mean. I won't get pregnant, by him." Seeing that Megan seems to believe her, and (dear Lord!) that Megan *pities* her, her plight, Lavinia recklessly (lyingly!) adds, "Although otherwise of course we're absolutely perfect, in every way. Potter is, well, he's just terrific. I'm sure you know what I mean, little Megan." And she gives Megan a long, probing look, faintly smiling (back in control).

By now Megan looks so flustered, so utterly confused, that Lavinia is able to reestablish their connection as she feels that it should be, to regain what is her necessary upper hand. "You know, Megan, it's really time you thought about getting married yourself," she says. "Isn't there some handsome editor down there?"

"Actually not. They're married, mostly, and the not married one is, uh, queer, I think. But he's very nice."

"Oh, swell. What a great environment you've picked. But Megan, you must know someone. You don't want to turn into one of those awful New York career women."

Surprisingly, Megan announces, "I think I'd like to earn a lot of money." Those words seem to have surprised her too; she looks taken aback, as though she had not quite intended to say that.

"Well, that's certainly the most sensible thing I've ever heard you say. But why not marry some nice rich man? Now that you're so thin and all. And Megan, I must say, that's a terrific suit."

A blush. "You like it? I just got it yesterday. At Lord & Taylor."

To have lunch with me, Lavinia thinks, and she is touched by this tribute, although of course it is no more than her due, from Megan. "Their things are nice," she concedes, of Lord & Taylor, "but you really should try Bendel's sometime."

After a small pause, Megan asks, "Well, what do you hear from Peg?"

"Well, she's absolutely wonderful. Of course she adores living in Texas, and sometimes they go to New Orleans for weekends. And all those adorable babies. Old Peg was obviously made for motherhood, it makes me so jealous. You know, I think you were pretty hard on her sometimes, little Megan. I don't think you appreciated the true old Peg." This is said with a very severe look, which ends in a forgiving smile.

"Probably that's true." Saying this, however, Megan does not blush; she does not even look particularly concerned. Lavinia doubts that Megan is even thinking of Peg, at that moment.

With her small frown Lavinia asks, "What do you hear from Cathy?"

Megan comes back into focus. "Oh, she really loves it in California. She says she is getting fat from all the great restaurants. Can you imagine Cathy fat?" Megan is smiling as she asks this, affectionately (quite fatuously, Lavinia thinks).

Lavinia gives her own smile, having just realized that she is as uninterested in Cathy as Megan is not interested in Peg, and she further reflects that it is odd how clannish the Irish are; even generations later, Megan and Cathy, those micks, are so drawn to each other, atavistically. "Darling Megan," Lavinia purrs, "if I can imagine and even see you thin, I can certainly see Cathy fat."

Megan's interest seems caught by this. "Maybe we're all changing in some profound way?" she asks. "Shifting roles, and identities. It'll be fascinating to see what happens in the next ten or twenty years. The next five, even!"

"Well, if you're thinking of a best-seller about our lives, or a movie, just give me at least three sons," says Lavinia, quite conscious of the sadness of her smile. "Tall dark thin sons, and they'll all go to Harvard. Or maybe one will rebel, and go to Yale."

Soon after that they separate, with a flurry of talk about getting together again, very soon.

Friends, perfect friends. Why not be friends forever, she and Henry Stuyvesant? That solution comes to Lavinia, as that evening she again contemplates her silver-mirrored face, and thinks of Henry. This time she is less meditative, somewhat hurried, though; people are coming for drinks before they all go out for dinner, and dancing, most likely at LaRue. Smiling, Lavinia calculates that all the other young wives will be in their pearls and black, whereas she has on her new gray chiffon.

But: *friends*. She and Henry Stuyvesant. The idea of such a friendship, with such a brilliant and attractive man, fills Lavinia with a warm and virtuous pleasure. She thinks of the Duchess of Guermantes and Swann, although *of course* Henry is hardly Jewish (and Swann wasn't *very* Jewish). But, if they could be friends for life, she and Henry, it would be like owning something wonderful, an enviably beautiful house in the country, or a lovely boat. Or jewels. And no one will ever quite understand the nature of their friendship, hers with Henry; there will be false rumors, suspicious speculation, as over the years they are so often seen together, lunching in the Oak Room, laughing together in the corners of large parties—even, on rare occasions, dining together, Potter having been called away to Chicago, or somewhere on business. Or maybe Potter could even be in a hospital, with some tiny minor operation, a hernia or something safe like that.

Perhaps tonight, as they dance, Henry will ask her out for lunch, and she will say, Yes, I'd love to, are you fond of the Oak Room, as I am?

There have been times, since her marriage and their move to New York, when Lavinia has experienced moments of discouragement with the accoutrements of her life, moments at which she has perceived her own apartment as discouragingly similar to those of her friends. They all live on the upper East Side; their rooms all are filled with family antiques, plus a few bold "contemporary" touches, here a Noguchi lamp, there an Eames chair. And everywhere a similar weight of wedding presents, the silver or crystal ashtrays, Paul Revere bowls, pewter cocktail shakers. And at such bad moments even their friends have seemed remarkably alike, and unoriginal. For some reason all the wives are blond, or almost; they all went to Vassar or Wellesley or Smith—Lavinia's having gone to Radcliffe is a little outré, in many eyes. The men all wear Brooks clothes, perhaps an occasional fling at J. Press or Chips, a wild pink shirt. They all work in law firms or brokerage houses. (She wonders: what kind of parties do Janet Cohen and Adam Marr go to, and where?)

On the night after her lunch with Megan, however, Lavinia's contentment with her apartment and her friends seems at least for the moment restored. Hers is the most truly elegant apartment of them all; the graceful effect of her (real) Louis Seize chairs is not marred by anything clumsy, Jacobean. And she and Potter are the only couple to have a Robsjohn-Gibbings dining room table.

And, as for friends, what other young woman has a friend like Henry Stuyvesant, who is standing just now beside that Robsjohn-Gibbings table, where the drinks are?

Henry looks across at her, at Lavinia, and he smiles. He takes off his glasses, and winks! as though he has understood everything that she has been thinking, all her plan. Without glasses his eyes are very beautiful, Lavinia again observes. So dark and thick-lashed, almost like a woman's eyes, and so intelligent.

Hours later, though, late that night, Lavinia's bright mood has entirely dissolved; she can barely remember any earlier optimistic hours, ever.

For one thing, they are not dancing at LaRue, they are listening to *jazz*, at some place way down in the Village—all the fault of that stingy George Wharton, whom Lavinia has decided that she despises. The Village and this jazz place were George's idea, and of course that dopey red-haired ugly Connie went along. "We can go to La Rue any time," George Wharton said. "Jackson's playing down at the Vanguard, let's go hear him." And tacky George also suggested a spaghetti dinner first, at some downtown place. (Well, maybe the Whartons are not really rich?)

And so, a dumb dinner over checked tablecloths, even sawdust on the floor—so utterly cornball. Candles dripping wax onto rivulets of more colored wax, down the sides of huge wine bottles, just like that tacky place in Cambridge that certain people (Megan) always thought was so terrific. The Oxford Grill.

And for some reason everyone was seated next to their husband —and so Henry Stuyvesant, with his silly date, some young deb, was not even at Lavinia's table. There she was, next to Potter, with her terrible private thoughts.

And now this ghastly jazz place, where the Negro with the trombone is practically blasting them all out of their seats.

It is the sort of place that Megan probably comes to, Lavinia thinks, and she looks around apprehensively, as though Megan really might be there (Megan twice in one day would be much more than she could bear). She sees a lot of college kids, and some older couples, not very attractive. But fortunately not Megan.

However, having Megan so much on her mind gives Lavinia an idea. Leaning across the table to where George Wharton sits, with ugly Connie, quite audibly she shouts, above the pounding music, "Oh, George, I had lunch with a very dear old friend of yours today," with one of her smiles.

"Oh?" Mean-faced Connie looks inquiringly at her husband.

"Megan Greene, of course. Such a career girl, and you wouldn't believe how thin she's got. You wouldn't know her, but on the other hand I guess *you* would."

"Megan?" Stupid George is actually blushing, as, ridiculously, Connie asks him, "Who is Megan Greene?"

"Now, George," Lavinia begins to lecture, but at that moment the loud music gets even louder, a long crescendo, as though that awful black man were purposely drowning her out.

Did Megan and George Wharton ever actually, uh, do it?

Lavinia considers that possibility through the next few long passages of music. George looked so miserably embarrassed at the mention of Megan's name (so gratifying: that should teach him not to make everyone have cheap Italian food, and listen to this God-awful music). And, did Megan really do it with all those men, the way everyone said she did? Where there's smoke there's fire, but still, Lavinia isn't as sure as she would like to be. At that moment an ugly, unbidden image has entered Lavinia's mind, of Megan, naked, and as fat as she used to be, with a dark naked man on top of her, pumping into her, battering, with his huge, uh, thing. Lavinia closes her eyes against this hideous vision.

Then, to dispel what she sees, she opens her eyes as wide as she can, and finds herself staring into the eyes of that trombone player, Jackson something, who is smiling—Christ, smiling directly at her, and singing, *to her*, "You are my baby, you my sweetest darling little baby"—*right at her.*

Horrible! Intolerable! He should be arrested. In Washington, D.C., he probably would be, for looking at her like that.

Lavinia jerks her head around, and the nightmare in which she finds herself increases as she sees that Henry Stuyvesant is not even looking at her (not with the knowledge, the understanding that could save her life); he is looking at his date, some silly black-haired girl who looks (why didn't Lavinia notice this before?) very Irish. Henry and that Irish girl are laughing, talking; with so much noise, that horrible trombone, it is impossible to make out what they are saying.

Saying nothing to anyone, and not even excusing herself (why bother? no one could hear her) Lavinia gets up and gropes her way through the noisy, crowded darkness, toward the ladies' room, which turns out to be as dirty as she had feared.

She throws up into the toilet.

Not feeling better, Lavinia is washing her face when Connie Wharton comes into the room, of all people she did not want to see. Connie, with her mean little pale blue eyes, who will undoubtedly ask some dumb girlish question about Megan.

Connie does not; she barely smiles, and she rushes into the toilet stall, as Lavinia fleetingly observes that Connie looks even worse than she, Lavinia, did (but then of course she began looking worse). Obviously something was wrong with the food, at that crummy Italian place.

But it seems only polite to wait for Connie, who might need help.

Emerging, Connie again just barely smiles, as Lavinia says something about spaghetti, a poisoned sauce.

At which Connie turns on her and says, "It's not the food. Don't be so dumb, Lavinia. I've had much too much to drink. Surely that must be apparent, even to you? But I can only say that if you were married to George Wharton you'd drink a lot too."

Lavinia murmurs something about being sorry—though precisely for what she would not have been able to say.

Seeming suddenly to feel a great deal better, Connie breaks into a smile, showing all her teeth and even further narrowing her little pig eyes (or so Lavinia perceives Connie's face). "Don't be sorry," Connie tells her. "You may congratulate me. I'm going to be first in our group to get a divorce. How I wish George had married your friend, Megan what's-her-name. Tell me, Lavinia, whatever was she like?"

"Well, actually she's one of the prettiest and the most brilliant girls I ever knew."

Connie sniffs. "In that case the more's the pity," she says.

16

A letter from Peg Harding Sinclair, in Midland, Texas, to Megan, in New York:

Dear Megan, You will be surprised to hear from me. Here it is almost Christmas, you will be surprised to hear how hot it is, down here. Yesterday 86, and this hot rain blew up from the Gulf. Dark sheets of hot rain, dark sheets of hot rain. You will think that a trite expression and typical, I am sure, of "Peg," but that is what in fact the rain is like. It hits you in the face like wet clothes on a clothesline. All this part of the country, this part of Texas, is made of clay, and in the rain the clay gets very slick. It is impossible. I have four children.

I am not the person that I seem to you to be. Anyway, I have been wondering if maybe you are not either. Are not what you seem. Are any of us? (Trite question, I am sorry.) I am writing this letter, maybe. Are you as fat and oversexed as you look, or used to look? Are your "judgment" and your "taste" as poor as Lavinia always said they were? Is it true that you are more intelligent than any of us? Lavinia is much more intelligent than you think she is, even if she is not as she appears, i.e., is not the Duchess of Guermantes. I did not have a "lesbian" crush on Lavinia, just a maternal one. And now fate has punished me with four children. (That was a joke, ho ho.)

Just when I thought I had that problem, children, solved, another arrived. Just a month ago. She is one month old today. Kate. There is something wrong with her, though. All babies spit up but not like this. So much, such big white curds· all over everything. Cameron can't stand the smell. There are a lot of smells that Cameron can't stand, in fact. Have you noticed this about other men? Do you know many men?

Do you think men have stronger noses than women do, or just weaker stomachs? When I can't stand certain smells I do stand them anyway. It seems to me that I have no choice.

Would this be an interesting conversation, if we were friends?

In any case there is something wrong with Kate. In Dr. Spock I read about something called "projectile vomiting" which means that a baby has something called "pyloric stenosis." Kate's vomiting looks projectile to me. In a medical book I read about pyloric stenosis. It is a narrowing of the tube below the stomach. Most characteristically it occurs in first-born sons who are born in the spring (never, interestingly, is there a recorded case of a female Negro, but maybe they just don't record such cases, female Negroes?). Kate's being a fourth-born girl, born in the late fall, maybe that is not what she has, or maybe it is. It sure looks like it. It is easily "correctable" by surgery, the medical book says. In the meantime I have to "let her cry" between meals. She can cry for a long time. Sometimes I go out into the yard so I won't hear her, but I still can. Our yard is not very large, here in Midland.

This is really crazy. How can I imagine that you would be interested in pyloric stenosis, or in my children?

But I have not read any good books lately.

Books and sex. "Megan doesn't care about anything but books and sex, fundamentally." That is what Lavinia said, but is it true? I have no time to read. I suppose you would read a lot under any circumstances, four children or five or six (Jesus, six), but I do not. Cannot. At night I fall asleep. About sex I have nothing to say. Really nothing at all. One more thing I am not good at, would be one way to put it.

I am afraid.

I do everything wrong.

Cameron—

Peg does not mail this letter; she shoves it into a pigeonhole in her desk, as just at the instant of writing her husband's name two things happen simultaneously: one, Kate begins to cry, and outside the sweeping rain begins again, dark sheets of it slapping the windows.

And so it is not clear to Peg what she had meant to say about Cameron, surely something, some explanation to Megan, about her life? Something that might catch Megan's attention, interest her?

The twins are in nursery school, and this year Rex too, thank God, none of them home until three. But it is now only two thirty, and Kate is not supposed to be fed again until four; suppose she is still screaming when the other children get home? How to explain such screams? If Peg can't bear to hear them, how about the children, who understand medical advice and "pyloric stenosis" even less than she herself does?

The screams are sharp, animal outcries.

Peg's breasts ache, and her stomach knots.

And outside the rain is so thick and dark, so hot and terrible. Everywhere in the house she can hear the screams. The screams. The screams.

She is wearing a loose old cotton dress, one that fits in the early months of pregnancies and the first few months after a birth. Or, perhaps it never fits. Anyway, in that dress Peg hurries through her house, to the kitchen, to the back door, back porch. She rushes out into the warm, lashing black rain, in her barren backyard. So new, nothing growing, no time to plant. And the soil is terrible, now all wet and slick.

She stands there in the rain, raising her face up to it, her clothes all soaked through, instantly soaked, and she thinks: I am having some sort of a breakdown. I am not all right. I am too exhausted. As she thinks the word "exhausted" an image comes to her of old elastic, all dingy, worn out. No give. Exhausted.

This new subdivision where they live in Midland is raw and flat. And expensive. The houses are not close together, and now in the heavy rain Peg can see only rain, no other house, or bush or tree or road. But she can hear acutely, unmuffled by all that intervening, falling, falling water—she can hear the screams of her smallest, newest child.

In an instant, moving far more quickly than when she ran out into the rain, Peg rushes back into the house, all soaking dripping wet; she rushes into the baby's yellow nursery. She opens her clothes to her breasts, and she snatches up the bright red, screaming baby, who for several minutes still breathes and gasps from all that screaming, who cannot at first seize the nipple.

Peg thinks two things: she thinks that she is wrong, she is doing just what the doctor said not to do, when Kate screams—and she thinks too that she is saving her child.

· · ·

By the time the older children get home from school, Kate is mercifully asleep, and their mother is herself again, in old Levi's from college and a big clean shirt, one of their father's discards. She is big jolly Peg again, their mom.

She gets out crayons and fingerpaints for Candy and Carol, the twins, and books for Rex. She goes into the kitchen and begins to cut up a chicken for dinner; she and Cameron will have steaks later on, since he gets home late and does not like to have meals with children, not really. He likes to see them all clean and already fed and ready for bed, and not quite conscious.

Peg goes back and forth between the playroom and the kitchen; if she doesn't watch the children the room will be hopeless. She makes their dinner, and then she gives them all baths, all the time praying that Kate does not wake up again. She cleans up their dinner. She puts in potatoes, makes the salad for her dinner with Cameron. Then she goes in to read to the children for a while.

Miraculously, tonight it all works out. By seven thirty, which is Cameron's coming home time, Peg is on the sofa with Rex on her lap, one twin on either side of her. Reading *Winnie-the-Pooh*, which is Cameron's favorite book. A perfect scene for him to walk into, or maybe she should have changed her dress? Peg (too late) wonders. Put on lipstick? However, why? Cameron after all married "good old Peg."

He comes in hurriedly, his hair distraught. He looks tired, with his worried eyes. He smiles at them all. "Well, old girl. And young ladies. Rex, how's my boy?"

The next day, for no reason that she can understand, Peg again tries to write a letter to Megan.

> Dear Megan, I am sure that I was writing a letter to you but it seems to be misplaced. Lost, strayed, but who would steal such a thing? However I do remember that the last word was "Cameron," and I know what I meant to say. To ask. There is something, actually several things, that I do

not understand. About Cameron. Men. Could you help? Do you know a lot of men? Understand them?

Cameron and I have a serious problem of no words. We have no words for anything that we do, much less for any of the parts of our bodies. I think of what we do as "doing it," and of his instrument as his "thing." We do it a lot. Cameron is very fond of numbers and I think he counts. I would not be surprised to find a calender of his on which he had noted dates and numbers, records.

But in some way Cameron is worried about his thing. I am not allowed to touch it. In and out of me like Dresden china in and out of some bag (joke, ho ho, Peg the bag). But is that usual, with men?

I read in a sex book about mutual touching, but we do not mutually touch. Does he take it out of me so slowly so as not to break it off? And then he goes into the bathroom, for a ritual wash. Well, I guess you would just say that is how Cameron is. Wouldn't you? I think I should not read sex books.

Another thing you do not know about me is how rich I am. Lavinia recognized it right off, she can smell a lot of money. I suppose any Guermantes could. But smart as you are I do not think you are very smart about money, fat Megan. I am probably about twenty times as rich as Lavinia is. Cameron knew that too. He knew my parents in Plainfield, of course, but he also has Lavinia's nose for money.

But Cameron wants us to be even richer than we are. That is why we are "living simply." We have no maid. No maid is better for the children, I am sure, or almost sure. The maids around our house in Plainfield were mean.

I just wish I were not so tired. We are putting all our money into oil, fields and wells. All my trust income and all Cameron's salary. All oil. I hope he isn't wrong about oil but he probably is not.

With love from your fat friend (ha ha).

17

Cathy hates California, or rather, she hates the portion of it that she finds at Stanford, around Palo Alto. She hates it more than she could admit to anyone, even to Megan. And she now recognizes that in some curious way she had anticipated that her sojourn in California would be somehow parallel or akin to Megan's in New England. She had imagined that she would experience the exhilaration that Megan often spoke of, as Megan described her own migration from one coast to another. Too late, Cathy perceives that this was a literary possibility, not to be actualized. For why indeed should California prove exhilarating to a prospective economist, an Irish Catholic from Philadelphia, who is secretly literary?

It does not; California fails to exhilarate. What Cathy feels is acute isolation, and deprivation. Depression. And she blames herself, of course: who else? Undoubtedly the capacity for enlightenment and for pleasure lay within Megan herself, the evident virtues and beauties and excitements of New England notwithstanding. Megan is an essentially joyous, receptive person, one happily open to new experience (slightly indiscriminate, one could possibly say, of Megan; Lavinia said it quite often, but was that really, in any final way, accurate?). Whereas she, Cathy, is just the opposite. She is withdrawn, and enclosed. She is generally hostile to new impressions, new ideas, and heaven knows hostile to new people, generally.

Everyone at Stanford appears to be so large, even oversized, and everyone is blond; Cathy has never felt so thin and dark. The boys all wear tight Levi's and clean tight white T-shirts; the girls wear pastel cashmere sweaters and matching flannel skirts. The girls' white socks are neatly folded down, as opposed to the gym socks they all used to wear at Radcliffe, turned up to their calves. These girls wear mocassins or saddle shoes (saddle shoes!), and strands of pearls, always pearls, a whole industry of pearls, offsetting those fresh California skins and pearly upper-middle-class teeth.

There are no Negroes. A few people might be Jewish but they just as well might not be. The same with Irish Catholics, except for a priest in Cathy's Milton class (she allows herself a few literary indulgences, from her strict economics diet); that priest, with his white hair and red face, is the most familiar-looking person around.

By contrast to everyone else, Cathy feels herself more Irish, more Catholic than ever, as well as scrawnier, darker.

Cathy comes gradually to realize that not only had she hoped to duplicate the excitement of Megan's going-East experience, she had also hoped to duplicate Megan, in a way. Not in her own person, no hope of that, Cathy turning into voluptuous, chattering, happily laughing Megan—but in California Cathy had hoped to find another Megan as a friend, someone bright and funny and offbeat. And naturally, no such luck. Just cashmered blondes, as bland as they are fair.

Even the architecture at Stanford is depressing to her. All that Spanish tile and brownish stucco. And the trees: huge dry ugly dusty palm trees, that rattle like snakes. The palms have the look of prehistoric birds, Cathy decides, in a state of terminal disease.

She especially hates the fall, in Palo Alto, everywhere dry blond grass, and warm winds. Nothing brisk in the air. No red leaves.

In the winter of 1905, William James, who was teaching at Stanford, wrote to his brother, Henry:

> . . . so simple the life and so benign the elements, that for a young ambitious professor who wishes to leave his mark on Pacific civilization while it is most plastic or for *any one* who wishes to teach and work under the most perfect conditions for eight or nine months, and *who is able to get to the East, or Europe, for the remaining three,* I can't imagine anything finer. It is Utopian. Perfection of weather. Cold nights, though above freezing. Fire pleasant until 10 o'clock A.M.,

then unpleasant. In short, the "simple life" with all the essential higher elements thrown in as communal possessions. The drawback is, of course, the great surrounding human vacuum—the historic silence fairly rings in your ears when you listen—and the social insipidity. I'm glad I came, and with God's blessing I may pull through.

Cathy copies out this passage, and she sends it to Megan, retaining James's original emphases, and she adds a few of her own, in red pencil; she underlines both instances of "simple," and also with two fierce lines she underlines "the historic silence, social insipidity." Another red line under the last phrase, "and with God's blessing." She simply signs the whole thing, Love Cathy—and that is her first letter to Megan from California.

The housing situation in Palo Alto, in and around Stanford, at that time is terrible, and has been for some years, particularly with the influx of World War II veterans, often with their wives. A low-cost housing development is too small to do much to alleviate this situation, and is of course out of the question for Cathy, who is neither a veteran nor married. Childless. A woman.

Many local homeowners have cannily appraised the situation and have turned it to their own considerable advantage. A well-off widow, say, with a too large house, and perhaps one guest room that she has not used for years, can rent out that room; if it has its own bath, she can get as much as seventy-five dollars a month. If she can divide that room in half, and somehow put in a vestigial kitchen, she can advertise an apartment for rent, plenty of room for a studious young man and his working wife, if they are careful not to have children or noisy parties, and if they can pay ninety dollars a month, or sometimes more.

And that is what Cathy has, a divided room, which was formerly an attic, with a hot plate and an icebox and a "separate entrance": rickety stairs which were once a fire escape. All this is on College Terrace, just south of the Stanford campus. For ninety dollars.

Paying that much rent is a little hard, since Cathy is trying to live on two hundred a month, which is what her father sends her. (What she guiltily accepts; she knows that he is opposed to graduate schools, for girls, and she plans to repay, as soon as she gets a job.) Next year, maybe she can get a couple of freshman sections to teach. Although there too, as with the cheap housing, the preference is to veterans, and to men. Girls can usually get money from home, that is what girls are supposed to do, according to the current line of thought. And Cathy has to concede that it may be to some extent true, but then she thinks, Suppose you can't? Suppose your family is seriously poor? Well, the answer to that one comes easily: a girl from a truly poor family goes to work or she gets married very young, she does not go to graduate school, and surely not to Stanford.

Not being given to self-pity, lonely is not a word that Cathy would use, as applied to herself, but that is what she is; she is acutely, excruciatingly lonely. She almost never has a conversation with anyone, only a few short occasional dialogues with some other student whom she encounters in the library, or in what is called the quad. Or in the Stanford Bookstore, where Megan said she worked, one high school summer. "Where I met my great love, George Wharton," is how Megan, laughing, in her way, has put it.

The only person whom Cathy meets in the bookstore is that priest, from her Milton seminar. Standing behind him in line, she hears him say a few words to the clerk (he has never spoken in class, so far) and she is then unable not to say to him, "Oh, you're from Boston!"

He turns and smiles quickly, his smooth face a shade more red. "Dorchester. How'd you guess? Are you from around there too?"

"Uh, no, but I went to school—I'm from Philadelphia. Ardmore, actually. Father."

Cathy feels her own face reddening, at the sheer impossible stupidity of this exchange. And how rude of her to remark on his accent. She is obviously out of touch, she thinks; isolation is making her more than a little nutty. (And then she does think the forbidden word, lonely.)

But the priest is saying, "Well now, Radcliffe, I'll be bound. You don't have the look of a B.U. girl. I'm a Tufts man myself, but of course that's a long way back."

"Oh," is all Cathy can think of to say. On her face she feels the presence of a simpering smile.

And so he finishes it off, their nonconversation. "Well, I'll see you in class," he says, and he moves away from her, out of the store and out into the alien California sunlight. He has a jaunty, athletic walk, more like a tennis player than a priest (but a priest could play tennis; why not?).

Despite the white hair, close up that priest looked younger than she had thought, Cathy muses later on, when she is "at home." He must be about her father's age, late forties, but he is thinner, healthier-looking than her fat, bold, adored-feared father. Why couldn't she at least have asked him how he likes it out here, which is not as dumb a question as it might sound. She could mention the quote from William James. Priests get lonely too, they like to talk. Cathy's mother is always befriending some priest, having priests to dinner, in the small Ardmore house. Cathy is used to priests (or she should be), to seeing them outside as well as in church.

She next thinks, daringly: Maybe I should invite that priest to dinner? (But suppose he said no!) And what could I cook for two people on a hot plate? Maybe ask him for a drink? A lot of priests like to drink. But what would I buy? And everything costs so much, Scotch, Irish whiskey (her father drinks Irish, drinks much too much of it).

He probably wouldn't come, no matter what I asked him to, Cathy then decides. What an insane idea.

She would like to telephone Megan, but is frightened by the probable cost of the call. She knows that what she needs, though, is a good long laugh. What with the strangeness of California, Stanford, everything, she is just a little out of control. Her thinking has got a little bizarre; she has never even imagined asking a priest to dinner before.

18

In New York, down in the Village, the quarters in which Megan lives are considerably smaller than those occupied by Cathy, in California. Megan has one room on the top floor of a brownstone on West 12th Street, just off Fifth Avenue—an impressive address, but she is in what once were the servants' quarters, four small rooms around a large, central (and entirely wasted) space, with a grime-filled skylight in the middle. Megan has one of those four rooms, and she shares the bath with two anonymous and seemingly identical old men, whom she almost never sees, their hours being somehow opposite to hers. The fourth room is fortunately unoccupied.

In her narrow room there is a single bed, and a table which holds alternately her typewriter and a hot plate. She has a chair, one bookcase. Her window opens onto a fire escape where she sometimes sits and smokes, on those chokingly hot New York summer nights. From that perch she can peer into what must be a dance studio, on Fifth Avenue (she finds later that it is indeed a dance studio, Martha Graham's). What she sees are portions of marvelously leaping, prancing bodies, long brown arms and legs, in black tank suits or tights.

For her room Megan pays fifteen dollars a week, from her salary of forty-five, also weekly, at the publishing house. She occasionally takes a few books from the mail room and sells them, but that does not bring in much cash, and besides, it seems so sordid, petty thievery—although she is assured that all the underlings in publishing do just that, that year.

Megan likes her room very much, and she was pleased to find it, in her favorite part of New York, even her favorite block. And it is handy to her job; she can walk over to Fourth Avenue by way of Union Square. When she can afford it she stops at the Fifth Avenue Schrafft's for breakfast. And that is her general rule:

breakfast out, and lunch at a counter, somewhere. At night she heats something on her hot plate, a can of soup or stew.

She enjoys coming back to her room at night, alone; to her it seems compact rather than much too small. It reminds her a little of her room in Paris, in the Welcome Hotel; this too is her absolute, independent domain.

It is not, however, a room to which to invite her friends, and sometimes Megan decides that that is just as well; she does not need another Danny moving in with her, for example. But at other times she strongly wishes for more space.

As it is, only two people ever visit Megan, in her 12th Street room: Jackson Clay, and Biff Maloney, the editor whom Megan told Lavinia that she thought was "queer," and who is by now a considerable friend. (The two men do not visit her together, naturally.)

Jackson very much objects to Megan's room. He snorts unpleasantly, derisively, whenever she refers to it as her apartment (which is how she thinks of it). For a while Megan does not understand what he finds so objectionable; after all he does not have to live there—there has never been even the slightest question of their living together, not at that time. And for a few drinks, a few hours of love, which is how they use the room, it is perfectly adequate. But since Megan is truly, deeply fond of Jackson, she tries to understand what bothers him about it.

"Look," she tells him. "It's really okay for me. I don't feel crowded. I love this neighborhood, and it's so cheap."

Evasively, he tells her, "I bet I could find you some place, more uptown?"

"But Jackson, I like it down here."

"Oh, the Village's okay. I been to some Village places I like just fine."

"Well, I know this is small, but I don't give parties here, I don't even want to give parties, for heaven's sake."

"Oh, parties. I been to enough parties to last me for good. But baby, I think about you, like when I'm doing a date in Chicago, or D.C., and I think about you in this room, and that really brings me down."

And at last Megan begins to understand: this small cheap room simply does not coincide with Jackson's view of her. To Jackson she is a superior woman, who should therefore live in grand surroundings. And while Megan does not necessarily agree, she is touched by his concern. Jackson is one of the nicest men she has ever known, if not the nicest.

They are linked, she and Jackson Clay, in ways that are both mysterious and strong. And interesting, to Megan; she gives considerable thought to the mysteries of their connection—God knows it escapes all the usual definitions. Certainly none of the current concepts of "in love" quite apply, although in their ways Megan and Jackson do love each other. But they are not jealous or even curious about other people in each other's lives, as people in love are supposed to be. Megan supposes that Jackson sees other women; well, he must—he is extremely handsome, sexy, attractive, and he spends so much time away, on tours. And she supposes that he assumes the same of her—although actually, for several years, the years of seeing Jackson most, Megan only makes love with him. But she sees no point in telling Jackson that; he might find it in some way alarming, or even embarrassing, her unsought fidelity.

And their needs to see each other are in perfect accord, seemingly; just when Megan has begun to wonder when she will see him again, when she feels that she must see him, suddenly there he is. From out of the blue he will call; he will tell her that he just got back into town, is she free? He'll come by her place long about seven o'clock.

Generally, almost always, Megan works considerably past the eight hours that she is paid for; but on the days that she is expecting Jackson she will leave her office at about five thirty, very early for her. In a happy anticipatory daze she will walk home (not having to stop for a can of stew, or soup). Sometimes she will buy a small bunch of flowers, fall asters or daisies; she has learned that Jackson likes these touches (they improve her "apartment"). Back home, she will take a long bath, at last emerging all clean and smooth and perfumed, all dusted with powder. Black underthings, a black dress, some makeup—and she is ready, waiting for Jackson.

But he is always late; she has come to think that his "long

about" means *late*, and during that time of waiting for him her blood does race, her heart beats anxiously. Perhaps, after all, she is in love with Jackson?

Then she hears those well-known, unmistakable steps, bounding, heavy. He always runs up her stairs; a big tall man, he is out of breath at her door. Handsome Jackson, in his sharkskin suit and camel's hair coat, his shining yellow-brown skin and wide dark eyes. Jackson, who kisses her with his whole mouth, her whole mouth, and all of their bodies. So eagerly, with love.

Jackson would like to help her out with money. He hints around at this, so that Megan has understood what he means before he is able to ask her, in a very low, strained voice: "They pay you okay, at that book house?"

"Oh, I guess so."

"You ever need a loan, or anything extra, you come to me, you hear?"

"Oh sure, Jackson. Uh, thanks."

But of course she cannot, would not ever ask Jackson for money. Even though she does need money, and he seems to have a lot, and they are friends. Megan is aware of the illogic of her view, but she is deeply prudish, in this way. And she knows that she is much more prudish than she would be if she were not so broke. If she were richer she could probably say something like, Jackson, I'm really in over my head at Lord & Taylor, at Bendel's—could you let me have a hundred, two hundred, five? Whereas, as it is, she cannot ask for the twenty or thirty dollars that she is usually short of, by the end of the month.

When Jackson is in town, and playing on 52d Street, Megan would like to go and hear him every night, if she could; she still is crazy about his music, that hot wild blasting trombone—and crazy too about the way he sings, those sliding lilts. And his eyes, as he sings to her.

Going to one of those clubs presents a problem for her, though. In those days it is almost impossible for her, a young woman, to go alone. And it is hard for her to ask anyone to take her there, unless by some odd chance she has a date, someone she knew at Harvard, calling her up, and whom she knows has enough money for the fairly stiff cover charge. (Saying to someone, Look, please let me pay half was just not done, not then.)

"You don't just know some guy, some guy like a brother, you could ask him to be your guest at the club?" sensitive Jackson asks her, as they discuss her coming to hear him, at the Onyx. "That way," he says, "I tell the manager you my guests."

Megan laughs. "But I don't have any brothers."

However, of course she thinks of Biff, at work.

One of the ways in which Megan sees Biff is at the counter of the corner Rexall's, where they both often go for sandwiches at lunch-time. She has concluded that Biff has no money either, other than what is probably a salary not much larger than hers (but somewhat larger; he has been there for two years longer, and men are always paid more, no matter what they do, *of course*).

Broke or not, Biff's manner is very grand indeed. He is a small man, barely taller than Megan is, with extremely curly, extremely red hair. Wide-spaced blue eyes, and freckles; he is the most freckled person Megan has ever seen. An Irish kid, obviously, from some never mentioned suburb of Boston. His accent and his whole demeanor, however, are the purest, perhaps even exaggerated Harvard, or possibly Back Bay. Old days in Cambridge are one of the things that he and Megan talk about, as Biff's huge eyes tear with nostalgia, remembering the best days of his life.

And so it seems quite natural for Megan to ask Biff, over grilled cheese and coffee, "Biff, did you ever go to any of those jazz places in Boston? The Savoy?"

"Oh, did I not!" The wide eyes widen expressively. "Although I must say, those places sometimes made me rather nervous. I was much more *comfortable*, really, at the Napoleon Club."

"I heard of it, but I never went there."

"Well, you wouldn't have, it's of another generation. But there used to be a wonderful singer. Johnny something. He was terribly Dwight Fiske. You know."

"Oh. Well, I was sort of wondering. Do you know a trombone player named Jackson Clay?"

"Not personally, but I've heard of him, if that's what you mean. He's rather sensational, I thought."

"Well, I do sort of know him. He's a friend of a friend." (Is this a necessary lie? Megan feels bad about it, but is not sure how else to explain.) "Anyway, when he's in town I can get in free, free drinks and all, with anyone I want. So I wondered if you—"

"But my dear girl, I'd be enchanted."

And that is how it comes about that Megan and Biff from time to time go together to the Downbeat, or the Onyx Club; they are admitted free, and guided to a table near the bandstand, near Jackson—who sings and smiles to Megan, and sometimes nods in a friendly way to Biff, Megan's "brother."

Biff must of course perceive what is going on between Jackson and Megan, although there would seem to be a tacit agreement among the three of them that nothing be made explicit. Never does Megan abandon Biff at the end of the evening in order to meet Jackson after the show (although Biff may have expected, at first, that that would happen, and would probably not mind). But for one thing, in a practical way, that would keep them there much too late. But more important, it strikes Megan as a very rude thing to do to a friend.

Also, as Megan gradually comes to understand, as she knows Biff better, he does not at all want to hear about her romantic or sexual life—any more than he would recount his own to her (assuming that he has such a life, which Megan sometimes wonders). Instead, in her room, to which he brings an occasional bottle of wine, or in his Horatio Street apartment, where he sometimes cooks supper for her, they discuss Proust, or Elizabeth Bowen, or E. M. Forster, all old favorites of Biff's, and more recently of Megan's. And of course there is always the endless bond of Henry James, their household god, as it were.

In terms of food, as well as of literature, Biff is innovative in Megan's life. His specialty is small rich stews of innards—tripe or kidneys, liver—which, under Danny's tutelage in Paris, Megan has tasted but not quite learned to like (at home in Palo Alto, Florence would never have cooked such things, of course not). But Biff's stews all taste quite wonderful to Megan, no doubt in part because they provide such a contrast to all her other meals, the bland overcooked canned meats which she heats up on her hot plate, or even the occasional restaurant steaks, with Jackson, late at night, in some Village bar and grill.

"Leopold Bloom food" is what Biff calls what he cooks, and he often adds, "*That* crazy mick. Although I suppose actually more Jewish. And how I wish I shared that particular strain. I might have been another Proust."

"That's interesting. I've often wished I were Jewish," Megan tells him. "In fact I do wish that." (Wonderful exotic Jewish parents, instead of so-ordinary Florence and Harry, she is thinking, disloyally.)

"It would be interesting to know how many people share our wish," says Biff, and they laugh: good friends, who trust each other.

Partly because she has no phone at home, in her "apartment," Megan is fairly often called at work. She discourages any but the briefest, arrangement-making calls, partly because of the geography of the large room in which she works: she and Biff, the underlings, are out in the middle, at wholly unprivate, totally exposed desks; upper editors are lodged in cubicles, which afford a minimal privacy, despite the lack of doors. Only the president and the financial vice-president of the company have proper offices, with doors and chairs and windows.

However, sometimes Megan is caught by a phone call—as one morning she is, most strangely, by a call from Midland, Texas.

First a long distance operator asks for her by name, and then, over humming, buzzing wires, an unfamiliar male voice says an unfamiliar name. "Cameron Sinclair."

Megan asks, "Uh, do we know each other?"

"I think we met at Barnard Hall. Briefly. I married Peg, Peg Harding. In fact we still are married. I'm calling from Midland, where we live."

"Oh? Well, how is Peg?"

"Well, not so well, actually. I think maybe overtired. Four children. A lot of work. You know. I, uh, wanted to ask you, if you wouldn't mind, about her letters to you. The doctor thought maybe, uh, if you wouldn't mind. They might shed some light."

"Letters?" Some urgency in his voice has made Megan feel that she should remember something that is nowhere in her mind. "I don't have any letters from Peg," she says, as she wracks her brains: *has* Peg ever written to her? She believes not. Lavinia has, certainly, and of course Cathy, but she is sure that Peg has not.

In an anxious voice "Cameron Sinclair" asks her, "You're sure you didn't get any?"

"Well yes, I'd remember. Honestly, I don't even remember a postcard from Peg, when we all took terms off from school."

"Oh, well. If you're sure. I'm sorry to have bothered you. Sorry."

Still sounding unconvinced, he has hung up, as Megan was in the midst of telling him that it was all right, he really hadn't bothered her at all—although of course he had. She is bothered, partly because she has the sense that he believed her to be lying. She is sufficiently bothered to find it necessary to call Lavinia, right away.

"I had the strangest phone call from Peg Harding's husband," Megan begins.

"Oh, poor Cameron. Well, actually poor Peglet. She's had a complete breakdown, she's been having shock treatment, oh, it's so awful I can't even think about it. Honestly, Megan, I always said you were awfully hard on her. You had no idea how much she admired you, how important you were to her."

"But what does that have to do—"

"Oh, I'm not making any connection. I'm not blaming you. Honestly, baby Megan, what a thin-skinned baby you always are. I just meant that I didn't think you understood poor Peglet at all. How complicated she is. How fond of you. Cameron told me she was always writing to you. He found a whole pile of letters to you. That's why he called me to get your number."

"But Lavinia, I never got a single letter from Peg. Honestly."

"You see? She never even dared mail them to you. Well, we'll just see how the shock treatment works. God, what a thing to think about."

"Yes."

"God," Lavinia repeats, "I've had nothing but bad news lately. You remember that ugly little Connie Winsor? Of course you must, she married your old flame, George Wharton. Well—" Lavinia drops to a whisper. "She's leaving George, the first divorce in our group. And everyone says she has this terrific crush on someone named Henry Stuyvesant. I'm sure there's nothing to it on his part, he's terribly attractive and I don't think he'd give her the time of day."

Biff at that moment begins to signal to Megan that she had better get off the phone; a senior editor approaches.

But not before Lavinia gets in a few more digs at Connie (interesting, as Megan and Biff observe to each other in a later conversation, how the rich are always most anxious to criticize those richer than themselves). "Some rich girls think they can buy anything they want," Lavinia sniffs. "Well, actually I have to go too. Funnily enough I'm having lunch with Henry Stuyvesant today. We're becoming the most terrific friends, and he's taking me to the Plaza."

19

The house near Fredericksburg is on a bluff above the Rappahannock, that house where once Lavinia hated to go, which now she
is crazy about, she cannot spend enough time there. The blurred,
once symmetrical shapes of a once formal, now ruined garden lead
down to the river. Those blurred terraces are all overgrown, re-
claimed by natural vines and grasses, wild and luxuriant, powerfully green—which Lavinia has had the great good sense to leave
alone.

From the house, the view of broad brown water is sometimes
obscured by so much growth, but from out on the terrace, its
ancient brick now restored by tasteful Lavinia, from the comfortable new wicker chairs and the deep wide sofa, you can see both
the river and its opposite small sandy shore, and sometimes boats;
people in canoes or small motor launches can be seen to look up
curiously at what must be a house, high up there on the bank
(surely that was a flash of glass, some windows?). But so many
trees and vines prevent any accurate view; no person is ever clearly
visible there, or even the shape of the house. It is perfectly private—
a lovers' house.

It is the perfect house for Lavinia and Henry Stuyvesant, who
have been lovers for almost a year, by the spring of 1952. This house,
this former "plantation," which was built by some original Harcourt, has in effect become their house. "Lavinia's retreat" is how
both Potter and her father, Mr. Harcourt, think of it.

For tax purposes the house was always in Mrs. Harcourt's name,
and when she died, one Christmas a couple of years after Lavinia's
marriage to Potter, the house went to Lavinia. And Lavinia simply
left it there, not even wanting to think of that drafty, creaking
wreck until one night she suddenly thought of the house (actually
on the evening after her first afternoon of love with Henry, while

she was having dinner at home with Potter). In that illuminated instant, her enraptured fatigue, she saw a perfect use for the Fredericksburg house; she saw days there of absolute privacy, with Henry. And in the same enlightened instant she was able to think very clearly that the house would have to be redone, of course; she even imagined the wicker furniture that would be perfect on the renovated old brick terrace, the soft chintz pads to be taken in at the end of weekends, or when it rained.

To Potter at that time she only said, "You know, I've been thinking about the house in Fredericksburg. It seems so wasteful. Just letting it sit there and fall apart."

"You're right there. If you wanted to sell it, well, with capital gains we'd have to buy something though. How about a nice place on the Cape?"

"No." Lavinia spoke musingly, in her way; she was visibly not listening to Potter, but he is fairly used to that. "I don't want to sell it," she told him. "I want to remodel. Maybe try my hand at decorating." And she laughed, her pretty old half–self-deprecating laugh. "I certainly can't make it look any worse than Mother did. In fact I think I'll go down for a couple of days next week."

"But I don't think I can get away—"

"Darling, that's perfectly all right. I'll stop off and see Daddy, and then I'll just push along in the station wagon. I can think better when I'm alone," and she laughed again.

Potter leaned slightly forward, intent on her face, "You look, uh, really pretty tonight," he said, with slightly drunken emphasis.

"That can't be true. I've got the filthiest headache, actually. That wicked Henry plied me with wine, at lunch."

"Oh, I forgot you had a lunch with Henry. How is he?"

"Oh, fine. We did the Oak Room."

"He's still seeing Connie a lot?"

"Oh, you know Henry and his girls. I don't think he was ever really serious about Connie. And she may just have needed an excuse to leave that dreary old George." Lavinia frowned, her interior look, which served to finish Henry as a topic for that night, at least with Potter. "I really think I'll go up to bed very soon," she said. And she went upstairs to lie awake for hours, with her thoughts of Henry.

Naturally, Lavinia had all along been aware of their true direction, hers with Henry, through all those jovial, pseudo-friendly phone calls: "Well, I finally told Connie that I thought I was wasting her time. Lavinia, tell me I'm not a total shit." "But of course not, but must you use those words? You sound like that horrible pal of yours, that Adam." (Inexplicably to Lavinia, Henry and Adam Marr have indeed become good friends; they too have lunch at the Plaza, and Henry goes up for weekends in White Plains.) "I feel like a shit," says Henry. "Will you have lunch with me, anyway?" Lavinia knew what was going on, really, during those phone calls, and the long, rather winy lunches, at which their hands so often touched, lighting cigarettes, as their fingers lingered, exploring, promising. It was all leading to the afternoon when over coffee Henry simply took her hand in his, no cigarettes involved, and he said, very firmly, "Come on. I've taken a room for us at the Wyndham. It's just across the street."

"But—"

"Don't be silly. No one cares who we are, and we won't see anyone. I've got the key."

The elevator is small, operated by an aged, limping black man, trimly uniformed—behind whose back for the first time Lavinia and Henry hold hands in a serious way, not looking at each other.

They arrive at a large, pleasant-but-not-smart room, overlooking 58th Street, in which they for the first time kiss, very seriously, and then violently, their hands groping, grasping, Henry saying, "Christ, Lavinia, so many clothes—"

Henry's body was a great surprise, so much dark hair, everywhere, such powerful thick dark hair, such power. And later, his beautiful eyes, larger and darker and moistly deeper now, his beautiful eyes meeting hers, as they lie back for a moment on a pillow. His smile, their smiles.

And even later, as they lay there in the vast tangle of sheets, in the late afternoon sunlight, hearing the increased momentum of cabs, the distant clop of horses' hooves—even then, as Lavinia lay in a dizzied, sensual swoon, a funny cool part of her mind was calculating, Oh, I must have come four times, at least, which almost makes up for the years of nothing—but is that a record, for an afternoon? Could Megan—ever?

"You can't go home now, it isn't even civilized," Henry told her. But Lavinia, who believed that her sense of him was absolutely accurate—she had after all put in a lot of time studying him, his moods and tastes—Lavinia believed that just to please Henry she must go, that going home was the civilized thing for her to do. She must bathe immediately, must reemerge from the bathroom all crisp and madeup and new. She must say goodbye to him sadly but with a very slight coolness, as though just possibly they might not meet again. As though she were not so seriously in love.

And Lavinia did all that, and all so quickly that Henry could hardly believe that she was gone (for tactical reasons they agreed that she was to go down in the elevator first), and she felt that he could hardly wait to have her back again. Just as she had planned.

The sad part is that for all her cleverness, her assiduous scholarship, in terms of Henry, Lavinia was absolutely wrong. Lavinia had created a certain "Henry" as her lover from scraps, and from her own demanding imagination.

She could not know that as Lavinia left him that day, Henry sighed for the lack of a woman who would stay with him, one who would not rush off to a husband, or even off to bathe. One who would not require an uptown hotel room, which he could not afford, not often.

In the meantime, he enjoyed her beauty, he enjoyed making love to her—and her evident enjoyment of himself. And he enjoyed watching Lavinia at her games. Women are much more complicated, more interesting than men are, Henry believes. He loves their complexity.

. . .

Now, on the terrace of the house that she has perfected for them both, on that misted April day, Lavinia is perfect. In a soft robe, she pours strong hot coffee into the gold-bordered (antique) French cups, she passes fresh croissants and sweet butter. In two pewter bowls tiny wild strawberries nestle against pale brown sugar.

Henry is not handsome, actually; his nose is too long, his mouth too wide, and he is so nearsighted. But just now, with his dark hair a mess and his glasses off, with his beautiful dark-thick lashed eyes (well, it's true, as he says: they are like a giraffe's), his face is perfect, Lavinia thinks. He must look like some remote Dutch ancestor, some brilliant brave captain, Lavinia imagines (although Henry has told her that all his people were farmers).

But Henry's looks can only improve with age, Lavinia is sure. Thick gray hair will distinguish him. She does not understand why so often he looks so sad—but perhaps she misreads his expressions, she tells herself.

It rained all last night. A soft, insistent intimate rain that drummed lightly on the roof, above the room where Lavinia and Henry thrashed about, a little drunkenly—more than their usual wine at dinner, and then with dessert some champagne. In their wide soft bed, in the rainy dark. And they woke to make love again, very slowly and soberly, in the silvery cobwebbed morning.

Now from the terrace the weather is seen to be clearing; there is even some pale sunlight on the long wet grass, beyond the tidy bricks, their island of order. And far down below the river gleams, through light mists.

"Curiously enough I know Governor Stevenson slightly," Henry is saying, looking up from the paper, his glasses back on and pushed down his nose. "And I must say, a perfectly delightful fellow. But then, so was poor Alger." With an unhappy smile he sips at his coffee, and then, looking up at Lavinia, an entirely different smile takes over his face.

He then says, "You know, I think I've never seen you so beautiful, Lavy? No makeup, I don't know why you bother. But just at this moment—honestly—"

He is quite right, she has never been prettier; and Lavinia even knows just how she looks. Normally pale, she now is faintly pink across her delicate cheekbones; her gray eyes which can be cool are now warm, almost blue. And her light, somewhat flimsy hair is softer, and full, in the light, moist April air. She feels beautiful, she feels the new color of her skin, and her eyes. Her hair. Her whole body.

Henry, in the daylight, rarely speaks in that way, and so Lavinia blushes, making herself even prettier, and rather recklessly she says the first thing that comes into her mind: "Really? I look different. Heavens, I must be pregnant."

Henry stares for a moment. Then he laughs, and he says, "You're joking, of course."

"Of course I am."

"But if you were, you know, I suppose you'd leave old Potter and run off with me."

"Oh no, I wouldn't do that. I could pass it off as Potter's. My father used to be quite dark. And when he was young he had terrific bones, like yours. Before they got all blurred."

Henry laughs again. "I suppose. Well, I guess that takes care of that. How quickly you work things out."

"Yes, I do."

"I never know what you're thinking when you frown," he says.

"Just concentrating," she tells him, as the tiny frown disappears. But what came out as an idle remark in the last few minutes has become a strong conviction: she is pregnant, by Henry. Of course by Henry; she and Potter haven't done it for several months—he is usually too drunk, and besides, she hasn't wanted to. She next thinks, As soon as I get back to New York I'll have to get Potter back into my bed. And she frowns again.

"Well, if you're not with child," says Henry, "then we don't have to have a sordid conversation about divorce. But tell me, do you really think I'd be such a terrible husband? Was Connie right, after all, not to marry me? I think I'd really like to get married, someday."

"Oh, Connie. No, of course you'd be a lovely husband. For someone. But I don't want you for a husband. I want you to be in love with me. Forever."

"What a practical little romantic you are."

Lavinia laughs, in a light pleased way; she has just come to several more highly "practical" conclusions. "I guess I am," she says. "More coffee?"

The baby will be a girl; of that Lavinia is fairly sure. And she will be born sometime the following January—perhaps on Lavinia's own birthday? A small, exquisitely beautiful dark baby girl, easy enough to pass off as slightly premature. And Henry will always love them both, Lavinia and her (*his*) daughter. And so, for that matter, will Potter, the putative father.

Lying in bed, in New York, in her own apartment, Lavinia is awakened by an awareness of Potter, who is next to her, of his sharp shoulder bones and his heavy, sour breath, and she begins then to think of names. Forms of her own name, which she then sees before her, as though engraved. Mrs. Henry Stuyvesant. Lavinia Harcourt Cobb Stuyvesant, and before that, for a decent interval, Mrs. Harcourt Cobb. All wonderful names, especially the last, she thinks.

But now there is not only Potter in her bed, to keep her awake, but from outside some unholy street sound, an ambulance, or something. More fully awake, much too awake, Lavinia stops thinking of beautiful babies, attractive new names, and she sees with absolute clarity that divorce is absolutely impossible for her. To divorce Potter and to marry Henry, no matter how long the interval between, even years, would be to admit both original error and later guilt. And worse, her (*their*) beautiful daughter would be exposed to ugly rumor.

With impeccable logic Lavinia sees exactly what lies ahead for her: pregnant or not, she will stay married to Potter, and she and Henry will be lovers, forever, for years, for a very long time. Her course is perfectly clear. And so why, as she lies there in the clamorous city darkness, the rainy April night, is Lavinia overcome quite suddenly with terrible tears? She has to choke them down, in order not to wake Potter. Why does she lie there, silently weeping and sleepless until almost dawn?

. . .

Lavinia believes very strongly in her own prescience, and not only in regard to Henry. She always knew, she thinks, that Peg would have a lot of children, even though for a while her children seemed not to make Peg happy. (Now, however, Peg is perfectly fine, back at home with Cameron and the kids, all well, herself again. Which proves that Lavinia was right all along.) Lavinia believes too that Megan will not have children, will not bother to get married even. Very probably Megan will do something quite unusual, Lavinia admits to herself, with a certain small reluctance. However, comfortingly, whatever Megan does will not quite work out.

When she thinks of Cathy, though, Lavinia worries, and for an apparent reason: Cathy is still in graduate school, at Stanford, and everyone says the economics department there is tops, if a little left-wing. If Cathy has a beau she has never mentioned him; however, after the disaster of Phil-Flash, she may just be keeping her love affairs to herself (as Lavinia herself certainly would, after a big mistake like that). But Lavinia senses some dark complexity in Cathy, she always has; she has always feared that finally things will go terribly wrong for Cathy.

Across the continent, in Palo Alto, California, Cathy does indeed have a "beau," although that would not be her word for him; in fact she has no word. But he is a man who is in love with her (insanely: he sometimes seriously thinks that he must have lost his mind). He walks through the flowery darkness of a spring night, in California, with everything in bloom, the acacia and apple trees, walnut blossoms, peach, the jonquils, ranunculus; and he is vaguely aware of flowers, some sweetness in the air, but his heart and his mind are all full of Cathy, her brown-black eyes and warm mouth and her delicately small breasts.

Along the streets that lead toward her street he hurries, in the old part of what is still, in the early fifties, a relatively quiet town, especially in this neighborhood of large, widely spaced Spanish-style or colonial houses, streets lined with stately palms, their fronds slightly rattling in the light spring breeze.

Tonight, as he does on a certain day of every month, this man is carrying a bottle of chilled white Alsatian wine (Cathy's favorite; she prefers it to champagne) to celebrate what is now eleven months of love, since the June night, which so moves him still that he can hardly bear the emotion of remembering. When they first.

He does not know what he will do on the seventeenth of the following month, to celebrate a year.

All those silly songs about love, to which in his life (with good reason!) he has never paid much attention now turn out to be absolutely true, this man is thinking, as he rushes through the tepid night, with his wine. Love does make you feel young; he could actually run, so light is the feeling in his feet, in all his body. He could run, he has so nearly forgotten his white hair and the fact that he is almost fifty.

He has forgotten that he is a priest, in a black suit, with a clerical collar; and that he is on his way to commit a great sin, again and again.

20

In New York, Henry and Lavinia are models of circumspection, or nearly so. It is her idea that they should "save themselves" for the times in Fredericksburg, their magical house on the river. In New York, as she sees it, they should continue their "friendship"; she cannot risk many dinners with Potter at which she is still flushed, out of breath, and even slightly drunk from a winy lunch, and an afternoon in bed with Henry. Odd bruises, here, there.

Thus Lavinia is able to have it both ways, or nearly: to have both the actual love affair and the appearance of an enviable, respectable if slightly puzzling friendship. She actually loves the occasional lunches in New York, after which they conspicuously *do not* go on out together; they do not go on down to Henry's Village apartment. And Lavinia is later able to report on the lunch in full detail, to Potter. "I'm not sure that Henry is exactly cut out for the law," she will muse.

"Oh really? I thought he was doing quite well. I know he's well liked in the firm." In the way of not quite deceived husbands, Potter is always eager to hear about Henry.

"Well, I just don't think his heart's quite in it." Lavinia dreams of the State Department, at least, for Henry. How handy if he were a diplomat, always traveling about.

Potter laughs, a little meanly. "He's probably too busy with his crew of young divorcées to have his heart in his work."

"Oh, darling, I'm sure you're right."

Another of Lavinia's stated reasons for not meeting Henry for an afternoon of love, in New York, is that there is nowhere for them to go, she says. Henry laughs at this, but Lavinia insists, very seriously. "We could always be seen. *Always.* Even if we aren't together. Anyone could see me leaving the Plaza at some odd hour, late some afternoon, or walking somewhere in your neighborhood, and come up with the wrong conclusion, which would actually be right, if you see what I mean." She laughs, charmingly. "Even if you were nowhere around," she adds. "It's not safe, unless we go to some really sordid place, and I just couldn't."

Henry is both too shy and too chivalrous to tell her that he is too busy and too poor to see her more often, and so Lavinia's arrangements work out well for both of them.

On an afternoon in May, however, Lavinia agrees to come up to Henry's new apartment, on Riverside Drive—to Lavinia, a very puzzling move. "But no one lives up there," she has protested, just not saying, No one but Jews. Although she and Henry do not talk about social issues, she suspects that he is "liberal."

He tells her, "Just take a cab. Honestly, Lavy, take two cabs, if you're worried about being followed." He laughs, and then he says, "I really want to see you."

Pleased by his urgency, Lavinia is also confirmed in what she sees as the correctness of her previous course: the infrequency of their hours together has made him more anxious to see her, as he is supposed to be; he should always be *dying* to see her.

This afternoon will be their first together for almost a month, since the couple of days that they had together in April, in Fredericksburg. Since the night that it rained and rained.

And Lavinia has news of her own. She is indeed pregnant, and this seems the perfect afternoon, the perfect time to tell Henry that she is. *Perfect.*

The weather is lovely. Even the shabby neighborhoods that Lavinia is forced to traverse on her journey uptown (much too far uptown) look prettier; even, at one corner, Lavinia sees an old man, probably Italian, with a barrow full of flowers, narcissus and daffodils, iris, peonies, hyacinth. On an impulse, and because she would like to be a little late, Lavinia has the cab pull over and wait, while she selects a bunch of the largest, the pinkest peonies, all delicately, exquisitely petaled. She will arrive holding them, in a bridal way, against her pale gray wool suit.

"But my darling, I don't think there's a vase in the place," says Henry, after their first long kiss, in his front entrance hall, once the door is firmly closed behind them.

"You must have a pitcher or something, a cocktail shaker, milk bottle?"

But they then begin to kiss, again, and somehow the forgotten flowers are left on the long hall table, and Lavinia and Henry move toward the bedroom, which has, Lavinia notes in passing, a perfectly nice view of the river.

An hour or so later, they both are dressed again, and washed, and seated in Henry's small living room. He has even made tea—touchingly, in the tiny kitchen. Handing Lavinia her cup, he says, "I'm really glad you'd come here today. I wanted you to see this place, and I wanted to tell you something, not over the phone."

Lavinia, who was herself about to speak, smiles expectantly, but her heart has chilled just slightly: what could he possibly tell her that would rival her great news? But she continues to smile, as she remarks, in a mock-scolding way, "Well, I hope your news will explain this eccentric move of yours. Not that I don't love it here. The nice view."

"Well, in a way it does explain it," Henry begins. "For one thing, the rent here is about half what I was paying downtown."

"Oh?" Lavinia has experienced further premonitory chills, at that unpleasant admission; she and Henry never talk about money, the cost of anything.

"It's just this," says Henry, with the most radiant smile that Lavinia has ever seen on his face, a transforming smile. "I'm going back to graduate school, to study history. You noticed how close I am to Columbia?"

Lavinia had not; never having been near Columbia, how could she have recognized it? Which she does not say; she only murmurs, in a noncommittal but encouraging way—while her heart seems to freeze.

"Eventually—does this come as a surprise to you, Lavy darling? —I'd like to go into politics. Or if that doesn't work out, to teach."

More surprised than Henry could possibly imagine, Lavinia at once decides that this is not the day to tell him that she is pregnant.

On the way home, in her taxi, controlling tears, Lavinia considers the incredible egocentricity of men.

Everything that we have always been told is quite true, she thinks: when it comes to women, only one thing really interests them, and that only on their own terms.

21

The Prettyware Party, to which Cameron, for some reason, has urged Peg to go, is in a new house which is very like their new house; both houses are "antebellum," although brand-new, in Midland, Texas. (Moving to a new house is one of the things that they have done since Peg's illness, along with a maid to help Peg, Cornelia, a Negro.) The floor plan of this house is identical to that of Peg's house, in fact, but just going into the two houses no one would know that.

This party house is Early American, all bright maple and bright chintz and ruffles and polished brass, everywhere there is something going on, everything shining and sparkling. Peg has never seen such a lively house, but probably that is because she feels a little tired; she did not especially feel like going out, only felt that she should, and was urged to.

Peg's house is all dark and heavy, with all those antiques from her mother, and from Cameron's mother, old furniture that now the children have battered with their tricycles and trucks. Her heavy dark house is a weight in Peg's mind; even with Cornelia to help her, it is such a mess. Especially now that she is sitting here at a Prettyware Party, in such a pretty light bright Early American room. (Is Early American a little too early for antebellum? Peg believes that it is, just as Victorian must be a little late?)

The hostess, whom Peg has not quite met before (Cameron knows her husband, who is also in oil) is Cindy, and she too is light and bright and cute, very small, with big yellow curls and small blue eyes, and a matching blue sweater and skirt, all twirly. "As cute as a button," Peg's mother would probably say, approvingly, if she should see Cindy, but her mother would not like this house. Peg's mother does not like for anything to be new, and even if it is new it must look as though you have always had it, like clothes—especially clothes. But Cindy is certainly cute, and her house is so, so gay; no wonder it was chosen for the Prettyware Party.

Cindy is the hostess, it is her house, but the girl who is running the party, the Prettyware person, is named Patsy. "Prettyware Patsy," she said, laughing, as she introduced herself. She has black hair that curls up at the ends, on her shoulders, a dark red mouth and a white sweater, and the most pointed, sticking-out breasts that Peg has ever seen. It is hard not to look at Patsy's breasts, they are so sharp and high up on her chest, so much more visible than her eyes, where of course you are supposed to be looking.

Peg herself has been meaning to get some new bras, she then remembers. Although it is hard to think of everything.

Peg got here on time, seven thirty, and for a few minutes it was difficult, introducing herself, being introduced to Patsy, having all the Prettyware Prizes pointed out, all that. But quite soon the doorbell rang—it tinkled; it is chimes—and there were two more girls, and then more chimes tinkling, more girls, and now the room is full of girls, who all seem to have been there before. All smiling. Friends.

Patsy is standing by the table in the front of the room, where the Prettyware Prizes are all spread out, pink cannisters and yellow bowls. Not the most fortunate color combination, Peg hears herself thinking, in her mother's voice. ("It is perfectly normal to think in your mother's voice, even your father's," her doctor told Peg, but then he seemed to think that everything she thought was the craziest was perfectly normal. He seemed actually pleased when she onced dreamed that her mother died. Only hostile dreams against your husband and children are bad.)

The picture window is framed in crisp sheer white ruffles, whereas the same window in Peg's house is draped in dark red velvet, from the attic of her family house in Plainfield. Perfectly good velvet, perfectly normal to have it there.

Cindy passes out pieces of paper and pencils to everyone, as Peg wonders what there will be to eat, later on. Surely, refreshments? Since her illness she is so hungry, so often, but at the same time she has trouble with eating.

Patsy explains the rules of the game they are going to play, in order to win the Prettyware Prizes. "Now, girls," she begins, in a mock-severe way, and then she laughs. Everyone laughs too, Peg among them, although she was a little late getting it out.

"Now, girls," repeats Patsy, "I want you to be ab-so-lute-ly honest. Anyone who cheats will get none of the delicious goodies that little Cindy has made for us."

Peg quails at that, as though she has already cheated and been deprived of delicious goodies.

"Now," says Patsy, with a lift of her chest so that her breasts point up even higher. "I'm going to ask you girls some questions that you will answer with a number. It's really very simple, simple arithmetic."

Peg feels an instant of sheer terror, which she knows to be unreasonable, not right, not perfectly normal. (What her doctor would have called "inappropriate," which is the opposite of "perfectly normal." But she can't help it, although that is something else that she is not supposed to say, or think, or feel. "Yes, Peg, of course you can help it, you *can*," the doctor said to her, quite frequently. The nurses said it too.) But she really is afraid of questions, and of numbers, adding, subtracting. She thinks of the nightmare of her checkbook (until she discovered that Cornelia is a whiz with numbers, oh, wonderful Cornelia). But now Peg wonders: if she does cheat, how will they know?

"Now, here goes with the first question. And remember, all these questions apply to this week only. We're not delving into your *pasts* tonight, girls." Patsy rolls her eyes, and everyone laughs. Peg laughs too, but was it too loud, her laugh?

"All right: have you ironed your husband's shirts this week? If you have, write the number ten on your paper. If you haven't, just don't write anything. See? I promised this was easy."

Most of the people—most of the girls seem to be writing something down, but several of them do not. Those who are not writing giggle. One of them, sitting near Peg, says, "Do I get a five for good intentions? I really meant to iron Larry's shirts."

Laughs all around.

Relieved, Peg decides that it is okay not to have ironed

Cameron's shirts, to be writing nothing on her paper. Other people didn't either.

The next two questions involve waxing the kitchen floor and cleaning out the oven. It is Cornelia who is supposed to wax the floor and clean out the oven, of course, although come to think of it, Cornelia hasn't done any of those things either, not for quite a while. But Cornelia looks so tired, and she moves so slowly, so saggingly around the house; Peg thinks Cornelia must be unhappy, and often tells her not to bother. She worries about Cornelia. And besides, really, what is the point of a perfectly clean kitchen floor, with four children in the house? And poor Cornelia: why should she be doing those things? She looks as though she had troubles of her own.

However, Peg is holding a blank sheet of paper, undoubtedly the only person in the room with no numbers, not one written down. She is scared: will anyone see? Will they ask for all the papers at the end, with names? If she cheated, how would they know? Would a representative of the company call Cameron, or Cornelia? Well, of course not—or would they?

The next question saves her, or so Peg believes, for a while. Patsy asks, "Have you written to your mother this week?"

And Peg has! She wrote her mother a postcard yesterday, explaining why she hadn't written before, children home sick with colds, would write soon. But do postcards count? Should she ask? No, of course they count; what Patsy said was, "Written to your mother." No need to ask. She writes the first number on her paper. Ten.

Then Patsy giggles, so that Peg knows, as everyone must know, that she is going to say something dangerous. "Now, girls," she says. "Tell me, have you kissed your husband this week? And you do know what I mean when I say kiss. Not some peck at the door." And again, the dangerous giggle.

Of course Peg knows what she means, of course everyone does, and in the quickest possible upward glance Peg is able to see that everyone in the room is writing down a number, of course they all are, and so does she: how could she not? And in a sensible, appropriate way, she reassures herself: no one, *no one* could possibly call Cameron on the phone to check on such a thing. "Mr. Sinclair, we're from Prettyware, and we're running a check on your wife. Would you mind telling us if it's true that you and she 'kissed' this week? Oh, you didn't? You don't, not anymore? Well, that's quite strange, Mr. Sinclair, she certainly said—well, she's lied. Your wife has cheated in the Prettyware contest."

Well, no one could possibly have such a conversation with Cameron, that was ridiculous. Still, as she writes the large TEN, under the other TEN that she got for the postcard to her mother (which very likely she did not deserve either), Peg is chilled with fear. Her stomach does not feel right; she would give a lot to get out of that room, out of all that Early American brightness.

Patsy clears her throat, and she sighs in an audible way, thus announcing that the next question will be innocuous, idle. "Now, girls," she says, "if any of you have spanked a child this week, and that includes slapping, any hitting at all, you have to take ten points off your score."

Several sounds of protest arise from certain corners of that room, but they quickly subside as several people mark a line through one of their tens. Peg's quick look catches them at it, but she can't tell how many people. It looks like about half the girls there. Less than half hit their children?

And for Peg the question was not innocuous; yesterday she slapped Candy at breakfast—Candy and Carol, her twins, now seven and too old to be slapped; it was terrible, it made her sick all day, sickly waiting for Candy to come home from school, and sick with worry, worrying that Candy might not come home, had been frightened away. It was so unfair; poor Candy had only been whining and saying she didn't want to go to school. Not eating her breakfast. But the thought of Candy at home all day, whining like that, when there were both baby Kate and Rex already at home with colds, and Cornelia out sick—well, Peg slapped Candy, and said she had to go to school; she was not sick. A light slap, not hard at all; still, it made Candy scream and scream, barely stopping in time to wash her face and get on the school bus. It was terrible— Peg's hand shakes as she makes a line through the Ten that she just put down, the lying ten, saying that she and Cameron had "kissed." So that all she has left is the ten for a card to her mother, just a card, when she should have written a letter.

But if she did not have that ten her score would be a zero, or would it be a minus number? It is hard to figure out, as she knew and feared that it would be. She needs Cornelia.

"*Girls.*" Patsy's voice is as deep as she can make it, probably. "Now, girls, this last is a *very important question.* So important that I want you all to close your eyes, as you think about your answer. Also, you will not want anyone else to know what you put down. Now girls, have any of you, this week, kissed *someone else's husband?* And I do not mean your father. If you have, subtract ten points."

Relief, or perhaps some stranger and stronger emotion makes Peg break out into a sudden and quite uncontrollable laugh; although her eyes are obediently closed she can hear her own laugh, the old loud jolly-Peg laugh that so many people, like Megan, at college, always disliked.

Looking up, Peg sees on Patsy's face an expression of the very purest dislike, even rage. But then Patsy changes her face back into a smile, almost, as she says, "Well, it takes all kinds, I guess. I'm so glad I was able to amuse you." It is clear that she thinks that Peg has somehow spoiled the game, and everyone else is looking at Peg as though they thought that too.

It is a horrible moment; Peg feels hot blood flooding up into her face, into her brain, and her stomach also seems to rise. From the top of her throat she manages to say, "I'm sorry, something just struck me."

But by then no one is looking at her, or listening; they are all looking at Prettyware Patsy, who is explaining that fifty is the top possible score: will everyone with a fifty raise her hand?

Several people do, and if they cheated no one will ever know— Peg is suddenly sure of that. Several more people got forty, all girls who iron their husbands shirts and kiss a lot and do not hit children and write to their mothers, maybe long letters every day, even. Who do not kiss other husbands, or who, if they did, would not think there was anything funny involved.

At last, in the confusion of people going up to the front to get their prizes, no one looking at her anymore, Peg is able to escape; she sneaks out the back of the room, knowing the floor plan as she does, and she finds a hall, leading as she knew it would to an outer door.

She drives home slowly, too early, wondering what there would have been by way of refreshments. What everyone else is eating.

22

Although she is not sure what she would have expected, Megan is still vastly surprised, arriving at Janet and Adam Marr's White Plains house. In the first place, she thinks, why White Plains? She has visited them before this in a variety of rented houses (they seem to move a lot; "our wandering Jew complex," Adam calls it) but in places that seemed somehow more plausible: Wellfleet and Provincetown, Westhampton, Westport. But now they have bought this staggeringly large house in White Plains.

With all Adam's new money and splashy success, three Broadway hits in two years, Megan would have expected a big house, of course, but this house is remarkably large, even for Adam's fantasy standards. Set far back from the street (North Broadway: could Adam have chosen a house for its street's name?) its dark wings spread out onto what can only be called grounds, acres of immaculately tended green lawn (a Henry James, English lawn, thinks Megan) with ancient sweeping trees. In one corner there is a clump of formal shrubbery surrounding a birdbath, and leading up to the house is a formally patterned brick walkway.

Megan now feels silly, walking up all that way, with her suitcase. She had the cabdriver let her out at the entrance, but as she approaches the house she sees that there is a circle in the driveway where he could perfectly well have turned around (where anyone

else's cab would have driven up and turned around). Drawing
closer, walking slowly, she sees too that the "grounds" are far more
extensive even than she saw at first; past the porte cochere and the
parking circle there are what look to be an orchard and a garden.
There must be at least three or four acres, in the middle of this
expensive suburb.

The house is fronted with a very long porch; at one end a long
swing hangs, with a table and some chairs. But no person is in
sight. Megan begins to wonder about the wine she brought, a
Beaujolais; in Paris they considered Beaujolais a real step up from
their usual *vin ordinaire*—but in White Plains, in this house? Not
to mention her clothes: could Adam and Janet, conforming to
their house, possibly have begun to dress for dinner?

Surprising they are still such good friends, really—Megan and
Adam and Janet have not seen each other for over a year, the
last time being a not terribly successful encounter at an after-
theater party, at someone's hyperchic upper East Side apartment. Adam was drunk, and noisily abusive to almost everyone
there; he was taking them all on, and perhaps in self-defense
Janet got drunk too, and sick. Megan felt worse than out of
place; she was wretchedly sorry that she had come at all. In what
she had thought was a good new dress, she was somehow never
introduced to anyone, and still too shy to do much about introducing herself. She felt nearly invisible—an unwilling witness to an
ugly scene.

This weekend, then, is to make amends for that admittedly bad
evening, and for the lapse of time since. (Adam even wrote an
apologetic letter, out of character for him, but it was funny and
bright and very warm, making fun of himself as a novice drunk,
"an arriviste mick," he said.)

Crossing the porch, Megan still sees no one around, and she wonders: could they possibly be away? *Could* she have come on the
wrong weekend? Almost wishing that this would turn out to be

the case, she goes up to the bright white front door; she lifts and lets fall the heavy gleaming brass knocker.

The door opens, and she is confronted with an enormous white starched apron, really immense; for a moment the apron is all that Megan sees. Also, the woman wearing the apron is so black it is hard to see her face, in that cavernous, shadowed entrance hall. Automatically introducing herself, Megan also extends her hand, but then as quickly retracts it, having registered the stark contempt on the other woman's face.

The black woman says, "They was expecting you. I'll take your bag," and she snatches it from Megan's hand, and begins a slow march toward the staircase.

Clearly Megan is supposed to follow, and she starts to do so, but suddenly, swooshing down the banister of those impressive stairs there comes a small boy who plummets to her feet. It is Aron, of course, much taller and thinner than a year ago, with Janet's dark pretty face.

He squats there on the floor near Megan's feet, looking up at her, not smiling.

She is not sure how to approach him, being unused to children, and generally shy with them. She says, "Hi, Aron."

Aron smiles; it is Janet's sweet tentative smile. He stretches his head toward her, and then he bites her leg, fairly hard, so that Megan cries out, "Jesus!"

"*Aron!* Aron, goddamn it, I've told you—" It is Janet, from the top of the stairs, then running down them and just not colliding with the big black woman, who has not even turned around during Megan's exchange with Aron, but who now says, "You, Aron. You come on upstairs with me."

Oh, thank you, Elvira, how good of you," Janet says, all in a rush, and then, "Oh, Megan, I'm so sorry, honestly, what a welcome."

But Aron has begun to scream, and so most of what Janet says is lost.

Janet picks him up. (How strong she is, Megan thinks; small Janet—and he is kicking.) She hands him up to Elvira, who is coming down the stairs toward them, scowling.

"Megan, you met Elvira?" Janet asks. Elvira's scowl deepens, as she turns to Megan, presumably in acknowledgment. "Elvira saves my life," says Janet, and, to Aron, "Aron, you can do some fingerpaints till dinnertime."

Janet is in her old familiar blue jeans and an old shirt, but in these odd circumstances, this White Plains mansion, with a big black maid and a small biting child, she still looks strange and unfamiliar to Megan.

The two women kiss a little awkwardly, and Janet asks, "Do you want to go up to your room? Oh no, let's have a cigarette first. God, doesn't that sound familiar?" She laughs as she leads Megan into a small, rather dark room; leaded windows, diamond-paned, do not supply much light.

The furniture there too is dark and stiff, small-scaled; Megan supposes that they bought the furniture along with the house, they cannot have chosen such stuff. The walls are lined with glassed-in bookcases, and the books are old and dark, leather-bound, and probably unread. Megan and Janet sit down on a sofa that feels like horsehair.

"*Shit*, where are my cigarettes?" Janet reaches into her pockets.

"Here, I have some."

In a familiar way they light up, draw in. They lean back.

"I just feel so terrible about that biting," Janet says. "He does it all the time. He bites anyone, but especially any new person. It's so embarrassing at the playground, his biting the other children. The mothers scream, and one old cunt even said something about tetanus shots. Honestly."

"It really didn't hurt," is all that Megan can think of to say, which is not quite true: small Adam has very sharp teeth, that is clear. "I was mostly surprised," she adds.

"It makes me feel so terrible," repeats Janet, hopelessly. And then, in a pondering way, "It's as though I'd bitten someone myself, you know? I feel guilty in just the same way." She stares at Megan, with the inward look of someone digesting a remarkable piece of self-knowledge.

Megan ventures, "Don't mothers always feel guilty about what their kids do?" Sinkingly (selfishly) she hopes that they are not going to spend much of the weekend in long talks about Aron, Aron's "problems."

"Not this guilty," Janet assures her. "I must really be identified with him, in some very sick way. I wonder if I should call Dr. Bilding. We're seeing a psychiatrist, of course, Aron and I." She has brought this out in a brave, somewhat defiant voice. "Of course Aron thinks he's just a friend that we go to see."

"Oh, really?" is all that Megan can think of to say to this.

"But why would he bite *you*?" Janet muses; it was not a question. "I mean, if he's acting out for me. I'm sure I don't want to bite you. I have almost no hostile feelings toward you, I'm almost sure."

"Oh, *Janet*." In spite of herself Megan has begun to laugh, Janet having finally sounded too ridiculous.

For a moment, with a tiny frown, Janet stares at her, and then with a giggle she says, "Oh, you're right! It gets crazy, it all goes around in a circle—" She giggles again, until she begins to cough, turning red and choking a little, with tears in her eyes.

They are both still laughing when from outside the house comes the sudden, violent noise of a fast-raced car, crushing crushed rocks, unbelievably loud; it could be heading right into the house, from the sound of it.

Immediately sobering, Janet exclaims, "Oh fuck, that's Adam. And Jesus, I'm not even dressed, or *anything*."

She gets to her feet, and for a minute Megan believes that Janet means to rush upstairs, to start dressing or whatever she feels that she was supposed to be doing. But something prevents her (it could have been an expression on Megan's face); she sits down again, saying, "Well, *shit*. I've had a busy day too." But in an agitated way she reaches for Megan's Chesterfields; she extracts and lights another cigarette.

Adam is somewhat heavier but splendidly turned out, in blue blazer and bright regimental-striped tie. He bursts into the small dark room, exuding energy; almost simultaneously he manages to scowl at Janet and to turn an enormous grin on Megan, like a searchlight.

By custom Adam and Megan do not kiss. Instead he hits her on the shoulder, with a force that implies affection, some possible sexual challenge, and a disciplinary sternness, a keeping of Megan in her place. The grin makes his eyes seem to slant downward at their outer corners, giving him a warm-clown look, although even grinning his mouth is tautly controlled.

"Christ, Janet, you're not even dressed, and it's almost dinner," he shouts. And then, "Old fat Megan, but shit, you're thin, you've lost your boobs. Go *home*, why do you think I invited you here, you dumb cunt?"

Megan finds herself grinning foolishly in turn, in sheer un-reasoning affection; she simply likes Adam, even his outrageousness —despite a number of negative judgments.

"Where's the kid?" Adam then asks Janet, but he turns to Megan before Janet can answer, saying, "You met my son the Jewish intellectual? He's planning to grow up and persecute me. His father the mick. He's just like his mother, a chip off the old cunt." Another grin, this one a little mean, as he turns back to Janet.

She tells him, "Aron bit Megan."

"Well, if that isn't cute. Or is it what you and that high-priced headshrinker call oral aggression? Which of course he must get from me, I'm a very orally aggressive person. Anally too, as a matter of fact. And *phallic*. Honestly, Megan, old fellow mick, the amount of Jewish bullshit that goes on in this house, it's enough to choke a horse." All that was said half-jocularly, Adam in performance. In a more direct and serious way he addresses Janet, "They've got dinner under way in the kitchen? They know we'll be eight?"

"Eight? But I thought—"

"I know I said seven. But I think Sheila's coming by later."

Janet looks at Adam, and seems to flush. Limply she says, "Oh."

"Well, old Megan, how do you like this spread?" Adam asks then—a rhetorical question. "Isn't it something? Did you see Elvira? The most hostile living nigger. A single-handed revenge on white exploitation. She may lead the revolution. I think she's good for Aron, a living lesson in the true nature of womanhood." And then, "Some old friends of yours are coming for dinner. You re-member Price, and Lucy? And someone you wouldn't know, but he's just getting big in state politics. Henry Stuyvesant. He's bring-

ing a rather dull woman, though, rich broad named Connie something, I don't know why he sees her."

Having been put off by his name—she assumed him to be one of
the new "social" people with whom Adam is increasingly involved—too tall, nearsighted Henry Stuyvesant is a pleasant surprise to Megan. He seems instantly likable, kind and intelligent, a
little shy, slightly awkward. And if he is rich, or social, those are not
important facts about him, as they surely were with George
Wharton, or even more with Lavinia's husband, Potter Cobb (of
course).

Connie Winsor Wharton is another sort of surprise, however.
Having assumed considerable beauty, Megan is startled by her
carrot-red hair, tiny pale blue eyes, and thin-lipped, unpretty
mouth. (*Why?* an insistent voice within Megan cries out, startlingly,
after so much time; why did George choose her?)

Striving for charity (people can't help how they look, or not
entirely), Megan watches Connie, observing her as closely as she
can, without appearing to spy. And she concludes that Connie is
a perfectly nice, unattractive, perfectly ordinary woman. She is rich,
of course, her voice is loud and somewhat rude, in the way of the
very rich. But George probably knew a lot of very rich girls. And
Megan wonders: could it have been Connie's very ordinariness
that he found so appealing? Are some men put off by extremes
of intelligence or even attractiveness in women—put off by superior
women? This is a new thought, highly puzzling, unwelcome, and
difficult to digest. And it is true; she is quite sure of that.

Henry Stuyvesant is on Megan's right; on her left is Price
Christopher, who tells her that he has left law school for business
school, a move which he seems to find it necessary to explain and
excuse to Megan. Actually she does not care in the least; she thinks,
For all of me he could have switched to anthropology, although of
course he never would—no money in it.

But, "Lawyers are really out for the big bucks in a very twisted,
covert way," Price tells her. "Businessmen are simply more honest.
Anyway, this Cold War is going to end in the big blast, and if

anyone survives it's not going to be some Village idealist, now is it. Of course I don't mean you, dear Megan. It's going to be the really rich, and that's just what I've got in mind for myself. All the way on the Scotch and lobster train."

Lucy, who (of course) seems to be a good friend of Connie's, is looking at Price and Megan with an expression which Megan finds difficult to read, but surely not pride? Megan is thinking that he must be somewhat drunk, or did he always sound so simpleminded? And, perhaps Lucy has heard this so often that she no longer cares? she is (happily for her) quite deaf to Price?

In any case, Lucy has made the transition from being a very pretty girl to a beautiful woman. Her fair hair is long and smooth, her dark translucent eyes serene. It then occurs to Megan that perhaps Lucy was brought up to believe that once married one does not have to pay much attention to one's husband. Not expecting much of marriage by way of companionship, much less rapport, such women can probably remain serenely married forever, to almost anyone.

The first course having come and gone (served by a young man even crosser and blacker than Elvira is), Adam rises to his feet. Picking up an opened bottle of red wine, with a great flourish he pours a large splash out on the spanking-clean white linen table-cloth. "Now, no one who spills will feel any shame!" he shouts. "And as the Jews say, enjoy!"

Not knowing quite how to respond, herself, Megan checks out reactions around the table. Janet looks mildly embarrassed, although surely Adam has done that before? It did not look quite spontaneous. Henry Stuyvesant too looks a little taken aback. Both Connie Wharton and Lucy Christopher look simply surprised; they can barely believe that *anyone* would *do* such a thing. Only Price laughs, and he claps enthusiastically. And, out of some dim sense that Adam's gesture has not gone over well, that he needs help, Megan too gives a feeble clap.

Price is muttering in her direction. "What an idiot, isn't he. I love to watch him making an ass of himself."

Megan stares, not sure that she has heard him right.

As Price goes on to ask, "I suppose you know all the news about your old pal Danny?"

"Well no, I haven't heard anything. He doesn't write." But the mention of Danny at that moment seems cheering, to Megan; for an instant his blithe, graceful presence is restored to her.

"*Well*," Price for some reason has begun to whisper. "You know that he's in London, and he's living with ———!"

He has whispered a name that Megan failed to catch, entirely, but she understands that she is supposed to have been both astonished and impressed. "Really?" she asks.

Price, with exaggerated eyebrow raisings, begins to imitate an English actor old and homosexual, although he still is whispering. "Well yes, my dear, Danny's found his true niche, or his true nature, as it were. Not to mention some juicy parts on the London stage—and offstage too, I would imagine. You'll forgive the dreadful pun? Dear Megan, how surprised you look. You didn't guess, or know?"

"Of course I knew," she furiously lies, hating Price.

Price looks at her in a cool and wholly contemptuous way. "No, Megan, I don't think you did know, actually. You girls are generally the last to tumble to certain truths."

This too has been said in the aging-homosexual voice, as Megan suddenly thinks Price loves to talk that way. *Obviously*.

She cannot resist saying, "Honestly, Price, your imitation is almost too good." And she remembers then some gossip that used to go around their particular group, in Paris: Price was said sometimes to go to expensive bars, like the Ritz, where he would let himself be picked up and taken expensively out to dinner by some fag, and then, when the pass was made, Price would feign absolute indignation; if necessary, he would beat the guy up.

"Thank you, Megan," Price now says, chillingly.

Turning to Henry Stuyvesant, who is not just then talking to Janet, as he has been, Megan asks him, "Do you ever see Lavinia, and Potter?"

"Uh, yes. Fairly often. You did hear about the baby, Princess Amy?"

Under no circumstances could she have said what it was, but something in Henry's voice, or his eyes, makes Megan for one instant imagine that he and Lavinia are lovers; they are, or have been, or perhaps will be, at some time in the future. But she next thinks, No, of course not, Lavinia would never have an "affair," not perfect, cool Lavinia. She says to Henry, "Yes, Lavinia sent me an announcement when Amy was born. But I haven't seen her. Them."

"She's very beautiful. The baby. I mean, everyone says she is. Lavinia seems very happy with her. And Potter," he adds. "Well," he continues then, "tell me about you. You live in New York? You work there?"

Infrequently asked what she does, or even if she works at all, Megan with some considerable enthusiasm tells him about a book that her house is publishing, on the Spanish Civil War, by two veterans of the Lincoln Brigade.

At this Henry's whole face brightens—with what could be relief at a new subject, and could also be genuine interest. "Oh, well," he says. "That's terrific. Do you know, I ran away from Milton Academy in nineteen thirty-eight to join the Brigade."

"Really? That's amazing. What happened?"

He laughs briefly, self-deprecatingly. "Well, actually they turned me down," he says. "I was just seventeen and unfortunately looked younger. I was a pretty protected kid. And then my family got into the act. Well, it was pretty much of a mess. And then I tried to make up for it, when I got to Harvard. Make up for not being in Spain, I mean. I kept track of all the battles, and I joined everything that said anti-fascist. I was a young fanatic." Henry has said all this as though telling a joke, but at the same time his tone is sad and regretful. He has taken off his glasses, taken out a handkerchief to wipe at them.

Observing that his eyes are very beautiful, so dark, soft, deep, Megan says, "I hope Senator McCarthy doesn't hear about you."

"Well, I doubt if he'd have time for all the idealistic under-graduates, back then. Anyway, I'm hardly important."

Henry has spoken as though his undergraduate time of idealism were an isolated period of his life, unrevisited—as though even to mention it is strange and unfamiliar. And Megan wonders: has he never talked about the Spanish War, all that, with Connie Wharton, or with Lavinia and Potter? Well, probably not. And on an impulse she tells him, "I'd be glad to send you a copy, when the book comes out." And then she is shy: will he imagine that she wants to see him again, looking for an excuse?

And is that even possibly true? Does she want to see him again, and if so, for what purpose—more friendly conversation? Yes. For love? Well, no. Yes? Maybe? There would be an interesting, almost Jamesian logic, Megan thinks, if she should have a love affair with someone who has also (possibly) been the lover of Lavinia, possibly the lover of George Wharton's former wife. But because she doesn't care at all, she thinks, she smiles at all this contrived complexity.

Henry Stuyvesant seems to believe, though, in the purity of her friendly intentions. He reaches and hands her a card, saying, "That would be great. I'd really appreciate it." With his glasses on again he looks both highly serious and more remote, a professor, possibly.

"*Mr.* Stuyvesant, please, no campaigning at the dinner table," Adam's heavy voice has broken in. "Besides, Megan there doesn't know a fucking thing about politics."

Megan blushes uncomfortably, and for the first time it comes to her very clearly that someday, somehow, there will be some sort of reckoning between herself and Adam. What he does and says goes farther and farther beyond "friendly teasing." Or, another possibility, at a certain point they will simply cease to know each other at all.

Her blush gone, Megan looks at Adam in an appraising way, and she sees the familiar warm-clown grin quickly painted onto his face, disarming, and so far irresistible.

That long formal dining room has high moldings, an elaborate marble fireplace, Piranasi etchings; and Adam's chair, the host's chair is heavily carved, ornate. Beyond his end of the room are long glass French windows, leading out to a small circle of lawn, some low flowering shrubbery, a surrounding wall of dark clipped cypresses. There is a single bench, stone, beneath those trees; just now, in the deepening June dusk, it looks entirely desolate—possibly no one has ever sat there.

Megan, looking out at that bench, at the strange surrounding trees, then formulates what she has been half thinking ever since she arrived, which is that this is an extremely strange house for Adam and Janet. And Aron. It simply does not make sense, for them.

Nor does the dinner make sense, really. Course follows rich course, new wines are produced, until Megan feels swollen and groggy, half asleep. As do almost all the others, from their look. Only Adam has remained alert; he even looks half expectant, still, excited about his lavish dinner party, as though it might yet yield up something marvelous.

Which it suddenly does: there is the sound of the car, from outside, a car furiously driven up over all that crushed asphalt. Brakes, a slammed door. By this time Adam is on his feet, and then out of the room. Some moments of a heavy, waiting silence follow. They all, in the dining room, look at each other in a questioning way, and at various instants, separately, everyone looks at Janet, and then away; she is seen to be staring miserably at her plate, at the half-eaten pastry into which she has just plunged a cigarette, ignoring the tiny silver ashtray placed beside her recently emptied wine glass.

Adam comes back into the room, grinning, followed by the tallest, the darkest, and very likely the most beautiful woman that Megan (and possibly everyone there) has ever seen. In a yellow satin cape. She is well over six feet tall, dwarfing Adam, of course, with mahogany-brown-black skin and wild frizzed-out hair (the style later known as an Afro, a natural, but not at that time seen at all, in New York; Sheila was sometimes credited with that fashion, its general use). But other than her color and her hair Sheila does not look "Negro," or African. Her flat, exotic features could be Egyptian, Oriental: wide slanting liquid, amber eyes, a long narrow nose, thin mouth, painted scarlet. She is more stylish, more fashionable than any fashion model could be. She is futuristic.

Adam is looking at her, this apparition from the night, with the most evident delight, with obvious lust and absolute admiration; and his look is observed by all his guests, none of whom quite dares to look back at Janet, again.

"Well, friends, this is Sheila," Adam announces, and he might as well have been announcing his intention to abandon Janet, there and then, and to run all over the world hand-in-hand with his gorgeous captive giant, with beautiful Sheila.

Sheila smiles, showing brilliantly white teeth, and she ducks her head, a shy queen, acknowledging obeisance.

One of the things that Megan thinks, observing this small but significant scene, is, Well, now Janet can go on to med school.

Another thought is, Oh, so that's what this house is all about. A place for him to leave Janet in. What a bastard Adam is.

23

Although they have talked about almost everything under the sun, the one thing that Peg and Cornelia (Cornelia, who works for her now) have never mentioned is the curious fact that they look very much alike; they are close to the same size, both being large, rather squarely built women—and that is only the beginning.

Like Peg, Cornelia has round blue eyes, although legally (and in practical terms—not voting, for example) she is a Negro. And like Peg, she has a large upturned nose and a wide full mouth. Only her skin is quite another color; Cornelia's skin is a shadowy pale brown, whereas Peg's is simply pale, either dead white or pink, the sort of skin that does not tan. Also, Cornelia has a long and terrible scar across one cheek, a souvenir from her first marriage, and of an emergency room that put off any aid to a bleeding Negro woman until all the white people (mostly drunks) were taken care of.

In the cruel Texas heat the two women perspire a lot, and each has trouble with what Cornelia calls the monthlies. They each have four children, although Cornelia is a little younger than Peg is. These and other affinities are discussed between them; what neither of them has ever said is, You know, we really look a lot alike. To Peg, this would seem a tactless observation.

Cameron though has noticed the similarity, and has said so to Peg. He thinks it is very funny. "Honestly, I've heard of pets resembling their masters," he has said, "but honestly, Peglet, only you could find a goddamn maid who looks like you."

"I didn't find her, the agency—"

"Oh, don't be so literal. You hired her, and she looks like you. That's all."

The truth is though that Cornelia is considerably prettier than Peg is. Peg recognizes this (it is one of her reasons for not pointing out that they look a little alike) and she has wondered if Cameron does. Perhaps not, she has concluded. For one thing, if he had he would probably have said so; he is not given to holding back things of a wounding nature; he does not spare Peg's feelings. For another (and this is a truth about Cameron that she does not like to admit to herself), he is the sort of white man who is literally blind to Negroes, in sexual or aesthetic terms; he only sees *Negro*, he does not differentiate. Which is not to say that he is more prejudiced than most people are (in the early fifties), or that he would treat Negroes in an unfair or cruel way. He would not (or so Peg believes, she has to believe). He simply does not see them.

Peg thinks that Cornelia is also smarter than she is, and she thinks that it is terrible that Cornelia barely got to finish high school, and had her first child at sixteen. Cornelia should have gone to college and then to med school; she could have been a doctor— Cornelia is the one who should have gone to Radcliffe. But no chance of that now, with all those children and no husband and no money, and boyfriends that are worse off than she is, usually. In addition to the problem, in Texas, of her "color," in terms of getting an education.

In any case they talk a lot, Peg and Cornelia; they are very close friends, although that is not exactly how they think of each other.

. . .

Peg still thinks of Lavinia as her closest friend, although since college they have seen each other hardly at all. On one of Cameron's recent trips to New York, on business, Peg got to come along, and she met Lavinia for lunch, and they were all supposed to meet for dinner later that week, Potter and Lavinia, Cameron and Peg—but after Peg was there for two days Cornelia called to tell her that the twins had simultaneously come down with chicken pox. Cornelia said she could perfectly well take care of them, but Peg took the next plane back to Texas; and so on that trip she did not see very much of Lavinia. But they have kept in touch by letter, and for years they have said that they would celebrate their thirtieth birthdays together, which are to occur within a week of each other, in late January 1956.

And the preceding fall Lavinia writes that it is really going to work out, after all: she and Potter are going to New Orleans. And then they will come on to Midland, to Peg and Cameron. *Perfect*, it will all work out perfectly, even though they can only be in Midland for one night; they have to get back to Amy—although their nurse is marvelous, a true jewel. She is Swedish, and Swedes make fantastic nurses, of course.

But, "I don't know why, the idea of that dinner is really making me nervous," Peg confides to Cornelia. "I can't even decide what to cook. And it's just the four of us, for heaven's sake."

"Some friends can make a person nervous, even if they's friends," is Cornelia's comment.

"Oh, that's right. But sometimes I think everyone makes me nervous. Except you, Cornelia."

Peg is not only nervous about the dinner; she is strangely depressed at the very idea of the visit, Lavinia coming to her house, seeing everything—and is that it? Is she afraid of what Lavinia will see?

However: she determines that she will be strong and "womanly," in the way that her doctor has recommended. No more sicknesses or secret rebellions.

Of course Cornelia will be a great help. The very idea of Cornelia is strengthening (just as the very idea of Lavinia makes her nervous? Peg drops this thought instantly).

Thoughtfully Peg remarks to Cameron, one night at dinner, "I think maybe beef Wellington, don't you? For Lavinia and Potter. Doesn't everyone like it?"

Having expected no answer—she was actually speaking to herself—Peg is surprised to hear Cameron saying, "Oh, great. You haven't made that for—for years." Not since you were sick, he means, and just does not say. And then he says, "But really, Pegs, if you're going to go to all that trouble, could we ring in at least another couple? I'd like to ask Barbara and Harold."

"Oh. Well, okay. You don't think they'd be bored? College reunion, birthdays, all that?" Peg tries to laugh in her jolly old way, but it does not sound quite right.

"Of course not. And you girls can take care of all that stuff ahead of dinner. You and Lavinia. Didn't you say they were getting here before lunch?"

"Mummy, what's beef Wellington?" Carol asks, from the foot of the table. "Will we like it?"

"No, you wouldn't like it at all. And Cornelia will feed you kids before we eat," says her father decisively.

Harold and Barbara accept—Harold is someone important, in another oil company. And Peg and Cornelia decide that yes, beef Wellington would be best. ("We'll show them folks we knows how to do," Cornelia giggles, in what Peg thinks of as her stage Southern Negro voice. She thinks a lot, still, about Cornelia going to college.) They will start with Cornelia's crayfish bisque. Cornelia's sponge cake for dessert.

Why, then, does Peg experience such leaden dread, whenever she thinks of Lavinia, the dinner, as though a thick black cloud had settled around her? Is she going to be sick again?

No, she *will not be*. (Remembering shock, she will not be.)

. . .

But:

On the very day of the dinner, the day that Lavinia and Potter are to arrive, the phone rings early in the morning, and it is Cornelia, who says to Peg, "I bleeding. Bleeding too bad to move."

"But Cornelia, Jesus. Every month. I mean, you've come here before, when you were—"

"Not like now. I bleeding too bad."

"Cornelia, what'll I do for the dinner?"

"You manage. You cook good."

"But, your crayfish bisque. Sponge cake."

"You make some other kinds. You ain't bought the crayfish yet, is you?"

"Oh, *God*. Cornelia."

"Well, if that isn't typical," says Cameron, informed of this emergency. "Peg, I don't like to say this, but I really think you've asked for it. You've practically made a *friend* of that woman, and so of course she takes advantage of you. She probably just decided that a dinner party would be too much work. Miss Scarface is just plain lazy. I know it's a cliché, but really, they all are."

"Oh, I'm sure it's not like that. She really sounded terrible. Sick." Saying this, Peg experiences a strong surge of guilt toward Cornelia, who did sound terrible, and sick; but she, Peg, was almost too caught up in her own panic to notice. Miserably she thinks, I cannot get through this day.

In an automatic way she begins, though, to do the chores that she had planned for that morning, once the kids are off to school, the dusting and silver polishing, rechecking the guest room for Lavinia and Potter, going out to the flower market, arranging flowers, putting bowls of flowers everywhere. She is aware of moving in a dull-witted, leaden way; it is hard to think of what comes next.

And then, about midmorning, there is a taxi pulling up. Lavinia Potter. Lavinia getting out. Long thin legs, a red suit. Potter in a dark business suit, carrying bags.

"Well, old Peglet, happy birthday! I can't tell you how glad we are to be here! If New Orleans isn't the tackiest—now, Potter, you know we hated it. Oh, Peglet, what an adorable room! and the flowers!"

In Lavinia's perfumed, blond, effusive presence, Peg feels heavier, duller. And much closer to panic. She is barely in control, she thinks.

But once Potter has gone off to the business that Peg suspects was the real reason for their visit, Lavinia takes charge. "Darling Peglet, just tell me the menu. In my way I'm madly efficient."

Which she is. This comes as no surprise to Peg, who has always known that Lavinia could do anything she wanted to. But she had forgotten.

"Oh, Peg," Lavinia scolds. "I just know you were too nice to that black girl, and so when you really needed her she let you down. Honestly, you just don't understand colored help. You're not used to them, growing up in New Jersey."

Too tired to argue, too confused, Peg is also thinking that Lavinia at thirty is even more beautiful than she was at eighteen, but she can think of no way to say this, and perhaps it is something that she is not supposed to say? But heavily, clumsily, she simply says, "Lavy, you look great, really great."

Very pleased, Lavinia frowns, in her special way. "Oh come on, I'm a thirty-year-old mother. Can you believe it? But you have to see Amy. She's very beautiful, no picture can give you any idea."

"I'd love to see her," Peg mumbles. She is thinking that a miniature Lavinia would truly be more than she could stand.

"Well now, let's see about your dinner," Lavinia bustles. "Peglet, no one does beef Wellington themselves, at home. It's a caterer thing. We'll just broil the steak. Just a lovely big plain steak. Very easy. And since your girl's not around to make her famous bisque, well, I know a really great trick with canned beef bouillon and tomato juice. Everyone loves it. Great short cuts, that's my specialty," and Lavinia laughs, her old charming complicitous laugh.

By midafternoon the dinner has been taken as far as it can go, for the moment, and so Lavinia and Peg settle in the living room with cups of tea. Finally, to *talk*. (Although, really, Peg does not want talk. With Lavinia there, the living room suddenly looks so shabby, everything so old and battered, as she herself feels old and battered, as heavy as her furniture. She would rather lie down, with the door closed. She would rather get in the car and drive out to see Cornelia; with Lavinia so close by, so disapproving, she has not even dared telephone Cornelia.)

"Well, do you ever see old Megan?" Making a huge effort, Peg has asked this question heartily (but perhaps too heartily? She has a sense of having said something wrong).

Lavinia frowns, in her old way. "Not much, really. Sometimes we talk on the phone. But you know, our lives are simply too different. They just don't overlap. And with Megan there's always been something a little, well, odd."

"I guess there is." Peg is finding it hard to pay attention. She is not thinking of Megan, really.

"Oh, Peglet, you know she's pretty difficult. It may have something to do with coming from California. Isn't her mother a car-hop, or something like that? But all those Jews she used to go out with, and recently she told me that she actually knows this Negro trombone player. Jackson something. She has actually *gone out* with him. And you know Megan, heaven knows what else."

"Megan has a Negro friend?"

"Yes, silly Peglet, what do you think I've been saying. A friend, and maybe something more."

"I think Rosa Parks is wonderful," is the next thing that Peg says.

"Who? Do I know her? Was she in our class?" Lavinia is genuinely puzzled, and she had wanted to go on talking about Megan, having quite a bit more to say. But, Rosa Parks?

"You know, Rosa Parks," insists Peg. "The woman on the bus in Montgomery."

"*Oh.* Oh well, really, Peg, I didn't know you'd got so political."

"I'm not. It's not that. I just think she was really—brave." At this Peg's weak blue eyes fill with tears. She is losing her nerve, all the nerve that it now takes to talk to Lavinia, that she will need for tonight. She is thinking of Cornelia, bleeding.

"In a way, I suppose she was very brave." Lavinia speaks slowly, judiciously; she is trying to be fair. But then, with more authority (and much more feeling), she adds, "She really started a lot of trouble, though. A lot of people are going to get hurt. And for what? Just so Negroes can sit on the front seat in buses?"

Peg reflects on this, and concludes that it is true: a lot of people will get hurt, and will it really do any good, finally? Lavinia is always right, she leaves no room for argument (even when she is not right, is wrong). Peg finds her spirits lowered, almost flattened out, as though Lavinia had forceably pushed them down. Almost with relief she suddenly remembers, and cries out, "Oh, God, I forgot all about our cake!"

Relieved to have the subject changed, Lavinia giggles; she felt that it had been getting out of hand, their talk. What is the point in even discussing such things? "Peglet, you just forget about doing any baking," she tells her friend. "Just give me your car keys and tell me where there's a good bakery."

"Oh no, I'll go too. But you're right, we have to buy one." The dinner has changed hands, Peg is thinking; it is now Lavinia's dinner, her project. But was it once Cornelia's dinner?

"Speaking of Negroes, as we sort of were," Lavinia continues, "do you all down here read much about Adam Marr? You know, the playwright that Janet Cohen married?"

"Uh, I can't remember."

"Well, naturally Megan used to be their practically best friend. I heard she was living with them in Paris. Although I don't think she sees them much anymore. But you didn't read that Adam Marr married that colored girl?"

"Oh. I think so. Something."

"Well, he did. Although I hear she's gorgeous. You know how some of them are. But he left Janet in some big old barn of a house in White Plains, of all places. I guess Megan goes up to see her sometimes."

"What does his wife do? The Negro that Adam Marr married."

"Oh, I don't think she does anything much. From what I hear being married to him's a full-time job, and then some. I think she used to be a model, you know a lot of magazines are using them now. Even *Vogue*."

After a pause, in a troubled way Peg muses, "I wonder how Cathy is."

"It's strange, I have this strong feeling that something really peculiar is going on with our little Cathy," Lavinia tells her. "I don't think she even writes to Megan anymore."

In its way, the birthday dinner is a great success.

As usual Lavinia was right: the soup is highly praised, and she laughingly (charmingly) refuses to tell anyone what it consists of. "That's a secret, just between Peglet and me," she says, with a small wink in Peg's direction.

And Potter and Lavinia get along with Harold and Barbara as though (literally, actually) they had always known each other. And indeed it turns out that they had known each other's cousins, gone to school with each other's best friends, had spent summer vacations at the very same places, and winter vacations too. Everything they say is familiar also to Peg, and those same names, same schools and summer beaches, winter suns—but it is as though she had never heard of them; she might be some accidental stranger in these people's midst, so acute is her sense of isolation.

Now they are talking about Senator McCarthy, whom one of them very much dislikes, ". . . although, you've got to admit, he got a job done that someone had to do," says Harold, looking piously boyish.

Potter Cobb frowns at his steak. "He was instrumental, at least, in doing a lot of damage to a friend of ours. Man named Henry Stuyvesant, just about to get started in state politics, a few years back in New York, with every kind of backing, and that name—" Potter grins sheepishly, embarrassed at even mentioning the possible distinction of a name. "Anyway, Henry had all this going for him, and some Broadway, Hollywood connections too. Darling, who's that fellow that married the Negro girl?"

"Adam Marr," Lavinia supplies, through tightened lips that only Peg observes, and wonders at.

"Well, Henry is a perfect prince of a guy, even if he does have some pretty funny friends. He hasn't always had the greatest judgment in the world. Would you agree to that, darling?"

Lavinia stares at her husband. Is it possible that she has flushed, just slightly?

Potter continues. "It seems that old Henry went through a fairly pinko phase as an undergraduate, the war in Spain, all that business. Well, some fellows from the senator's office got in touch with him, and they just said he'd better forget about public office. He wanted to fight them, but of course he'd have really ruined himself, that way. But the poor fellow really took it hard."

Lavinia is up on her feet, but smiling. "Darling Peglet, we're the maid, remember? Come on, let's clear this stuff off, or we might get fired." She achieves a laugh.

In the kitchen, standing at the sink, efficient Lavinia unaccountably breaks a wine glass, as Peg is bringing in the dinner plates. Lavinia holds up a furiously bleeding index finger. Her eyes are full of tears as she exclaims, "Oh, shit, shit! Why does Potter have to be so stupid? Who wants to hear about that ass of a senator? I hate politics."

Peg holds the finger under cold water, and then produces a Band-Aid. For the first time that day she feels that she knows what she is doing.

And almost instantly Lavinia recovers. She smiles. "Oh, Peglet, you're so good to me!"

Together, Lavinia and Peg bring in the birthday cake, with their thirty candles, and everyone claps and sings Happy Birthday to "the girls."

The next day, Peg cannot get Cornelia on the phone. No answer, even. But that is impossible: even if Cornelia isn't there, where are all the children? You can't just vanish if you have four children, as Peg would be the first to know. Someone has to be taking care of them, always.

She thinks of driving out to Cornelia's house, but then she reasons that if no one is answering the phone, there can't be anyone at the house.

In an idle way, she stares at the phone book, then notices that a couple of numbers are scribbled there, in Cornelia's schoolgirl writing.

She tries the first number. A man answers, a Negro man. "I never heard of no Cornelia Smith," he says, too loud, and he hangs up.

The second number produces a shrill woman, also a Negro, who says, "She owe you money, it your tough luck, white lady."

"She doesn't owe me anything, I just wanted—" But that person has also hung up.

At last, trying Cornelia's house once more, Peg gets the small faint voice of a child, who says, "She gone to the hospital."

Once at the Negro hospital, that afternoon, it still takes Peg more than an hour to find Cornelia, an hour of surly and/or stupid bureaucrats, of corridors crowded with gurneys, wheelchairs, ambulatory patients, in their shabby hospital robes. Large wards of beds, full of men and women who are not Cornelia.

Peg has left her own house in a hurry, having errands to do on her way to see Cornelia: she stopped by Cornelia's house with some hastily bought presents for the children, and she has with her a present for Cornelia. (She did not even stop to call Lavinia, to say goodbye, she now guiltily thinks.) Nor did she get dressed up; she is wearing the old college Levi's that she had put on at breakfast. And now, confronting one hospital official after another, including a succession of hostile nurses, she wishes that she had got dressed. No one cares in the slightest whether or not she finds Cornelia Smith, who is there for an unknown and probably suspicious ailment.

The smells of disinfectant and of medicine have begun to give Peg a headache. As she hurries through those corridors and wards she gets glimpses of bloody bandages, of faces drawn in pain, and of tearful visitors, sitting miserably on the hard waiting room benches. She sees tiny fearful (Negro) children in oversized wheelchairs, or on crutches.

But finally, in a narrow white bed, in a roomful of beds, she comes to Cornelia: Cornelia, ashen-faced, dopey, weakly crying.

She barely smiles as Peg comes up to her, she only murmurs, "Miz Sinclair."

Peg takes her hand; she is thinking how beautiful Cornelia is, more beautiful than Lavinia ever was, even.

"Miz Sinclair, they done took it out. They done took everything out of me," Cornelia cries.

"Oh, Cornelia, how do you mean? What was wrong?"

"I ain't no more woman, they done took it out."

"A hysterectomy? Is that what they said—did you hear that word?"

"Yes'm, they say that." And Cornelia cries harder, sniffling, holding her fist to her nose and wiping at tears.

Wishing she had a handkerchief or even some Kleenex to offer, Peg feebly says, "Oh, Cornelia, oh, that's too bad."

"They just took it all out!" Cornelia begins to cry harder, her words making what she feels worse.

Peg wonders if her visit is doing any good; she does not feel helpful, or cheering.

"Cornelia," she tries to ask, "is there anything I could bring you, anything you need? I took some things over to your house for the children, just some food and a few clothes, some toys, so don't worry. They all looked fine—"

"I just need to be back where I was before," Cornelia moans.

"But Cornelia, now you won't have all that trouble every month. And you really didn't want any more children, did you?"

"No'm, I didn't, but I might, some year. Somethin' could happen to these ones that I have." And she cries and cries.

Peg has brought Cornelia a pink silk nightgown; having had no idea what to bring, she was caught by a display of gowns, in the department store where she went to look for children's toys. Deciding that it might at least be a diversion, she holds out the box, as she says, "Here, I thought you might like this."

Quieted, for the moment, Cornelia takes and begins to unwrap the present; she even smiles. But then as she parts the tissue and comes to the actual gown, her tears begin again, coming harder and faster than before. "But I got no more use—," she gets out, with the most terrible plaintiveness.

After a dull, uncomprehending moment, Peg suddenly understands that Cornelia believes her sexual life to be over: the nightgown will not do her any good, with men. And of course she, Peg, must tell her that this is not true. Which seems impossible. They don't talk about sex, they have no words for it.

"Cornelia, what you think isn't really true," she clumsily attempts. "I mean, you can still find some nice man, who loves you." For a minute she is too embarrassed by the transparent silliness of what she is saying to continue: Cornelia has never yet and most likely never will find a nice man to love her. Peg forces herself to say what is more nearly true. "Cornelia, you can still have intercourse. Have sex, if you want to."

But do you want to, Peg would like to ask; did you ever enjoy it, really? Or do you feel, possibly, as I do, that it's something you have to do for men?

Cornelia gives her a look of sheer disbelief, in which there is some anger, as though Peg were willfully misleading her, one more treacherous white person, meddling where she has no business to be.

Peg touches her arm. "Cornelia, look, I'll come back tomorrow, okay? And you be thinking about what you need. Cornelia, tell me, what's the name of your doctor?"

"But if the tumors weren't malignant, I don't quite see—" Lack of medical information makes Peg stop, and she wonders, how *can* women know so little about their bodies? Or, do men really know much more about theirs—or ours?

Ignorance, coupled with habitual shyness, awkwardness, make this phone conversation with Cornelia's doctor almost impossible. But Peg is forcing herself, very hard. She feels herself to be Cornelia's champion, her only possible savior.

The doctor snaps, "Fibroid tumors. Besides, do you want her to have fifteen children before she's forty? Some of them do, you know."

Hanging up, some minutes later, without much further enlightenment, Peg thinks, I only want her to get well and stay with me forever. I love Cornelia.

24

"Darling, you must tell me, how do you like our house now?" asks Lavinia of Henry Stuyvesant, on a Thursday afternoon, near the end of a remarkably hot and wet month of May. This particular day has been clear, but billowing heavy gray clouds hang just above the fields across the river, the Rappahannock, and the light is unnatural, too bright, so that the meadow grass even from this distance looks unreal, its green bright and poisonous (or is it simply that my mood is poisonous? Henry wonders, focusing on the meadow).

On the terrace, where they now sit sipping lemonade from fluted champagne glasses (why champagne glasses? Henry has never asked Lavinia this, but now he wonders), the scent of roses and wisteria is almost overwhelming, like spilled perfume. The very air is burned out, decadent (to Henry).

Trying to remember what Lavinia has just said, Henry replays her last sentence in his mind, a trick he has taught himself at political meetings; it works, thank God, ". . . do you like our house now?" He rehears her sentence, with its light but marked, ironic emphasis on *our*, and *now*. It is her special tone, and in his own, expected voice he answers her, "Oh, it's absolutely splendid, never better."

Looking around, Henry tries (and knows that he will fail) to notice what she has done to the place since they last were here; she is always doing something. He cannot even recall, precisely, just when they were here last, and the effort of trying to remember everything exhausts him. Which adds to the weight of another worry growing in his mind, just now, having to do with the night ahead, and Lavinia's clear anticipations, her preconceptions, as it were, of their "love," of how lovers behave, what they do. Henry smiles at what he perceives, now, as the absolute inappropriateness of all the words that he and Lavinia ever use, talking together.

Involuntarily he then thinks of Adam Marr, his sometime friend, who would inevitably say to him, "What's bugging you, man, is if you can get it up or not," and he can hear Adam's "Negro" laugh. And his own hyperstilted, impossibly refined response: "Well, old man, it isn't quite all that simple. This particular situation requires, well, considerably more than my simply 'getting it up.' You'd have to know Lavinia." He smiles again, aware of irony, and pain.

"Darling, whatever are you thinking?" asks Lavinia, smiling to his smile, speaking in her reasonable voice. She is almost always reasonable—the most reasonable, rational living romantic, he has always said.

And so he answers reasonably, and truly. "I was wondering if it would rain."

This simple statement has an unlooked-for success, however; Lavinia, ardently gray-eyed, picks up his nearest hand with hers, hers so tended and ringed, and so talented, in some ways. She says, "Darling Henry, I was thinking of that too, that night. And I now forgive you for not noticing the new awning."

Henry smiles warmly, as though also remembering a certain romantic night, presumably of rain, and then mercifully he does remember: a night in this house, "their" house, a windy night of wild crashing flailing rain, an overstimulated night (were they drunk?) of making love wildly, repeatedly. He remembers how they stared at each other, amazed, in the intervals of lightning, at each other's white naked bodies, flashed into exposure, and at that time so passionately new.

And he understands that for Lavinia it could have been the night before, or last week; her memory is less sullied than his, by far, and her high notion of love does not admit of change. She retains her view of their love, of him and of herself; it is necessary for her to do so. She even believes that Amy is "their child," and that Amy was conceived, now that Henry fully recalls it, on that particular rainy April night.

Because he chooses to, perhaps, Henry believes that the child is Potter's. Certainly that tiny girl has no look of him. In any case, in a legal sense she is Potter's child, and for the child herself that is the emotional reality. It is also, from Henry's (Marxist) point of view, the correct position.

Lavinia sighs. "If only we had the whole weekend. If I didn't have all those *people* coming tomorrow."

"You mean, all your new best friends?"

Teased, Lavinia turns girlish, daddy's girl; she almost pouts as she pleads, "But I have to have friends. You're never around, you're always down at your precious Chapel Hill, with all *your* new best friends." She adds, half seriously, "All Communists, I suppose."

Lavinia, I am a Communist. Henry does not say this, although he would like to, since it is the truth.

Driven, as he sees it, from elective political office by the McCarthy committee, Henry continued his graduate work in history at Columbia, and he then became an instructor in the department at Chapel Hill. Offered several choices, his record having been outstanding, he chose North Carolina with an informed and calculated look at the civil rights movement, his new passion. Once down there, Henry found, or came to believe, that the most active, the liveliest, and brightest Movement people were party members, and he was urged to join. And so, after some months of indecision, hesitations, he did join the Communist Party—it was all done very discreetly, since the Smith Act had forced the whole party underground, at that time. Especially, one did not tell nonmembers of one's membership, not even sympathizers. (Thus, Adam Marr, a flirtacious nonmember, kept urging Henry to join.)

To Lavinia, Henry only says, quite mildly, "I do like Chapel Hill. It's old and very pretty, and I like the people. Most of them." He adds, "Adam Marr's speech down there last week was quite sensational."

"Oh, I'm sure. If you say, uh, 'fuck' every other word, it's bound to be a sensation."

"Actually he was talking about writing plays. We have quite a famous group, the Playmakers, and a wonderful old theater—Greek revival. Where Adam spoke."

Lavinia laughs. "Darling, you sound so patriotic. Like a convert. What is it you call yourselves down there, the tar babies?"

"Tarheels."

"Well," says Lavinia, after a moment, with a small frown at the now dissipating clouds, the clearing air. "I guess it's not going to rain, after all."

"I guess not. But it's wonderful to have such a handsome new awning."

25

In June of that year, 1956, during which the four friends all turn thirty, Cathy and Megan arrange to spend a few days together, in Carmel, California.

Megan has ostensibly come out to see her parents; actually she has wanted to see Cathy, but so far that has not worked out very well. Both Megan and Cathy have been constrained, during their lunches; Megan has felt that they were not quite themselves. Her own problem has been quite simply her worry about her parents, who seem suddenly old, or nearly: Florence, still working as a carhop, looking more brazenly dyed, more foolish (to Megan) in that perky uniform; Megan is torn between irritation and pity for her. And Harry, her father, still so hopeful that his store will be discovered, or that he will discover among the "junque" a genuine antique.

Megan does not know what, if anything, is bothering Cathy, but Cathy surely does not look well; in fact she looks so unwell that it has been hard for Megan not to ask her what is the matter. To begin with, she has put on a lot of weight. And she is pale; her always vulnerable skin is blotchy, her dark hair too long, and lank. She looks unhappy and cross, and her manner, even with Megan, has been snappish, stiff.

At last Megan does bring herself to say, "Honestly, Cath, you look a little pale. Let's do go to Carmel. We'll walk on the beach a lot, it'll do you good, and me too. I need to get away from *them*."

A wan smile. "You're probably right," says Cathy.

And so, having agreed that it would be wiser to avoid a weekend, on a Tuesday morning they head westward, toward the coast. They have also agreed on the shoreline route.

These days Cathy has an old red Ford convertible—it wildly occurs to Megan that Cathy's car could once have been Phil-Flash's; this is an aged, beat-up version of his grand car. And Megan wonders if Cathy thought of Flash, as she chose and bought this car. But she cannot ask; even mentioning Flash would seem a mistake, so great is the contrast between this pale, blotchy overweight Cathy, indifferently dressed, and the Cathy of ten years back, all curled and pretty and proud of going off with Flash. (The fact that Phil-Flash was on the whole a jerk now seems less important than that with him Cathy was confident, and happy. As she so visibly now is not.)

Taking back roads, they are heading for Pescadero, and all that terrain is deeply familiar to Megan: the rounded hills shaded with live oaks, eroded red clay embankments, the occasional fruit orchards where now, in early June, the blossoms are just wilted, fallen onto the barely yellowing grass. Pine trees, clumps of cypress and manzanita, eucalyptus.

One clearing, then, in a pine grove just off the road, suddenly looks so familiar that Megan is startled; she might have dreamed of it the night before. But just as they pass she recognizes the place: it is where she and George Wharton used to park and neck, with such passion, such ignorance and frustration. That was almost half a lifetime ago, Megan now thinks, and she considers that sixteen-year-old girl, her former self, with some affectionate pity and some embarrassment, for her intensity, her innocence, her simplicity.

After the foothills is a pleasant area of farmland: heavy white fences that surround cropped green pastures, large prosperous white houses. And then with no warning they come to the sea: flat blue and shining, lapping against coarse gray sand, against barnacled rocks. In the warm summer air the scents of salt and fish are strong, wafted on a light wind.

"This was really a good idea, don't you think?" asks Megan, tentatively, as Cathy turns left, heading south and down the coast.

"I guess," says Cathy.

"My life in New York has been so crazy lately," Megan tells her; is she explaining the unease that she feels now with Cathy, trying to blame it on New York?

"Really? Mine too, I guess," is Cathy's laconic contribution.

"I had a really insane weekend up in White Plains with Janet Cohen. Marr." Cathy's enclosed silence is making Megan babble, she realizes, and she wonders if this has always been the case, that she talked so much with Cathy for the very reason that Cathy said so little. In any case, she begins to tell Cathy all about the White Plains weekend.

Part of the craziness was that Adam Marr was present, and Megan soon understood from Janet that this was often the case. Divorced from Janet, and now married to Sheila, Adam still, quite often, arrived for weekends in White Plains—and if Sheila minded she was never heard from to that effect.

"I can't exactly not let him come up," was Janet's explanation. "You know, because of Aron. And besides, I guess I still do care about Adam, in certain ways. I worry about him. This sounds silly, but I think he's changing into someone I don't quite know, and it's as though I'm trying to stop him."

"I see what you mean," agreed Megan, not quite seeing.

"I think he's a little nuts," Janet added, and then, flushing: "He thinks we should have another child. Together. *Really.*"

"But Janet, Jesus, that's outrageous."

"Of course it is. Adam is outrageous, that's his shtick." But Janet sighed in an affectionate way.

Megan considered the implications of this preposterous idea: First, did Janet mean that she and Adam still went to bed together, well, fucked, as Adam would put it, when he spent weekends with her in White Plains? Probably she did mean just that. And Megan further thinks, How can Janet, after the cruel way that Adam left her?

Not wanting to say that, of course not, Megan asked instead the most reasonable question that came into her mind. "But suppose you get into med school?" Janet had told her earlier that she had applied at Yale. "You can't have another child, not now."

"Oh, I know. The last thing I need is a baby. But Adam has this obsession about having kids."

"Let him have children with Sheila, then."

"He doesn't seem to want to, or maybe she can't? She is so thin."

Megan snorted. "He doesn't want Negro kids?"

"Oh no, you know Adam's not like that."

"I think Adam's seriously crazy," said Megan, seriously.

"I really hope I get into med school." Janet's voice was plaintive. "That would solve almost everything."

"Oh, I'm sure you will." Supportive Megan.

This conversation took place on the house's narrow porch, in the long summer dusk, before dinner. Adam had gone off somewhere with Aron, announcing that they were coming back with lobster for dinner, and that some other people would be coming too. He would take care of everything, he said, in an arrogant way that implied that only he *could* take care of everything. Listening, absorbing, Megan thought, He's really a fascist, where women are concerned. (The very idea of Janet having another child, with him!)

And that night at dinner it was exactly as though Adam still lived there; he had in no way given up his territory. Sheila, as a fact, was much less present than she had been on the night when she was so visibly anticipated by Adam; if Adam thought of her now, he did not say so. He was too busy with his party.

By midnight the rooms were all crowded, people had seemingly drifted in from everywhere, in their flashing foreign cars. The din in the house was cacophonous: people shouting and laughing harshly, too loud, somewhere records playing, hard rock. And everywhere a lot of smoke, clouds of grayish, yellowish smoke, scents of marijuana. Smells of spilled drinks and too much perfume. The sort of party at which everyone screams at once, and all the clothes are much too bright.

Almost all the guests were celebrities, of one sort or another. Very public people: Megan could pick out many of the faces, actors and actresses, famous directors, blockbuster writers. What later came to be known as media people.

Scattered here and there were a few exceptionally pretty young women, nonactresses, to whom no one paid the slightest attention. They were unknowns, and no one had time for them, that night. As Megan explained to Cathy, the party was all about ambition, various forms of self-promotion; it was the least sexy party she had ever been to.

But Adam loved it, every frantic heightened pulsing minute of his party. He was a famous person, among other famous people, and his awareness of success, of arrival, made him raucously jovial, loudly and quite impersonally friendly to everyone—so that Megan wondered if he and she actually were friends, any longer.

She was slightly disappointed not to find Henry Stuyvesant there again, they could have talked, she thought. But she recognized that Henry was in most ways the direct opposite of these people, a quietly thoughtful person, rather shy, she thought.

Another thing very much on Megan's mind, as she and Cathy speed south on the flat coastal highway, is the fact that the publishing house for which Megan works has just been acquired by a Texas oil conglomerate. And she tells Cathy all about this too.

Every day, at work, the lesser editors, the salesmen, and the secretaries were assured by the senior editors that this will make no difference; the house will maintain its high literary standards, high quality, etcetera. It will make no difference.

"Which of course is a patent lie," as Biff put it to Megan. "Of course it will make a difference. Frankly I find it ominous as hell.

But besides being basically lazy, I am also basically a whore, and so I will stay on. But you, dearest Megan—truly, I think you might think about a move. Much as I personally would deplore it."

"Oh, I am thinking. Seriously. But for me there's the problem of women never becoming senior editors anywhere, anyway."

"That is absolutely true." Biff sighed heavily, his whole small body sagging with dismay. "Oh, but I can see the writing on the wall. You'll leave, and you'll be a terrific success somewhere else, and then who on earth will I talk to? No more laughs, no one else around who *reads*."

"You're probably wrong. Where on earth would I go? You know that all the other houses are just as bad, in their ways. But why don't we leave together?"

"Holding hands and skipping along, like some comedy team? Well, that's an adorable idea—but just perhaps not."

But then a couple of days later, and not quite coincidentally, Megan had lunch with a literary agent, Barbara Blumenthal, whom she has liked and admired for some time. Barbara is a very successful woman, who manages at the same to be quite simply *nice* (or, perhaps her niceness is not simple at all). In the course of the lunch Barbara suggested that Megan might come to work for her. (Barbara has heard of the big oil takeover; she heard of almost everything first.) Barbara mentioned a handsome salary, plus percentages and commissions.

Some odd fate must have been at work, at just that moment, Megan thought: in the instant when Barbara had finished making her offer, across the fancy restaurant she, Megan, looked up and saw Lavinia—Lavinia out to lunch with a young blond woman who looked rather like herself, both so carefully, expensively gloved and coiffed, bejeweled. Catching sight of Megan, Lavinia smiled brightly and waved. But Megan could feel Lavinia taking in Barbara, could see Lavinia's quick appraising glance, and could almost from across the room read Lavinia's mind, her summation of Barbara: a real career woman, Jewish, looks aggressive, overweight, her suit needs pressing. Which of course would leave out almost everything of importance concerning Barbara.

Aware that her attention had wandered (when it perhaps

should not have), Megan explained, "That's an old friend of mine from college. I don't see her very much anymore though. You know how that goes."

Surprisingly Barbara commented, "She looks so much older than you do."

"Really? Beautiful Lavinia? Actually we both turn thirty this year—she already has, I guess."

"She looks so much more—more rigid than you do. More set in her ways."

"Well, I guess she is." Understandably pleased, Megan smiled.

Barbara inhaled, then stubbed out the long cigarette. "I've got to stop this," she said. "I cough." And then, "Take a lot of time, Megan dear, but please give me some thought. I think you'd like the business."

And so on the extraordinarily beautiful coastal drive, sitting beside silent, opaque Cathy, there is a great deal for Megan to think about: Janet and Adam. Her job. Biff. Barbara Blumenthal. And the rest of her life.

She observes with something approaching shock that not a single one of her concerns at this moment has to do with a love affair, not even remotely. She has not seen Jackson Clay for, dear God, a couple of years; there has been no one else. A few months back she had lunch with her old friend former section man Simon Jacoby, now married to Phyllis and working in his father-in-law's investment firm, and Simon suggested that it might be nice if they "saw each other a little more." But Megan said no, she was just too busy, just now.

She tells Cathy a great deal of what she is thinking, and is unable to resist adding, "Can you imagine? Barbara Blumenthal thinks I look younger than Lavinia does. I have to admit, I was sort of pleased when she said that."

"Well, of course you were pleased." With a visible but honest effort Cathy adds, "I think probably you do. To me you look about seventeen."

. . .

The Mission Inn, where Megan and Cathy have chosen to stay, is at the farthest, southern end of town, past the English cuteness of the shopping area, and the expensive, dangerously dramatic houses that perch out on the rocks, above the violent sea.

The Inn itself is rather shabby, low-key: a cluster of cottages, overlooking a pleasant meadow of wild flowers, where horses amble about and graze. A slow river winds through the meadow to the sea, where there is a wide sandy beach, at the river's mouth. Families picnic there with their dogs and children; they swim in the river or in the sea, which is bright and cold.

All this is visible from the little cottages: the meadow, with its flowers and grazing horses, some cows, and the river. The bathers and picnickers, dogs, and the sea. And further along, the stark silhouette of Point Lobos, a cliff of sharp rocks, harsh dead trees, and large black birds, swooping down.

Megan and Cathy have the cabin that is farthest from the central lodge, closest to the meadow and the sea. There is a narrow porch, a small living room, and smaller bedroom. Tiny kitchen, tinier bath. Megan insists that Cathy take the bedroom, she will be fine on the studio couch in the living room, she says. For an instant, then, as Cathy is putting her things away, Megan strongly wishes that she were there with a lover, not with Cathy. The cabin's very shabbiness seems to Megan highly romantic: love stripped down to its essentials—privacy, quiet, and a bed, with the further bounty of that view.

And very possibly Cathy could have just the same wish? It is impossible to tell, with her. Also loneliness of that sort is seldom if ever mentioned, in 1956—much less straight lust, a sense of sexual deprivation.

Cathy has brought along a bottle of Irish whiskey. "Actually a contribution from a friend of mine," she explains, her mouth small and ironic. And her quick glance at Megan admits that "friend" does mean lover. The glance though also says that she does not want to talk about him, not now, and maybe never.

They have drinks on the rickety porch, seated on hard warped and rusted aluminum chairs; they watch the big horses who now lumber playfully, ludicrously, in the summer dusk, among the flowers near the river. And they talk about money.

"It's very tempting," says Megan, who has been speaking of the offer from Barbara Blumenthal. "I could end up rich. Biff says Barbara is really rich, although I must say she doesn't look it. But somewhere along the line I picked up some puritanical prejudice against richness. I thought good people were poor. Which probably is true."

"Some of us Christians tend to believe that," says Cathy, with her small smile.

"Yes, that too." Megan is quiet, musing, before she goes on. "And all that exposure to Lavinia certainly had its effect. Not to mention Henry James. I got the idea that being rich was a sort of state of grace, only all right if you didn't work for it. If you have money at all you're supposed to have inherited it."

Cathy laughs. "But you're tempted."

"I really am. The truth is, I'm so tired of being broke, and that stupid old room, and old clothes. And New York, Lord, it's so full of things to buy, it's so tempting."

"Even San Francisco is, these days. Not that I get up there much." Cathy's tone is level, hard to read.

After a small pause Megan says, "I'm very glad we came here. It's so beautiful. And look at those silly horses."

"They think they're elephants."

They laugh, and just at that moment the horses become quite still, as though suddenly self-conscious.

Cathy laughs again. "Can they possibly have heard us, do you think?"

"Well, maybe they're especially sensitive? They felt something?"

Although Cathy is appreciably more relaxed now, with the drinks and the foolish familiar talk, to Megan she still looks and seems not well. In repose her face is pinched and sad. And it is still impossible to ask her what is wrong.

Megan wonders about the donor of the Irish whiskey, who is

presumably Cathy's lover. And it comes to her that, of course, Cathy must be involved with a man who is married. No wonder she is upset, what a mess for Cathy to be in. Megan has seen several New York friends through such affairs, lonely girls in offices, and she thinks, Oh, poor Cathy, to go from Phil-Flash to a sleazy arrangement like that. Oh, how unfair.

They have more drinks; they decide to have dinner in the Inn's dining room, not many yards away.

In the candlelight, at their small window table, Cathy looks even worse, so that at last Megan is unable not to say, "Cathy, you just don't look awfully well. You're okay?"

Cathy gulps at her wine, then quite deliberately she puts down the glass. She does not quite look at Megan as she says, "It's a slight case of being pregnant, I'm afraid."

"*Oh.*" Megan in her turn gulps down some more wine. The baked potato on her plate looks suddenly unsightly, all packed with sour cream and chives—and the rare beef looks painted, something unnatural.

"And, as a Catholic," continues Cathy, in her high, thin voice, "I can't even consider an abortion. Besides, it's too late."

Much more wine will make her drunk, Megan knows, if she doesn't eat; on the other hand, why not get drunk? She asks, "Do you know what you're going to do?"

They are sitting next to what has been the same view of meadow and river, the sea, that they saw from their cabin, but now the dark has blotted everything out. If the horses still are there they are invisible. But through the night air, through the just-opened window there comes a heavy sound of waves, pounding the sand. Megan shivers, thinking of so much water, the sea, the cold.

"I'm, uh, going to a place in Colorado, when it's time," says Cathy. "People who, uh, place them."

"Oh, Cathy. Jesus."

"Precisely." A wan smile.

Megan then asks, "The friend who gave you the Irish, uh, you still see him?"

"Oh *yes*."

That emphatic word says almost everything to Megan; saying it, Cathy has looked almost happy.

And so Megan is compelled to ask, "But Cathy, couldn't you somehow get married, or live together? All of you? Almost everyone can get a divorce these days, somehow." Tears of earnestness well up in her eyes; she is getting drunk.

Cathy looks at her. "You haven't guessed what's wrong?"

"He's married, I guess. His wife is sick, or crazy? Mrs. Rochester, locked up?"

Oh, if it were only that, is what Cathy's faint smile implies, as in a high dry voice what she actually says is, "He's a priest."

In all her thirty-year life, this is the single most shocking sentence (so far) that Megan has ever heard; her mind balks at it, her imagination stops. She closes her eyes, sees long black skirts, naked male legs. A *priest*.

Cathy is saying. "I thought you would have figured that out."

"No, I would never have thought of a priest. Everything else, but not that. For one thing, I've never even met a priest."

For some reason this last remark strikes both of them, Cathy and Megan, as being extremely funny. In a soft, hysterical way they begin to giggle; they laugh until tears run down their faces.

And that is the sum of the conversation that weekend, between Megan and Cathy on the subject of Cathy's "friend." The priest.

26

By 1960, Megan has been associated with Barbara Blumenthal for just over three years, and she is earning well over five times what she did at the publishing house. She is sometimes dizzy with all the money that she now has; having so much within her reach, such a lot of choices, makes her even greedier, she finds. She considers the proverbial greed of the very rich, and believes it to be true, even if the *riche* is very *nouveau*, as in her case, and by most standards not really rich at all.

Taking Barbara's advice, she has put a lot of money into Xerox, but that money only earns more money, giving Megan more choices, more possibilities.

She would like to send money to her parents. She hinted at this, and was roundly, almost angrily, turned down by Florence. And so instead she sends them "things," coats and dresses for her mother (does Florence wear them? She never says). A stereo.

Megan has discovered, though, one source of financial pleasure so intense that it troubles her, which is the pleasure she derives from handling her bankbooks. She keeps that information meticulously up to date, immaculately accurate: her checking and savings accounts, records of stock transactions. She even keeps track of her cash on hand, the amounts of money in her purse, in two separate drawers in her bedroom. All that adding and counting takes up a lot of time, which Megan *enjoys*, terrifically enjoys, and that enjoyment strikes her as highly suspect. If she heard it described as a habit, a secret pleasure of someone else's, she would find it repugnant. Obscene.

But on the whole it has worked out extremely well, the association between Megan and Barbara Blumenthal. As never-married Megan has sometimes thought, they are rather like a good marriage; they complement each other, in the way of some married couples. Barbara, although basically a very kind person, tends to be brusque; she can't help it, she is simply not "good with people." She is perhaps good only with her husband; she has been married to Norman, a corporation lawyer, since high school, and they seem to get along well. Barbara is at her best with contracts, figures, percentages, whereas Megan can handle money only in a private way.

Megan, on the other hand, *is* good with people, she finds. She is tactful, she manages to make both writers and editors feel sufficiently important and admired. Everyone likes her, which makes Megan almost as dizzy as being rich does, so unaccustomed is she to anything like large-scale popularity.

"*You* talk to her," Barbara will say, clutching at her straw-dry blond, uncontrollable hair, gulping smoke from her cigarette: the secretary, paper-thin Leslie DuVal, has just announced that Jane Anne Johns is on the phone, and Jane Anne is *upset*.

Soothingly, but with a sound of honesty, Megan will come on the line. "Jane Anne, you're absolutely right, they did say they'd get back to us this week. I'll call them the minute we hang up. No, I'm not at all worried that they won't like it. If they don't it only means we can go somewhere else with it, and in the long run I'm sure you'll be much happier."

And Jane Anne Johns, a Gothic novelist, calms down. She loves to talk to Megan. She is a very nice, now very old woman, with blue rinsed hair and a French château in Miami. She is given to diamonds and orchids and white mink coats. She is a great success. Her novels are consummate trash, a fact Megan tries not to think about; she is thankful that she does not have to read them, she only sells them, serialized, to magazines. Barbara handles the book and movie and TV contracts, and presumably she has read the books, although Megan seriously doubts that she bothers anymore.

"Ah Megan, you're great," sighs overweight Barbara, as Megan hangs up the phone—smiling Megan, successful (again) with Jane Anne. "Let's face it," Barbara goes on, "how could we pay the rent without Jane Anne? Megan, if you run off and get married I'll shoot myself," and she laughs, in her hoarse, barking way.

This is an old joke between them, Barbara's joke, actually, and Megan has worked it out that Barbara would not make the joke if she, Barbara, thought there were even a chance that Megan would leave her to get married. And, Megan has further concluded, Barbara herself is quite unconscious of her own certainty as to Megan's matrimonial prospects; she is just making a tired joke and at the same time telling the truth, that she does not want Megan to leave.

But, although there is certainly no one whom Megan wants to marry, Barbara's assumption is a small needling irritation to Megan;

is she so clearly unmarriageable? She knows better, of course, than to make the old connection between unmarriageable and unattractive. Still. And then it occurs to her that perhaps she is perceived as unmarriageable for the simple reason that she does not wish to marry? She would like to think that this is true, and it sounds quite true, to her.

Leslie, the secretary, does not seem to share Barbara's cloistered view of Megan, though. She announces phone calls for Megan, when they are from men, with a thin, derisive smile, as though to say, Of course I know what you're up to, with your friends, even if you never confide in me. Leslie is given to long conversations about her own life. Megan believes that Leslie sees her, Megan, as an essentially nonserious person. And very likely Leslie, who is ambitious, hopes that Megan *will* leave, married or not. In any case, it is with particular derision that Leslie announces, one August afternoon, that a George Wharton is on the line, for Megan.

Incredibly enough, as she later thinks of it, for a moment Megan is not entirely sure who that is. Then, largely from sheer surprise, she gasps into the phone, "Oh, *George*," in what must have sounded very much like her old tone, with him. She has undoubtedly given an impression of much warmer enthusiasm than in fact she feels, both to George and to her audience, Barbara and Leslie.

She then hears an embarrassed laugh from George, on the other end of the line, and she realizes that it would have been better if she had told the truth: For a minute I didn't know who you were.

"You sound so, uh, like yourself," he tells her. "I, uh, got your number from Lavinia."

"Oh, of course." And of course it was Lavinia who told Megan a few years back that George's wife Connie had left him, and that she, Connie, had a crush on Henry Stuyvesant. And Lavinia had further said that George had moved from Mass. General Hospital to Columbia-Presbyterian. And how natural, Megan now thinks, that George should be a friend of Lavinia and Potter's. Rich people always seem to know each other.

"I don't suppose, could you possibly, uh, be free for dinner?" George asks.

"Oh, I'd love that. Terrific." Megan hears her own voice, sounding as she must have sounded fifteen years or so ago, when she so warmly, eagerly rushed out to him; whereas now, as she thinks of it, she would actually much rather stay at home and read manuscripts, as she had planned to do. As she usually does, these days.

"You look a little rattled," is Barbara's comment, as Megan leaves the phone.

"Well, it's just an old friend. Whom I'm not sure I especially want to see. But when I was sixteen I was out of my mind about him. He changed my whole life."

Barbara laughs, and coughs. "You must have changed quite a lot. That doesn't even sound like you. Out of your mind, my sane old Meg?"

"I have changed a lot."

Instead of moving uptown, which with a job in the East Fifties might have seemed more logical, newly prosperous Megan has simply moved downstairs, to a fairly large apartment in her same old building on West 12th Street. She now occupies a long narrow space; "Procrustean, it must be," Biff has remarked. "It's making you so thin!" Her living room faces the street; she has a small, rarely used dining room, a kitchen, bath, rear bedroom. The bedroom has of course the view that she has always had, more or less, when she lived upstairs, and partly for that reason, perhaps, she tends to spend most of her time there. Her bedroom is where she works or reads, looking out to the same old fire escape, same trees.

She likes her living room least; it is overcrowded and cluttered, and always a mess. Her fault, of course, but she cannot seem to clear it up, nor can she somehow bring herself to hire someone, a maid, to clean up her messiness. Tonight, though, as she surveys the disordered room in which she will soon receive George Wharton, she feels an annoyance with herself for that foolish scruple: she is busy, she needs a cleaning person, other people need jobs. Too late, in a frantic way she begins to pile the coffee table's books and magazines into tidy stacks, to put her records back into their jackets, on their shelf; but it is hopeless.

Hopeless, too, is a decision what to wear. A wool dress, or velvet pants? Her closets now bulge with clothes, shelves of sweaters, rows of shoes. However, standing there in her bedroom after her bath, towel-wrapped, expensively scented, Megan recognizes that she is suddenly no longer a successful working woman. She has been transformed back into a fat young girl from the provinces with all the wrong clothes, and a violent mania for a young man who will never introduce her to his parents, or teach her to sail, or to "clam."

In an angry, impatient way she snaps herself into some heavy black lace; she pulls up red velvet pants, a red silk shirt, as she thinks, But I look like a flag. A red flag.

The doorbell rings on time, and Megan opens the door to a tall thin gray person, who frowns slightly as he says to her, "Is Megan—?" in a quickly familiar, flat New England voice. He then grins and says, "By God! I wouldn't have recognized you, you've got so, so—"

"Thin?" Megan helps him out. But perhaps he had not meant simply thin? Had he, conceivably, meant beautiful, or rich? Very likely not—just thin.

"Yes, thin," George tells her. "But you look, uh, *great*."

In an awkward way they grasp at each other's arms; their faces bump together in what was probably intended as a kiss.

Stepping back Megan asks, "Well, won't you have a drink? What can I get you?" Should she have remembered what he drank?

"Uh, how are you fixed for beer?"

Beer is the one thing that Megan does not have. She thinks it is fattening, and also she does not know anyone who drinks beer, certainly not Biff, who is the person most often there for drinks.

But of course, beer is what George always drank, and she along with him, in those Oxford Grill days, although she never really liked it much. Megan would have assumed that beer was a taste that most grown-ups got over; surely George might have taken to

Scotch, or gin? "I'm really sorry," she lies. "Would you settle for champagne?" That was supposed to be funny, but as she says it she realizes that it was not.

"Actually I never touch the stuff. Could I have a Scotch, if that's easy?"

"Oh, of course." Going off for the Scotch, Megan is thinking several things at once: one, that really rich people often don't like champagne—it's the originally poor, like herself and Biff, who think it's a wonderful drink. Or people in B movies. She is also thinking that it is going to be a very difficult evening.

She is more than right about the difficulty of the evening. Over drinks, his Scotch and her sugarless old-fashioned, they first discuss his work at Columbia-Presbyterian. He tells her a couple of grisly medical jokes. Of his colleagues there he says, "A really great bunch of guys." He tells her about his recent trip to Scotland, with some of those great guys, for salmon fishing and golf; there seems to have been a medical meeting thrown in, somehow. His summer plans include all the weekends he can arrange for on the Cape, where his parents still live, and thrive. "They're pretty old-timers now but in great shape, and really game. Dad can still outsail me. You met them, didn't you, uh, back then?"

"No, I didn't. Actually."

"Really? I thought you had."

He asks a question about her work, and Megan tells him a couple of very short anecdotes about writers he has heard of (anyone would have).

They agree on the beauty of Amy, daughter of Lavinia and Potter.

They do not talk about Connie, not at all, although surely George must know that Megan knows something of that chapter in his history?

Nor do they reminisce, in any way, about their own past connection, whatever it was. And Megan inwardly concludes that there is not much to say about it: what can you make of some beery evenings that later included a lot of sexual mauling? She can vividly remember, still, the hardness of the riverbank where they lay and thrashed about, under some bridge, in the cold. The dirt and grass stains on her clothes; she remembers all that, and how she thought of him with such passionate intensity, all the time.

He looks rather badly, George does, a gray ghost of the dashing boy she knew. His skin, always tan from all that sailing, is grayish white, and his blue eyes have also grayed. All his facial muscles seem to have tightened up, and the skin is tight across his bony nose, his big jaw. In that taut face his teeth look too large—or, perhaps this is how he has always looked, a heavy-jawed, rather large-nosed man, whom she perceived as radiantly handsome?

Their conversation is in fact so sketchy, so impersonal that for a moment Megan crazily wonders if he is really sure who she is. Does he know just when and where he knew her?

But then he asks an almost personal question. "Do you ever go back there to, uh, California? To see your parents?"

"I did go about four years ago, in fact. To see my parents and a college friend of mine who lives out there now. Cathy Barnes. I guess you never met her."

"Uh, I guess not. And actually I don't think I met your parents."

"No, you didn't." Moved then by an impulse which she does not entirely understand—perhaps just to get his attention?—Megan decides to tell George the story of Cathy. "It was quite an extraordinary visit, all around," she begins, and then plunges ahead. "Cathy and I went to Carmel together," she says, in a rush, "and she told me that she was pregnant. She looked awful."

Giving some evidence of attention, George comments, "Not married, I suppose."

Why does he suppose that? Megan wonders. Am I the sort of person, in his mind, whose unmarried friends would turn up pregnant? Quite probably; no wonder I didn't meet his parents— and he's quite right, of course. She looks at him. "No, she wasn't married. But she's a Catholic, and so, no abortion. And then it turned out that the father of the baby is a priest."

George is frowning—less from shock, Megan sees (and surely she had meant to shock him?) than from sheer distaste: she has told him something quite unpleasant, involving people he would not at all care to know. "Well, priests," he mutters.

Almost angrily, Megan continues. "She was going to give the baby up for adoption, it was all settled, and then a couple of months after that she wrote me that she'd decided to keep it. I thought that was really brave. And she did keep him. A little boy, Stephen. They live in San Francisco. She's an economist with some firm out there, and her mother moved out to live with them. I guess she mostly takes care of the baby. Little boy."

George has not been listening quite, but then with an effort he brings himself back, to ask, "What happened to the priest?"

"I don't know. She never mentions him. She never did mention him, actually. Would you like another drink?"

"Uh, well, yes. I would."

Over the next drink they talk about Adam Marr, who by now is so public a figure, so famous, that everyone knows almost everything he does. He has divorced beautiful black Sheila and married a very tall Chinese lady, Fusai, who in two years has already borne him two children. He is frequently in gossip columns, being given to well-publicized drunken fights, as well as to multiple affairs. "The man's liver will wear out before he's fifty," is George's prediction.

Megan has just remembered a minor coincidence. "Actually his former wife is an intern at your hospital," she tells George. "Do you know her, Janet Marr? Dr. Janet Cohen Marr?"

"We've got quite a lot of interns, but not too many of them ladies. Naturally. But I think I do remember a Janet Marr, though. Rather on the small side, and rather dark? Uh, Jewish?"

"Yes, she is small and dark. And Jewish."

"Considered very able, I believe. Well, where would we be without the Jews? In medicine, I mean. And the Scots, of course."

Megan sighs. "I have no idea."

"So, our Dr. Marr used to be married to that playwright fellow. Well, poor little woman."

He has said this so feelingly that Megan laughs, as she thinks how Janet would dislike hearing herself so described. Poor little woman indeed.

But there must be, mustn't there? something behind this mask of silliness and pomposity that George presents. Megan senses that he is extremely shy, all hidden.

Perhaps for that reason, kindliness toward him, at a certain point she says, "Look, everything's so crowded at this hour, in restaurants. We'd have to wait. Suppose I scramble some eggs? And there's cheese, and onions. Unless you're terrifically hungry?"

George looks grateful, almost happy; Megan hopes that this is not only because, as she now remembers, he is rather tight. Happily he next says, "But you'll let me get some wine? Otherwise that sounds terrific. It really does. But I insist on the wine."

Megan directs him to the wine shop on 8th Street, and in his absence she peels and slices onions and potatoes; she is working toward an Italian omelette that Biff has taught her.

George returns with a good Beaujolais, as Megan is beating up the eggs. She has forgotten to put on an apron. "This is awfully good of you," says George, with more feeling than he has revealed all evening. "Restaurants, they all seem so much alike. You can get so tired."

She asks, "You eat out a lot?"

"Well, yes I do, since—" And that unfilled blank is his first and only reference to the departure of his wife.

A bit of egg has of course spattered onto Megan's red silk shirt, but nevertheless, over dinner George remarks, "I must say, you are looking really great. First-rate," and then he looks down, as though he has gone too far, conversationally.

Megan understands then that she was silly not to have recognized before, which is that later they will (of course: what else has all this been about?) go to bed together. What else, besides sex, did they have in common, ever? George has known this all along; very likely this knowledge has been one factor in his shyness.

And now, shy herself, Megan looks across at him; for a split second their glances lock, before he looks down, and away.

But their going to bed will be all wrong, Megan knows. It is in every sense too late for that, and besides, she does not really want to.

. . .

George helps her clean up the kitchen. "You're getting that terrific blouse all wet," he accurately notes.

Obediently she ties a dishcloth around her neck.

George says, "I would give anything not to have to go home right now," and he puts his arms around her.

His words had less the sound of a question than of a plea, and so it is from sheer kindness that Megan tells him, "Well, you really don't."

She was right, though, that it would be a mistake. Nothing works, at all.

In the concealing dark, George tells her, "Well, uh, I guess I'm not quite as fit as I thought I was."

"George, please don't worry. It's okay." Megan herself is exhausted with the efforts she has made in "helping" him, lengthy and unavailing.

He asks, "But can I see you again? I'd really like to take you out."

Megan kisses his mouth, considerately holding her body away from his—the scene of his failure. She says, "Of course."

"Actually, I'm probably more tired than I think. In fact, if you don't mind, I think I'll just push on home. Get some rest." All this has come out in a jerky rush.

Relieved (breakfast with George would have been as impossible as sex with him turned out to be), Megan tells him, "Of course." Not saying, In fact I'm really just as tired as you are. Intending a small joke, she then asks, "You'll forgive my not seeing you to the door?"

"Oh, absolutely. You mustn't think of it. But can I, uh, get you anything?"

"No. But thanks."

Very hurriedly he dresses, and after an awkward, hurried kiss he is gone.

· · ·

Waiting for sleep, as she lies there Megan reflects that if the situation had been somehow reversed, if it had been she, a woman, who had failed to respond in a sexual way to a man, in bed, he would very likely have chosen not to see her again, and almost surely he would not have worried about the effect of that decision on her ego, her "feelings."

But as it is, Megan feels that for the sake of George's male ego she will have to see him again, and she believes that most women would react in just that way.

And what does this mean, she wonders? Are women nicer than men? stronger, more protective? Although she stays awake, unwillingly, for hours, Megan comes to no conclusions.

27

"Do you know, we haven't seen that nice Father Mallory since he dropped in that afternoon, and it was Stephen's second birthday?" remarks Cathy's mother, with a look up from her knitting.

"I guess that's right." Cathy does not look up from her book.

"Such a nice person. I always thought we should have asked him for dinner. He took a real interest in Stephen, I thought."

Cathy does not answer, but this is not in itself unusual; many of her mother's small remarks, her little questions float out into the space between them, like soap bubbles, in the small square living room. Once Stephen is in bed Cathy has to use the time for her reading, journals of economics, mostly; her mother, widowed Mrs. Barnes, understands that, but she is by nature a chatty person, small and warm-spirited, a plump little sparrow of a woman, and sometimes things come to her mind and she says them aloud. Now she sighs and says, "I guess I miss knowing priests in a social way. You know we always did, back home."

Cathy looks up from her book. "Father Mallory has left the

priesthood, someone told me," she says in her usual dry voice, as though this were not a remarkable statement.

Mrs. Barnes stops her knitting. "Well! I know a lot of them are these days, but it always seems so—so surprising, especially someone you've met. And he seemed so—so—"

"I believe he's getting married," brings out Cathy, relentlessly.

"Getting married! Well! Well, I suppose that's a reason to stop being a priest, all right." Mrs. Barnes tries to laugh.

"I guess it is." Cathy closes her book. "I think I'll go up to bed."

"That's right, darling. You look really tired tonight."

Cathy and her mother and Stephen, now four, live in a small house in the Richmond district of San Francisco, an unfashionable and vast area of mostly older houses, in the western segment of the city. Theirs is a cottage, with an actual white picket fence around it, which Cathy, in her sardonic way, finds quite funny. "I'm living with my bastard son, surrounded by white pickets," she once wrote to Megan. But the house has a nice yard for Stephen and Stephen's dog, Arrow, and Stephen goes to a local public kindergarten, quite nearby. Mrs. Barnes markets and cooks and cleans; sometimes she has a neighbor in for a cup of coffee, during the day. Her maiden name was Mulcahy, and that is the name that Cathy chose for Stephen; he was christened Stephen Mulcahy. The neighbors are told that Mr. Mulcahy, Cathy's husband, died in some unspecified sad way; they assume some form of cancer, and that is what Stephen has been and will continue to be told: his father is dead.

Mrs. Barnes was told, and believes, that Cathy had a love affair, became pregnant, and (a good Catholic girl) she chose to keep the child. And how Mrs. Barnes rejoices that Cathy made that choice! She is crazy about Stephen, a winsome, handsome, dark-haired child. Her private idea is that the man was married; an extremely reticent family, she and her daughter do not discuss intimate matters, no more than she and her husband ever did; she would not have expected details. She would never, literally never in a million years have dreamed of a priest as the father of her grandson, any more than at first Megan would have, as the lover of her friend.

Megan has been instructed by Cathy to present the same story of the departed lover to Lavinia and to Peg; it is always possible that one of them might show up in San Francisco. "Everyone seems to, sooner or later," Cathy remarks. "And I can't exactly pass off Stephen as just some kid I'm taking care of."

Cathy Barnes and Thomas Mallory have not been lovers since Stephen's birth, or since a couple of months before.

Heavily pregnant, infinitely weary, she told him, "I can't. Not now. Probably not anymore. Ever."

"But I love you more than ever. You're more beautiful." Even he could see that actually Cathy looked terrible, swollen and blotched, she was not in fact more beautiful, but he did love her more. He was besotted with love for her, and crazed with guilt and anguish. "I'll do anything," he said wildly, but meaning it. "I'll, uh, *leave*—leave the priesthood. I mean, quit. Not be a priest. I could teach. We could get married."

"No." With her small dark eyes Cathy regarded him coldly, and clearly.

In a low, defeated voice he asked her, "Can I see the child?"

"I'll see." Her regard was pitiless (he felt). She added, "There's my mother to think about."

He left, and she burst into tears.

The birth of Stephen (Mulcahy) in January 1957 was prolonged, and difficult. At some point, during her fourteen hours of labor, a kindly, very likely Irish, red-haired nurse said to Cathy, "Your priest has stopped by to see you. Now, isn't that thoughtful?"

"I don't want to see him."

The nurse registered disbelief: no one refuses to see her priest. "But, a minute?"

"No."

.   .   .

Mrs. Barnes arrived the following day, in time to do everything that Cathy had neglected to do, in terms of readying the nursery for Stephen (which turned out to be quite a lot), and in time to bring them home from the hospital, her daughter and her new grandson, Stephen Mulcahy.

Stephen, as babies go, was an easy baby—much easier, Mrs. Barnes often exclaimed, than Cathy had been. He finished off his bottles at a satisfying rate, and he slept a lot, soon adjusting to an all-night sleep schedule which made it easy for Cathy to go back to work, when he was six weeks old.

What Cathy mentioned to no one, certainly not to her mother, was what she described to herself as a severe postpartum depression. She lay awake, ravaged with anguish, nameless grief, a sweet, piercing agony. A wild sense of loss, incomprehensible, relentless. Postpartum depression. But what had she lost, exactly?

"I could be the priest who comes for tea, or a drink, for the Lord's sake," says Thomas—Father Mallory. "I'm good at that. I do it all the time. Your mother will love me."

"I know she would. I'm just not sure I could stand it," Cathy told him. "Acting all that out. And Stephen."

"How is he? What's he like?"

"He's a good baby. I guess. Nice-looking. Dark."

"I was dark," says white-haired Thomas.

Even though Stephen was "good," and apparently content (if a little solemn, for a baby), Cathy sometimes thought, and continued to think, that she should have had him placed as she originally planned to, with some nice, merry, loving couple, maybe in a nice suburb, like Palo Alto, or Menlo Park. She could have given him to a nice young woman who would stay home and play with him all day, and in a couple of years they would adopt a younger brother for Stephen—or perhaps the fact of Stephen would overcome the young woman's infertility problem; Cathy had read that this often happened. Stephen could have lots of brothers, sisters, a whole family of kids.

Whereas she, Cathy, must be chaste for the rest of her life. Not to kiss any man again. No sexual joy.

This is absolutely clear to her, a moral command.

Thomas Mallory, Father Mallory, came for tea, for drinks several times; and Mrs. Barnes loved him and he loved Stephen, and Cathy could not bear the sight of any of this love. Watching those three people, all of whom in separate ways she herself loved, passionately—her mother, Stephen, and Thomas—watching them as they warmed to each other turned Cathy as cold and stiff as cement; she felt herself an upright cement slab—as her mother giggled and Thomas laughed and Stephen turned in a questioning way toward her, Cathy, his mother.

"Such an interesting man," commented her mother, later on. "It's nice to see priests sometimes, in a social way. And I'm sure they get lonely too."

Cathy made an unfathomable sound, but her mother was used to such noncomments; her husband, Cathy's father, had made the same sound quite often, even when she had said something important.

"And he's so nice with Stephen," Mrs. Barnes went on.

"I cannot stand it," Cathy said to Thomas. "It's that simple."

"But—"

Extreme suffering was apparent in his voice, and in all the lines of his face, and in the fact that he could not speak of it. Moved, despite herself, despite other feelings and judgments, Cathy next thought: I cannot do this to him, it is too unkind. Inhuman. She said, "My mother really liked you. Why don't you go by when I'm not there?" Painfully adding, "See Stephen."

His eyes blurred. "But not you."

"No."

Cathy bore that arrangement for as long as she could: coming home to hear that Father Mallory had been there for tea, for a drink, had brought a toy for Stephen. She bore all that, when it happened, and also bore the dread that it might; on any given evening her mother might say, "Well, we had a delightful visitor today!"

And then there was the more awful possibility that he would still be there when she got home; he would have managed to "forget" the time, in order to see her. For Cathy assumed, always, that their mutual deprivation was shared. That he, like herself, lay wracked with longing, alone.

On Stephen's second birthday, a Tuesday, Cathy came home early to hear that she had just missed Father Mallory, who had seemed to be in more of a hurry than usual.

Mrs. Barnes had invited some five or six neighborhood children in for cake and ice cream; she had bought soap bubble kits, little jars of liquid with blow-through rings on top. The children were enchanted, the small house was full of the shimmering, translucent spheres. As Cathy thought, This is really too much for me, his just having been here, having just seen what I now see. He has just seen Stephen, that day in a blue starched suit that his grandmother had not been able to resist, at the City of Paris.

A few days later Cathy called him. Father Mallory.

His jaunty voice was the first surprise. "Oh, I'm quite fine," he told her. "I'm glad you called. I've been wanting to talk to you."

With an effort Cathy made her noncommittal sound.

He seemed to breathe deeply. "I wish I could see you," he said. "To tell you—I am leaving the Church, the priesthood. I mean I've left." He sighed. "I don't think I ever had the true vocation." He sighed again, and seemed to brace himself. "And there's someone I want to marry."

Shock at once penetrated each cell of Cathy's being, became ice in her veins. She barely stopped herself from crying out, in sheer disbelief. She was choked by a welter of emotions which she could not at that moment have sorted out, or named.

"It was being with you, loving you, and then Stephen," Thomas Mallory ran on, "that showed me the sort of life I was meant to have. Next year I'll be fifty, and it's not too late. And Mary wants children too. I hope someday that you—that I—"

But Cathy had hung up.

And, after the night when her mother remarked on not seeing Father Mallory since Stephen's second birthday, and Cathy said that she had heard he was getting married, Cathy never mentioned Thomas Mallory again, to anyone, until she died.

Cathy thinks of Megan fairly often, and sometimes she writes, although she often observes herself telling Megan that she has not much to say. But how can she write to Megan about Stephen's progress at nursery school, kindergarten, first grade, or her own progress in the mammoth superstructure of corporation taxes?

However, Megan turns up in her dreams (as Thomas Mallory never does). In some dreams, even, she, Cathy, seems to have turned into Megan. In those dreams she is a violently sexual Megan; in one, she Megan-Cathy has "sexual congress" with a handsome Negro trombone player (Megan used to mention one named Jackson Clay, and Cathy always assumed that they were lovers; in an interested way she has followed his career). The violence and the vividness of that dream were troublesome, embarrassing. Vicarious sex, though, as far as she knows is not a sin.

Cathy has, in effect, no social life. She and her mother do not go out together; it would somehow seem silly, getting a baby-sitter to go to a movie with your mother. Occasionally they will take Stephen to the zoo, or to Ocean Beach, or to some restaurant in Chinatown. Or Cathy will go out to dinner and a movie with some other young working woman. She has no intimate friends, in the sense that she and Megan were intimate, but she knows a few women, about her age or a little older, who are perfectly okay for a short evening out. Some drinks, a little light talk. None of them is especially interesting; there is no one whom Megan, for example, would want to know (in Cathy's imaginings all Megan's New York friends are exceptional people).

Cathy lives in a state of peaceful resignation. She puts almost all her money in a bank, for Stephen. It is rather as though, she thinks, she were her mother's husband; she and her mother are like an old married couple, with an accidental but welcome late-life child.

Mrs. Barnes, though, is a highly social being; she magnetizes people—most recently, a widower neighbor, a retired Italian florist, Mr. Piscetti, who likes to go dancing in the Lochinvar Room, at the Mark Hopkins Hotel, a place that Cathy has tried and failed to imagine.

"I am baby-sitting for my mother, actually, who is out dancing at the Lochinvar Room," she writes to Megan. "Have you ever been there? My mother admits it's a little silly. There is something called the Kiltie Bar, and they wear funny clothes, but she likes the band, and she likes to dance. She likes Mr. Piscetti. I hope you think this is funny? I hope I do?"

28

The house in which Peg and three other civil rights workers are lodged, in the summer of 1964, is just outside a small town called Edenborough, in the hills of north Georgia. It belongs to an old couple named Sawyer, Nora and Clyde. The Sawyers are intensely religious, nominally Presbyterians, but what they actually practice is their own; it includes total abstinence from alcohol and cigarettes (their views on sex are not known), and a militant abhorrence of social inequities, legal or economic, especially those due to color of skin. Nigger lovers, they are sometimes locally called, and that is accurate; they are.

Thus, Nora and Clyde provide comfortable lodgings and generous meals to Movement workers, who come that summer to register Negro voters. But no one can smoke or drink on the premises. The Sawyers are nice about it, but very clear: "We don't hold with drinking anything alcoholic, and so if you young people

can just refrain while you're stopping with us, we'd take it kindly."
They are nice people, both of them rather gray, and thin; they look
somewhat alike, as is said to happen in cases of unusual com-
patibility. They share a deceptive look of frailty.

In their early years, in the thirties, just out of Black Mountain
College, the Sawyers built this house themselves. It is simply
constructed, large and square, two stories and an attic. It sits on
a hilltop, in a grove of oak and pine, overlooking a valley of green
cornfields, in the summer, and a brighter green thick border of a
creek. It looks west to other hills, all gently rounded, green.
Because of this view, which is invariably, richly beautiful, newly
so in each changing season, the Sawyers' final addition to their
house was a long, broad porch, with a sloping green-shingled roof,
now overgrown with thick wisteria vines—and just now, in mid-
summer, overhung with lavender blossoms, hanging heavily, falling
finally to the drying grass below.

Coming in late from work, that August, Peg is exhausted to the
marrow of her bones from so much walking, or driving in a jeep
over perilously rutted roads; and her brain is dulled from so much
talking. And sometimes she is afraid. But always she is struck by
the peacefulness of that house; its restful lack of clutter (as opposed
to the "plantation" house, in Midland, where she still lives) is
balm to her soul, she loves its bareness. It is even miraculously cool,
that house, on most of the sultry, heavy summer nights, as though
an actual kindly god loved the Sawyers, and sent winds to their
house. Or, more plausibly, by some fortunate accident the house
is situated so that it catches any possible passing breeze.

Peg is always grateful for the quiet house, for her narrow but
private room, in the slanting attic, for the good meals and the light
cool breezes, all that; but sometimes she acutely needs (or believes
that she needs) a drink and a cigarette. Of course she feels guilty
about these baser needs, although the other workers seem to share
them; they are fortunately no more saintly than she is.

Down a white dirt road, about a quarter of a mile from the
Sawyers' house there stands (still, incredibly) an old tobacco barn:

a big square log cabin, chinked with mud, from whose high rafters the tobacco leaves once were hung to dry. The floor is dirt, red clay, and all around the big bare room are low, uneven stones, a primitive bench. The only windows are high up, near the eaves; through these openings the baking, drying sunlight used to enter, making motes and beams in the rising red clay dust. These days, or rather nights, the tobacco barn is where the guilty Movement workers sneak off for moonshine and cigarettes, appropriately enough: sooner or later everyone makes that joke about going out to the tobacco barn for a smoke.

No one knows whether or not the Sawyers know about this practice; the accepted, comforting theory is that they do but pretend that they do not.

Walking down that road alone, one black night that summer, Peg is especially tired, and fearful: this is the first of August, and three civil rights workers, in Mississippi, have been missing since June 22.

Peg has been out trying to register people to vote with a new friend, Vera, who is another worker. Vera too lives in the Sawyer house (as does Henry Stuyvesant: an as yet unknown coincidence). Vera is a social worker from Los Angeles, a Mexican; she is very dark, so dark that at first Peg took her to be Negro. She is very beautiful, Peg thinks, so proud and thin, with amazingly lashed eyes. All summer, on the streets of Edenborough, as she walks along with Vera, Peg has been aware of suspicion, an angry distrust from the town's street corner loiterers, the men and boys in dusty jeans, smoking thin cigars or pipes. Not talking much, just staring, unabashed. To Peg they look both stupid and dangerous, and even the women seem inimical, in their flowered dresses, their shielded, covert faces—even as they smile and say, "Hey, how you." Thin smiles, and cold bright eyes.

In a conscientious way Peg has given some thought to how she and Vera must appear to them, to these not-prosperous low-mountain Georgians, who have probably never been as far from home as Atlanta. These people would look at Peg and Vera, and they would see dark Vera, probably to their eyes a Negro, "cullud."

And herself, big white Peg, whose jeans no longer fit—she keeps losing weight, she is often too tired to eat, who has given up on her hair and just pulls it back with a rubber band.

Since late June, when those three workers disappeared in Mississippi, Peg has seen, or thought she has seen, even more suspicion on those pale guarded faces, as though she and Vera, connected to those who have disappeared, were dangerous themselves—as people might feel suspicious of the family members of persons dangerously ill. She and Vera are viewed as being where they do not belong; they are there to stir up trouble, and nothing good will come of it.

(And Vera is so sensitive, vulnerable, despite professional training; if anyone did anything to Vera, Peg would kill, would die for her. She loves Vera ferociously, as though Vera were Cornelia and Lavinia in one, and all Peg's daughters. She knows that there are several ugly names for what she feels about Vera, and she is determined that no one, least of all Vera, must ever know.)

Even in the outlying country cabins where the black people live, those small clapboard boxes raised up from the dirt on brick stilts—even out there, that day, Peg has been aware of more resistance, more possible hostility than usual. Innately polite, these country people always masked suspicion as a lack of interest. "I'm just not studying to vote," they would say, with warm, evasive smiles. Today, though, at three separate houses, all reached after miles and miles of impossibly rutted, narrow roads, Peg and Vera were summarily turned away. "We don't want to hear nothing 'bout that," they were told, just before the firm flat final closing of the door.

Now, on the hard white road, in the warm August night of no stars but strange white looming clouds, a night unnaturally still, Peg is scared. The sweet-smelling, ancient roadside privet could conceal anyone; and what better place for an ambush than the tobacco barn itself?

Sternly, Peg tells herself that this is very foolish indeed; for one thing she is simply not that important, to anyone. She also tells herself that she does not really need a cigarette or a drink. She could perfectly well, with perfect safety, turn around and go back to the big safe house behind her. Which she almost does.

She is alone because Vera said she was just too tired; she couldn't wait to go to bed. Another man, Charlie, who also lives at the Sawyers, has gone to Atlanta for a meeting of some sort. The most recent arrival in the house is someone named Henry Stuyvesant, whom Peg has barely met, and they have not talked at all. In any case, Peg is not sure at this moment where he is.

She and Vera were too late for dinner, and instead made sandwiches in the kitchen; one of the generous customs of the house is a constant supply of sandwich makings, sliced cold chicken and tomatoes, homemade mayonnaise and good crusty bread.

Henry Stuyvesant (what a silly name, Peg thinks) could be anywhere at all. He could in fact be out in the barn, where Peg is headed. Thinking of that possibility, Peg very much hopes not. He seems nice, but something about him terrifies her: he is so serious, so intent, with an air of seeing everything at once, and judging, probably. And so tall, taller than Cameron, even, thinner, more elegant. The possibility of Henry Stuyvesant is almost more scaring than that of being alone.

And there ahead of her is the century-old barn, on its lonely knoll, darker against the dark night sky. A staunch survivor. Its windows emit no sound, its face is blank.

There is a prearranged signal so that none of the workers will scare each other, nor be scared: three whistled notes, whip-poor-will. Peg does this now, standing outside in the thick sweet darkness, and as no one answers, she thinks, I just won't bother going in, looking for the jug of booze, bourbon that I surely do not need. I'll just have a quick cigarette, right here, right now.

But someone in white clothes, a white person, at that moment emerges from the barn's open front door, ghostly, in the shadows. For an instant Peg is frozen in panic, which then becomes more ordinary fear, actually shyness, as she sees that it is Henry Stuyvesant.

"Oh, *hi*," they say to each other, in much the same tone.

And then Henry says, "How very nice. I really wanted a drink but I was holding off. Wanting some company."

"Oh, me too," Peg says, feeling choked. But she follows him in, follows his white back into the cool shadowy room, the big space that is darker than the night. Big clumsy Peg, who at that moment wishes that she were anyone else at all.

The bourbon and a supply of paper cups are kept in a hollowed-out place under one of the long stone benches. Henry gets them out, as Peg, shaky-fingered, lights her cigarette, and sits down close to the door. As far from him as she can.

With a small flourish Henry hands her the half-filled paper cup; he says, "Well, cheers. I needed this. How about you?"

Is he smiling? In the darkness, she can't tell. Peg makes a sound that is intended as assent.

Very likely sensing her unease, Henry is quiet for a while; then, in a slow, undemanding way he begins to talk, almost as though to himself. He remarks on the similarities between this north Georgia countryside and Chapel Hill, where he teaches. The two areas are more alike than not, he says, and both of course are vastly unlike the New England countryside where he grew up. He then mentions Cambridge.

At which Peg, who is breathing more easily by now, can say, "Oh yes, Cambridge. I was there for four years. In school. I loved it."

At Radcliffe?

Yes.

Which gets them almost immediately to Lavinia. (Although, as Peg remarks later to Vera, you do not exactly expect to find a friend of Lavinia's doing civil rights work.)

"Oh yes," Peg now gasps, "I knew her very well. Or, I mean I spent a lot of time with her. She was the most beautiful girl around, I always thought. I mean, I sometimes thought we must have looked sort of funny together. Like some beautiful small white monkey and a big, uh, elephant."

"My so-called friends at prep school used to say I looked like a giraffe," Henry tells her. He is smiling—she can see him now.

"Oh, really?" Quickly seeing the accuracy of this (he does; he looks tall and awkward, and his eyes, like giraffes' eyes, are beautiful), Peg laughs, very much in the old jolly Peg way—although to herself it has the sound of someone else laughing, some ghost.

"In a way I sort of took care of her, I guess," she continues, speaking of Lavinia. "Mothering. I must have been practicing up to actually be a mother. And then I was supposed to be in her wedding but I was home having another baby."

Henry asks, "You have a lot of children?"

"Oh yes, four. But the oldest two, the twins, they're nineteen, and they're pretty nice girls, usually. I bribed them to help Cornelia so I could come here this summer, and I bribed Cornelia to stay with all of them for the summer. Cornelia's the, uh, maid." Two hundred dollars apiece for the girls, Candy and Carol, a crazy sum, she knows that perfectly well; Cameron would have a stroke if he found out. And even worse, from Cameron's point of view, two thousand to Cornelia, which he will never know about though. Especially since it will let Cornelia quit work in the fall, when Peg gets home, and go to the Teachers' College.

Peg has said none of this last to Henry, of course; she only thought of it, fleetingly. She now tries to go on about Lavinia. "They came to see us, Lavinia and Potter, a few years ago," she tells Henry, "and Lavinia was wonderful, and beautiful, and such a help. I had been sick, a nervous breakdown, I guess you'd call it. She was really nice, and we wrote letters, but some things I can't explain to her."

"Coming down here, for example," says Henry, in a quiet way.

"Well yes, exactly. Only for me it's up, not down. We live in Texas. Midland," she explains. She is thinking that because in this strange, still shadowy darkness Henry's face is still almost invisible to her, he is less frightening than he might be, if she could see him. What comes clearly across to her though is his niceness; he is nice and kind and intelligent, remarkably so. And Peg is not so foolish as to believe that everyone she meets in Georgia, everyone in the Movement, in "good works," is necessarily nice, or kind or even smart.

Out of some odd necessity, she now tries to explain further about Lavinia. "I don't mean to say that there's anything really wrong between us now," she tells him—but perhaps she is over-explaining, is talking to herself? "Although of course," she quickly continues, "she's so polite that even if there were something the matter I wouldn't know that there was, not necessarily. If you know what I mean." This has been a new thought, to Peg, the notion of the deceptiveness of Lavinia's "politeness."

Henry laughs, in an understanding way, and for no good reason it then flashes through Peg's mind that he and Lavinia could have been lovers, have had an affair. But then Peg thinks, Oh no, Lavinia would never do that, she would not sneak around.

(Does Lavinia like to, uh, "do it"? Peg has wondered about this of course; does she cry out, like women in D. H. Lawrence, a few other writers? Peg herself of course does not, she cannot, ever, something wrong. She is not at all sure what it would be that women would do together, but she thinks about it.)

In his quiet voice Henry asks, "Your husband didn't mind your coming here this summer?"

"Well, actually he did mind quite a lot." Peg is surprised to hear herself saying this, to a relative stranger. She is so surprised that she goes right on. "But a few years ago when I was sick, with my, uh, nervous breakdown, I was really off my nut, if you want to know the truth. And that made him a little afraid of me, if you see what I mean."

Henry does see; she can tell that from the quality of his listening, his silence, his murmured, Oh.

"Also, this is a funny thing to say," Peg goes on, "but I have more money than he does. My family, I mean. And when I got to be thirty my trust fund went up a lot, to more than he makes, even in oil. Although of course he is going to be very rich. But now he thinks that my money makes me a powerful person. Which must be the whole point, don't you think?" She gives a sudden big jolly-Peg laugh, echoing in the lofty barn, in the silent dark.

Henry laughs too, but in a surprisingly sad way. "Well, I'm sure it beats being poor."

"Oh, God, of course. Honestly, I'm not that silly. I know you have to have money," she tells him piously. "I only meant that money gives me a kind of, uh, hollow power over Cameron, my husband." This need of hers to overexplain things, in an apologetic way, is something that Peg and her doctor have discussed, but it is still very hard for her not to, sometimes.

The oddity of being with Henry, so comfortably, as easily as old friends, or cousins, then strikes Peg with such force that she stops talking. (For one thing, nonsexual friendships between men and women were so very rare, in those days.) Peg, the big old cow, and dark, distinguished Henry. But, she next thinks, that is exactly the point. If I were good-looking, pretty, we would not be here like this. Henry would have to make a pass at me, if I looked like Lavinia, for example. Even if I looked like Megan, with those breasts, and her pretty blue eyes.

At that moment Henry laughs, so that Peg searches around in her mind for whatever it was that she last said; surely nothing about Megan's breasts?

"Hollow power," is what Henry next says, as though he were quoting her. "That's good. It's what I think I've always had, people responding to something that has nothing to do with me, like my name. It makes me nervous."

His tone has made Peg giggle, its wry self-deprecation, even some sly self-pity.

"You're right, it's really funny," he tells her then. "And in a way of course I've loved it."

With no idea what he has meant, Peg is quiet, and reaches for another cigarette.

Even in the dark, Henry has sensed or felt her gesture, and he reaches to light it for her, so that for a moment his face is illuminated—just long enough to intimidate her (again) with its authority. He is not so much handsome as impressive; so dark, so defined.

Now really scared of him, and shy, Peg gets to her feet. "Oh, I didn't realize how late it was," she mumbles foolishly, and she looks at her watch.

Sensing her shift in mood Henry tells her, "I think I'll have another smoke out here. You can get back to the house okay, by yourself?"

"Oh *yes*." Peg stubs out her just-lit cigarette, and she mutters, "Well, bye," and she hurries up the path. She is thinking, Well, of course we can't really be friends, how silly to think that, even for a minute.

But she is wrong.

Waking early, on the following morning (August 5, 1964), Peg is the first person in the kitchen; already, just past 6 A.M., the air is heavy with threatened heat, maybe rain, maybe thunderstorms. She has just put on the kettle for coffee, and a saucepan for boiled eggs, and is about to slice some bread when Henry comes in. He first looks surprised at seeing her there, and then he smiles widely; he is pleased to see her, clearly happy. "Oh, how great! Good morning," he says. "But you should have stuck around last night. I began to feel sorry for myself, and I had another drink, which I really didn't need. It's all your fault. While you were there I wasn't thinking about myself, or not much," and he laughs, in a friendly-brother way. His eyes are a little red, Peg sees, as he takes off his glasses, and his dark, dark hair is uncombed.

Feeling a blush, Peg asks, "Can I boil you an egg? Two eggs?"

"Sure, two. I'll do the toast. Lord, it's almost too hot for toast already, don't you think?"

In this incredibly companionable way, they are having breakfast together (which Peg might have known, had she thought about it, would be broken by some disaster), both in their unironed white cotton shirts.

When Vera comes in.

Pale brown-skinned great-eyed Vera. She says, or rather she croaks out (her voice is terrible, broken): "You guys hear the news last night? They're dead. All three of them. They found them yesterday. All three murdered." By now she is weeping—as is Peg, as Henry is. "They found them buried in the dirt," says Vera.

29

In the early sixties, before it became fashionable, Adam Marr developed an obsession with the war in Vietnam. That distant and to most people, including the President, alien conflict pervaded his mind, his conversation—and his plays. Previously he had written dramas that were described as "psychological," or "contemporary," having to do with love and sex, marriage and divorce, an occasional violent death, a murder—and so far his plays had been immensely successful. The few bad reviews, the dismissals of Adam as "melo-dramatic," "sensation-seeking," or, routinely, "pornographic," did nothing to hurt Adam at the box office—any more than did his very public, fairly frequent brawls in bars, his hinted-at liaisons with young actresses and "models."

But especially after President Johnson's Tonkin Resolution, Adam's style and mode entirely changed. He wrote a series of one-act plays that were all either overtly or sometimes indirectly about the war. Even when the ostensible subject was a soccer match in Australia, he was writing and preaching against the war.

These one-acts were produced off-Broadway, and were variously received. Bloodthirsty, trivial, warmongering, passé, obscure, and blatant: those were among the words used by his negative critics, in addition to the old staples of Marr criticism: violent, obscene, sensational. Other, younger critics, and a few old leftists, found the new plays powerful, eloquent, brilliant. "At last Adam Marr has found a subject matter commensurate with his formidable talent," said one young critic, in the venerable *Partisan Review*.

Megan is generally in agreement with the latter group, and she thinks his new plays are by far the best work that Adam has ever done.

But somehow she and Adam have not seen each other for several years. For one thing, her life is as intensely private as his is public. Following the example set by Barbara Blumenthal, and also her own inclinations, Megan never goes to the places considered "in," she is never seen at P. J. Clarke's or the Russian Tea Room or Elaine's; she does not even go to the Algonquin, or the Oak Room, at the Plaza. All of which are favorite haunts of Adam's; he has seemed especially fond of the Oak Room (curious, to anyone not knowing him as well as Megan does); he is even careful to behave well on those premises.

However, after seeing the second of his new plays, the soccer match, Megan is so moved, so really overwhelmed, that she goes home and writes a note to Adam.

To which he responds with a phone call, and an invitation to lunch. "Your note was exceptionally kind," he says to her over the phone, in a formal, quite unfamiliar tone, and then, more recognizably, "I've missed you, you silly old bitch."

She is to meet him in the Oak Room at one on the following day.

Early September; it is Labor Day weekend, in fact.

And there he is. Megan spots him standing at the bar, the moment she shyly enters that large, dark, and crowded, rather intimidating room: Adam in dark gray flannels, blue button-down shirt, and black knit ite (his Oak Room costume?), the too curly hair slicked down. Adam, coming toward her with his broad twisted smile, and a drink in his hand that turns out to be sherry.

"My God, you're so thin," is his greeting, after their classic non-kiss; but he looks at her approvingly, so that Megan decides that she has after all worn the right dress. (Dressing, she remembered harsh words from Adam to Janet on that subject: "You dumb cunt, you still dress like a college girl.")

He leads her to a small window table that he has evidently reserved.

"*Thin*," he says again, and grins, as they sit down. "But actually you look terrific." That last in his most Harvard voice.

Away from Adam, Megan has tended to see him at his worst,

which is surely his most conspicuous side: his drunken or even sober arrogance, his racist obsessions (all the crazy talk about Jews, sometimes blacks); his compulsive obscenity (she does not like, has never liked being called a cunt—does anyone?). His real cruelty to Janet. And, recalling all that, Megan has wondered at what she has to recognize in herself as unshakable vestiges of fondness for him. How can she even think of liking Adam Marr? she has often wondered.

However, face to face with Adam, across the small table, Megan is very much aware that she does like him, and not for the first time she wonders if what she feels for Adam is sexual, after all? Certainly it does not seem so. Emphatically, she does not want to go to bed with him (but would she, if she had not first encountered him attached to Janet, so to speak? She still thinks not).

What it seems to be is simply affection, the affection of old friends who sometimes fight. Maybe this is how women feel about their brothers? Not having had one, Megan cannot precisely know.

All through that lunch, though, Adam is at his interested, kindly, noncombative best, so that Megan realizes that she had forgotten just those most appealing qualities of his. He can, for instance, be more genuinely "interested" than anyone; his curiosity is infinite, and real—as when he asks Megan about her literary agent life, in detail, perceptively.

She explains, as he listens carefully, and then he says, "I get an impression that that's *all* you're doing, though. Which is not a criticism. I'm just remarking that you're not in love."

"Oh. Well, no." It is possible that Megan is blushing; she can't tell.

Adam stares out the window, half frowning at the green rises of Central Park, as Megan wonders apprehensively what is to come.

Returned to her, Adam speaks much more hesitantly than usual. "You superior women have a real problem for yourselves, don't you. Just any old guy won't do. You wouldn't like him, and even if you did your strength would scare him, even make him mad. You know, that's actually one reason I had to dump Janet, though I can't say I knew it at the time. I began to have some black suspicion that she was stronger than I was. So I dumped her for that dumb dinge. Poor Sheila was dumber and more cowardly than anyone. What you need"—Adam is visibly winding up this remarkable set of admissions—"what you need is a hero."

Megan is silenced, suffering from a variety of shock. Not seeing herself as "superior," or as especially "strong," she is intrigued by Adam's view, though at the same time she wonders: is he simply inventing her, as though she were a woman in one of his plays? She recognizes the probability of this.

But for Adam to say that he left Janet because of a perception of her strength is extraordinary, fantastic. In fact it is so fantastic that Megan is convinced that, should she ever remind him of this view (which she never will), he would deny it, as being *her* fantasy.

Adam suddenly laughs. And, as though continuing with his last thoughts on Megan's need for a hero, he snorts, "But you seem to go in for antiheroes. Very fashionable, Miss Greene. That silly little French queer, Danny. Whatever led you to him, I wonder?"

This has been a serious question, and so, very much liking him at that moment, Megan tries to answer. "I'm not sure," she says. "Partly pity, I guess. He was so thin, and so broke. I guess you could call it maternal. Besides, we were just friends. And I think it's harder to have good judgment in another country. You suspend all your usual standards, or something."

"Your old pal Henry James did pretty well with that idea. Dining out on it, so to speak."

Slightly surprised at even this degree of awareness of James on Adam's part, Megan half agrees. "I suppose." And then she asks, "Do you still see Danny? Isn't it odd that he's never called me here?"

"He's a coward. I told you, inferior men are afraid of you, Megan. Anyway, he's gone back to Paris. I couldn't make an actor out of him. God knows I tried. And maybe all I sensed in him was that basic dishonesty. His playing a role. Acting male."

"What's terrible is that I can hardly remember him at all."

"He didn't really touch you," Adam speculates, but his voice is vague; he has lost interest in Danny. Then he scowls, "Did you know about Aron?"

"Uh, what?"

"He's a fucking queer. A Jewish fag."

"How do you know that?" Megan has simply asked the first question that came to mind.

"Janet told me. And do you know how she knew? He fucking told her. Can you imagine that, a boy telling his own mother that he's queer?"

"Well, it might be better than not telling her?"

"Aaaah." Adam makes his well-known sound of disgust. "Don't give me that psycho claptrap." But, are there tears in his eyes?

"Well, whatever he is," Megan tells Adam gently, "he's awfully nice. And really bright."

"You're a nice woman. Most of the time." Adam has regained control, and some cheerfulness. "Even if you are a little too big for your britches, as my sainted mother liked to say." He grins, so that Megan wonders if he really *has* suffered over Aron's being "queer"; she believes that he has, and she wonders why Janet told him. Janet had already told Megan about Aron: Janet, new and cool, saying, "Adam will have a fit, but I actually think it has more to do with genes."

Perhaps fortunately, at that moment Adam and Megan are interrupted; someone, a man, has come up to their table. Tall, extremely tall and thin, and dark, with large dark nearsighted eyes. Henry Stuyvesant. Of course, and with a surge of warm liking, Megan remembers meeting him at Adam and Janet's White Plains house, all those years ago.

Adam stands, the two men shake hands, they make hearty sounds of greeting, as Adam asks, "Do you know Megan Greene?"

Henry and Megan reach toward each other to shake hands, at the same moment they both say, "But we met—" and they laugh. As Megan thinks: he liked me too?

"You never sent me the Lincoln Brigade book," Henry then reminds her. "You said you would, and all these years I've been waiting. You'd just published it, remember?"

"Oh, I know I meant to. Maybe I could find it." She did not send it, Megan now remembers, out of sheer shyness; she was so afraid that he had not really wanted the book, that he had been merely polite about it, and would misinterpret her gesture of sending him the book.

"That's a splendid tan, old man," Adam intervenes. "Good summer at the Vineyard?"

"Uh, no. Actually I'm just back from Georgia." Henry smiles, curiously apologetic, or embarrassed, and then he turns back to Megan. "Funny, I met a friend of yours down there. Peg Sinclair. We mentioned you; I mean I told her I remembered meeting you," and he smiles. "She's so nice," he adds. "I really liked her."

"Oh, Peg—how strange. I'd heard from Lavinia that she'd gone there. But how is she?"

"Well, she's okay. We got to be quite pals, down there. And then funnily enough, it turns out that we're distant cousins."

"All rich Eastern Protestants are distant cousins," Adam intones, and then he laughs, as though this was a joke.

Still looking at Henry, Megan thinks, Suppose I call him tomorrow and say that I have that book, which I can probably get, and to please come over for a drink? Please make love to me?

"You're probably quite right," Henry is saying, to Adam. "Although if I were really rich I don't think I'd be staying at the Gramercy Park." And then, "Well, I'm awfully glad to have met you again, Megan Greene. I hope it won't be so long before the next time."

They exchange a smile, a look; then he is gone.

As though Henry's presence had in some way been constraining, Adam in his absence becomes very garrulous. Gossipy. He asks Megan if she knew that Price and Lucy Christopher had just had their fifth child. "Very curious," he says. "Almost every one of their kids has been born exactly nine months after one of mine. He's still competing with me, I swear he is. Or actually fucking me, through Lucy, poor woman. And I understand quite a lot of other ladies too. But he doesn't really have the courage of all those erections. Price is a tease."

Half listening, still thinking strongly of Henry—the puzzle of his extreme attractiveness, to her; is it simply that she hasn't been with anyone for so long? is hard up?—in an idle, careless way Megan remarks that she didn't realize Adam had five children.

"Well, of course I do. Janet didn't tell you? Fusai is marvelous, the best one yet. Shit, I think I knocked her up the first night we met. And the kids are beautiful."

Megan does not tell him that Fusai is a whole chapter of his life that she has missed, nor that she and Janet do not talk about him very much, anymore. When they do meet, which is rare, both being busy, they talk about their work. Janet is doing cancer research. Megan talks about her books and writers, her growing unrest with her professional life. Not Adam's marriages and children.

Even the conversation about Aron's homosexuality was unusual, for Megan and Janet; it only took place because Janet's conversation with Adam had been the night before.

"In fact the Nip is a great woman," Adam continues (as Megan wonders: does she know you call her that?). "Sometimes I think she could be my final wife, but then I start to fantasize about number six, or *seven*."

Adam grins his corrupt-priest grin, which is very appealing, and Megan laughs. Seeing Henry Stuyvesant has made her light in the heart somehow.

After lunch Megan and Adam separate, near the fountain in front of the Plaza; he gets into a cab, going off fast, and Megan in a leisurely way starts walking down Fifth Avenue, toward her office.

The day has turned very warm; most people look uncomfortable, the businessmen in their suits, the women in from the suburbs in silk dresses and light wool coats. But there on the corner of Fifth and 57th is a group of hippies, in their ruffles and rags, bare arms and feet. Several of them have bad skin and vacant stoned eyes, hollow smiles. But Megan notices that one of them, a boy who seems to be their leader, looks clean and alert, and happy, not just doped. He is tall and dark and nearsighted, in rimless glasses, but he looks, astonishingly, very much like Henry Stuyvesant. He is carrying a sign that says MAKE LOVE NOT WAR, of course. As Megan goes by, he gives her a friendly, sexy wink, to which she finds herself responding, and smiling, smiling.

. . .

That hippie boy is the start of a curious phenomenon, in Megan's life, one that persists for several days: she sees men who might be, who almost are, Henry Stuyvesant, everywhere. This is especially strange in that Henry's face and his stance, his way of walking, are all quite unusual: how is it possible that she sees that many men who are that tall, dark, wide-eyed, *serious*, with strong wide mouths? But the delusion is so strong that Megan begins to fear that she well might see the real Henry and dismiss him, not speaking, as one more figment of her seemingly deranged imagination.

Idling in Barbara's office, one day after lunch in early October, Megan asks, "If you saw the same face and body, on a great many different people who actually have other faces, what would you do —would you go to a shrink?" (This is odd: in her own tight voice Megan has heard an echo of Cathy's voice.)

Barbara laughs, then coughs. "I assume somehow you mean a man's face? Someone you know?"

"Well, yes. But not very well."

"I'd call him and take him out to lunch. Or invite him to dinner. I think maidenly modesty is going out of style. Thank God." She coughs again. "Is that what you wanted me to say?"

In a happy way, Megan laughs.

But first she makes a call to Biff, who is still at the publishing house near Union Square. Biff is now plump and sleek with success, terrifically busy, in a professional way, but he always has time for a chat. His voice, along with his girth and his worldly success, has grown; it is not so much larger as deeper, more resonant. And his laugh too is richer and deeper.

After some preliminary bookish gossip, Megan asks if he remembers a book they published in the early fifties, on the Lincoln Brigade.

"But of course I do. Its total sale was something under six hundred copies. How could I forget a sales figure like that?"

"Well, the point is, I really need a copy. Do you think there is one, somewhere around?"

"One can only look."

"The thing is, I'd like it as soon as possible."

"Well, I wouldn't dare ask why. I only remark that it's a curious book for which to develop a sudden raging need."

Megan laughs. As she often does, she is thinking how much she likes Biff.

"However," Biff continues, "by an odd chance I have a necessary party to go to, in your neighborhood. If you could give me a drink quite promptly at six, I would come by with the book. *If* I find it. Shall I call you?"

"No, of course not. Come anyway. I haven't seen you forever."

"Perfect."

Knowing Biff, Megan knows that "promptly at six" will mean sometime near seven, with luck; nevertheless, herself a prompt person, she begins to wait at six. And she nervously plans the phone call to Henry, in case Biff does not bring the book, has not found it, or has possibly forgotten all about it. Biff is well-intentioned, at least in her direction, but often overcommitted, a little scattered.

And without the book, just what will she say to Henry Stuyvesant? She knows that a simple invitation to dinner is what she should do, that would be "correct," and liberated. But still. She then comforts herself with the thought that she may not even be able to get in touch with Henry; he was staying at the Gramercy Park that day, he said, but she believes that he usually lives somewhere in the South, is teaching there. And she *will not* call Adam to find out Henry's whereabouts.

However Biff does arrive at six fifteen; a record, of sorts. And he brings the book. Biff, pink-faced and puffing, in a splendid new-looking checked gray suit. "Darling, your stairs are more and more too much for me," he wheezes. "Either you must move or I must lose some weight. Perhaps both? You don't see yourself in something really smart, uptown? With an elevator, for the dear Lord's sake? For my sake, for that matter."

"You're an angel to bring the book. Let me get you a drink."

"You note how wonderfully I do not ask why you wanted it." Biff's large blue eyes blink soulfully at Megan.

"You are wonderful, I always say so," she counters, and she goes off into the kitchen.

Henry Stuyvesant is immediately reached at the Gramercy Park.

"Uh, Henry? This is Megan Greene. We, uh, met with Adam Marr—"

"Megan! of course, it's really good to hear from you. And odd that you should call at just this moment: I got in ten minutes ago, I'm up here for some meetings."

She tries to laugh. "Well, I know it's several years late, but I did get the book for you. The Lincoln Brigade one."

"Oh, that's really good of you. I'd almost forgotten, but you're kind."

Naturally enough, Henry has sounded a little surprised, Megan thinks—both at hearing from her, she assumes, and at her bothering to get him a book which he cannot really have wanted very much, ever. And so it is hard for her to continue with her plan; she has to force herself to plunge ahead. "How about your coming for dinner, here?" she asks abruptly, and then begins to explain, "I haven't cooked for a while, and you get so tired of going out, and that way I could give you the book. And where I live is very easy to get to. It's just off Fifth. As a matter of fact when I used to work near where you are, I always walked." At the end of all this she is out of breath.

"That sounds really swell. No one has asked me to dinner for ever so long." A pause. "But I do hope you mean very soon? I have to get back down to North Carolina in a couple of days."

They settle on the following night, at seven.

. . .

Megan spends an inordinate amount of time planning and changing menus, and planning and changing her plans for her clothes, for that projected evening. She finally forces herself to desist from both preoccupations, and she tells herself that any good dinner will do, or any dress (but: short dress or long? or velvet pants? silk shirt or sweater?).

It is the hottest October on record. What summer leaves are left on the city's trees go limp; in the narrow concrete-floored garden behind the building where Megan lives, in the Village, the big ferns droop dustily to the paving, in their death throes. On such a night, eight or ten years back, she would have sat out on the fire escape, two floors up from where she lives now; she would have sat there praying for a breeze, and envying rich people who will sit out the heat in air-conditioned restaurants or hotel rooms. Now she herself has an air-conditioned bedroom, to which she has repaired from time to time, that day, between frenetic intervals of food preparation, of polishing wine glasses and silver. Of killing time.

Henry is mercifully prompt, for which he gracefully, laughingly apologizes: "I'm sorry, I can never manage to be late," he tells her, at the door. "Always boringly on the nose." And he adds, "You won't mind my state of undress." He is so tall, entering her room, just slightly stooped. He carries his coat, a striped seersucker. He is also carrying a brown paper bag: white wine that turns out to be miraculously still cold.

Greeting him, taking the wine—"Oh, lovely, thanks!"—what Megan most clearly reacts to is his face: she sees that she was wrong in imagining that anyone else could look like Henry Stuyvesant. His is the strongest, the most original and interesting face that she has ever seen. Its planes are as balanced as chords, its black eyebrows authoritative, mouth wide and firm. His expression is intent, highly serious. He is just now seriously concentrated on her, Megan feels.

And now, she thinks, we will go through an evening of silly

conversation; it will be hours before I can even think of touching his mouth.

She takes the wine into the kitchen and stands there for a minute, catching her breath, as she continues to think about the evening that stretches ahead, on this hottest and heaviest of nights. And quite suddenly, although she likes Henry very much, it all seems unbearably depressing: the drinks she is about to make, the obligatory talk about mutual friends, it having been established that Henry knows both Peg and Lavinia, and Adam and Janet— quite possibly there will be quite a lot of Adam. They will talk about some books, and his summer in Georgia. And, being both more intelligent and more polite than most men are, and more truly fond of women, Megan senses, he will ask her about her work, and she will say what she has just begun to think: that she doesn't like it, much.

And maybe, at the end of the evening, after too much to drink, there will be some exhausted, half-drunken exchange of love. That is how it goes, these days, when you ask a man to your apartment for dinner. It is what you both expect. Whereas Megan would give anything in the world for some permission, *now*, simply to trace the shape of Henry's wide mouth with one forefinger. Just to touch his mouth, right away.

She returns to the living room with the requisite tall cold glasses, gin and tonic; she hands one to Henry and she sits down near him, on her broad smartly and newly upholstered sofa. And then she smiles; she can feel the smile involving her whole face, her mouth and eyes. She looks at Henry. What she has just thought is, Why do I need permission though? Why not just touch him?

Henry smiles too, of course. He sips at his drink, though, before he says, "I insist that you tell me what you just thought, to make you smile like that."

Megan puts down her glass. She reaches toward him, and with one chilled wet finger, very slowly she traces the outer line of his mouth, that small firm ridge, as delicate and sensitive as a vein. As lovely to her touch as she knew it would be. "There," she says. "That's what I just thought of doing."

He reaches then and does the same to her, touching her mouth as slowly, as lingeringly. His finger also cold.

A little later, after kissing, Megan murmurs, "My bedroom's air-conditioned, actually," and then she laughs, very quietly, as he does.

They get up, and Megan starts toward the hall, her bedroom, but Henry stops her for a moment, holding her arm. "You make me so happy," he tells her. "The way you are. Already. You really do."

That promising mood, of a rich and happy leisurely time, remains with them all night, in Megan's big cool room, her wide bed; her room seems an island, remote, in the surrounding sea of heat, the thick black night.

"The way you come to me," Henry tells her, at some point. "It's just extraordinary."

"Well, it is for me." She is shy, pleased.

"And your breasts. I never met such a generous woman."

In that chilly room sweat cools on their wet, slick bodies. In an interval of rest Megan pulls up a sheet and the nearest light blanket, covering them both. Some weird half-light from the pre-dawn city beyond her delicate curtains has made Henry just visible to her, but only his face, and already she misses that long strong pale body.

Somewhat later, simultaneously awake, they both look at their watches; it is almost five, on the following morning.

"Lord, no wonder I'm starved." It is Henry who says this, but it could as easily have been Megan; she is suddenly awake, and she has never been so hungry.

Foolishly, she says, "What a hostess I am. Now you'll never come again for dinner."

"Oh, will I not."

They laugh.

Megan offers, "I'll bring things in. You stay here." For a moment she has liked the notion of serving him in bed.

"No, don't be foolish. We'll forage, rustle it up together, okay? I'm a handy man in the kitchen."

Megan likes this even better.

In an amazingly familiar way, for comparative strangers, they get up. They go into Megan's kitchen, they set about making huge sandwiches from her carefully prepared dinner. Greed and sexual exhaustion combine to make them dismissive of nonessentials, like tidiness.

At Megan's round pine table they sit drinking wine, eating messy chicken and cheese and avocado. An unreal pale light comes in from the street, making paler their drained, pale faces.

Very solemnly Henry says to her, "I think maybe this is the favorite night of my life."

Not considering what she is going to say, Megan answers him seriously. "Do you realize that in less than two years I'll be forty?"

30

In some stupid movie that Lavinia and Potter once saw together, a man prefaced his advances to a lady (although they were already in bed) by saying, "My dear, would you consent to do me the greatest honor—"

It was fairly funny at the time, Lavinia thought, but to Potter that line was hilarious, excruciating, hysterical, to a degree that he repeats it *all the time*. In bed with Lavinia, fumbling at her night-gown, Potter will stage-whisper, "My dear, would you consent—" Fumbling, reaching with his dull, hot, unarousing fingers.

No, she has wanted to scream at him; no, don't touch me, I have the curse, I'm bleeding a lot, my head aches, I hate you. You never make me come. She does not say any of these things, of course not, not even the ones that are true.

Even, most of the time she still thinks of herself and Potter as "happily married"; they almost never fight, never yell at each other, and they look wonderful together, still—she is sure of that. And they are very popular, invited out everywhere, all the time. It is just that she cannot bear for him to touch her. "My dear, would you consent—" *Jesus:* no—no—no—

Is she in fact frigid? Is that what has happened to her, along with almost reaching forty? And, would it be worse to be frigid in an absolute sense, or only frigid with your husband? Logical Lavinia cannot quite work that one out, not yet.

In the old days with Henry Stuyvesant, though, she came every time, or almost, and so quickly; they both would be trying to slow themselves down, postponing, in those long sultry nights in the river house, near Fredericksburg, in smells of rain and honeysuckle, wet grass and earth-wafting river smells. Or anywhere, hotel rooms in New York, making love with Henry she would come again and again—although now she does not even like Henry, and they never see each other. Everyone says he is a Communist, and he has no money.

Nevertheless, ten years or so ago she was wildly in love with him; she cannot pretend otherwise to herself. Which should have given her some clue as to his character, Lavinia recognizes, with an inward smile of pure irony. It is clear by now that she only falls in love with shits. Harvey the crippled crook, and then terrible Gordon Shaughnessey (thank God he died), and then Henry. Whereas, with Potter Cobb, her nice husband, with whom she was never, never "wildly in love" at any moment, she is sexually bored, she is frigid.

Is it simply that Potter is so exceptionally nice, is not a shit—or would she at this point, at this age be frigid with anyone?

Oh, if only some friend were around to talk all this over with, Lavinia sighs to herself—in her yellow silk bedroom, just redone. What fun we could have if old Kitty were around, instead of dead, her liver ruined, at thirty-eight. "Well, in that case you'd just better find yourself some other rotten guy," is what Kitty would say, probably—with her yelping, coughing laugh.

Or even Peg. Although of course with Peg the tone would have to be serious; she could only hint at the nature of her problem, using words like "exciting" instead of "sexy," and of course "respond" for "come." In the old days, good old Peg would have reminded Lavinia of the essential goodness of good old Potter, her lovely little daughter, and her several lovely large houses. But now, with Peg, who knows? On his last visit to New York Cameron Sinclair (who is terribly nice, both Lavinia and Potter have decided: does this make Peg frigid with him?)—anyway, Cameron told Lavinia and Potter that Peg spends absolutely all her time with some friend she met in Georgia, a Mexican girl, from Los Angeles, "even if she's really rather pretty." Cameron said. At this point Lavinia cannot imagine any conversation with Peg, who never writes, much less a womanly talk about sex. (But did Peg ever, uh, go to bed with a black person, down there in Georgia? This thought is so shocking, so *wild*, that Lavinia actually cringes, and then giggles, silently, furtively.)

Megan then enters Lavinia's mind, possibly by association; there were always those rumors about Megan and that colored trombone player. Another rumor, however, makes Lavinia thrust Megan from her consciousness, as fast as possible. This rumor began with Potter, though, a notoriously inaccurate, unobservant person. However: Potter *said* that he saw Megan and Henry Stuyvesant walking along lower Fifth Avenue together, *holding hands*. Potter was in a cab, coming up from Wall Street—and Potter was so often wrong. Very likely for some reason or other he had been thinking of Henry, and then he imagined that he saw him. This happens all the time, Lavinia knows: when you think of a person you believe that you see him; she herself used to see Henry everywhere, when they were in love. Very likely it was Megan with someone else, some other tall thin man whom Potter saw. Though surely Megan is a little old for holding hands? (Lavinia snickers at the thought.) Or very likely it wasn't Megan at all. Was neither of them. Not Megan. Not Henry. (Lavinia has trouble putting both their names into the same sentence, even.)

But there is something just slightly odd in Potter's attitude toward Henry, Lavinia has noticed. It was Potter, in fact, who explained to Lavinia about Henry's not being rich, after all.

"You only thought he was rich because of his shoes," was what Potter said, and the worst of that remark was its at least partial truth; Lavinia had once loved Henry's shoes as much as anything about him. She loved and admired such good, old highly polished shoes. People with no money do not preserve their things in that way, she thought; she was remembering the almost new cars that poor people turned into rattletraps, so quickly, driving around the country roads of her childhood, in Maryland and Virginia, in the thirties. "Henry is the original poor relation," Potter had continued. Henry didn't even have a trust fund, said Potter.

When Henry and Lavinia were in love, the subject of money never came up, of course. She simply assumed, from everything about Henry, beginning with his wonderful name, that he was everything he seemed to be, i.e., very rich: his schools and accent, clothes, his friends, or most of them. It still amazes Lavinia that she could have been wrong, in that way.

It is almost as though Potter somehow knew about Lavinia and Henry, but of course that is impossible.

Since Henry, there has been no one, no lover in Lavinia's life. Although several men have tried with very obvious invitations to lunch, or to *tea*, for heaven's sake. And since she is almost always, well, frigid with Potter, Lavinia is worried about her skin, and the circles under her eyes. Sex is the only thing that really works for your skin, she has always known that. You can spend a fortune on creams and oil, massage, but without good sex, well, forget it.

However, except for the sexual part, Lavinia does not really want to have another affair. For one thing they're very dangerous; almost always someone finds out, no matter how discreet you are. Someone sees you somewhere where it's odd that you should be. For example, Price Christopher, who is still a friend of theirs, sort of, is almost always having an affair with someone or other, usually someone who is also one of their friends, and one way or another Lavinia and Potter always know. Price may be a little less discreet than most people are (there was the girl he always took to the Russian Tea Room, of all dumb places), but still, things get out.

But: her skin, although perfect, to Lavinia's practiced scrutiny looks dead. Deeply disturbing. Frowning into her mirror—probably making lines!—for a moment Lavinia even entertains a fantasy in which she telephones Henry and suggests that they spend, maybe, an afternoon a week together? She could rent a tiny apartment somewhere, and maybe—

But then she remembers, entirely and vividly, their final day together, in Chapel Hill.

Hot. That is the main thing that Lavinia remembers about that very old, very pretty, and absolutely terrible small town. So hot! Hot at the incredibly tacky Raleigh-Durham airport—to which, on an impulse, just phoning Henry that morning ("Darling, I'm coming down to see you in an hour! Isn't that fabulous! I couldn't wait," which was not her best impulse, as things turned out), she flew down from Washington, an hour away.

Instead of taking her right out to his cabin and making love to her, making love all day, as they sometimes did, just doing it for hours (which is all that Lavinia had thought about, not seeing him for almost three weeks), instead of anything like that, Henry insisted that she must see the campus, the university, for God's sake. He showed her the Old Well, and the Playmakers Theater; in that awful heat, in her heels, they walked through the Arboretum, all those damn exotic plants, with name tags, and wisteria blossoms fallen all over those gravel paths, swollen, like awful bugs. And those skinny young girl students in their next to no clothes, with their long straight hair and good tans.

At last Henry took her to the stadium, of all absolutely crazy choices for an intimate conversation, which perhaps he had never even intended to have; very likely not. They walked past a really ugly red brick tower, the bell tower, on more graveled paths, between clipped hedges, down more paths and through some scrubby pinewoods to a huge open stadium. No one there of course, but still, a stadium.

The benches were green, old flaking paint that would stick to Lavinia's pale linen skirt, but at that point she hardly cared; her feet hurt so much, from all that goddamn gravel.

"You must admit, this place really has it all over Soldiers' Field," said Henry, in a satisfied way, and they sat down on one of the topmost, highest benches.

That possibly innocent observation had an instant and cruel effect on Lavinia: it took her back vividly and violently to Soldiers' Field, at Harvard. Oh! twenty years ago, or more. She had to close her eyes against the vision: a dazzling New England fall day, a Saturday, the Princeton game. The sky a cold, electric blue, and the stadium packed, milling crowds, the Crimson band. And Lavinia: she could see herself in her wonderful dark red coat, lined in gray kid (Daddy had worried so much about the cold weather in Cambridge that he had been very generous); she could see her own lovely pink skin in the marvelous air, could feel the perfection of her skin—and she was with *Gordon*, Gordon Shaughnessey, so handsome, in his ROTC uniform. Oh, she had loved him so much, so innocently, so happily—as they watched the game, and thought about being together later on, after all the parties, a little drunk and kissing, hours of kisses. Oh, Gordon, how could you let me go like that! Lavinia inwardly cried out, even then, even twenty years later. Tears came to her eyes. "I think North Carolina is a terribly tacky state," she burst out, passionately, to Henry.

In a preoccupied way (and it occurred to Lavinia that he had been somewhat less than absolutely *with* her, ever since she got off the plane) Henry observed, rather academically, "That's how people from Maryland often seem to feel, I've noticed. Or Virginia. Even South Carolinians generally feel superior to Tarheels, as they call us. It's curious." He even laughed.

"Us"? Lavinia did not ask.

Well, are we going to sit in this stadium all day? Lavinia would have liked to ask that also, but did not. She only muttered, "Well, I think all those people are right, it is quite tacky. Red clay all over."

"You should never go to Georgia, you wouldn't like that either," Henry unhelpfully told her, just then.

"I most certainly hadn't planned to."

And then, putting his arm around her in a way that was much more friendly than sexy, Henry announced, "Beautiful Lavinia, the worst possible luck about this afternoon. Just after you called someone phoned me about a meeting. It begins at four—" He glanced at his watch, a brand-new and very cheap one, Lavinia noticed (which could or *should* have been a clue). "That's a couple of hours from now but it's over in Hillsborough. And the worst of it is, I just can't promise when it'll be done with."

Lavinia forced a laugh. "Well, in that case, Henry darling, I guess you'll just have to cancel the meeting." She reached her mouth up to kiss his cheek, like a little girl.

"Actually, my darling, I can't do that. It's, uh, important."

With more courage than she knew she had, and much more tenacity, Lavinia kept at it. For one thing, she could hardly believe what he was doing. "Well, that's perfectly simple, then," she told him. "We'll drive to Hillsborough together, and you can park me in a bar, or something. You appear at your meeting, and if you promise to leave early, as soon as you can, I'll be good and not pick up anyone." And she laughed, naughtily.

"Lavinia, there are no bars in Hillsborough. The state's dry. And I can't take you out there."

Realizing at last that he was serious, Lavinia allowed herself a small strike. "One of your Communist cell meetings, I suppose."

As though she were a perfect stranger, in a cold way Henry explained, "Actually I broke with the party some time ago. But I have certain loyalties, certain obligations. I suppose I should have explained some of this to you before. But it had so little to do with 'us.'" (Was his "us" ironic? Its effect was chilling, to Lavinia.) "One of the things we were doing," serious Henry explained, "in our cell, as you put it, was establishing a credit union for black people, in Carrbro. That's where most of them live, around here—"

"Fascinating," Lavinia murmured, just not saying: But what about *me*? She got to her feet. "Well, I really seem to have picked the worst possible day." Her words were a triumph of lightness, she felt, a victory over her suddenly leaden heart. "I do hope you have time to drive me back to the airport? I don't suppose there's a taxi."

"Just," said Henry, looking again at his cheap new watch. And saying again, "I am sorry."

And that was all. Hardly need for him to say, I don't love you anymore, you have ceased to be important to me. They drove those silent dozen or so miles to the airport with those dismissive words playing through Lavinia's brain, however; past all the hated, eroded red clay, past turgid brown creeks thickly overgrown with honeysuckle vines. Small rickety unpainted houses with bare yards, chickens, skinny black children. The tackiest state, so hot, so *terrible*.

At the airport, with one of his darkest, most beautiful looks, Henry kissed her quickly; he kissed her before she could stop him, actually, and he said, "I'll write to you, I'm extremely sorry about today, Lavinia. You were beautiful to come, it's just—"

"Oh, darling, please, please don't write, I know how busy you are," and Lavinia smiled, and hurried into the plane, not looking back. And even on the plane she did not cry; she hurried back to Potter and Amy, who had not expected her for a couple of days— "I need a tiny vacation to myself," she had told them, and the maids, so daringly. Even then she did not cry.

However, Lavinia now reminds herself, there is less than no point in thinking of Henry; he might as well be as dead as Gordon Shaughnessey. As forgotten as crippled Harvey Rodman. And there is really no point in worrying about her skin, which everyone else admires. Even the new girl at Arden's, generally such a little bitch, who was giving Lavinia a facial the other day, remarked on her fantastic skin, and she did not say, For your age. (And she got the large tip that she deserved for once.)

If Lavinia wanted worries over skin, though, there is Amy. Amy, as though on purpose, as though visiting some judgment on her mother, has terrible acne, the poor child, but still, it is hard to bear. Pimples. Pustules that no tetracycline or anything seems to affect. Thousands of dollars to dermatologists, in New York and Washington, down to Johns Hopkins, even to Boston—Mass. General; they made a special trip up there to a man who was supposed to do miracles with adolescent skin. But no, that beautiful little girl, that fairy princess has become a living rebuke to Lavinia, her mother (although she is no longer sure what she is being punished for, having convinced herself that the child is surely Potter's, as Henry said all along). And not only pimples: Amy, at only thirteen, has gigantic breasts, as big as Megan's were before she got so thin, but Amy is thin, so thin that those breasts look grotesque; and the doctor said, all the doctors all said that plastic surgery would be a mistake, at that age; you have to wait. (But wait for what, for those bosoms to get even bigger than they are?)

Thank God, at the moment Amy is away at camp, in Vermont. *Invisible.* Just nice perfunctory misspelled schoolgirl letters.

Down in Fredericksburg, where now they often go together, Lavinia and Potter have frequent weekend guests, house parties; actually that has become the true function of the river house, a place for entertaining.

However, on a particular hot Saturday night in August 1966, they are alone. They will have dinner alone, together, and spend the evening alone. Which is one of the reasons that Lavinia dallies as long as she can at her dressing table; she is wondering what on earth they will talk about.

Although Potter is several years older than Lavinia, and she is a few months past forty, Potter continues to have his hair cut as though he were twenty-one, a crew cut. Short gray hair. Lavinia hates it.

Not that she would want actually long hair, Beatle hair, hippie hair (oh, Jesus, the very idea is ludicrous) but something other than a 1942 crew cut. Something attractive, dignified. And he dresses that way too, as he always has, in old Brooks clothes. Worn-out button-downs and gray flannels. Old navy blazers and regimental ties.

But even though it is Potter, her husband, whose very hair and clothes she does not approve of, with whom she is to have dinner, Lavinia makes an effort at being beautiful herself, and all through dinner she talks, and listens, and *laughs*.

. . .

After dinner, since no one else is there, they go out on the terrace for coffee, in the heavy, humid darkness, the still air full of river smells, and honeysuckle.

Potter, who has taken off his blazer and hung it neatly over the arm of a wicker chair, now stands and stretches. He is near the bench where Lavinia is sitting, her long legs in silk trousers, and looking at him, Lavinia thinks, At least he's stayed thin; I could not be married to someone fat.

Raising white shirt-sleeved arms above his head, and then down, in a discouraged gesture that Lavinia recognizes, Potter says, "Well, it looks like they're really going to run Nixon in '68."

"Richard Nixon? But that's crazy, he's all washed up. That awful speech about not having him to kick around anymore. And he's so—so *awful*. So ugly."

"As you would say, my dear, he's thoroughly tacky, in fact he's tacky as hell. I absolutely agree. But there's some very big money that says he'll run."

"Oh, I don't believe it." However, Lavinia reflects that at least they are having a conversation. So often they are as silent as some terrible cartoon couple, some terrible low-class marriage, with the TV on and no one even speaking.

Potter laughs. "I would like not to believe it myself, my dear. But I truly think the Vietnam war has wrecked the Democrats, so almost anyone we run will win. And, I repeat, the really big money boys really like Nixon."

"But, couldn't they find someone, anyone more attractive? Lord, even Rockefeller." Lavinia knows that she sounded a little silly, she could hear herself, but that is how she has always talked to men, beginning with Daddy. (Only Henry, sometimes, drew her into "intelligent conversation." The kind of talk that she might have had with a woman, even. And see where that got her.)

Sitting down beside but not too close to Lavinia, Potter continues. "There's one really mysterious fellow. He's supposed to be the richest man in Washington, and no one knows where he got his money. Rather odd-looking person, a cripple."

"What's his name?"

"Oh, Harvey something. Rodman, I think."

"Harvey Rodman?" Lavinia has spoken much more loudly than she meant to; everything within her is suddenly out of control. Racing pulses, heated blood: her brain has come alive, is galvanized.

"Surely you don't know him?" asks Potter, reasonably enough.

Lavinia can hear the slight frown in his too-familiar voice, as she says, "Uh, no, of course not. But I think he came to our house a couple of times. He was sort of a friend of Daddy's."

"Odd friend for your father to have, even 'sort of.'"

But Lavinia is not really listening; she does not have to listen to Potter anymore. Her whole life is on the verge of a tremendous change, is wonderfully changing. By now she is perfectly calm and controlled, in charge, as she asks, "But you've met this Harvey Rodman, the mystery man?"

"Just for a minute, one Sunday at the Hay-Adams. He keeps a suite there."

Perfect. Good Potter has told her the one thing that she needed to know, which is where Harvey lives. And with a pleased and secret smile Lavinia also thinks, And good for you, dear old Harvey, you've improved a lot, the Hay-Adams is so much nicer than the Shoreham. Still: she smiles more deeply, remembering certain afternoons at the Shoreham, in Harvey's suite there. Lord, how young she was then—and how perfectly beautiful.

Potter asks, "Is that thunder? You know, it feels like a storm."

"Oh, it really does! How terrific." Lavinia even reaches for Potter's hand.

Black rumbling thunder, and then a sudden brilliant crack of lightning illuminates the whole lurid night sky: their majestic green garden, boxwoods, the fountain. For one instant it is like a stage set. Then total blackness again, thicker and darker than before, it seems. And then rain, suddenly heavily pounding, spattering the terrace where Lavinia and Potter still sit beneath their awning, as though transfixed.

"Oh, it's so cool!" she breathes.

"Shouldn't we go in, though?"

. . .

In the course of that night, during that long, wild heavy summer storm, at least two remarkable things occur. One is that Lavinia does not think of Henry, not once. Whereas, for years, any sound of rain and especially a summer storm would bring him back, alive.

The other exceptional event is that after Potter has murmured, "My dear, would you consent—" and begun to touch her, Lavinia can feel herself "responding." And yes, she does actually come, with Potter.

31

Strangely, and very gradually—and mostly through letters, a long correspondence—after almost twenty-five years of knowing each other, Megan and Peg become good, trusted, and trusting friends. In the mid- to late sixties. Further strangeness is the fact that money, Megan's money, plays a considerable part in their newly forged rapport.

It happens in this way: possibly to atone for, perhaps to wipe out the letters that she had written to Megan when she was so sick (although of course Megan never saw those letters), Peg begins to write small news bulletins to Megan, now that she is well and strong. She tells about going to Georgia. She says that the woman who used to work for her, Cornelia, whom she really liked, is in a teachers' college, and doing well, and Peg is really pleased. She says that since her summer in Georgia she has been involved with various rights groups. She has met Martin King, and Dr. Abernathy. Her kids are all okay, she adds.

And Megan answers with small news of her own, what's going on at the agency, her affection for Barbara, her dislike of Leslie, who is now Barbara's assistant. ("Could it be because she's so thin?" Megan asks Peg, in a letter; and, "Do you think we were both so drawn to Lavinia because she was so much smaller than we were?") She tells Peg that she thinks what Peg is doing is really great; could they use some more money? She, Megan—"funnily enough"—is doing very little but work, these days, she earns a lot; she would like to do something good. She sends off checks.

Peg sends back warm, appreciative thanks, and further news.

"I feel slightly silly saying this to you," Peg writes, "but it won't be a big surprise, I don't think. I am very much in love, and very happily, with a woman. Vera. She is lovely in every way. For a long time I had an idea that I must be homosexual, but I thought that just meant I should live alone, or not with men. But Vera was there in Georgia, that summer, and we went from being friends to being in love. She is wonderful. She is Mexican, originally, and was a social worker in Los Angeles. Funny, down here a lot of people suspect her of being black. You can see why I am not writing any of this to Lavinia, and I do not know what I am going to do about Cameron. But I think we can work it out."

Megan indeed is not wholly surprised; rather, she is very pleased, and she is touched at Peg's writing to her in that way. She does not call Lavinia, with whom she is barely in touch anyway, but she does call Henry—both because they talk so much, about literally everything, and also because Henry speaks so affectionately of Peg, whom he seems to regard as a sort of sister.

"Well, that's really good," says Henry, informed of the Peg-Vera connection. "And she's right, Vera is lovely, and nice. She struck me as a little fragile, maybe, but Peg will take care of her."

"Yes, it's what she always does." Megan sighs.

"But that's really okay, don't you think?"

"Well, sure. Someone has to." Megan laughs.

They talk, and talk, and laugh a lot, about everyone, everything—and so the fact that they have never, or barely, mentioned Lavinia is marked, to Megan, who continues with her old assumption that there was something between Henry and Lavinia; that they were lovers, at least for a while. Not wanting to know, in fact terrified of knowing, she would never ask; also, she would hate to hear chivalrous Henry lie, as he might, if she forced him to.

And actually they have never gone in for discussions of former lovers; a certain shy delicacy is a shared quality between them, Megan and Henry. They probably and quite correctly assume that for each of them the other is entirely wonderful—a marvel, quite superior to any predecessor (even if Lavinia could be counted in that group).

Perfect lovers, perfect friends. Why then is she not perfectly happy, spending time with Henry, or even time away from him? Megan ponders this, and she concludes only that no one ever is— perfectly happy. Although absolute misery is a condition that she is fairly sure most people reach, at one time or another.

Henry's back is beautiful, the most perfectly beautiful human back, in Megan's view. Long and hard and smooth, cool to her touch, lovely wide shoulders narrowing down to rise again in a lovely rounded, hard ass. She could stroke his back forever, Megan thinks.

She bends now to kiss the small knob at the top of Henry's spine. His skin is fragrant, delicious. She kisses him everywhere.

How can she even imagine misery, here with Henry?

And she loves the town of Chapel Hill, in the warm bright blue October air, smelling of pines and leaves, oak and maple and poplar of every possible color, green to yellow, gold and red, bright brown. Megan gives some thought to the difference between a New England fall, and one down here, down South (she leaves out California, where almost nothing happens, to signify fall). It is the difference, she dreamily concludes (she is sitting on Henry's side porch and drinking coffee, waiting for him to come home from his Saturday morning class), the difference between scarlet and gold: Cambridge is scarlet, the leaves and electric cold brilliant air, whereas this Southern air is golden, with its gentle winds, and slow descent of leaves. The murmurous pines, and the swollen creek, whose rush to the sea she can just hear from where she sits, in the heavy sun.

· · ·

Henry's house is small, but it is not precisely a cabin (that was Lavinia's fantasy of it); it is rather a dignified old structure, one-story, once a farm. It is somewhat south of town, near Morgan's Creek—down the highway that goes on to Pittsboro, Southern Pines, to South Carolina. And the twin of Henry's house, just visible from his porch, lies across what was once a cornfield, now plowed over, dead, but the shape of furrows may still be discerned in that rich and crumbling dirt.

Two of Henry's closest local friends live in that other house, the Jacobses, Ralph and Irene. They have long been politically involved together (Ralph, an economist who also has a law degree, was largely instrumental in setting up the famous credit union, for Negroes, in Carrbro). Now they all are active in the local anti–Vietnam war movement.

Megan admires the Jacobses; they are clearly admirable, intelligent, principled, energetic—even handsome people. Small and neat and dark, they look rather alike; they could easily pass for brother and sister.

But evenings with Henry and Megan, Ralph and Irene never seem quite to work out. In a conscientious way they all four work at being friends, everyone asks polite and interested questions of each other, but there is always a sense of pointlessness in their encounters—or, worse, of something just wrong, barely beneath the surface. (So that Megan comes away wondering why: why do we have to go through this? It isn't fun, which is surely the point of friends being together? But she cannot quite bring herself to say this to Henry.)

Adam Marr sometimes provides a moderately successful conversational staple, though, for the four of them. The Jacobses are interested in Megan's early view of him, the undergraduate fiancé of Janet Cohen. And somewhat to her surprise Megan finds that behind Adam's back she tends to present his favorable aspects; she defends him, even.

"In some way he was always really compelling," she says, of that early Adam. "What you'd call a strong presence." As she speaks she is seeing that early, young Adam, in his messy khakis, on the terrace of Barnard Hall, in the sunlight; 1944. His intense blue eyes. "He has a wonderful voice," she tells them. "You listen even when you know it's total nonsense. And sometimes of course it isn't nonsense; he's right at least half the time, and he's always interesting, I think."

"He sure caught on to Vietnam a long time before most people did," Ralph puts in. "Although I don't think it's accurate to call him a radical anymore."

"He calls himself a conservative." Henry is ironic, leaning back in the Jacobses' best bentwood chair, firelight on his shadowed face.

"I just see that as part of Adam's baronial pose," Megan ventures. "Along with that crazy White Plains house, and his new digs on Central Park West."

"Of course you're right," Henry agrees. "Surely his 'conservative' isn't anyone else's."

Encouraged, Megan follows her own line of thought; with a heady, slightly guilty sense of betraying an old friend, in the interests of entertaining new ones, she adds, "There's always been something rather social-climbing about Adam, I've always thought."

But Megan's observation does not go over very well, although she believes it to be quite accurate, and believes too that her betrayal of Adam was a generous present to them all. Even Henry looks a little baffled, and Megan then realizes, Well, of course; he would not be sympathetic to a view that at least in part explained Adam's affection for himself. Henry will not admit that he himself could be socially climbed upon. And the Jacobses' faces show an even deeper bafflement; social climbing is a sin that they cannot even contemplate, and surely not in an undoubted "genius," a man whom they have long considered, ideologically, as one of themselves, however he may quixotically refer to himself as a conservative. But, social climbing? Adam Marr?

Henry and Irene Jacobs (obviously attuned to each other, Megan objectively notes) break the ensuing silence almost simultaneously: Henry saying, "Well—" and Irene, earnest, well-intentioned, "What I don't see is why he keeps getting married."

But this remark does not work out much better than Megan's did. It brings up what Megan has sensed the Jacobses as wondering: well, why don't Henry and Megan marry? Are they afraid to?

Well, perhaps we are, Megan now concedes to herself; heaven knows they don't discuss it much.

And then everyone begins to speak.

Megan says, "Because he really dislikes women, I think." As she wonders: has Henry never married because he likes women more than any other man does?

And Henry, "Yes, marriage is how he gets rid of them. You could call it the Blue Beard syndrome."

Followed by:

Ralph. "Interesting, how often anti-Semites marry Jews."

Agreeing, Irene names several known couples who follow that pattern.

That is, then, one of their better, more successful evenings together. However, walking home in the chilled October dark, stumbling across the ancient corn furrows in her smart New York boots, it is clear to Megan both that she has drunk too much wine, in her nervousness, and also that it would have been a better evening for the three of them without her.

"The three of you get along so terrifically," she tells Henry later, as they are both quickly undressing, in his unheated bedroom. "It's like a good triangle," Megan says. "I throw off the balance. In fact I think they're both in love with you, in very harmless ways, of course. What we used to call 'unconscious.' And they don't understand the fact of me. They don't know what they feel."

"Will you please stop talking and come to bed? I know what I feel: cold but concupiscent. Is that how you feel? Megan, come here."

But how would it be if they were, in fact, actually married? Megan of course has wondered about that, has sometimes mulled it over. Where, for instance, would they live? Would Henry look for a teaching job in New York? They could both easily live on what she earns, and very well, but Megan cannot quite see Henry as "kept," and besides, what would he do? Or, conversely, what would she do in Chapel Hill? It would seem silly, somehow, to marry and still live in separate places, Megan thinks, despite various recent magazine articles to the contrary. Maybe she could find something useful to do down here? As she thinks this, Megan is stricken with a vast distaste for the work that she does, in New York: all those nonbooks decked out for marketing. So much execrable prose. The sheer unreality of it all.

She is thinking all this as she lies drowsily, warmly awake, next to sleeping Henry, after love. She wonders about that too: would they make love as often living together, married? Well, very likely not, how could they? every night? But maybe an occasional passionate return to earlier habits and practices?

In the morning what could be considered an amazing coincidence occurs, which is that Henry, just waking, turns and reaches for Megan to kiss, and then he says, "You know, I really think we should get married. I really want to, don't you?"

It is like the several times that they have waked to similar dreams. Only now, to her vast surprise, Megan feels a rush of new blood to her heart, lovely new crisp air in her lungs, as she gasps, and then laughs. "Well, I guess *so*," she tells him.

"I love you, just amazingly," says Henry.

32

However, Megan and Henry do not marry right away, as they might have been expected to do, having once made up their minds and being of certain ages: Megan by now is in her early forties, and Henry is five years older.

For one thing, the November that follows their October morning of decision is that of Richard Nixon's election to the presidency. Both Megan and Henry find it surprising that this event should be a factor in their personal lives, but the truth is that they are both so depressed by Nixon that they are stunned into a sort of immobility. "I simply cannot believe it," they repeat to each other, in a sort of litany with minor variations. "He's so terribly, transparently dishonest. Self-serving. *Creepy. Ugly,*" they both say, from time to time.

Nixon's election has managed to shatter their personal hopes, along with their wishes for the general future; they do not exactly say this to each other, but that is more or less the case. These days, when they talk about what will happen now, they do not mean to themselves. The Vietnam war will go on forever, they hopelessly say, or at least until everyone is dead—both countries beaten back into the Stone Age, in the immortal words of that general. Civil rights and libertics pushed backward, social progress all shrunken, because of "defense" expenditure.

Noting the political tone of almost all their conversations, these days, Megan observes to herself that this in itself is very odd. Is it indeed simply because things are so bad? Are she and Henry simply reacting in an intelligent, responsible way? Or, is she herself becoming a more political person because that is what Henry is? Or (yet another possibility) is the personal connection between them now on the wane, as it were?

And none of the possible answers to any of these questions is cheering, in any way.

In fact, for Megan this is one of those periods when everything in her life is going so badly, along with everything out in the world that she observes and reads about, that she could almost believe in the onset of some era of plague, of universal misfortune.

One of these terrible events (perhaps, in its way, the worst) is a call from Cathy—California, where at the time of the call it is only about nine o'clock, but midnight in New York; it is entirely out of character for Cathy to have forgotten. It is also out of character for her to be a little drunk, which almost immediately she announces that she is. With apologies, of course.

"Oh, Megan, I'm so sorry, I've waked you up. It's just that I'm a little, well, more than a little drunk."

"Cathy, it's all right, I just happened to go to bed early." Megan does not say that Henry is there with her in bed; they went to bed early, together, which somehow they had not managed to do for several weeks.

"Oh, Megan, I'm so sorry," Cathy repeats. "Stephen's at Mother and Bill's, and I've been drinking this brandy."

"But Cathy, why? I mean, are you okay?"

A silence, during which Megan imagines that she can hear the hum of transcontinental cables, in the dark. She knows of course that she cannot, but she can imagine California, now in November, in early nighttime. The whole north coast muffled and blanketed in fog, probably. Winds, foghorns. Megan shivers, there in New York, in her overheated room, next to warm Henry.

Cathy says, "I've been taking these tests, and there seems to be something wrong. You know, uh, malignant."

"Cathy—"

"Oh, and I woke you up! Megan, I'm so stupid. I forgot the whole time thing—"

"But Cathy—"

"Megan, I'll be okay. I'm sorry. Honestly."

"Cathy, will you please tell me what you're talking about. I *am* awake."

"Well, I had all these, uh, aches and pains. More than my normal share, I mean." Cathy laughs, one short harsh note. "So I had some tests, and it isn't good. My bones aren't good. I did not pass the test with flying colors, you might say."

"How many doctors did you go to?" Megan hears and is appalled by the sharp impatience in her own voice.

"Well, just one, actually," Cathy admits.

Yes, and probably some ignorant biased Irish Catholic, Megan does not say. But she had that thought, very clearly, and again, she is appalled by herself. What she actually does say is, "Well, Christ, Cathy. You have to see a lot of doctors. That one could be absolutely wrong. They make mistakes all the time. Even lab tests are wrong, all the time." Her voice is cross, uncontrolled.

"Oh, Megan, I feel so bad that I woke you up." Cathy's voice is dim, fading out.

"You mustn't feel bad, please don't."

"Megan, good night. I'm *sorry*."

And Cathy hangs up, a tiny click, three thousand miles distant.

Megan lies awake, next to Henry, who is soundly sleeping at her side. She can still hear her own impatient, unsympathetic voice, without warmth, none of the affection, the love that she actually feels for Cathy. It is enough to make her cry, which she does, softly, in the clear November eastern dark. She does not want to wake Henry, partly because she cannot bear, yet, to say the words to him: "Cathy has cancer." Even to herself she does not quite say them.

Then, a week or so later, Barbara Blumenthal leans back heavily in her chair, in her office; she looks straight at Megan and she announces, "I seem to have cancer, Megan. I hate to just throw it at you like this, really, I'm very sorry." She looks away, toward the grimy window, the thin December sunlight on gray buildings, other grimy windows.

Looking back to Megan, who has not managed•to say anything, yet, Barbara continues. "I'm partly trying to get used to the word. Not to mention the whole idea." She laughs and coughs, and apologizes. "Sorry." Looking at Megan, her large eyes tear. "Poor Norman," she says. "He just cries, he can't stop. God, what a thing to do to him."

"Oh, but Barbara—"

"Well, I know. Not exactly a ball for me either." Barbara wipes at one eye with an already wadded Kleenex. "Megan, I'm really sorry."

Wanting to take Barbara into her arms—big Barbara, all of her —Megan cannot quite make that gesture (nor, probably, would she have been able to embrace Cathy, in that way, if she and Cathy had been together when Cathy told her about her illness).

Megan simply stands there, still and helpless, saying, "Barbara, I'm so sorry, that's terrible."

"Well, it's terrible to put it on you this way."

"Jesus, Barbara, please don't apologize." (Cathy, don't apologize!)

"Well." In a determined, executive way, Barbara puts her hands down flat on the desk before her, and she looks up at Megan. "We have to talk about what you're going to do. I really forced my doctor, what a jerk, I had to twist his arm, almost, but he finally admitted that I'd be damn lucky to go on working for another six months."

"God."

"Well, I know. This is so sudden and all that. I repeat, I'm very sorry to throw everything at you."

"*Please*, Barbara."

"Well, the point is, I'm going to divide the majority of shares between you and Leslie. I know you're not crazy about her, Megan, but you've got to admit she's first-rate with contracts, my stuff. Norman will have the rest, of course; in a way you'll be working for him, but you know how easy he is."

"Well, Jesus. I just don't know."

"Well, think." And Barbara smiles her old warm reassuring smile, or almost.

That night, as they so often do, Megan and Henry have a long expensive conversation, North Carolina to New York. Having told him about Barbara as briefly and factually as possible, Megan then muses, "It's so odd, about the agency. Ten years ago I would have thought something like that was the greatest thing that could happen to me. All that money. Knowing everyone, and all that. *Power*. But now all the inner voices that I can hear are saying no. They're telling me to get out of the whole thing. And not just because of Leslie."

"I've corrupted you," Henry tells her. "Turned you into an un-American." He laughs gently, then clears his throat. "But that's terrible about Barbara. Terrible," he repeats, with emphasis, although his voice is oddly distant.

"Yes, and Cathy. It's more than I can think about. Or cope with. All this cancer. Death. Jesus Christ, why doesn't Nixon have cancer?"

Henry laughs, but some condition of their phone connection makes the sound fade in and out, eerily. Unclearly he says, "I'm afraid things don't work out like that, generally speaking."

"Isn't there some Catholic heresy about evil being in charge? Is that Manichaean?"

"I'm not sure. Ask Cathy."

"I guess. At least she'd think it was a funny question. Probably. She might laugh."

Some minutes later, hanging up, Megan reflects that this has been a conversation during which nothing at all was said about themselves; for various reasons, they are no longer discussing, making plans.

33

Peg and Cameron Sinclair are invited to the inauguration, Nixon's, but to Cameron's dismay (rage, horror, panic: he thinks she must be getting sick again) Peg refuses to go.

On the day when Cameron triumphantly divulges the fact that they have been invited, Peg simply announces that she will not, will not go. "No," is what Peg says, and all she will add by way of explanation is, "I don't like him."

Cameron responds reasonably—very reasonably, considering. "Of course you don't like him," he tells her. "No one does. The fellow has no class at all. But he's the only person who can turn this country around."

"But maybe in the wrong direction?"

Is this one of Peg's infrequent, never funny, slightly disturbing jokes? Cameron wonders, as he stares at her large, familiar blank white face. He finds no clue. And after a silent moment or two he decides that she was not joking.

How little they have talked to each other, over the past few years especially; but it has been forever, really, now that Cameron thinks of it. It is astonishing, in a way, how little they have spoken. And for the first time this fact strikes him as very sad; more often he has concluded that it is just as well. If they talked a lot all kinds of garbage might be exposed.

For instance, although both the twins are up in Berkeley, doing God-knows-what (being hippies, very likely; they don't come home), Peg has continued to write to them, which he, Cameron, will not do, not until they shape up, come to their senses. He is farily sure that Peg even sends them money. Rex, thank God, is just the opposite, a natural athlete, an SAE at Tulane, and headed for law school. He can't tell yet about Kate. But Cameron has often thought that it was just as well they did not have the boring conversations about the kids that most people seem to be having, these days.

However, Cameron is aware that he has little knowledge of any of Peg's real ideas about the world, about this country, even assuming that she has any such ideas, and he is not too sure. He is only aware of her very overly permissive feelings about her children. And about colored people, come to think of it.

Peg would like to pin some bigot label on him, Cameron firmly believes, to make him out a real KKK type of guy. But he fooled her on that one; when she wanted to bring home, for a visit, that colored girl she met in Georgia (they said she was a Mexican, but it was obvious to Cameron: a dinge), he was perfectly nice about it, which must have surprised Peg a lot. He treated Vera just like any other guest.

And so, now he gets this quite unexpected, inexplicable nonsense about not liking Nixon. Not wanting to go to the inauguration. (He could understand Peg better if she drank, for instance; a lot of Midland wives do. Poor Barbara had to be carted off to that place in Connecticut, finally. But Peg barely drinks.)

Immersed in these thoughts, and in the further not-quite-new question: what does she do all day, and, almost more urgent, where does all her money go? Cameron does not at first entirely grasp what Peg is saying, but then he does: first his name, and then an impossible sentence: "Cameron, I want a divorce."

He sighs, very deeply. She must be sick.

But then she says it again, adding something even crazier. She says, "Cameron, I want a divorce. I'm moving back to Georgia. With Vera."

34

Lavinia, on the other hand is not invited to Nixon's inauguration, although by that time she is the lover (mistress may be the dated but more accurate word) of Harvey Rodman; and he is even more powerful, more important in the new administration (closer to Nixon) and also even richer than Potter said he was. (And of course Lavinia does not want to go to the inauguration.)

But it has all worked out perfectly with Harvey, from Lavinia's point of view; perfect, from her first tiny note, in which she simply said that she had been pleased to hear that he was doing well, to his instant call, and then more calls, and then, finally, their meeting, her allowing him to see her again—in New York, for lunch, at a very discreet restaurant. Many more lunches, in New York and Washington, not to mention all the flowers/presents/impassioned pleas. To all of which Lavinia finally and most gracefully yielded.

Harvey adores her, he always has. He finds her absolutely, totally enchanting. When they are together he feels that he owns the world, he says, stroking her still (to him) perfect skin, on her thin taut thigh.

And when they are apart they are always closely in touch, no matter how fantastically busy Harvey is, all over the world (he is in international monetary funds). There is always a connection between them, if not an actual phone call or a letter, a long cassette of love.

Or a present. Not even Lavinia's banker knows how much *stuff* she has stored in her vault (she has had to admit to herself, Harvey's taste in that direction is the tiniest bit on the vulgar side; she was forced to tell him that she really doesn't care for anything large).

Or flowers. A new myth, created of necessity between Lavinia and Potter, is that she is extraordinarily, irredeemably extravagant when it comes to buying flowers, especially the most delicate, the farthest out-of-season.

Another myth, and one much closer to the truth, is that Lavinia is extremely clever, investment-wise. Of course Harvey cannot actually give her money (he would like to, though, and the idea gives Lavinia a certain perverse thrill), but giving her stock seems acceptable to them both (and almost as thrilling to Lavinia as dirty cash would be). He then advises her when to sell, where next to put her profits. How not to pay taxes. And Lavinia has developed a considerable skill at these transactions on her own. And so, her financial acumen is not really fictional at all; she is wonderful with money, it is just too bad that she has not been really rich before, has not had enough to play with.

Lavinia of course does not in the least want to meet Richard Nixon, or any of those people. But she thinks about him, she thinks about all of them; she feels, through Harvey, the impact of their terrific power. He does not talk about politics with her, but he does let a few things drop, always showing her how close in he is. "It's exciting how few people we've managed to get it down to, just a very few, in total control. There's not much spreading around these days, baby doll, in terms of real power," and he laughs, excitingly.

. . .

At Lavinia's instigation, she and Potter travel a great deal, during those early years of the seventies. Amy is safely (they hope) at Radcliffe now, and Potter is sufficiently advanced in the firm to be able to take time off, more or less at will. "Heaven knows we can afford it," says Lavinia, with a light, modest laugh, in the course of persuading Potter that a couple of weeks in Rome, in October, will make her perfectly happy.

Which is of course where Harvey is to be, at some international monetary conference. Harvey stays at the Hilton, where the conference is; Lavinia is at the Hassler, with her husband. It is very easy for her to murmur, one afternoon, that she really doesn't care about seeing the Vatican: "All those crowds, all those Catholics." (She has always been able to make Potter laugh; amusement is one of her valuable qualities, for him.) She would really like an afternoon of shopping, on her own. And how perfectly natural for her to come back to the Hassler, a little late, a little pale and tired, with an incredibly beautiful antique gold filigree necklace, with yellow sapphires—and to decline very prettily to say how much it cost. "I won't buy another thing for months, I promise. Although actually it was a terrific bargain, in a way."

Although Lavinia has never quite admitted this to herself, one of the best aspects of this love affair with Harvey is that since almost all of their time together is spent in bed, she can easily forget about his crippled legs. He and she do not go out together (or almost never, only in the very remotest places), and so she never has to walk beside him.

In bed she is not taller than he is. She is simply more beautiful; it is her body that is made love to, not his. She does very little for Harvey, along those lines.

Inevitably, having had only two lovers in her life (so far! but you never can tell), comparisons occur to Lavinia's lively mind, although these days she has a little trouble bringing Henry back in any clear way. But out of intellectual curiosity, really, she makes the effort, and she is able to remember pretty well how it was with him, with Henry. What strikes her most, and with an angry force, is that it was she who was most "in love" with Henry. It was she who kissed, as much if not more than he kissed her; she kissed him everywhere, even putting his, uh, thing in her mouth, although she really didn't want to. She would never do that with Harvey.

And if that memory were not enough to make her hate, despise Henry Stuyvesant, there is his continuing affair with Megan Greene, who is basically disgusting. She always has been. Megan, a dumpy, dowdy girl from California, who even thinned-down and in expensive clothes (well, fairly expensive) never looks quite right. And heaven knows where Megan kisses Henry (Lavinia has a little private giggle, at that salacious thought).

Whereas, it is Harvey who adores *her*, who kisses her, strokes her whole body with his hands, and then his tongue. He makes her come three or four times in an afternoon—which makes him so pleased with himself, with so much success, with *her*.

Afterwards Harvey bathes her. She lies there in perfumed foam, in the bathrooms of their various hotels, all over the world. She lies back, in Amsterdam (the Amstel) or Paris (the Crillon), in the scented steam, and Harvey very gently, delicately washes her, everywhere.

It is almost the part of their time together that Harvey likes best, Lavinia feels.

In fact everything with Harvey is perfect, is marvelous—her whole life is perfect, until a strange afternoon in Juneau, Alaska, of all crazy places. In June 1972. June 17, in fact.

First Lavinia went alone to San Francisco, on the pretext, to Potter, of seeing Cathy, her old classmate, now so sick. And actually she did go to see Cathy, in the hospital, which was not exactly a cheering visit.

To begin with, the enormous white hospital was Catholic, of course, nuns all over the place, priests hurrying along the corridors, and everywhere those awful crucifixes.

Directed at last to Cathy's room, Lavinia first thought that she must have been sent to the wrong place; just like those nuns—they can tell a Protestant. The person in the bed there, her head all wrapped in white, had no look of Cathy at all. But then in Cathy's voice that person spoke; she said, "Lavinia." Just a statement; no particular surprise and less welcome in her voice.

"Oh, Cathy. Yes. I've, uh, come to see you."

The room had more flowers in it than Lavinia had ever seen, a shocking amount of flowers, really; the place looked like a vulgar florist shop, and also they dwarfed the spray of yellow roses for which Lavinia had just paid a lot of money. Still, she had bought them, and so, unnecessarily, she added, "I brought you some roses," holding them out.

Cathy's laugh was new and sharp, a small bark. "Coals to Newcastle, indeed. Or maybe whores to Paris? Curiously enough, my mother's married to a retired florist, and he tends to keep me rather oversupplied. But thanks, Lavinia."

Only her voice was familiar; that white swollen face, the puffy hands could have belonged to anyone. And that awful bleached white cotton gown, with the same material wrapped around her head (dear God, could Cathy be bald now?).

Staring straight at Lavinia (reading her mind?), Cathy announced, "In fact I'm as bald as a ball. This chemotherapy is really great stuff." Her voice had tiny cracks in it, like a slightly scratched record.

"Oh, Cathy, that's terrible."

"They say it may grow back, but I rather think not. These good Sisters can be the most terrible liars." And then she said, "One of the problems with cancer is that it can be so fucking slow."

Did Cathy used to talk that way? Shocked, Lavinia was almost sure that she did not; only Megan would sometimes use those words, that she probably got from that terrible Adam Marr, or Janet Cohen. Could this person, just possibly, not be Cathy after all?

Reading Lavinia's mind (*again*), Cathy said, I'll bet you'd hardly have known me, right?"

Lavinia murmured something—helplessly, incoherently.

"Well, you might as well sit down, mightn't you? And tell me what brings you to adorable San Francisco."

"Oh. I, uh, came to see you, really." Lavinia could feel herself flushing, as she said this.

"Oh, come on now, Lavinia. Don't be silly. You're not a nun, you don't get to lie to me." The barking laugh again.

There was no possible answer to that non-joke. Lavinia busied herself with sitting down, putting her bag on the floor beside her. She was still holding the superfluous roses, which fortunately looked very well against her dress: a striped silk, black and yellow, in which she had been shivering, in the San Francisco summer fog that she had heard about but been unable to believe in. She had been unable to imagine a climate other than the one that she was in as she packed, New York's summer heat. It was rather like trying to imagine yourself another person (at which Lavinia had never been successful): how would it be to be Cathy, dying of cancer?

"Those roses are *perfect* with your dress," unnervingly commented Cathy; in an ironic way she had underlined perfect, as they all used to do—Lavinia sharply, painfully remembered, that funny language of the four of them, the four friends who possibly never really liked each other. The language that she, Lavinia, had always insisted derived from the Duchess de Guermantes, from Proust.

"Perhaps you should take those roses along to wherever you're going next," Cathy then suggested.

"Oh, don't be so silly." Lavinia had not wanted to sound so sharp, but she had just come to a sudden and clear decision, which was that, even dying, Cathy did not have to be so cross, so *rude*. Nevertheless, Lavinia then asked very gently, "How's your son getting along—Philip?"

"Stephen." Cathy frowned, and looked away, and then she was quiet for a while.

Lavinia floundered: should she not, after all, have asked about the boy? Of course she had never, not for a minute believed that fishy story of Megan's, Cathy's brief marriage to someone instantly dead—but maybe that was true? maybe he too had had cancer? Is anyone absolutely sure that it is not contagious, or somehow passed on?

Cathy cleared her throat. "Actually Stephen's fine," she said. "Remarkably. He lives with my mother and Bill, her husband. It's as though—" (a long pause) "as though he had been meant to be there, all along. With them." Her new, quick alarming laugh. "If anyone believed in that kind of master plan."

In the pause that followed, Lavinia recognized—and very likely so did Cathy—that that was it. They had covered everything they had to say to each other, possibly. However, how could she possibly leave after only ten minutes?

"Did you hear about Peglet's divorce?" Lavinia next brightly attempted. "So crazy, and she's moved to some old house in the country. In Georgia, of all places."

"Is that crazy, necessarily?"

"Well, uh, in the circumstances. You may not know this, Cathy, but Peglet is an extremely rich girl. *Extremely* rich."

"Oh. Well, you're right, I didn't exactly know that." A pause. "But do you mean that extremely rich people don't get to live in old houses in Georgia? I would have thought that to be a virtue of richness, you could live anywhere."

Lavinia laughed in a feeble way, and only added, "Well, at least she's had the sense to take a friend along. Some social worker she met in Georgia that summer is going there too." A pause, before she went on, "And of course now Megan's the head, or joint head, of that really successful agency."

"Oh yes, since her boss died of cancer," was Cathy's quick response.

"Well yes, I guess she did. Barbara Blumenthal."

Cathy laughed. "Well, there sure seems to be a lot of it around." Abruptly, then, she lay back and closed her eyes. "Nap time, I guess. You'll forgive me?"

"Oh, Cathy, of course. I'm sorry, I didn't mean to stay. Uh, I'll call you before I go." Unable to go over and kiss Cathy goodbye (that was probably all right with Cathy, she looked already asleep), Lavinia got up and tiptoed out of the room. She had to get away from all those garish flowers, in their awful plastic containers. Away from Cathy.

Once out in the corridor, though, Lavinia noticed that she was still carrying the roses she had brought. Too ridiculous; still, no point in their being entirely wasted. They would help her hotel room a little, her supposedly view suite, in the Mark.

She pushed through the hospital's swinging doors, passing more nuns, more priests (how ugly they all were, no wonder they're celibate) and went out into the foggy cold that she had been told about, but not believed.

She had to wait quite a while before getting a taxi—as she would have to wait, with not much to do, all the next day, until her late afternoon plane to Juneau.

She did not, therefore, arrive in Juneau in a mood that was exactly upbeat. That grim visit with Cathy left her disturbed and vaguely guilty; she wondered what she could have done, otherwise, in the face of such determined unpleasantness from Cathy. When she had thought at all before of dying people she had believed that they could be counted on to behave in a quiet, somewhat distant way, like saints. But Cathy, who was never notably sweet-tempered, was much worse than ever; in fact she was terrible, and the more Lavinia thought of it the more marked (the more inexcusable, really) that terribleness became. When you came right down to it, Cathy was extremely rude.

Also, the descent into Juneau is frightening: a narrow passage between steep mountains, sheer cliffs of rock, and below a bluish-white field, which someone at Lavinia's elbow identifies as a glacier. The Mendenhall Glacier. The air outside the plane is gray with fog, or maybe rain—and dark, and dull.

She walks into the terminal building, meaning to head straight for the baggage pick-up area. The room is full of foolish-looking, mostly fat, and all very dowdy people, who must have come to meet someone, see someone off. But suddenly there among them she sees

Harvey, off to one side, frowning (and shorter than anyone, any grown-up, because of his terrible legs). His face is perfectly all right, just a plain man's face, which, curiously, away from him Lavinia can never quite remember. However, at the sight of him standing there like that, despite being so "madly in love" with Harvey, Lavinia's heart drops, coldly. So that he will not limp over to her she rushes toward him, though, her face smiling, beautifully. Reaching him she bends down and they kiss, passionately, although Lavinia can already see that he is annoyed. He is preoccupied with something else, having nothing to do with her.

Together they move toward the luggage place, as Harvey explains that the hotel at which they were to have met has turned out not to be, after all, the very best one; there was no way to let her know where to go and so, unprecedentedly, he has come to meet her. However, the hotel problem is not what is most on his mind—nor is she at the moment foremost; Lavinia can tell. And she prepares to wait, probably to listen to some boring news about the group called CREEP that he talks about a lot, these days. (Lavinia thinks the name is extremely funny, and she can never remember what those initials stand for—something about re-electing the President, *that* creep. Harvey laughs too, sometimes.)

As they stand there together, among all those awful-looking people, in the awful light, Harvey's small hand holds Lavinia's, which is fortunately even smaller. As she often does, Lavinia takes in the fact that they are by far the most elegant, the richest-looking people in that place, no comparison. In that dreary, dowdy company they could be visiting royalty, and perhaps they are being taken for exactly that, at just that moment. However, as though she herself were one of those staring people, looking at herself, at Harvey, Lavinia at the same time senses that there is something wrong, in a visual way, with her and Harvey. Something morally amiss is suggested by her height and beauty, coupled with Harvey's too-short crippled legs, his dreadful ungainly walk. They should not be together, aesthetically; from an exterior *or* moral point of view, they look like two people who are up to no good, and their sin is much darker and more complex than the simple fact of adultery.

. . .

The room in the hotel to which Harvey has moved them is tacky beyond belief (piss-elegant, Megan would probably say, which of course is awful, but sometimes quite descriptive): gold threads in the draperies and a huge painting of big white bears, on black velvet. But they do have windows overlooking the harbor; there are boats, shining silver-gray water, and across the way some darkly wooded islands.

"Strange, it looks sort of like the coast of Yugoslavia, doesn't it," Harvey remarks, as for a moment they stand there, contemplating Juneau. Then, "Christ, come on, let's go to bed," and he pulls her along with him, to bed.

As always, Harvey undresses her; he makes love to her with his usual eager vigor. He makes her come twice, although she notices that he does not come, himself.

A little while later he orders champagne; good, they do have Dom Pérignon. And he tells her his worrying news: some Cubans have been caught breaking into Democratic headquarters. In the Watergate.

35

Letters from Cathy to Megan, excerpted; 1972–73:

Lousy Lavinia came to see me, such a surprise. I had a strong sense that I was her excuse to be somewhere else, and I responded "appropriately," i.e., by being horrible to her. All the saint went right out of me at the very sight. I was even glad that she had worn all the wrong clothes, probably the first time in her life that happened, i.e., she had on summer silks, in which she must have frozen. In any case, it was my feeling that she was "up to no good."

You are very nice to offer to come to see me. My feeling really is, no. I look terrible and you would be upset. Even hardhearted Lavinia was upset. Your letters are great. I enjoy writing to you. I repeat: it is kind of you to offer, and it is good to know that you would come if I asked. Okay? You can hear what I'm saying?

One thing about dying is the time that it is a waste of (do you like that sentence?). I can no longer kid myself that I am engaged in any other activity whatsoever. I am dying, and the process seems to get slower every day. If only I weren't stuck in this religion which prohibits the "easy way out."

Stephen is fine. I have made my mother stop bringing him here. She is much better at motherhood than I was (am, would be—this dying messes up tenses, along with everything else). But did God have to give me cancer to get me out of the way? I would willingly just have given her the kid.

Aren't the Watergate hearings fun? I have fallen in love with the eyebrows of Senator Ervin.

I now seem to be having what is called a remission, and I can't tell you how that enrages me. It is like going back to GO, without passng anything worthwhile or collecting anything. I have really had more than enough cancer time already. My mother brought me a lovely book, however, which you have no doubt already read a dozen times. *Cranford*, by Mrs. Gaskell. That Victorian coziness is so comforting, like being born into the right family after all. It's too bad the afterlife can't go backwards, or around in a circle, if you see what I mean. In that case I could die and be reborn as a Victorian spinster, in some English village, which would certainly beat being an unmarried Catholic mother, in what we call modern America. Are you going to marry that Henry Stuyvesant? I never think about the Father (cap's a mistake, but honesty makes me let it stand) of Stephen. Thank God for that.

I think the remission is over. Would you really come out? I think I need to see you.

At that small note, which unaccountably took five days to get from San Francisco to New York, Megan instantly calls her travel agent. The first flight she can get on is the next morning, a Friday, and it goes from Newark, rather than JFK, to Oakland, rather than San Francisco, all of which is all right.

She will call her own parents once she has got there and seen Cathy, Megan decides—sitting at her important cluttered desk, at her important East Fifties address. And she plans to call Cathy's mother late that afternoon; surely she will be able to find the letter on which Cathy, with the prescience which has seemed a part of her illness, has given Megan her mother's new married name, and her telephone number. "In case you ever have some hurried need to know how I am," Cathy wrote.

Megan tells Leslie that she will be in California—"for at least a week, probably."

"No problem."

Megan reflects that she cannot stand people who say "no problem." And that it is qute unnecessary to explain to Leslie the nature of her mission in California.

Later that afternoon, that Thursday, there is to be a book party at one of the big uptown hotels, to which Megan feels that she must go; the publisher is extremely important (viewed, currently, as "hot"), and Megan has been at times much less cordial toward him than she might have been, professionally. (She privately regards him as an idiot, but how could he be? she has asked herself.) In any case today seems an opportune time for her to show up, if briefly. However, since she is leaving so early the next day, must pack and all that, she decides not to go home to change before the party.

About five, then, Megan begins to look for Cathy's mother's new name and her telephone number, which surprisingly she finds right away; she herself had neatly written them down in her address book, just under Cathy's name and her hospital address. In any case, she must now call Mrs. Piscetti—her number has an old San Francisco prefix, SKyline, which is enough to make Megan sadly, briefly sigh for California, as she dials the familiar area code, 415.

"Uh, Mrs. Piscetti? This is Megan Greene, we've met—I'm Cathy's friend—"

"Oh, Megan, of course. And how very good you are to call."

Megan hears the light hint of a brogue in Cathy's mother's voice. She tells her, "Cathy wrote me that she'd like to see me, and so tomorrow—"

"Ah, Megan." The force in Mrs. Piscetti's voice has interrupted Megan. "Ah, Megan," she says. "But Cathy left us. The day before yesterday. Tuesday it was, when she died."

"Oh, Jesus." Gone suddenly cold with shock, Megan clutches the phone to her ear, as Cathy's mother goes on talking. "In her sleep—no pain—a mercy—"

"I think I'll come to California anyway, if that's all right," is all that Megan can find to say, and she adds, "I'll call you when I get there. If you could see me—"

"Well, Megan dear, of course."

In a numb way at the same time Megan decides, hanging up, that she will go on to that party anyway; she will do everything as though Cathy had not died, and she were going out to see her (as though magically that would make Cathy less dead; as though Cathy would go on writing letters, having stronger, more convincing remissions).

In a dazed way she begins the walk up Fifth Avenue, past all the store windows which at this season blaze with splendor, gold and velvet and furs for the coming holidays. Which Megan barely sees. But, looking down certain side streets in the East Sixties, then Seventies, she is struck by the absolute uniqueness of a particular New York look: the old irregular sidewalks, thick old trees, the small rise of trim white steps, with iron handrails leading up to heavy substantial black doors, polished brass mail slots and name-plates. No blocks in Paris look quite like that, she recalls, nor in San Francisco, where Cathy is. Cathy was.

She then realizes that she is looking at New York in a strange, elegiac way, as though she would not come back, ever, from her trip to California. Which is foolish; she is only going for a week or so, and not exactly to see Cathy. She is no longer certain why she is going out there, being simply led by an impulse that instructs her to continue as she was headed, more or less, before Cathy died.

She then thinks, How odd that I didn't call Henry. Of all people he would know how much I cared about Cathy. Thinking of not calling Henry, of Henry, Megan suddenly and quite irrationally feels as though Henry too were lost, gone, along with Cathy. Ridiculous: they were together the weekend before.

In an unconscious way she has walked along one of those so characteristic New York blocks, not quite stumbling on the uneven sidewalk. She has reached her destination, Madison Avenue. And, as she turns the corner, again heading north, she is accosted by a mammoth travel poster, in a window (later she thinks of, finally remembering, the scene in *The Informer,* and Victor McLaglen, Gippo, caught by a poster whirled around his legs, advertising escape). This poster shows an almost naked couple on a beach. Bright blue ocean, palm trees. Come to Hawaii, at a new bargain rate. Its appeal is so improbable, so trashily unreal, that Megan thinks, Well, why not? Why not do just that: go to a trashy, un-likely place, and lie there anonymously, in the harsh, leveling sun-light, impersonally, for a week? She notes that the airline involved is the same one on which she is traveling to San Francisco, which seems some sort of sign, in her curious, numb mood. She could fly to San Francisco, she could go to see Cathy's mother—and then go on to bake in the sun, to sweat everything out of herself, to forget everything, in Hawaii.

Although she is early, the party which is Megan's actual destina-tion is already crowded, and smoky.

The first person she sees, though at a distance, is the hot young publisher, Benny, for whose sake she is here. He is not hard to see, in his pink suede blazer, with his conspicuously blond hair, his famously frightening pale blue eyes. Although he is married, and the father of several children, this man's appearance and his rather high voice ("he sounds so much like Truman") both give rise to constant rumors as to his sexual direction: "But of course he's gay," is whispered, or sometimes loudly, drunkenly asserted, up and down Madison Avenue. To Megan, however, this seems not to be the case; to her he comes across as not in any sense a sexual person, he is as sexually neutral as anyone she has ever met. And all the talk about how he published and extravagantly promoted a novel by a certain beautiful boy is nonsense, she believes; Benny was drawn to that book in a business way, and to its author by a pure and violently commercial instinct, which turned out to be quite sound: the book made hundreds of thousands for Benny's house, as he knew that it would.

That piping voice, too, is easily overheard, as it pronounces, "I've been reading, or rather, rereading—God, it came out while I was still at Hotchkiss—and you won't believe this, but it's the most absolutely perfect, wonderful novel. I am totally serious, and I am talking about *The Fountainhead*. The scenes in that book, the strength—"

Unable to comment, Megan veers instead toward the bar, where she is given a double martini, a drink that she has not had for almost twenty years, since early Village days with Jackson Clay, she recalls, with a vaguely painful pang.

"Of course I'm not really interested in films made since 1951," is the next full sentence that reaches Megan. "My all-time favorite is *The Red Shoes*. What's your favorite, darling Megan?"

"Oh, *The Informer*, maybe. I guess."

"Oh, what an adorable Irish thing you are, dearest Megan." And off he goes, Benny, the hottest publisher in town.

To her horror Megan realizes that the strong drink is simply giving her a strong urge to cry.

She decides that she will not risk talking to anyone else. She will walk around the room very slowly, but as though with some reasonable intention. Always smiling. "Making an appearance" would precisely describe what she is doing.

"But a seven-figure paperback sale? That's quite a bundle."

"My guess is he'll never finish it."

"Everyone knows, they're all dykes over there, and even those that aren't pretend to be, including himself."

"But he just left William Morris."

"She came back from the Coast with the most heavenly new pills."

Megan manages to stay in that overheated, overcrowded room, so full of violent conflicting odors: perfume and the sweat of anxiety, liquors, aromatic foods, plus all the smoke from cigarettes, pipes, cigars—she endures all that, and the noise from those urgent tongues, the hundreds of them, all spouting idiocy, for almost half an hour, without giving way to any of the impulses that almost overwhelm her; she does not throw up, or cry, she does not rush out of the room.

In a dignified way she finally leaves; outside she finds a cab quickly. From its window she gulps at air, in the rush down Fifth Avenue.

Back in her own private, welcoming apartment she irons a few things, she sews on a button. She packs, and makes a few obligatory phone calls: breaking next week's lunch dates, winding up business.

At last she does call Henry, but no one answers, at his remote Carolina cabin. Megan feels that she can hear the emptiness of his house, in those echoing rings. It occurs to her to try him at the Jacobses' house, where he well might be. But then she does not.

She goes to bed and to sleep, having managed to think of Cathy peacefully, unsentimentally. Not having cried.

The only thing that Megan neglects to do is to call the airport the following morning to check on the time of her flight. And, arrived at Newark, not too surprisingly it turns out that there is a two-hour delay before her plane will leave.

Panicking, for an instant this seems to Megan the one thing too much for her to bear: two hours in the Newark airport? in this large, confused, and entirely unpromising room? But she cannot afford to panic, and with an effort she brings it under control. She looks around and finds the ticket office of her airline, at which there is another poster beckoning her to Hawaii.

In a resolute way Megan goes up to the counter, at which, providentially, there is no line. And, a yet greater gift from fate, there is an intelligent, pleasant, and slightly shy young woman, black and plump, softly pretty. With whom, in a remarkably short time, Megan arranges to change her trip: she will fly directly to Hawaii, stopping in San Francisco only to change planes. She will spend five days on Maui, in Lahaina. Then two days in San Francisco, before coming back to New York.

At the end of all those arrangements (which included reservations at the Pioneer, at Lahaina) Megan thanks the woman who was so helpful. In a conversational way she says, "I can hardly believe this is happening. I'd never exactly meant to go to Hawaii."

A slow smile. "Well, I really hope you like it there."

"You've been?"

"Well, no." A slower, fainter smile.

Megan smiles back and hurries off toward her plane, which is loading now.

36

Megan's flight to Hawaii goes so smoothly that she is barely aware of what is happening. At one instant they are taking off from Newark, then flying over the blood-red fall woods of northern New Jersey, and in what seems almost no time later they are sailing over the endless bright and relentlessly blue Pacific. (Or, perhaps she slept through some of that flight? She made the change in San Francisco as a somnambulist? Megan is aware of some deep, pervasive fatigue, and she wonders, Is tiredness my substitute for mourning Cathy?)

The small monkeyish steward instructs everyone in some rudimentary Hawaiian words, all of which have a silly, baby-talk sound. He makes rather primitive sexual innuendoes, at which everyone in Megan's vicinity laughs, a slightly hysterical combination of relief (the flight is almost over) and embarrassment at the sheer idiocy of what is being said.

For the first time then since seeing the travel poster on Madison Avenue, Megan begins to wonder seriously at what she is doing: is it after all preposterous? Also, it occurs to her for the first time that she has no clothes for Hawaii with her, not even a bathing suit. However, the instinct that has carried her along so far remains strong; doubts do not attack her again until she has taken the small plane from Oahu to Maui, and a taxi to the Pioneer Hotel.

A pretty boy escorts her up to her room; with an enormous iron key he opens the door. He smiles, pleased at his tip, and leaves her there.

Megan sits alone then on the white edge of her very wide bed, under the slow, wooden-bladed fan, and she looks out through narrowly louvered windows, to palm trees, blood-red bougainvillea, and the flat blue sea. Closing her eyes against too much newness, she is simultaneously assailed by a confusion of impressions from the past few hours, like a rerun film: she resees the ghastly garish Honolulu airport, wild synthetic tourist clothes on everyone, horrible glutted souvenir shops, dolls, costumes. She sees the light plane shuddering above the shining water. Sees endless golf courses, and the tawdry little town. The lobby of the Pioneer, which is crowded with spacy, sun-bleached kids, and pale middle-aged alcoholics. And she wonders: *why*? why here? She thinks: I must be having some sort of breakdown. This is craziness. Nothing about where I am makes any sense.

But, if she sits there alone, if she does nothing for long enough, Megan is aware that she will indeed break down. She will go crazy.

In a resolute way she stands up. She opens her bag, unpacks a few things; going out to buy some clothes has to be her next step, she thinks.

Here in Hawaii, so many time zones west of New York, it is still midafternoon—although Megan feels that she has been traveling all day, which in fact she has. It is hardly surprising that she is incredibly tired.

But then suddenly, like a present from the recesses of her own mind, it comes to Megan (she has stopped even pretending to unpack, to be going out to shop) that somewhere she read that Jackson Clay had moved to Lahaina, and was playing some small clubs there. Clubs *here*.

Pleasure at the very thought of Jackson is infinitely soothing to Megan, as though a smooth hand had touched her face; she thinks that even if she cannot get in touch with Jackson, which is highly possible, the very idea of his nearness is comforting. And she thinks too how remarkable it is that even after so much time, over fifteen years, she will feel no hesitant shyness about telephoning Jackson. Picking up the phone book, beginning to look for "Clay," Megan could almost believe that she came here on purpose to see Jackson, to be comforted by him. (Perhaps after all there is a rational motive to this seemingly crazy trip.)

In any case, that is what she says to Jackson, a couple of hours later—in the now wildly disordered, sweat- and dope-smelling, sexy bed.

Exhausted beyond exhaustion, lying just away from him, Megan says, "You see? I came to see you. I knew you'd be here." She reaches to touch his smooth, slightly fleshier yellow-brown chest.

He says, "You did right to come." Aside from having put on a little weight, Jackson is unchanged; to Megan, he is no less beautiful. As always, his wide smile involves his eyes, just barely slant; as his mouth widens, white teeth shine—in the darkening, cooling room. He adds, "But honey, you're way too thin. I don't think your life is right for you, there in New York. And I know. Me, I had to get out of there."

"That's probably true." Megan had meant to say something else; she had something more to tell him, but whatever it was she drifts away without having said it, her mind emptied, body drained. She drifts off into a dreamless black space. Rest. Peace.

The next time Megan wakes up, Jackson is looking at the luminous dial of his watch; he is saying, "Holy shit, I got just ten minutes to get there."

But his movements remain deliberate, as he gets out of bed and reaches for clothes, very slowly putting them on.

He stops to ask, "Baby, you sure I can't get you something to eat?"

Megan smiles, and then laughs, though faintly; it is hard to make a sound (they have smoked so much dope!). She feels such pleasure at his niceness, though. It seems to Megan at that moment that no one was ever so simply kind. "Oh no," she murmurs. "I'm okay. I'll just sleep."

"—lunch," she believes he has said, as he kisses her mouth, then her breast, as he says, "This's the only place you not too thin."

She would like to laugh, in a grateful, acknowledging way, but she is asleep, before Jackson is out of the room.

The next morning, though, Cathy's death rushes back over Megan, like a penance visited upon her for forgetting—for so long. It is overwhelming. In the hot bright white sun-flooded room, in that unreal, entirely unlikely place, she thinks of Cathy, but not Cathy as she knew her, not her brightest, funniest friend. She thinks of Cathy dying, for all that time, alone in her white hospital room, everything smelling of drugs, of death. She hears Cathy's voice, the familiar, now silenced voice of Cathy's letters, saying, "If only they would let me go home. Actually any home would do. I am not 'more comfortable' here. I hate doctors, everything they do to me. Please come out here. I need to see you."

All those words and more play and replay themselves in Megan's inner ear, in Cathy's wry, self-deprecating voice—until in a blind way Megan rushes up and out of bed, she gets into her foolish New York silk shirt and skirt. She goes out into the bright flowery air.

She has breakfast—she eats enormously.

She buys a bathing suit, some white pants, a couple of shirts.

And then it is time to come back to the Pioneer. To meet Jackson.

To get back into bed with him.

For that is what they instantly do, all those five days—a time that Megan later sees as a time of true derangement; she was having a breakdown, of some sort, after all. And so was Jackson, he was burning himself out on drugs.

They make love and smoke dope, and when at some point Megan tells Jackson that she does not feel quite right, quite well, he gives her a small green pill. Which sends her off into crazy dreams: some terrifying, with weird, horrifying landscapes, a Doré *Inferno*.

Returned to "reality," her bed in the Pioneer Hotel, in Lahaina, Maui, Hawaii, and Jackson Clay—reality turns out to be as crazy as her dreams. Endless fucking, an endless orgasm, that seems to hollow her out.

In the rare lucid intervals when she is able to see Jackson with anything like clarity, Megan notes that he does not look well, really. His very wide-spaced, barely slanted eyes are reddened, and smaller in their surrounding fatty flesh, and his skin is darker, a murky yellow brown. His hands shake. She does not dare ask if anything is seriously wrong; the truth is that if there is she does not want to know—not now, she could not bear it.

She does, though, ask Jackson what the green pills are.

He laughs and cups her breasts, and he kisses her before he says, "They just called greens, round here. They like some native potion." He laughs again, an infinitely affectionate sound—but the affection is for the pills as much as for herself, Megan feels.

She says, "I really don't think I want to take any more."

"Baby, that's all right. You just don't."

What Megan most would like is just to hear Jackson play again; she realizes this after two or three days of only sex, high doped-up screwing, crazy naps. But Jackson's music was what drew her so violently to him, at first, all those years ago. On 52d Street.

And so, Jackson takes her to the club where he sometimes plays, late at night—her last night in Hawaii.

The club itself is ghastly. Although in a dim way Megan has been aware of where she is, Hawaii, she was not prepared for the parodic Hawaiian-ness of that place: the horrid profusion of gaudy, hideous flowers, the cruelly phallic birds of paradise, the hideous red plastic-looking anthurium, the febrile orchids. And the sick-sweet smells of other flowers, fetid, lurking in that small dark overheated cellar room. Even, as Megan and Jackson descend the narrow stairs, down into the smoke, there is horrible "Hawaiian" music playing, electric ukuleles; and on the small stage a very fat, very dark woman, topless, is dancing in a hula skirt, her big breasts swinging wild.

It is horrible; as in one of her green pill nightmares Megan, though seated at an inconspicuous corner table with Jackson (at least she does know where she is, and with whom), Megan believes, or feels, that that dark fat undulating woman is herself. There is fat dark old Megan, dancing—dancing in Hawaii, among sickening smells of alien, putrefying flowers.

But then she is not sitting with Jackson, she is there seated alone, and the dark fat dancing woman has disappeared. But up there on the stage is Jackson, with his horn, and behind him a small upright piano, someone playing, and a big bass, a bass player standing there, providing a gentle rhythmic background for Jackson, who is *playing*: his fantastic powerful always new sounds! his wild inventions, lovely lyric sweetness, his pure sounds of sex.

Suddenly sane, Megan thinks, as she listens, I'm really all right, then. In some way Jackson is okay, and so am I. Her eyes fill, at her awareness that he is playing for her; his horn slides toward her, his wide dark brown eyes on her, he is talking to her, saying everything.

And that is the moment that her trip was all about, she is later, slowly, to realize. She came there to hear Jackson play.

The next morning she does think of Cathy again, but now she is able to think of Cathy alive, Cathy brighter and funnier than anyone. No longer dying.

To break the flight back, Megan has, as planned, a twenty-four-hour layover in San Francisco, an expensive room at the St. Francis, which overlooks not Union Square but a curious concrete courtyard, with a small fountain and some small plumy ferns. That look gives her an odd sensation of being already back in New York—or that San Francisco has at last become New York.

Bracing herself, she dials the number that she has for Mrs. Piscetti, Cathy's mother. But the phone rings and rings, and no one answers.

Inwardly promising herself to try again, Megan goes out for a walk.

On Geary Street, as she passes the theaters, she sees that in one of them *Nicaragua*, one of Adam's greatest successes, is currently playing. Thinking of Adam in a friendly way, she smiles, and continues her walk, turning upward toward Nob Hill.

Back in the hotel, very tired, Megan decides that she will not even call her own parents, but that decision somehow shocks her, and instead she dials the familiar number.

The phone rings for a long time as Megan thinks, Well, of course, Florence is off carhopping and Harry is off—somewhere. Just what her father does on her mother's work nights is something that Megan has not considered before, and now she has barely time to, before Florence answers.

"Hello?" Florence sounds muffled, distant, or sick? But Florence is never sick.

"It's me, Megan." And Megan tries to explain: between planes, hardly any time. As usual, she notes to herself, she is making excuses, when in fact her mother has asked nothing of her.

But then Florence does ask something. "I'd give just anything to see you now," she says, in an almost pleading, unfamiliar way. "We could talk—"

"I *know*, I *do* wish we could," agrees Megan, meaning: I know I've never talked to you, and it may be time. "But now I just can't, I'm burned out, and I have to get back," she says. "I'll call you from New York."

"Well, that just might be the very best thing—a long-distance gab can be a real treat." The old Florence—perky, folksy—and perhaps pretending? Megan resolves to call her soon, for a long conversation.

She dials Mrs. Piscetti's number again, and still gets no answer. She concludes that they must be away.

She orders dinner in her room, with a good bottle of California wine.

She writes a long letter to Jackson, which she then tears up.

And the next day she takes an early plane to New York, Oakland to Newark, again.

"You're the only person I've ever seen just back from Hawaii without any tan at all," is the dead-pan comment of Leslie DuVal.

"Well, I had a lot to do there."

"Oh. Business?" Poor Leslie, chatty by nature, is frustrated, always, by Megan.

"Well yes, sort of. Private business."

"*Oh.*" Leslie sniffs. Desperately concerned with style, Leslie invents her own fashions; it is her form of fiction, Megan understands. That day she is wearing black net stockings, a tight black skirt and very high heels. "Well," she now says to Megan, "you won't mind if I'm a little late back from lunch? I'm doing it with Benny."

. . .

She goes home early.

Tired and aimless, disoriented in her own apartment, Megan's attention is suddenly caught by the preening voice of a news announcer; coming in, out of habit she must have flicked on the radio. He is talking about Christopher Street, and a slight breathiness in his delivery indicates that he has something big on his mind. "Christopher Street, where there have been several ugly incidents of what is known as 'fag-baiting' or 'queer-bashing' tonight added a new horror to its list. The famous playwright Adam Marr, out walking with a young actor, Donald Stark, neither of them, uh, known homosexuals—were assaulted by three men. There was an exchange of insults, and shots were fired by the men in the car, who escaped. They were not identified by passersby. . . . Not expected to live . . . Survived by . . . Shock . . . very successful playwright . . . wives . . . children . . . successful . . ."

Megan manages to turn off the radio, that horrible self-approving voice. She manages to sit down. She finds that she is trembling, and not weeping but covering her face with her hands as though she were.

She does not, of course, for an instant believe that Adam is dead. Nor Cathy.

After a while, when she can, Megan dials Janet's number, and is informed by an answering service that Dr. Marr is unavailable at this time. Is this an emergency? Well, is it? Dr. Marr will call.

Megan considers making herself a drink, and decides on tea instead, partly because boiling the water, heating the pot—all that tea ceremony will take up a certain amount of time.

Fortified, but hardly comforted, by her cup of tea, Megan telephones Biff.

Biff's voice is so tight that at first Megan thinks he must have guests, except that in that case he would explain, "Darling Megan, I couldn't be busier. Could we just possibly talk tomorrow?" Tonight he says nothing of the sort; in a dull-sounding way he asks about her trip and then, in answer to her question ("You've heard the news?") suddenly and entirely unexpectedly, entirely out of character (as Megan has known his character), Biff begins to shriek: "Of *course* I've heard the news. Lord God, don't you know anything? It could have been me! Megan, can't you tell I don't want to talk to you? I don't want to *see* you!"

Shocked, wounded, and most of all terrified, Megan hangs up. She believes that in some way she can understand Biff's outburst, his panic and rage, and she can tell herself that it really has nothing to do with her.

She goes to bed, and lies awake. She is wholly terrified of the world, all its lurking evils. Cancer. Crazy cretins bearing guns.

At some point her phone rings. She does not answer.

That night, and for days, for weeks to come, Megan finds it impossible to think of Adam—dead. Instead she continuously sees him, with the most incredible vividness, as first she did see him, on the steps of Barnard Hall, the soldier who for one instant she thought might be George Wharton. Adam, the skinny too-curly-haired boy with the violent hot blue eyes, Adam saying to her, "You know, if you'd lose some weight you'd be one terrific tomato."

And of Cathy too Megan thinks in earlier, middle-forties scenes. Cathy alive, in all her distinctiveness, her private quirks—her odd voice and odder wit. Cathy herself.

Of all the various known and available therapies, Megan chooses work, at that time of her life. Instead of getting out of the agency and doing something else, as she has from time to time considered, if vaguely, she throws herself back into it. She works ten and twelve hours a day, and also she walks back and forth to work every day.

And she almost succeeds, sometimes, in numbing the pain of Cathy's loss, and the shock of Adam's.

She does not call her mother.

37

In Georgia, after the deaths of the Sawyers (mercifully occurring within a single year), their house was bought by a sporting type from Texas, in the probate sale. He soon became disappointed with the local game, the scrawny rabbits and tough old squirrels not being just what he had in mind, and he took out his chagrin on the house, in the form of total neglect. The Sawyers' lawyer, a family friend, wrote to Peg, who had kept up with the Sawyers. Would she possibly be interested? Would she not! And so, when Peg arrived, she found too a great deal of work to be done; rescue work, so gratifying! She has probably never been so happy in her life, as she sees to propping up the sagging porch, arranges for the sanding of floors, discusses drains.

She loves everything about the house: its history, beginning with the Sawyers, just down from Black Mountain with their dream of a house, and its later service as a shelter for civil rights workers; and its situation, the broad view of hills and meadow, everywhere green. She is crazy about the heavy gray wisteria vines that frame the porch—her porch.

Apart from the rudimentary, necessary repairs, Peg is remodeling the top floor, and the attic; what was once a long gallery of bedrooms, ideal for the days when she and the other rights workers were there (including Henry Stuyvesant), she now wants as a long, large, and very private, very beautiful room, with a lovely view, for her own very private life, with Vera, whom she loves beyond words. (A love that includes the most passionate gratitude. "You gave me to myself," she has said, to Vera.)

The fact that Vera is often sick makes her an even more romantic figure, in Peg's view. And Vera never has ugly, minor ailments, as Peg herself sometimes does. During the first winter they were together Vera had pneumonia, and then an allergic reaction to antibiotics that almost killed her. How rare and valuable she is, to Peg—how beautiful, how loved. How unlike Peg.

Vera is considerably more realistic, more down-to-earth than Peg is, both because she has been in social work and because she has had quite a few more love affairs than Peg has, with women, sometimes men—"You would have found someone, sometime, if you hadn't met me," she tells Peg. And then, very affectionately, since she is truly fond of Peg (if not "in love"), "But I don't have to tell you, I'm sure glad it was me."

"Yes, you do have to tell me. Tell me that often, please."

In that first spring of beginning work on the house, Peg's house, the air inside is full of sawdust and fresh smells of new-sawn pine, sounds of hammering, sawing, the occasional protesting screech of a nail pulled out; and the voices of the young men who are doing the work, kids, actually. (And Peg is in trouble, fighting hard with the local union, because some of them are black.)

Surrounding the house, outside, the woods are full of spring. Sudden sprays of dogwood, white against the pines, like fountains. Budding maples, poplars, crepe myrtle. Peg walks everywhere, smiling to herself; she pushes aside the damp strong green boughs, brushes at cobwebs, and looks down at the thick carpeting of wet dead winter leaves, and brown needles—to see, with a rush of delight, a small patch of yellow dogtooth violets, or yellow or purple or white wild iris.

Sometimes alone, sometimes walking there with Vera. "Vera, look! Anemones, there by the waterfall!"

"Peg, you're too much. A person would think you never saw spring before." Vera touches her arm, and laughs, in her gentle way.

"Well, actually I might as well not. This is different."

The tobacco barn still stands, more crumbled now, with big holes in the plaster chinks, but still imposing. In fact Peg does not quite know what to do with it, if anything. The best plan seems to be to let it alone, let it fall down in its own dignified way.

At the moment Candy is sleeping out there—Candy, a twenty-eight-year-old disaster of the sixties, of drugs and God knows what else (Peg does not want to know any more than she does). Candy sleeps out there in her ancient filthy sleeping bag, which is like a baby's totem blanket, Peg has thought. But Peg thinks too that personal dirt and too-cold fresh spring air are less damaging to Candy than whatever her sleeping arrangements used to be, in her pads in San Francisco and Seattle, Vancouver, Anchorage, and back to San Francisco, where Peg finally found her.

Sometimes, sometimes for days, Candy is perfectly fine. She washes her hair and smiles, and sweeps up sawdust and eats at mealtimes, with Peg and Vera and the kids who are working there. She never talks when anyone is around, but that is all right at those meals; she is just a pale thin young girl, with short clean blond hair. Candy Sinclair.

But then, it is as if overnight her hair can go dirty and drab, and her eyes shift to a look of such anxiety as Peg has never seen, on anyone. Panic, terror, and a horrible wild nervous impatience. At those times she will follow Peg around all day, talking in an incessant and almost senseless mutter: "Do you think it could rain? I think it looks perfectly clear but who can tell? About anything? People come and go when you weren't expecting them to do anything at all. My periods make me feel terrible. I hate blood. Once I missed for four months in Anchorage. Just the cold, I guess, and I wasn't eating much. I hadn't been fucking, I don't think. Do you think it will snow down here this winter? Are we still going to be here next winter, do you think?"

Having listened to this, with variations, for several months now, Peg is almost able to turn it off, simply to keep on with whatever she is doing. At intervals she smiles at Candy, in a way that she hopes is reassuring.

At other times the content of Candy's rambling is genuinely alarming: barely whispering, Candy confides, "Along with the Thorazine they implanted this radio set in my head. It's tiny, that's why the scar is so small you can't even see it. But I can't turn it off, and people are telling me these terrible things. Like, I'm scheduled to go to Washington and be a call girl for the government, it's part of the Watergate deal. I'm supposed to, uh, go down on all those guys, and let them, uh, do it to me, anally. It'll hurt! They talk about this stuff all the time, but I don't think they know where I am. They don't know you've got this Georgia hideout for us."

Helpless Peg can only stroke Candy's hair, and say, "Darling Candy, that's terrible, that's horrible for you. But maybe they'll stop."

And this gentle reassurance seems to work a little, sometimes.

Vera is a considerable, kind help. "You're doing exactly right," she tells Peg. "Most people, including doctors, try to tell kids like Candy that what they feel isn't true, they don't have radios in their heads. But for them it is true, they do have radios, and they do hear those voices. I think you're wonderful with her."

What Cameron has said to Candy, Peg gathers, is: *You are crazy, no daughter of mine can be crazy, you have got to stop saying those things.* "Did he mean I'm not really his daughter?" Candy has asked.

"Darling, no, he just meant he was upset. Of course you're his daughter." And you are the result of that ghastly drunken coupling, Peg thinks, and of course does not say.

At other times Candy is saner than anyone. When Megan calls to tell Peg that Cathy has died, it is Candy who comforts her mother, pointing out, "In an odd way it all seems to have worked out right. Cathy's child, and her mother, and her mother's new husband. Was Cathy married to the father of her child?"

"I don't know. At first Megan said she was, and he died, but Lavinia always said there was something funny going on. 'Funny' seems an odd word for it all, somehow."

"Well, Cathy must have felt sort of good about the way it worked out. Her mother getting married and taking care of the child."

"I don't know if she felt good about anything." Peg sighs.

. . .

Lavinia also calls about Cathy's death; she and Peg have a brief, awkward conversation about that (Peg has already heard how "rude" Cathy was, on Lavinia's visit) and then Lavinia goes on to scold Peg about her new living arrangements (about which she knows very little).

"I'm sure you know what you're doing, dearest Peglet," says Lavinia, clearly not sure at all, "but I can't believe you did right in leaving that nice old Cameron."

"Well, I hope I did."

"He did say you'd taken your maid along."

"*My maid*? What on earth is he talking about?"

It is true that Cornelia has said she will come to visit, but surely that is not what Cameron meant? "I'm living here with Candy and a friend I met here before, that summer I spent working here," Peg halfway explains. And then, with more courage than she would have known she had, she adds, "Possibly because my friend is a Mexican-American Cameron chose to refer to her as my maid."

"Oh, well, yes, I guess." Lavinia trails off, and they both get off the phone as soon as possible.

And then, on one of her "good" days Candy announces that she is tired of the tobacco barn; she wants to move into the house.

"But darling, where?" Peg would also like to know for how long, but she cannot ask that, not of her daughter. Nor could she expect Candy to know.

But Candy's modest request has the (perhaps intended) effect of making Peg feel guilty for the very large amount of space that she, Peg, has had in mind for herself and Vera, that whole long room. Of course they do not need all that.

She also wonders what, at close range, as it were, Candy will make of her own connection with Vera, but decides rather easily not to worry; she somehow concludes that whatever Candy thinks could in no way be harmful to herself, to Candy.

· · ·

In a gradual way, Peg begins to notice that on those good days, Candy seems to have a particular friend among the kids who are working on the house: a small, very thin, very black young man, the probable youngest of the group—he looks about sixteen.

Peg sees Candy and Russell, who is smaller than Candy is, engaged in serious, rather hurried private conversations, here and there, during Russell's coffee breaks, or at lunch.

With Peg, Candy does not mention Russell at all, and so Peg sees fit not to ask, but she wonders about their connection, and she worries, a little. Although they never seem to smile at each other, Peg of course considers the possibility that they are lovers, and then chastises herself for doing so. She knows nothing at all about Candy's sexual life, she does not want to know. But she has to admit that she finds that possibility disturbing. Mainly because she does not think that Candy is well enough, really, to handle anything as serious as sex. Peg has never believed that the young are as light-hearted about sexual matters as they say they are; if they were they would all be much happier, wouldn't they?

"Russell is really upset," Candy tells Peg, one day (one good day). Candy's tone, though, is so tense, so enforcedly calm, or so it seems to Peg, that Peg is frightened, for Candy. She cannot quite focus on Russell's upset.

Candy continues: "His sister gets out of jail next week, he says she got into a fight with her husband, and she cut him so he wouldn't kill her. But they locked her up, not him. And now she's getting out, with no place to go, and her husband's going to be looking for her. And Mom, do you think she could stay here with us for a while?"

Even as Peg is saying, Yes, of course, her mind is running ahead, to her own long dream of a bedroom, which she now begins to see that she was not supposed to have. It will be diminished by one, by two, and who knows who will come next? She sees that she should perhaps have left the house as it was. She and Vera could have the attic (or half the attic).

The next day, a Saturday, about midafternoon, from nowhere strange yellowish heavy clouds appear, all around the green horizon, and distant rumblings of thunder sound. Peg summons Vera to come and sit out on the porch, to watch.

Vera laughs at her. "It's just a thunderstorm. You're so funny, you think everything that happens down here is strange and wonderful. Like Oz."

Peg cheerfully agrees. "I guess I do. It is Oz, for me."

They sit in adjacent rockers, on the long wide-open porch—like an old couple, people who have been together forever (like the Sawyers), Peg thinks, and she next thinks: dear God, please let us be that, an endless couple.

The sky darkens, and is split by a single crack of lightning, and then, in the weird sulfurous half-light, the threatened rain pours down.

"You're not cold?" Peg asks Vera.

"No, it's so warm out. And you're right, it's wonderful to watch."

Peg tells herself to stop worrying over Vera's health—and in fact Vera has never looked better. Her delicate dusky skin is lightly flushed, her dark eyes clear. She is not only pretty, she is a healthy young woman, Peg firmly tells herself. To Vera she says, "It's a little worrying, all these people suddenly moving in. And this summer Cornelia wants to come to visit. And Megan."

Surprisingly, Vera takes this up very seriously. "I think we have to talk about where we're going," she says.

Peg's heart clenches: does she mean, she'll move out if all those people come? She'll find someone else, some new woman, or a man? Too quickly she says, "Well, they don't have to come, I mean we don't have to have Russell's sister, or anyone, if you don't want—"

"But we do have to, and I do want. And I want to stay with you, silly Peg." Vera reaches out to Peg, her long cool fingers close around Peg's wrist.

Peg's skin burns, at that touch. She says, "Well, all right."

"We just have to talk about what we're going to do with the house," says Vera.

38

Half waking from the lively nonsleep of a drugged insomniac, at 4 A.M. (too late for another pill), Lavinia, alone in the house in Fredericksburg, begins to contemplate the rest of her life. Ahead she can only see, like giant impending tombstones, a row of unbearable anniversaries, all close at hand: the day on which her father will have been dead for a year; the anniversary of Watergate, which sent Harvey Rodman finally off to the Bahamas; her fiftieth birthday; her thirtieth college reunion (Christ, thirty years since that hopeful—well, fairly hopeful, very pretty June?). And the final tombstone, the largest, marks thirty years of marriage to Potter, which will require an enormous party, and she simply cannot, cannot do it.

What she will do, she thinks—what she often, almost always plans at that hour—will be what she thinks of as "take-some-pills." She will do it very carefully, too: she will not eat a big dinner (perhaps no dinner is best, just a lot of wine?) so as not to throw up, and live. So disgusting—an ambulance, stomach pump, retrieval. Everyone's curiosity as to why, and their flowers, sympathy. Herself looking awful. No. She will go about it properly, systematically, scientifically (she smiles to herself just slightly at that last). She will very successfully take-some-pills. Instant sleep, lovely, permanent sleep.

If she could stop smoking, could possibly, conceivably just quit, Lavinia thinks, several hours later, over morning coffee and her third cigarette (possibly her fourth, if you count the one in bed, at five)—if she could possibly stop smoking her skin would most assuredly improve, not to mention the dry cough that seems to attack her voice, especially at the end of phone calls.

Dry. Dry skin, a dry cough, a dry, uh, "place." (At that moment she curiously recalls Henry Stuyvesant, who used to talk, or whisper, rather, about her "lovely cunt," a word she has never brought herself to use. In any case, not lovely now.) Hot, dry. Would an ice cube possibly—God, she might try anything—would an ice cube there do anything for her?

Sipping coffee, smoking, in the prettyish (it should be redone) breakfast room, on the cold Virginia morning, Lavinia is wearing a long white quilted satin robe, which is warm but rather old, at least three or four years old, but whoever except Potter will possibly see her in it? It is even somewhat stained, she then notices, looking down, with the interesting interior frown that no one is there to observe. Lavinia has then an instant of pure déjà vu: with a lopsided jolt of her heart she sees that her robe could be the old one she always wore around Barnard Hall (although it is not, of course not; nothing lasts that long, thank God).

However, in 1943, or '44, '45—for years, whatever she wore (it didn't matter) Lavinia was so beautiful, a rarely lovely young blond girl, who could get by with wearing anything at all. Whereas now—now she needs everything she can buy, all the Laszlo and Elizabeth Arden, the Valentino, Gucci, everyone. She needs them all desperately, and still they are not enough.

All the men she has known have loved her clothes, Lavinia recalls, with a diffuse affection that includes both the men and the clothing. Even Gordon Shaughnessey (she won't think how long ago that was, *will not* count back), even poor Gordon always loved the silk and lace panties she used to wear, on top of her lace garter belt. She thinks of Gordon touching all that silk and lace that he never actually saw, since they never took off clothes, never actually (thank God, Potter had to have his virgin) ever did anything but touch.

Even Henry Stuyvesant, who turned out to be such a horrible radical Communist—Henry always loved, or said he did, the dresses that Lavinia wore, the scarves, the tiny bras, from France.

Whereas, whatever Megan wore would be just not right, no matter where she shopped or how much money she spent. Lavinia sits up taller and she almost smiles at this, her most cheering thought in hours. Something to do with coming from California, probably, or more to the point, with coming from nothing, in terms of family. No real family, no money.

Style in dress is rather like an accent, one's way of speaking, Lavinia concludes; a notion that she finds extremely interesting. No matter how people try to change they can never really hide where or from whom they come. Poor Harvey Rodman, with his careful (well yes, too careful) Ivy League clothes, and that perfect Princeton accent (and at least that part was true; he did go to Princeton); but sometimes some other telltale vowel would escape, and Lavinia would be reminded that before Princeton there was probably a public high school, and not the quite uncheckable Midwestern Catholic military place he named. Just as Megan's shoes or her gloves or her makeup or something would always be *just wrong*.

But it does not make Lavinia happy to think of Megan and Henry Stuyvesant together—even if she is quite sure that Henry must wish that Megan had more *style*. And they have been together for years, although of course with Megan so busy in New York and Henry still (incomprehensibly) down there in Chapel Hill, they probably do not spend much time together. And of course she, Lavinia, could always get Henry back, if she should condescend to do so.

That last sentence, like a tiny bead, a bright gleam among Lavinia's now habitually shadowy thoughts, drops entirely from her mind, for most of the hours of that day, as she goes about doing nothing: some phone calls, reading, out for shopping, eating, resting. She achieves nothing but further steps toward age: aging, drying, gravity pulling at everything, all of her sagging downward, until she begins to wonder: Why not now? Why not today, to take pills?

But then that small sentence about Henry reappears, this time expanded and much more clear: I could get Henry back, if I condescended to do so, and then make sure Megan found out, and then I would drop him cold, Lavinia thinks. Of course she will do no such thing, but the certainty that she could—she could ruin everything, for them both!—makes Lavinia smile, for the second time that day. And it makes her decide that no, no: no need to take pills just yet. She might as well stick around for a while and see what happens.

Although she rarely drinks at all (well, Potter drinks enough for both of them, God knows), she decides to have a glass of wine with her dinner.

"It's odd that you should call," says Henry Stuyvesant.

Lavinia laughs, rather sadly. It is about ten, that night, and all the monsters that haunt her mind are out in force. And so, having more or less planned that her tone with Henry would be frightened, close to panic, even, she now finds no need for pretense. She is frightened. It is raining outside, and cold, with a bellowing wind, and the images in her mind are worse than any possible weather. "I called you because I hate everything so much," she now says to Henry, "and I didn't use to. I mean, when I knew you I was okay, and now I'm not."

A pause, before Henry clears his throat. "Well, dear Lavinia. You mustn't feel like that. Although we all do sometimes, I suppose."

"Oh, Henry, please don't lecture me. I honestly can't bear it."

"I didn't mean to, Lavinia. I'm upset at how you sound. I'd like to help."

They settle, at last, on his stopping by the next day. He is driving up to Washington, then going on to New York. They do not mention Megan.

After all that wind and rain, the following day is brilliant, washed all clean and perfectly clear, except for some low-lying silver mists down on the river, far below Lavinia's house.

All day she has moved in a dreamy, tranced way, avoiding Jethro, the black man who is there to clean. Everything that Jethro does makes so much noise, the vacuum, with all its attachments, all the cleaning water that he runs; Jethro even makes furniture polish whine.

With a cup of tea and then a small blue bowl of soup Lavinia wanders wherever Jethro is not, sometimes resting, or at least just sitting down for a while. Every now and then in a surprised way she observes that she is crying.

She is still in her long white robe (still stained, with some ugly blood at the back, she has noticed) and she knows she should change, before Henry comes. I will change into something beautiful and then take some pills, she thinks, but does neither.

Jethro leaves around six, as usual, and then the house is empty and perfectly quiet. So quiet, and it occurs to Lavinia that the phone has not rung all day. Picking it up she discovers that the line is dead, out here a not at all unusual occurrence. But sinister, just now.

Of course Henry will not come to her at all; he was simply "being nice," when he said that he would. He was hoping to get her through a bad night, maybe thinking that she was drunk, and would be over it in the morning. Nice Henry.

However, with Henry not coming there seems no point in taking pills—nor does there, for that matter, seem to be much point in not taking pills. In "sticking around."

In that suspended mood Lavinia decides, at least, to bathe (maybe take pills in her tub? not tonight, but maybe later on? She had not quite thought of that before. However, it is probably not a good idea, after all. The water might wake her up, or else make her all swollen, a bloated corpse. Very Grade B). She throws a lot of flower-scented foamy lotion into the tub, hoping to make her bath last an hour or so, thus to take up—to kill off an hour.

This old house, which was built a couple of hundred years ago, between the Revolution and the Civil War, like an elderly person seems to creak the more, with its increasing age. And its sounds are unreliable; generally they signify nothing. Lavinia, in her cooling bathwater, tells herself these things as she hears what could be (but undoubtedly is not) the distant opening, the closing of the front door of her house.

She turns on more hot water. Lying back, just for a minute or two she runs her hands along her body, so beautifully smooth, so lightly, lightly oiled.

But unless she is crazy, delusional, which most surely is highly possible, there are footsteps on the stairs.

She is slightly groggy from so much immersion in warmth and steam, and what she thinks is, Well, good. Someone has broken in, to murder and rob me. I won't have to take pills. I wonder, will he rape me first? Don't they usually? (And if he does, will I come? Does anyone, being raped?)

Strangest of all, the intruder—and there really is someone, she can hear him—the intruder knows her name. She can hear herself being called, "Lavinia, Lavinia where in hell are you?"

She recognizes that Henry Stuyvesant has arrived, at last, and probably does not mean to murder her, or to rape. She sighs, before answering, "I'm in here."

Watching the gold doorknob as it turns, a motion that seems infinitely slow, she has time to think: Could some murderer have learned to impersonate Henry's voice?

But it is Henry, though, who comes in to her, the old tall giraffe, with his thick glasses and old tweed coat, his receding, graying curly hair. At the sight of him, uncontrollably and quite incomprehensibly Lavinia bursts into tears. Sitting up in the tub, in all those stupid bubbles, one arm covers her breasts (though small, they have fallen a little, in all those years); with the other hand she tries to shield her eyes—getting soap in, making everything worse.

Henry quickly sits down on the heavy white rug, beside the tub (or squats: his knees creak, like her house, as he does so). He reaches toward Lavinia, touching her back. She feels scratchiness, then smells wet tweed.

He is saying, "Jesus, I must have scared you, Lavy, I'm really sorry. My goddamn carburetor, damned old car—damn Detroit! I tried all day to call you."

Through sobs, she manages to say, "It's not that, I wasn't afraid. Oh Henry, that's what's so frightful, I wanted someone to come in and kill me. So I won't have to kill myself. Oh Christ, if you knew how I hate my life."

"Come on, now."

"Oh, it's *true*, I hate everything. Potter, and Amy, and everyone I know, and *me*. Christ, how I hate being me."

"Lavinia, come on. Get up out of that cold water. Right now. Later we can talk all night, if you want to."

She has stopped crying; she is looking at Henry, his thick fogged glasses, big nose, wide mouth.

He says, "Come on, I mean it. Shall I help you out?"

"No, you go on into the sitting room." But then she begins to cry again—crying, shivering, everything out of control, nothing as intended, as meant. She is an ugly white old woman, all gooseflesh, crying, crying, and every single minute getting older, uglier. It no longer matters at all if Henry sees her fallen breasts.

Making what seems the most enormous effort of her life, Lavinia stands up in the tub; she reaches past Henry for a towel—but of course he can already see everything, even (probably) the two white hairs that hurt too much to pull—except that his glasses are still so fogged, he might not see.

Henry wraps the towel around her, and rubs.

It is like an embrace but it is not one, not really, except that Lavinia suddenly longs to be *kissed*—to be healed, to be blessed. She looks up at Henry, who now has taken off his glasses, in so much steam; she sees his eyes, so dark, so thickly lashed, so beautiful. In what she believes to be her old familiar voice (in control), Lavinia says, "Henry, I can't tell you how sorry I am, I've been acting so crazy."

Henry says, "The truth is, you've never been more beautiful."

Even as Henry is making love to her, in the broad soft bed that for so long was theirs (the Porthault sheets are new, however, or relatively new; they were presents from Harvey)—even then, as Henry kisses her lightly, perfectly, a far part of Lavinia's mind continues to think: How strange, what I meant all along to happen is happening, but somehow not as I meant it to.

And she thinks, He must do this to Megan too, but I don't care; she is awful, and I am very beautiful, lovely, everywhere.

"I guess I've just been, well, extremely depressed," Lavinia tells Henry, the next morning, over a rather scanty breakfast (hardly anything but cold cereal and instant coffee in the house, no eggs or milk). Lavinia laughs, at the same time giving him her old serious concentrated look. "I'm not aging well," she says. "But today, I must say, everything seems gone. All the horrible things, I mean."

"I should have been a doctor." Henry smiles, then frowns. "But there are some things you could do, you know. About being depressed, I mean."

"Oh, I know. A shrink, or some encounter group. A face lift, a vigorous exercise class. If you knew how I hate exercise."

"Honestly, I wasn't thinking of any of those."

"Not even a shrink? Oh, I'll bet you were. But I know, you'd want me to get 'involved,' to join in some left-wing groupie thing." Lavinia can see that she is successfully annoying him (but *why?*).

Henry only says, "No, I don't want you to join anything," but he sounds cross.

"It's odd how much Amy is like you," Lavinia comments, as though she had never said this before. "Not in looks, of course, but her ideas—pure *you.*"

"Lavinia, for God's sake, we've been through all this. She simply is not—she is not my child. Just because you've decided not to like her."

Lavinia laughs, her old light self-admiring laugh. "Not like my own daughter? Don't be silly, of course I love Amy. I just didn't like her living in that Berkeley commune, or whatever it is. With those Hari Krishnas, or whoever. Or being so fat," she adds, with feeling.

"Well, you must admit that Potter's quite a lot fatter than I am."

"Oh Henry, why do we always quarrel? Do you know? Do you and Megan fight?"

Henry frowns, severely. "No."

That is all the mention of Megan between Lavinia and Henry, that day. When Henry leaves, as he quite soon does, Lavinia does not say (although it crosses her mind that she might do so), Give my love to Megan.

But Megan stays in Lavinia's mind all that day—curiously, almost more than Henry does. She wants very much to talk to Megan, but even with her excellent mind working hard at this problem (perhaps too hard?), it takes her quite a while to work out what she will say.

"Megan darling, I know it's late, but I've had such a day."

It is about four thirty, but Megan so far has sounded surprisingly relaxed, not so cross and rushed as she often does, these days. She merely asks, "Where are you, Lavinia? You sound so far away."

"Oh, just down in Fredericksburg. You know, resting up. Doing things around the house."

"Oh." Megan does not sound especially interested in Lavinia's house, but then she never has.

"Well, it's about Amy. I've been meaning to call you. I know how busy you are, but Amy has this friend, her boyfriend, I guess— they're all so strange about sex, these days. Anyway, Amy insists that he writes absolutely terrific poetry. And she knows that I know you. And so I said I'd ask."

Startlingly (and rather irritatingly) Megan laughs. "This seems to be children-of-friends day," she explains, and laughs again. "I just had a really nice long lunch with Aron Marr. You know, Janet and Adam's boy."

"Oh, really? I'd heard he was, uh, queer."

"Well, I guess he is homosexual, yes." Megan's voice has stiffened. "But I think he's written a very good novel. So ironic in a way that he should." (Lavinia has sensed that Megan is not thinking about *her*—is more or less talking to herself.) "I wonder how Adam would have reacted to his son's being a good writer."

Who in hell *cares*, Lavinia does not say. But it is annoying for Megan to go on, as she now does, about this silly little Jewish fag, when she, Lavinia, called to talk about her daughter and her daughter's talented friend. Also, every time Megan has ever mentioned that awful Adam Marr, since his very sordid death, she has sounded almost mournful.

In a heedless (or perhaps deeply thought-out) way, Lavinia next says, "I meant to ask Henry about all this with Amy, but then just as he was leaving I forgot."

"Leaving?"

"Yes, this morning."

A pause—has Megan hung up? But there was no click. And then Megan says, very clearly, "I assume that this call was really to tell me that Henry has just been to see you in Fredericksburg?" Unused to direct accusations, Lavinia improvises. "Oh now, Megan baby, don't be so 'uptight,' as the kids say. I assumed you two had some really civilized arrangement, after all this time." She suddenly recognizes that she has not felt so well in years; in fact, it could be all of thirty years ago, when she used to have such a good time teasing Megan, so easy to bring her close to tears.

Not crying now, her voice a little sharp, Megan only asks, "Lavinia, do you have any idea at all how totally out of style you are?"

Lavinia is working up to a light, careless laugh, which she will follow by saying, Well, somehow I never thought you'd be quite the person to give out instructions on style.

But it is too late; there is the click, and Megan is gone (for good, as things turn out; that conversation is to be their last).

And Lavinia is left to laugh all alone at the utter hilariousness of a reprimand to *her*, from Megan Greene, on the subject of style.

. . .

Lavinia does not come down to Fredericksburg again until the following March, and then, once more, her visit is for a recovery, of sorts. This time she has even brought a nurse, an Englishwoman, Miss Riggs, whom Lavinia calls Riggsy—striving for a somewhat warmer, cozier tone, or perhaps to make her sound even more English.

She has been through a lot though, Lavinia has; her poor face is still all swollen and black and blue and yellow, the most horrible bruises, but all that will disappear, her doctor has promised, along with the tiny scars behind her ears. She looks perfectly ghastly, so fortunate that no one but Riggsy is there to see her. However, even Riggsy has a disapproving look, Lavinia has noticed. Odd, in a nurse, who must have seen almost everything; and she wonders, is Riggsy just possibly "gay"?

Her face does not hurt, however, as awful as it looks; it just feels uncomfortably tight. But her breasts do hurt, the most frightful pains there, constantly. For which Riggsy will not give her quite enough drugs; it is really sadistic, Lavinia decides; nurses clearly become immune to pain, they do not care.

Riggsy is large and plain and absolutely shapeless, "my English pudding," as Lavinia has described her on the phone to a New York friend (she hopes, out of the hearing of Riggsy). Lying back, in such pain! among all her lace and linen, in her bright room full of roses, spring flowers, Lavinia in an idle way wonders just who it is that Riggsy reminds her so much of, and then, of course: it comes to her that Riggsy is Peg all over, a big square unattractive woman whose laugh is too loud, who is (probably) a lesbian.

And who (probably) does not approve of beautiful rich women. Nor of plastic surgery.

The following June, Lavinia and Potter decide to have their thirtieth wedding anniversary party down in Fredericksburg— quixotic, in the view of many of their friends; they have almost never been known to spend any time down there together. However, Lavinia just laughs, and she exaggerates the trace of a Southern accent that is always somewhere in her voice, as she tells her friends, "It'll do you Yankees good to get a touch of Virginia air in June. You just wait till you smell some real home-grown gardenias, and lilacs."

And (so typical of Lavinia, everyone feels) it all works out to perfection, a great deal of the perfection having to do with Lavinia's incredible efforts, her engineering skills. Guests are happily distributed between the Hay-Adams, in Washington, and the Princess Anne, in Fredericksburg. Lavinia has let it be known that she is just not having any house guests; thus no one's feelings are hurt, no friends are perceived as being more intimate than other friends.

And all of Lavinia's efforts are rewarded with a perfect June day. Soft, clear, and blue, and everything is in bloom, the lavender wisteria drooping heavily, sensually, everywhere; the roses, azaleas, honeysuckle. And Lavinia's terrace is literally a bower of potted flowers, all at their most hothouse perfect pitch of loveliness.

Lavinia herself feels quite wonderful, even; she looks better than she has for years, and everyone says so.

She and Potter have an early breakfast that day, just coffee and English muffins and a lot of brewer's yeast pills, for strength—on the terrace, alone together. And that day Potter looks perfectly all right, not red or swollen, not that hungover look that Lavinia has come to dread, and to hate. He does not say anything mean, as he sometimes does. No nasty cracks about marriage, nothing about how much all this is costing. Nothing has been said about a present either, but that is perfectly all right: Lavinia can pick out her own present later.

In fact Potter hardly speaks at all, at breakfast, which under the circumstances is really quite a relief, Lavinia having so much on her mind.

In all of that long and very strenuous (but wonderfully rewarding) day, Lavinia makes only two mistakes, and both quite unavoidable, actually.

The first mistake is opening a letter from the agency from which she got poor Riggsy (such an error, all around: she was forced to send Riggsy away a week earlier than planned, she simply could not stand that long fat white face around any longer). And so, Lavinia might have known that the letter would contain no pleasant news, or information; she could so easily have simply put off reading it until the next day. However, she did not put it off; she opened and scanned the letter, and instantly realized that she should not have: poor Riggsy had died of an overdose of sleeping pills.

There was nothing accusatory in the letter, of course not; they know who pays for these overpriced nurses. The agency simply wondered if Mrs. Cobb had noticed, had observed, had thought— well, of course she had not, had nothing to say.

Lavinia quickly digests this most unpleasant, really awful news; she decides at once that she will simply not answer the letter—well, why should she? The woman is dead, isn't she? Too depressing, but she will simply put it altogether out of her mind, as soon as possible, and that is what she does: Lavinia's control over her own thoughts has always been admirable. She stops thinking entirely about poor Riggsy, but not before she has had this curious idea: Lavinia thinks, Old Riggs did exactly what I had planned to do, she did it for me, so that now I don't have to. Ridiculous? Well, really. And then she forgets all about Ms. Riggs. For good.

Lavinia's second mistake is in answering the telephone when it rings, about eleven thirty that morning. Crazy of her, with all the help around, and the help for the help, but Lavinia does, she answers the phone herself and she finds, at the other end, her daughter, who is in Washington, of all places. Of course Amy is quite unaware that it is her parents' anniversary, Amy would never keep up with anything that reasonable, that adult, that "square."

"Well, darling, what an absolutely lovely surprise. Oh, we're just down here for the weekend, a sort of impulse. Well no, angel, it would not be very convenient for you and your friend to come over, it just wouldn't. Not today. We do have a few friends around, and it just would not work out, they're just not your type. You don't mind my being just a little frank? No, Megan Greene is not here, and actually she was rather rude about your friend's poetry, I thought I told you last fall, or whenever it was. And actually I've heard a rumor that her agency is not doing well at all, so I'd just forget all about her if I were you. No, I've never heard of the Tabbard Inn. Well, N Street, near Dupont, that's certainly a good address, it must be a very nice place. Amy darling, if you're really that hard up I'll get a check in an envelope right away, and I'll send it to you by one of our guests. How's that? a mysterious stranger with money. Someone who's staying at the Hay-Adams, which is very near you, will deliver it to the Tabbard Inn tonight. Well, darling, that's just the best I can do, possibly, and to tell you the truth I thought I was being rather hyperefficient. You know you're not the most appreciative little girl in the world, Amy dear. Oh God, Amy, Jesus, *shit*—of course I know you're not little."

Fortunately Lavinia is so busy that she is able to recover from that conversation almost instantly, and without the headache that communications from Amy usually afflict her with. She only briefly wonders, as always, *Why?* Why huge-breasted acne-scarred Amy, why Amy, for my daughter?

But she writes out a check (not quite as much as Amy asked for, no point in spoiling her even further); she puts it in an envelope and she remembers to give it to friends who are going back into Washington tonight, at some time or other, after the party.

During all that day, some dream or story or perhaps a literary reference, something she read long ago keeps running in and out of Lavinia's mind. It has something to do with shoes. She herself is wearing the most beautiful red kid sandals, perfect with the flowers on her dress.

And then sometime during dessert, the peaches floating in champagne, she does remember: of course, she has thought of "The Red Shoes of the Duchess," at the end of *Guermantes Way*.

Lavinia smiles happily, remembering her old awed affection for Proust. She has always meant to reread him, and now she surely will.

In every particular, her party is a most tremendous success.

39

Hanging up from her conversation with Lavinia, that November afternoon, for a while Megan simply stands there by the window of her small, impossibly crowded office. She looks down into the gray bleak windy street, into light, barely visible flurries of snow, the season's first. In the sudden, unanticipated cold the pedestrians walk more stiffly, braced against wind, tightened up; they keep their hands in their pockets, chins thrust down into collars.

I can hardly bear the thought of winter, Megan is thinking. And next summer I will be fifty.

And: How could Henry? she thinks. How could he? Lavinia, of all women—all people in the world. The person I most would mind about.

The thought of Henry "with" Lavinia is making her almost physically sick, and her own conversation with Lavinia, played and replayed in her mind, is an endless wound.

And, to make what is already intolerable worse, she is supposed to see Henry that night. He is coming up from Washington to see her, what would have been, without Lavinia, a perfectly natural arrangement between them: Henry driving to Washington for meetings of some sort, the next day driving on up to New York.

(Or, Megan now miserably, horribly thinks, perhaps he has stayed over in Fredericksburg before? I am only now finding out? I am the "last to know.")

. . .

Of course she could call it off; she could even call Henry now and say that she *knows*, she never wants to see him again. Henry is visiting some old left friends up on Riverside Drive in the afternoon; she knows how to get in touch with him (she thinks!). But—but; in her present state of mind an evening alone with her thoughts seems almost worse than the forthcoming evening with Henry will be. Besides, she is too old to be so cowardly; she and Henry have had a fairly adult connection, they have in their way been true friends. She has got to face him. Nor can she pretend not to know, which would be another easy way out (the way that Nixon so often liked to boast about not taking).

At least Leslie is out for the day. Thank God, no Leslie to almost bump into, in their increasingly cramped, sometimes suffocating, too intimate space (or is that simply how Megan feels, sometimes?). Leslie has gone up to Connecticut to see—to see whom? Someone important, a writer; Leslie had met her and wanted to go—but who? Megan knows perfectly well who it was that Leslie went to see—and she cannot remember. She is losing her mind; there are flurries of snow in her brain, like a TV screen, forgotten in the night.

Furthermore, on this worst of all days, she is quite hungover, not so much from too much booze as from too little sleep, too many rooms full of smoke, along with all the evening's too rich food, and wine. Her nerves feel scraped down, raw; her eyes are sore, her stomach uneasy. Her state is not surprising, nor are any of her symptoms remarkable, in view of the night before: for Megan this included a large hotel cocktail party; an uptown bookstore reading, with champagne; a heavy restaurant dinner, French (pre–nouvelle cuisine), oversauced, overcreamed. And as though all that were not far more than enough, Megan then went on to a SoHo loft party, to celebrate someone's (dear God, again, please, *whose?*)

new book, where she drank one very tiny glass of brandy—which could have been poisoned: at this moment Megan feels that indeed it was.

The fall publishing season, then, was in full swing, despite the economic uncertainties of the late seventies—and it was the sort of evening that makes Megan hate herself, and hate her work. She is sure she must be insane to go through all that.

Biff frequently tells her that she is in fact insane. "You simply don't have to do that anymore," he lectures her. "Do you really believe that John will die of hurt feelings if you don't show up at his reading? Or Betty, if you don't go along to some ludicrous restaurant bash? You don't catch Linda at any of those amateur nights, and I can tell you that I've heard from someone who'd know that she now makes almost three hundred G's a year."

"Linda's a different kind of agent. Leslie's going to grow up to be Linda."

"Well, she's certainly *chez* Elaine more than often enough. But dopey Megan, I know, you're the old-style maternal sort. But couldn't you modify those instincts just a little?"

"Biff, I am not maternal. Why do you have to call just being nice to some people by a word like that, putting me down?"

"Oh, Meg, you're so liberated."

"Of course I am, I always have been, sort of."

"Well, in that case I wish you'd liberate yourself from some of your imaginary obligations. Let Leslie take over more. God knows she'd like to."

He is quite right of course, and Megan laughs, and thinks that really she likes Biff better than anyone she knows.

Are gay men really nicer than so-called straight men? At times this has seemed a possibility.

Henry too, Megan has to admit, has pointed out that she expends herself in ways that she does not have to, and does not enjoy, in connection with her work.

"But what else would I do?" Megan has asked him.

And that of course is the problem, to which neither Biff nor

Henry nor Megan herself has an answer. She is working too hard at work at which she is only moderately successful—she is not good at contracts, negotiations, all that, in the way that Barbara was, and increasingly she leaves such things to Leslie; other young women, agents (Linda), are better at what she does.

In a word, she finds her work unsatisfying; is this, then, her midlife crisis—is that what she is actually facing?

And, are some of her symptoms (today's, especially) possibly menopausal? Would that explain the rage that she feels, that no sight of snow or swirling wind can cool, at the thought of Henry spending the night with, making love to, *fucking* Lavinia? Is this burning anger merely further proof that she is a middle-aged woman, is almost fifty?

Megan's fury then shifts to that diagnosis itself, to those labels, so useful for dismissing the complaints of women. I would be furious if I were thirty-five, she thinks, with absolute certainty. Or sixteen, for God's sake. What Henry has done, what I feel about it has nothing to do with my hormonal condition, but rather with my whole life, my history.

Looking down at the flurries of snow, now thicker, coming faster, a fine white cloud in the lowering darkness, Megan thinks, Oh good. Henry won't be able to get downtown. No cabs. Nothing.

However, Henry not only arrives at Megan's apartment on time, he arrives with their dinner, cartons and cartons of Italian delicacies from their favorite delicatessen, things to be variously heated or cooled, somehow dealt with, put somewhere. And two bottles of wine, a chilled white, a red to be opened, to breathe. "I wasn't sure about getting out to a restaurant," Henry explains, looking kind and tired, his familiar look. "I had one hellish time getting a cab," he adds.

Guilt offerings, Megan is thinking, and, with some pain. Of course he is tired, a night like that, and then a long day's drive.

However, fussing with all that food gives them something to do.

It is soothing, even, to Megan, who for a moment allows herself the possibility of *not* confronting Henry with her knowledge; she thinks of the balm of an ordinary evening with him, the good food and wine and random, easy talk. The familiar foolish jokes and distant reliable good music, from NCN. Her clean and comforting bed. Love, if not explicit, simply present, in messages from warm skin and nerves, from flesh to answering flesh.

But that is impossible. Now out of the question. Out.

Do men actually become handsomer with age, or is that a culturally determined view? In the popular mind, do gray hair and lines make *them* distinguished, whereas women simply age? Megan believes this to be true, one more inequity. However, it is surely true (aesthetically, objectively) that Henry has never looked better. Once a gangling, too tall, nearsighted young man, as he approaches sixty he looks very good indeed. Somewhere along the line his hair has stopped receding; remaining thick, it has turned silvery gray, a heavy ruff, framing that high and noble-looking brow. Without glasses (he has taken them off, being so at home, so familiar with Megan's kitchen), his eyes are always beautiful, dark and wide, the thick lashes darker in contrast to gray hair. These days no one would think of giraffes when they think of Henry.

It is truly enraging to Megan at that moment that Henry should look so *good*, only kindness and intelligence in evidence on his face.

"Someone drank your wine." Henry laughs as he says this, pouring more into her glass.

It is true; by habit a slow sipper of wine, Megan has gulped down her first glass in not many minutes. Faintly she says, "I guess so."

"This snow reminded me of the time we went up to the Cloisters, and it snowed," Henry is saying. "Remember? Another November, I think. But was it last year, or the year before?"

Abruptly, then: "Lavinia called me today," Megan tells him. "She wanted me to know that you, uh, spent the night with her."

Across the small table, the dishes of exotically, expensively seasoned foods, they stare at each other. Megan and Henry, lovers, now instant enemies.

It is Henry who blushes. "Well," he says. And then, "What an odd thing for her to do."

"Not at all, that was the whole point. Don't you see that? How stupid you are!" Megan hears her own too loud voice, strident, ugly and hateful.

"I suppose you're right, given Lavinia," muses Henry, thoughtfully—academically, "objectively." "That's not how it seemed at the time."

"Oh, I'll bet not!" Now Megan feels her own face redden, her blood heating, everywhere. How she would like to hit him, oh, scratch his face! Crazily flashing backwards, irrelevantly, she wonders if this was how her mother was: did Florence scream and yell at Harry? Megan thinks how she would love to throw something, red wine, or the soup, which is extremely hot.

"Is there any point in telling you I'm sorry it happened?" Henry asks her.

"No!" screams Megan.

"Megan, darling, please—"

"Lavinia, of all people in the world!"

For this is what Megan has been thinking all day, in various ways: Lavinia, who represents, as it were, everything that Megan has come to despise, most of whose ideas and aims are indeed despicable. Lavinia the bigot, the proud, beautiful, and irrevocably rich; unimaginatively, self-righteously filthy rich. And, almost worse, Lavinia the former condescending friend, who knows: who knew that Henry is Megan's lover now, who chose to tell Megan. "Jesus, don't you see that?" she cries out to Henry, from the depths of her helpless, degrading rage.

"But I thought you always knew about Lavinia—," he begins.

"Knew that you had an affair with her—that you used to—fuck? Yes, I did, and it didn't exactly make me like you any better, ever."

(But is that true? On the other hand, perhaps it did? Lavinia was part of her attraction to Henry? How *sick*.)

"I went to bed with someone when I went to Hawaii, when Cathy died," Megan now tells Henry (and why? why now—for punishment? She does not quite know, but goes on). "But it was someone you don't know. Who doesn't know you. I mean, it had nothing to do with you."

"Your reasoning is very interesting." Henry's voice has gone hard, and dry. Bone dry.

"It's you, you've ruined everything!" Megan cries.

Henry stands up. "It sounds to me as though we've both ruined everything," he tells her.

They are staring at each other, still, their eyes full of rage and disbelief. Their eyes might melt, in that violent heated terrible glare.

It is Megan who breaks it. "Okay, just go!" She shoots out the words at him, and then forces herself to look down, at her hands, which grip the edge of the table as though she were drowning.

She continues to clutch the table as she listens to Henry's receding footsteps. The closing door.

Gone. As Megan thinks, "for good."

40

"I am living in a lovely house out on California Street. I am with some lovely new friends." These are the first and seemingly innocuous sentences of a letter that comes to Megan from her mother, Florence—a letter that, reread, sounds so alarming, so wrong, that Megan, never a dutiful nor even a particularly affectionate daughter, begins to make arrangements to go out to California, to rescue her mother.

This letter arrives on a day early in March, a March that closely resembles the previous November, and the day looks much like that on which Megan last saw Henry Stuyvesant: the terrible final fight, about Lavinia. This day too is gray and full of snow, and unseasonably cold; now, as then, from her high office window Megan observes the pedestrians down on 57th Street walking stiffly, defensively, braced against chill winds.

This is the month during which, in balmier Virginia weather, poor Lavinia is recovering from her face and breast lifts, which Megan of course does not know about. Nor, for that matter, does Henry Stuyvesant.

The first thing that seems odd or wrong about Florence's letter is the return address, "out on California Street." The numbers in the address are familiar to Megan, dimly but certainly; as they come into focus she remembers paying bills to that address, to a doctor's office she once went to. It must have been right next door to her mother's lovely new house, or a couple of houses down. Except that there were no lovely houses around, Megan clearly remembers: more doctors' offices, a mortuary, a motel, and a rest home, the last two almost indistinguishable from each other, both very ugly, one-story redwood structures.

Megan first thinks, Well, silly old Florence. If she's living in a motel, why can't she just say so? Can she be managing one, with Harry?

She reads on.

"You father sure surprised me when he left, or rather when he said for me to leave, but I guess the wife is always the last to know, ha ha. Well, dumb old me, but I never would have thought he had the energy for a *younger woman*. To me forty-five is plenty younger, a chick. But I sincerely hope they will be very happy together, and I was very happy to let them have the house, especially with me being 'out of a job,' which I guess a lot of folks are, these days. But there is no point in my living next to the Bayshore anymore. I never did like it out there, and I know you didn't either, Megan. Harry's welcome, I say."

It is all false. Wrong. *Impossible.*

The telephone operator in San Francisco is no help. Chilled, with rising fear Megan hears that there is no number listed for Mrs. Florence Greene at that address, and that the operator does not know what building is at that street number; they do not give out numbers like that. It is clear that if anything further indeed were known, he would not tell Megan, not this operator. Not this phone company.

Megan then dials her father's number, the old awful near-the-Bayshore house, and then his shop, WE BUY JUNQUE. No answer at either place, and Megan thinks, unkindly, The old bastard. Off with a chick indeed.

Obviously Florence is in the rest home, and Harry put her there—so convenient for him. And for all Megan knows there is really something wrong, some physical problem that Florence has not seen fit to mention; Megan over the years has never exactly been a sympathetic audience for her mother—she knows that.

All the rest of that morning, through several dozen phone calls, some dictated letters, and three appointments, Megan thinks of Florence, in the "lovely house out on California Street." By early afternoon, her first lull of the day, through which light snow flurries still vaguely drift, it is clear to Megan that she has to go out there. To see Florence, find out what is going on.

Leslie is out "doing lunch" again with Benny, the still hot, still young publisher.

Megan and Biff have discussed this slightly odd connection. "If either of them was even remotely like anyone else, in a sexual way," Megan has observed, "I'd think they were having an affair. Off screwing, in some hotel."

"Well, you're certainly right that they're not like other people, in that way," Biff has agreed. "Maybe they go shopping together. Or maybe they go to hotels and do something really sinister, like trying on each other's clothes. God knows they're both thin enough, they'd probably fit," sighs portly Biff.

"I did hear that Benny and his wife are separated."

"Benny married at all is more than I can contemplate," sniffs Biff.

"Well, he loves those little girls."

"Darling Megan, of course he does. But wait till they grow up. So clever, his clearing out before that happens."

"Do you think that's how he loves Leslie, as a skinny little girl?"

"Or a little boy. Well, quite possibly. Although I rather see a naked lust for power as the great bond there. It's a marvelous substitute for sex, I'm told."

In any case, the Leslie-Benny connection has provided a theme and many variations for gossip between Megan and Biff, and undoubtedly for many other New York publishing people as well.

Megan and Henry Stuyvesant have exchanged a few letters since their ugly "final" quarrel, the preceding November. He being more in the wrong (his episode with Lavinia being "worse" than Megan's with Jackson Clay—in what Henry termed Megan's odd logic, but which he has accepted), in any case Henry wrote the first letter to Megan; he wrote several letters before she answered. His tone was sad, regretful rather than specifically apologetic. He seemed most to mourn the loss of their friendship, and indeed in important ways their connection has been precisely that. They have always talked so much to each other, have talked, and talked, and talked. Possibly because she felt the same regret Megan has responded in kind; she and Henry began a correspondence which had the sound of two people sharing a loss. Sad old friends.

And so it is to Henry that Megan now writes and explains her flight to San Francisco, on the following day. "She is obviously in a rest home," Megan writes, "and trying to sound as though she were not. Putting a good face on things, which is what she's always done, now that I think about it. I guess I do that too, sometimes. And of course one reason that I'm going out to see her is guilt for all the times that I didn't. Anyway, I'm off tomorrow.

"I've been trying to imagine Florence old. She is just the same age as the century, which at least makes it easy to remember. Born in June."

In these old-friends letters that pass between Henry and Megan, two things are never mentioned: one, Lavinia, and his defection; and two, the possibility of their seeing each other again, Henry and Megan. And if those omissions seem odd to either of them, that too goes unsaid.

Two days later, in the St. Francis Hotel, in San Francisco, Florence Greene is talking to her daughter.

"What I loved about that work was all the friends," says Florence. "You wouldn't believe all the folks I got to know. The whole trick to it, the trick to being a carhop, is to work real hard and fast but be friendly too, when you get to take a breath. And it's plenty hard work, I can tell you that. Folks hassle you, some don't act nice. Guys coming on. But if you can take all that, and still be nice and get your work done, well, you've got yourself a lot of friends. You're a person folks will want to come back to, just to see her. And I have to tell you, Megan honey, I was really super good at what I did. I got to be the fastest with the orders, and I was the one the most folks came back to see. And of course I don't mean any of that sex come-on stuff. As you well know, I was almost a middle-aged woman when I started out there. Although, to be honest with you, there was sometimes a little of that. For a while, at first. Well, sometime I'll tell you. Or maybe I won't.

"But it was mostly the friends, just plain old friends. Local folks were lots of my friends, of course. That figures. Folks from Mountain View, down to San Jose, over to Cupertino. And city folks, coming down from up here in San Francisco. After a few times they'd get to know me enough to call my name. 'Hey Florence, I bet you don't remember us.' You would not believe how many people said just those exact, identical words to me. But the thing is I did remember them, I could call to mind exactly what their order was, the time before. You know, cheeseburger, hold the fries, no onion, special onion rings. Whatever. I have this kind of a trick memory. I can bring back any order, as soon as I see the person's face. So it's really lucky I got into that kind of work, although I know both you and your dad were dead against it, at first. Do you have a specially good memory, Megan?

"Anyway, when I could recall like that those folks got such a kick, it was like some present I'd given them. They'd get excited, and I guess it was one of the things that made them come back again, to see if I still remembered. People coming back, some of them from really far away. Friends all over the country, and some of them would even send me postcards from the rest of their trip, or from when they got back home. You won't believe this, Meg, but there was one couple from England, used to visit in Woodside, that's a fancy place, you remember—lot of horses, pictures of horses in the paper, with their people. Well, these visiting English got to know me, sort of, and they used to write to me, from there. This funny sounding town, Chipping-something. Funny, how I can recall what they ordered every time but not the name of their town.

"Well, friends from all over. Always something to look forward to, every day. No telling who might show up. I can tell you, I really miss it now. And while the place was still there, and I wasn't, I used to wonder what they'd say to folks who come there, asking for me. Well, it stands to reason, some of them must have? I left my new address, when I moved, but I wonder about the postcards I used to get. The drive-in's all tore down now, a big old office building put where it was.

"Now Meg, don't look so sad. It's all okay, things work out, some way. I'm just telling you how it was, my good old times."

Megan is less sad than embarrassed, disturbed at these revelations of her mother's strong, eager needs, so like her own. The needs that made her, too, so "good with people."

. . .

Florence, in her late seventies, looks, well, odd. Her hair, for so many years bleached and dyed a brassy bright blond ("waitress blond," Megan, to her present shame, has termed it, to herself), now has grown out several inches, at least two, past blond to white, a bright clean white, as startling in its way as the blond hair was. Her face is weathered, tanned. "Rain or shine, I walk my five miles a day, and sometimes more. I like it outdoors," Florence has explained. "May have ruined my skin, though. Doctors tell us everything too late, it seems like to me." Her skin is less ruined than it is intensely wrinkled. With her small nose and round brown eyes, and the violent band of white hair, she has the look of a monkey, an impression increased by the animation, the energy involved in all her gestures, her facial expressions.

"Well, we don't look much alike, that's something you've escaped," Florence has commented, to her daughter.

"No, but I really wish we did. I've always wished I were thin and blond," Megan tells her, as Lavinia crosses her mind.

"Well, what I would have given for a shape like yours. Nobody's content with themselves, have you noticed? But I probably got myself in plenty of trouble without a shape."

"Well, me too. With."

They both laugh, a little warily—still sizing each other up, still questioning.

The rescue of Florence, once launched, turned out to be less difficult than Megan had imagined.

First, she remembered that in the office they had a San Francisco telephone directory, the fat book of yellow pages. Under Rest Homes she found what came to a single page of listings, and on that page, easily enough, she found the address that Florence had given her. "California Pines," the place was called.

At that time it was eleven thirty in New York, thus eight thirty in San Francisco, a perfectly reasonable time to call a rest home, Megan decided. But still she had to force herself; her hands shook and she didn't trust her voice. She was sorely afraid of whatever she would find out about Florence. Afraid of Florence.

A creaking, elderly voice answered the phone, which in her panic Megan assumed to be the voice of Florence. But no; however this person would summon Mrs. Greene, right away.

And Florence, who arrived with merciful alacrity—she could have been waiting for Megan to call—Florence was instantly reassuring. Her voice, if not young, was clear and strong. How smart of Megan to find her, Florence said, and how good of her to call. Although she, Florence, was perfectly all right, never better. It is pretty silly, actually, her being in any rest home. The truth was, she took sick the winter before and finally she had to have an operation. Her gall bladder, it turned out to be. And that damned Harry arranged for her to go from the hospital to the rest home. And since then she's just not quite had the gumption to get out of there, just too lazy, she guessed. And she did like the people, although most of them were too old to be much fun.

"But we can't just gab on like this, this call must be costing you a fortune," she said to Megan.

Megan explained about WATS lines, and then she said that she wanted to come out to California, to see Florence. And at that point the conversation became very strained, and difficult.

Florence repeated how well she was, what a lovely place, what lovely friends. No need for Megan to go to any trouble. She went on and on until Megan concluded that Florence hated and was deeply ashamed of where she was.

She had to come to San Francisco on business, Megan lied. She had booked a double room at the St. Francis; would Florence please just meet her there? That way they would have a chance to talk, maybe plan something. Maybe, even, Florence could come on to New York for a while?

And that is as far as they have got, with plans; the next day Florence, in the car that Megan has rented, will go back out to "California Pines" to collect the rest of her things (it is clear that she does not want Megan to come with her). Megan will attend to the business that brought her out here. And then they will take an early afternoon plane for New York. Florence has been assured that Megan has plenty of money, plenty of room. She, Florence, will visit "for a while."

. . .

The last time Megan stayed at the St. Francis was for the short
visit that terminated in New York with the horrifying news of
Adam's murder. Megan now thinks about Adam—and about Cathy,
remembering that she did not call Mrs. Piscetti again, having once
failed to get her.

And she decides against calling her now; it is easier to imagine
or to assume that they are all well and happy, Stephen growing up,
college, all that.

She does wonder about Cathy's priest, the father of Stephen:
where and how he is, and if he thinks much of Cathy, and of
Stephen. Very likely he has more children, by his wife? Megan
does not wish him well.

Adam's murder has remained unsolved, a "random killing."

But Megan is in fairly close touch with Aron Marr, son of
Adam; his novel is coming out the following fall, two book clubs
are interested, and Megan believes, and has confided to Janet, that
it will do well. "Maybe just as well Adam's not around to see that,"
is Janet's wry response. "I'm not sure that he could cope with a
successful writer son. And Jesus, a novel about a gay relationship."
Megan thinks that Janet is probably right.

"It was when I lost my job that everything went bad," Florence
tells Megan. They are on the plane, flying east, just now above the
sharp and snowy Rockies. "It's supposed to work the other way
around, I know," says Florence. "The man gets laid off and there
goes the marriage. But with us, like I say, it was me laid off, 'retired,' is how they put it, and even though Harry still went off to
that old shop of his every day, there I was at home every night,
which he wasn't used to, nowhere near.

"He'd got into the habit of going out a lot, he told me at first,
eating out by himself, which at first I believed. You see these old
guys in restaurants, with their papers, halfway flirting with waitresses
and looking perky enough. And at first I got sort of a kick out of

fixing for myself, fresh salads and fruit things and funny breads, all food they'd never heard of at the drive-in.

"But then it began to strike me pretty funny. There we were, me and Harry, old married folk, supposedly, and legally that was true, we surely were. And every night him getting all fixed up to go out by himself, as he said, and me cooking fancy suppers just for me. So I made this little suggestion that maybe we could combine what we were doing, now and then. Sometimes he could maybe take me out, and other times I'd cook up something nice for him.

"And then, well, Harry acted like I'd made some immoral proposition to him. That's a men's trick, I've noticed—have you ever, Meg? When you say something they don't like to hear or that makes them feel someways guilty, the first thing you hear is that you're the one that's crazy. Have you noticed?

"Well, he acted so peculiar that I knew something must be up, so I just up and asked him, was there some good reason we could not go out at the same time and to the same place?

"And then, at last it came out about this lady, this kind person who took him in to feed while I was *gallivanting*, that's the very word he used, I swear it to you. Gallivanting out at the drive-in, he said. Well, if toting trays and clearing off slop and always moving faster than you can, if that's gallivanting I guess that's what I was doing.

"I said to him, in that case maybe we should see a lawyer, so's he could divorce me and set up with this nice lady, this forty-five-year-old chick. Well, that's another men thing—they all hate that word, divorce. They act like it's some bad invention that women thought up. Always want to have their cake and eat it, men do, is what I think. Cowards, most of them.

Megan is thinking, perhaps irrelevantly, of Henry, who never said that she was crazy. Who is not a coward. Who did not want to have his cake and eat it, unless you count Lavinia, whom Megan does not believe he has seen again.

· · ·

About that, Megan is right. Henry will be invited by Lavinia and Potter to their wedding anniversary party, and he will decline.

"Maybe there'll be some kind of work for me to do in New York," says Florence, above the Mississippi River. "I know I'm too old for waitressing, although in some ways it seemed an ideal sort of life for me." She laughs. "Maybe you and me could open a restaurant?"

Megan is becoming somewhat adept at reading her mother's mind, and has noted that although Florence says a great deal, she also leaves a lot out. And so Megan now says, "Well, sure. But you don't have to be in such a hurry to get busy again. I have my work, and there's a lot for you to see in New York."

Megan is also wondering what she will do with her mother when she herself does stop working, a step that she considers more and more often.

It is clear to her that Florence will live forever.

Epilogue

June 1983. Georgia. A softly blue day that seems both a respite and a reward, after the punishing cold rains, the ferocious storms of the winter and spring just preceding.

In the relative cool of midmorning, Megan has begun to set the table for the people in Peg's house: Megan herself, and Florence, Peg, and Vera. Henry Stuyvesant, a weekend resident. Jackson Clay, who has been "visiting" since April. And two current temporary guests: Peg's son, Rex Sinclair, and Megan's old friend Biff, who has come down from New York to celebrate Florence's eighty-third birthday—today. Biff and Florence became great friends during Florence's sojourn with Megan in New York. Lovely friends —and Megan thinks then of the first sentence in Florence's letter to her from San Francisco, the letter that incited her rescue mission: "I am living in a lovely house, with some lovely friends." Megan smiles, thinking that this could more accurately describe her own current situation.

She is distributing place cards, which seems a very silly effort for this particular group, but Florence herself has made the cards, painting small blue flowers on them all (forget-me-nots, Megan decides). Remembering old rules about not seating husbands and wives or lovers together, and considering the impossibility of applying those dicta to these people, Megan smiles further, and concludes that they might just as well sit where they usually do.

The brutally cold and wet past winter and the cruel spring of freak snowstorms, rains, and floods have left in that area a strange legacy of growth. In the distance, where the creek overflowed and remained overflowed, its gentle slow water turned into ravaging, churning mud, on those beaten banks bright new honeysuckle vines have started up from the old; and in the meadow, the ancient furrowed field that lay half the winter under heavy snow or muddy waters, tiny wild flowers now insanely bloom, riotous colors, among brilliant upshooting leaves of grass.

Around the house, Peg's house (they all still think of it as Peg's although in legal fact it now belongs equally to Peg and Vera, Megan, Florence) more blooms: Vera's roses, everywhere, in bushes and climbing over trellises, all the way down along the road to the still upright tobacco barn (now converted: Megan lives there, Henry stays there with her on weekends). White roses, yellow, palest pink, and the deepest, most brilliant scarlet. And wisteria, gone mad: now, after a false, aborted start in April, it blooms and falls all over the porch, all heavy and full, sensuously lavender, fragrant.

It is all so lush, so too beautiful, really, that Megan wonders if the group of new women who are expected tomorrow, whom she is driving to Atlanta to pick up tomorrow, won't be just a little daunted, or depressed? The contrast could be too much?

The house is run now as a temporary shelter, a way-station hospitality house for the homeless, mostly women but sometimes men too. There are nine in the group that Megan will pick up tomorrow, from an Episcopal church in Atlanta. Megan and Peg are in close touch with churches in Washington and in Atlanta, which themselves have served as shelters, over the long and viciously punishing winter.

The task of driving, picking up new people, has fallen to Megan through a process of elimination: neither Vera nor Florence drives at all, while Peg genuinely hates to; and Henry, who still teaches at Chapel Hill, is there only on weekends.

Actually Megan does not much care for driving either, and she is still uneasy with the big old cumbersome VW van out on the road, but under the circumstances these seem inadmissible feelings.

Once, though, one of the women whom Megan was driving

down from Washington—it was late at night; they had been slowed in Virginia by car trouble, had to wait for a new generator, in the rain—that woman, who was sitting in the front seat next to Megan, quietly pulled out a long curved open knife, from her big shabby plastic bag. "You just pull over, I'll take all of everyone's money, now," the woman said, softly, but with a sort of desperate violence.

Megan pulled over off the highway, in the wet hot black Southern night, smelling of privet and red clay dust—they were in South Carolina, near the Georgia state line. "I don't think anyone has any money on them but me, and I don't have much left," Megan told the woman, in a small polite voice that later struck her as ludicrous.

She had chosen this particular woman as her front seat companion on the simple grounds that she looked even worse than the rest, her face more sadly sagging, with great dark sunken eyes, her heavy body creaking with defeat. As Megan handed over the few dollars, all she had left after paying for the generator (the small-town garage had refused her credit cards), she thought, You'll be lucky to make it through another day.

Not having even asked for money from the other women, or for Megan's cards, the woman climbed out of the van, went off into the rain.

Megan had to give up the money and let the woman out, she thought at the time; she had no choice—feeling the fearful breath of the five other shabby women from the backseats of the car.

But later it seemed to her that she had handled it all wrong: surely some kindly, cajoling phrases would have worked? The woman didn't really want to go off like that, probably. And that incident still frightens Megan; recalling the fearful glitter of those huge old eyes, Megan closes her own eyes against it, and she shudders, chilled.

In any case, for both acknowledged and for hidden reasons Megan dreads those drives. One dark and impossibly "neurotic" fear is that they simply won't like her; they won't speak, will be silent, surly. And sometimes that has been much the case; there are long drives during which no one responds to anything Megan says, to her tiny efforts at jokes, at reassurance.

Nor does it all go smoothly when the formerly homeless people are actually settled there, either. There have been some scaring illnesses among them, bad personal episodes, racist incidents (a woman objected that Jackson was sleeping down the hall from her room, and used the same bathroom; another woman whispered to Peg that she *suspected* that Vera might have "a touch of color" in her). Accusations of theft, when small valuables have been misplaced. A man who insisted that Henry looked at him "suggestively." Several people with seemingly chronic depressions.

By now, naturally, strong relationships have developed between this house and the nearest doctors' offices, the small local hospital, and the local police—all these connections of an exemplarily cordial nature, thanks to strenuous efforts from all.

But what they are doing seems still a plausible venture, as they all say to each other from time to time, Peg to Vera to Meg to Florence, to Henry, recently to Jackson; they accomplish at least a small amount of good. A few weeks, in some cases months, of good food and rest generally prove helpful to the people who come to them. "We don't hurt anybody, ever, and it's a whole lot better than leaving them out on the streets," as Florence has put it.

Also, the variety of personalities offered by the house works out; there is someone for everyone, as it were, some possible temporary friend. A woman who was somehow turned off by Megan might take up with Vera, or with Florence. Peg, or Henry. Jackson, for the past two months.

Perhaps the most useful task of all, and the hardest, is the effort made to find jobs, or at least some plausible, affordable housing to send the people on to. Or dredged-up families, or friends. This is how Megan spends most of her time; she has a room full of files, which she keeps meticulously complete and up to date. She spends hours and days on the phone and writing letters, following possible leads. She lavishes considerably more care on placing these people than she formerly did on placing books, as Henry has pointed out to her. "Obviously, you think that any person is valuable." "Well yes, I guess I do. And I'd really had it with all those nonbooks."

Megan, like Florence with her drive-in customers, makes a lot of friends. People send her postcards.

She (Megan) worked out an interest in the agency, which Leslie now controls and very capably runs (despite the fact that she and Benny now are married, and that they have somehow produced a daughter). Megan spends most of each October and May in New York, at the Gramercy Park—ostensibly to see to her business there, actually because she loves New York, still, especially during those months, and she needs time away from Georgia, from that work, even from her friends, and her mother.

It is fortuitous that Florence's birthday occurs during a rare interval when there are no needy guests. Or only Rex and Biff, both of whom could be considered family.

And other celebrations, too, are involved in this day: their project, and loose arrangement for living and working together, has been going on for almost exactly three years, since the summer of 1980 (just before the election of Mr. Reagan). It was during that summer that Megan and Florence, who had visited Peg several times, and talked about the possibility of developing a shelter, moved down in a permanent way. And Henry came down to visit, and to help, and he continued both to visit and to help. In his view he is a sort of weekend husband to Megan, which is not precisely how she sees it herself.

In any case, three years, and there they still are. Peg and Vera. Megan, Florence. Henry.

And: this present June marks forty years, *forty years*, that Peg and Megan have known each other, a fact that until the actual lunch they have somehow not really talked about.

. . .

At the last minute Megan chooses a conventional seating arrange-
ment, men alternating with women; thus, she is seated between
Henry and Biff, on the sunny, wisteria-sheltered side of the porch.
And Peg, between Rex and Jackson, is across the table.

Midway through lunch, or nearly, then, Megan leans across
the table to tell Peg what has obviously been much on her mind
all morning. "I can see it all so clearly!" she says. "Forty years, I
don't believe it. I can see the three of you coming into the smoking room at Cabot, Cathy in those dumb green pajamas, with
calomine all over her face. I was talking to Janet Cohen, and
right away I knew Lavinia didn't like her, before I even *knew*
Lavinia."

Peg frowns just slightly, at the effort of recall. "I don't remember that so much as seeing you in Hood's, and all those bran
muffins we used to eat." Now gray and lean, and lined, and considerably happier than she was in those old days, Peg smiles in a
tolerant way at her glimpse of that former bulky, awkward self.

"Oh yes, Hood's. I used to look at you three and think being
friends with you would be the greatest thing in the world. You
all looked so *Eastern*."

Although he has heard much of this before, Biff is still the most
ardent listener in the group. "Oh, how I remember those freshman
feelings," he now puts in. "My first year at Harvard I fell in love
with everyone I saw."

"I hated everyone at Tulane," says Rex, with a handsome
scowl. "What a bunch of assholes."

Peg regards him with some concern, wondering as she often
does what to say to him, and concluding, again, that it doesn't
matter.

Partly to fill in what has become a silence, Megan rushes on.
"What I can't remember, though, and sometimes I try to, is a
conversation that Cathy and I had, much later on, after we all got
to be friends, sort of. It was about those old boarding school books,
where there were always four friends. You know, Grace Harlow,
all those?"

It is Vera who laughs, who says, "Oh yes, the most wonderful trash. I used to gobble them up. It drove my poor upward ascendant folks nuts, they wanted me to be an intellectual."

"Seems to me like they got pretty much what they wanted, girl," Jackson tells her in his most phonily "Negro" voice.

Megan persists with her memory, though; she has clearly given some thought to the theme of four friends. "It seemed so perfectly *us*," she says. "Those girls in the books. We were classics. Always four of them, and one was kind and jolly. That's you, Peg."

"Yes, and too big and noisy, 'jolly.' I know." Peg grins.

"And one was rich and beautiful and rich and wicked. Lavinia, naturally. And one was poor and innocent and slightly simple, from the provinces. That's got to be me, although Cath and I used to argue, she thought it could be her. But I always thought she would have to be the mysterious fourth."

They are quiet, Megan and Peg remembering Cathy, until Henry says, "I do wish I'd met Cathy. I think she *was* mysterious."

"That's true, she was, and I wish you had too. You would have liked her," Megan tells him. But Cathy would have been intimidated by Henry, at least at first, she further reflects—as she was herself, years ago, meeting him at Adam Marr's improbable White Plains house.

"Well now, I wish I'd met the beautiful rich wicked one, that Lavinia." It is Jackson who has said this, and he is mildly surprised when no one responds, at all. Only, after a pause Megan tells him, "It wouldn't have worked out for you, Jackson, gorgeous as you are."

They smile at each other—good friends, occasional and very secret lovers.

Jackson's first visit to the group there in Georgia lasted for a month; his second, eight months later, lasted for three.

Megan and Peg believe that the real reason he visits is that he has laid out a fine seven-mile run: down their hill and across the furrowed meadow to the creek, several miles on a path along the bank, and back across the fields and up to the house. He does this every day. He also helps considerably, as they all do, in the running of the house. He likes to cook, and he is, like Megan, "good with people."

Megan thinks, though, that now this stay with them is almost over, despite his run. He spends more and more time listening to music in his room, at the end of the attic. He combs every music store in Atlanta for new tapes, of new groups. Megan believes that he is getting ready to play again.

Megan has a recurring fantasy concerning Jackson that no one knows about—surely not Henry, Megan's weekend lover, her almost-husband, and in many ways her closest friend—and surely not Jackson himself.

In the fantasy, Megan and Jackson drive down to Atlanta and register at a hotel.

Like sexual addicts, which perhaps they are, or very young lovers, which clearly they are not (but perhaps with a kind, late-middle-aged persistence of vision they see each other as young: Jackson as hard-muscled, as taut, and Megan as smoothly voluptuous as when they first met, some thirty-nine years back), all afternoon they make love, in that room. They exhaust each other's bodies and imaginations, they lie soaked in sweat, in secretions, in their sea-smelling bed. They laugh a lot, they bathe and dress and drive back home, to their separate quarters.

Henry of course knows that Jackson once lived in Hawaii, and he has undoubtedly worked it out that it was Jackson with whom Megan "went to bed," as she told him, after she had confronted him with Lavinia. And he has very likely concluded that since he no longer "sees" Lavinia, Megan and Jackson no longer make love either. Megan would not do what he himself would not, is how Henry would think. Probably.

Megan has had more than an occasional flash of guilt, at even fantasizing a betrayal of such trust. Henry and Jackson are even friends, in their way. Would it be worse to betray your lover with his friend, or with an enemy (Lavinia)? Megan is not sure.

In the meantime Megan has her strong fantasies.

. . .

This day, which belongs to Florence, is wonderfully warm, clear, and blue; it seems the first day of summer, after all the cold, the cruel rains of that preceding spring (some of the women whom Megan will pick up tomorrow are flood victims, still out of their homes and without possessions. Uninsured, of course, since they were poor to begin with).

"Florence, you really lucked out on the weather," Peg has told her. "God must really like you. But of course we all know you would have served us salads anyway."

"Of course I would have," Florence tells Peg—she tells them all. "We could right now be eating cold salad in the rain, right out here on this porch."

(Florence will live forever, they all think, and hope.)

"Florence darling, I'll bet you've never looked better in your life." It is Biff who says this, but it would have been any one of them.

"You just won't believe I was ever young and cute," Florence challenges.

"Oh, I do," Biff assures her. "But in a way, don't you feel a lot better now?"

"Of course I don't, dummy. I creak and I forget most things. But in most ways I do feel pretty good."

Megan's attention has wandered over to Rex, across the table, and she wonders, as she has before, just how Peg feels about this handsome, *awful* boy.

Which leads her to wonder, too, about children she herself might have had. By Henry, or by Jackson—or both? She has read somewhere about multiple insemination, and observed its results in litters of kittens, but she does not know whether this is possible with humans. How very embarrassing, if it should happen. Although both these men, in their separate ways, are quite superior.

Years ago, very young, Megan used to think of having a child by Jackson, a tall beautiful tawny girl, she thought, with Jackson's wide-set liquid eyes. However, more often, more realistically, she was in a state of panic at the thought that she could be pregnant.

Now she does not regret not having had children—too many people do, quite obviously.

Peg is thinking of Rex, as she watches him barely eating, and frowning, disapproving of everyone there. His extreme handsomeness is harder to explain than his difficult character is, Peg believes. His black hair and dark blue eyes and his graceful body seem an aberration, a mockery of herself, and of Cameron. She sighs, and thinks then that at least her other kids are all right. Even Candy has come out of her trouble; she is at Davis, studying to be an assistant to a vet. She is living with a man whom she only describes as "really nice." Peg hopes he is.

And she hopes that Vera will never leave her, never find a younger, prettier woman to love. Or a man.

And she wonders why (oh, why!) she can never take anyone or anything for granted. All winter, when it snowed so much and hail came down like bullets, and the creek kept flooding over, Peg desperately feared for herself; she began to feel that she did not deserve to own such a beautiful house, and that it would be taken. She wonders: is the "virtuous" use to which they have put it a propitiation, of sorts?

Henry Stuyvesant, curiously, is still thinking of Cathy, the only one of the group of four friends whom he never met. He wonders if she sounded as much like the others as those three do to each other, in terms of inflection. He would never tell Megan how much she reminds him of Lavinia, when she speaks. In fact if it were not for Megan he would almost never think of Lavinia, whose beauty he now remembers with a tiny sigh. He sighs too for her extreme intelligence, and her remarkably shoddy values.

Henry hopes that Jackson Clay will soon move on, that Megan is right about his plans. An old jazz buff, Henry tells himself that he misses Jackson's music, and, as a friend, he is sure that Jackson would be much happier, playing. But he also wonders if Jackson and Megan still make love sometimes—or if they ever will again.

And he hopes very much that his own new book will do well, at least some good reviews: a history of the American political left, 1925–1975, being published by the Press at Chapel Hill, in 1984. Good God, Henry thinks: *1984.*

Henry would of course help her carry in the dessert soufflé, not let her drop it, Megan is thinking, as she looks over at Henry, next to her. There in the sun, in the heat of that day, she can actually smell his warm clean familiar skin. He is wearing a striped cotton shirt, blue and white, that she likes very much; it is so old, has so often been laundered, that its texture is silky. She now very lightly touches his sleeve, his arm, and they exchange a small smile, of the most intense affection.

The drinks at that lunch provide a curious study in contrasts. Biff, whose tastes have always been rather grand, and who is now rich enough to indulge them, has generously provided a case of champagne. ("Such a practical drink," he has said. "You can drink it with anything.")

However, both Jackson and Rex Sinclair, for quite different reasons, stick to milk. ("Booze is for assholes like my old man," Rex has said.) Vera never drinks. Nor does Florence. "I'm too old, it makes me dizzy." Which leaves a lot of champagne for Peg and Megan, Henry, Biff.

The overflowing, heavy, fragrant wisteria provides some shelter from the sun for Megan and the others on that side of the table; still, all the warmth and the wine combine to produce a certain blurriness in her mind.

Which is probably at least in part why she has this thought, of which she is later ashamed; she thinks, Why do we have to be a shelter? Why keep driving to Atlanta, to Washington, for all those people? We could all just live here together, we could keep busy.

Especially after Jackson goes. Just Peg and Vera, and Florence. Henry and me. We'd be fine.

However, dismissing that not-even-practical idea (what else would they actually do, with all their time and space?), Megan recognizes that she is experiencing her familiar apprehension; as always, she is dreading the drive, the new people.

And she recognizes too that that is precisely what she is going to do, as always: she will get up early and take the van to be checked at the local garage, in Edenborough; by nine thirty or ten at the latest she will be off, down the white, red-clay-lined highways, past the pale green summery meadows, and over still-swollen rushing brown muddy creeks, past densely leafed-out woods—to the city, Atlanta, where nine women who need a place to stay are waiting for her.

Henry and Jackson are clearing off the table now. Rising, Biff offers to help, but he is turned down. "No help from temporary guests," he is told.

In a few minutes Megan, who has decided to do it by herself, will get up and go in to get the frozen soufflé. Her mother's birthday cake. With the 8 and the 3 on top. June 1983.

A NOTE ON THE TYPE

The text of this book was set in Electra, a type face designed by W(illiam) A(ddison) Dwiggins (1880–1956) for the Mergenthaler Linotype Company and first made available in 1935. Electra cannot be classified as either "modern" or "old style." It is not based on any historical model, and hence does not echo any particular period or style of type design. It avoids the extreme contrast between thick and thin elements that marks most modern faces, and it is without eccentricities that catch the eye and interfere with reading. In general, Electra is a simple, readable type face that attempts to give a feeling of fluidity, power, and speed.

W. A. Dwiggins began an association with the Mergenthaler Linotype Company in 1929 and over the next 27 years designed a number of book types, including Metro, Electra, Caledonia, Eldorado, and Falcon.

This book was composed by Maryland Linotype Composition Co., Inc., Baltimore, Maryland. It was printed and bound by The Haddon Craftsmen, Inc., Scranton, Pennsylvania.

Typography and binding design by
Amy Berniker